♡ Marina Giotteb Sorlos

THE LAST
Daughter
OF
Prussia

MARINA GOTTLIEB SARLES

A NOVEL

Wild River
BOOKS

Published by Wild River Books
P.O. Box 53
Stockton, New Jersey 08559
www.WildRiverReview.com

Distributed by Emerald Book Company

For ordering information or special discounts for bulk purchases, please contact Emerald Book Company at PO Box 91869, Austin, TX 78709, 512.891.6100.

Design and composition by Greenleaf Book Group LLC and Alex Head
Cover design by Tim Ogline
Map illustrations by Scott Deal
Cover: White Stallion image © Mariat 2012. Used under license from Shutterstock.com; background image © istockphoto.com/Vikarus; leather texture image © istockphoto.com/Joe Cicak; girl's face © Christine Matthai.

Publisher's Cataloging-In-Publication Data
(Prepared by The Donohue Group, Inc.)
Sarles, Marina Gottlieb.
    The last daughter of Prussia / Marina Gottlieb Sarles. -- 1st ed.
    p. : ill., map ; cm.
    ISBN: 978-0-9839188-2-0
    1. World War, 1939-1945—Prussia, East (Poland and Russia)—Fiction. 2. Germans—Prussia, East (Poland and Russia)—Fiction. 3. Romanies—Prussia, East (Poland and Russia)—Fiction. 4. Prussia, East (Poland and Russia)—History—20th century—Fiction. I. Title.

PS3619.A75 L37 2013   2012949948
813/.6

Part of the Tree Neutral® program, which offsets the number of trees consumed in the production and printing of this book by taking proactive steps, such as planting trees in direct proportion to the number of trees used: www.treeneutral.com

Printed in the United States of America on acid-free paper   Tree Neutral®

12 13 14 15 16 17   10 9 8 7 6 5 4 3 2 1

First Edition

To the memory of my grandparents,
Edith and Walter von Sanden,
and to the people of East Prussia
whose voices were silenced.

I Want to Wander Home

I want to wander home
In torn beggar's clothes,
On peaceful, lonely pathways
That no one else would know.
And should my feet be bloody
And all my strength be gone,
Yet, shall I keep on walking,
Until I see my home.
My beggar's staff may slip
Slowly from my hand,
But my soul shall be in heaven
In the grave upon my land.

—EDITH VON SANDEN

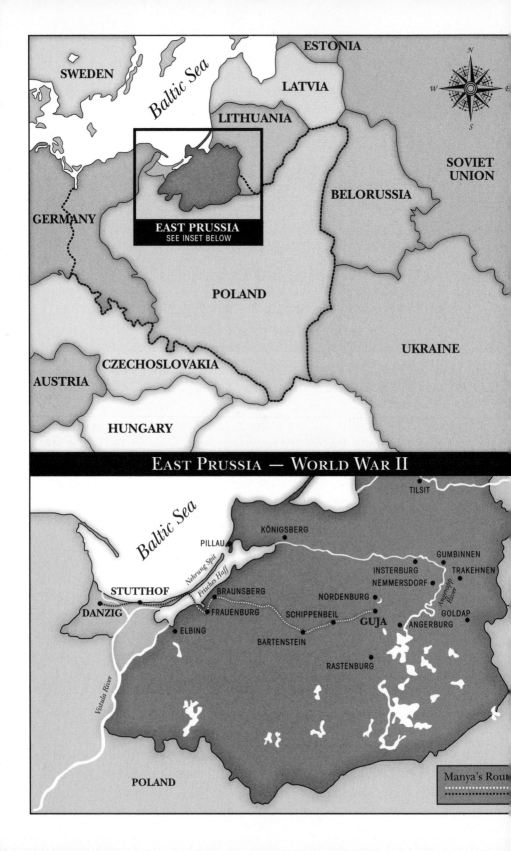

SWEDEN

Baltic Sea

ESTONIA

LATVIA

LITHUANIA

GERMANY

EAST PRUSSIA
SEE INSET BELOW

SOVIET
UNION

BELORUSSIA

POLAND

UKRAINE

CZECHOSLOVAKIA

AUSTRIA

HUNGARY

EAST PRUSSIA — WORLD WAR II

Baltic Sea

TILSIT

KÖNIGSBERG

PILLAU

GUMBINNEN

Nehrung Spit

INSTERBURG
NEMMERSDORF

TRAKEHNEN

BRAUNSBERG

Frisches Haff

NORDENBURG

STUTTHOF

DANZIG

FRAUENBURG

SCHIPPENBEIL

GUJA

Angerapp River

GOLDAP

ANGERBURG

ELBING

BARTENSTEIN

Vistula River

RASTENBURG

POLAND

Manya's Route

PROLOGUE

The Last Daughter of Prussia is the story of Manya von Falken, a young aristocratic woman, and Joshi Karas, her Romani friend and childhood companion with whom she falls in love during the evacuation of East Prussia at the end of World War II. Many of their experiences were inspired by true stories passed down by members of my family and documented in their diaries.

Often called "The Great Trek," the evacuation of East Prussia claimed the lives of nearly half a million women, children, and men who were attempting to escape the Red Army as it advanced on Berlin. But underneath cold statistics, what really happened during the harsh East Prussian winter of 1944–1945? Whose stories were silenced? For though "The Great Trek" remains one of the largest mass evacuations ever recorded, it is rarely discussed. Manya von Falken is a fictional character, but she could be any strong-willed daughter of East Prussia who was swept up in that life-threatening wave of terror and fleeing refugees.

Until 1944, East Prussia, the easternmost province of Germany, had been only slightly affected by the war. The people, misinformed by Nazi propaganda about the true state of military affairs, believed that Hitler's *Wunderwaffe* (superweapon) would make Germany victorious. Then, on October 22, 1944, it was reported that a Russian battalion ambushed the small East Prussian village of Nemmersdorf, shooting the grandfathers who weren't enlisted in the army and raping and killing nearly every woman and child. News of this massacre and the atrocities committed spread fear throughout the countryside. The East Prussians realized that they were in grave danger, but by then the harshest of winters was upon them. Adding to their panic was the fact that Hitler and one of his Nazi henchmen, *Gauleiter* (Governor) Erich Koch, had protracted the evacuation of all civilians, demanding that they stay and fight or be shot as traitors.

Trapped between two dangerous forces, the people defied orders. Gathering their lives in boxes and buckets, they harnessed their horses to carts and wagons and fled westward into the icy unknown. Targeted by Russian bombers and artillery, they traversed a dangerous, frozen lagoon— the only escape route open. In many places, the bullet-riddled ice collapsed, sending thousands to their watery graves.

My grandparents, Walter and Edith von Sanden, were part of this perilous journey. They survived, albeit with broken hearts. I know because I saw the emptiness in their eyes when I was a child. And I read their diaries.

I wrote this story for them and for those who did not survive. I wrote for the shocking number of German women and children who could not break the taboo of silence over the rapes they endured at the hands of Russian soldiers. To have been violated in that way surely made them ashamed, but to have been part of a German nation guilty of genocide kept them silent. From accounts I have read and stories told to me firsthand, many women felt that they were paying for their country's sins even while they were being raped. It is understandable that the Russians were full of wrath after Hitler's invasion had left more than 20 million of their countrymen dead. But the systematic rape of women and children has always been an unfair act of wartime retaliation.

The Romani people of East Prussia, often pejoratively called Gypsies, also faced disaster. The character Joshi Karas, a Romani, came to me as I was reading my grandfather's book *Schicksal Ostpreussen—East Prussia's Destiny*. I learned that a group of Romanies lived on my family's estate and that my mother and grandparents were very friendly with them. One night, they disappeared. When my grandfather went to the police to inquire about them, he was warned that associating with "asocials" was a crime punishable by death. Later he discovered that his Romani friends had been shot or carted off to a concentration camp. I based Joshi's story on this account. Some Romanies were sent to Auschwitz, but the closest death camp was Stutthof, near Danzig (the port city on the Baltic coast to which many refugees were headed, including Manya in this story). I used Stutthof as Joshi's ill-fated destination. The female warden, Elisabeth Martens, also is a fictional character, but sexual exploitation of prisoners by both male and female wardens has been documented in accounts about concentration camps. It is estimated that 1.5 million Romani were murdered in Germany from 1935 to the end of the war.

Last, within this chaotic arena of Nazis, Russian soldiers, and fleeing families, the Trakehner horses—East Prussia's symbol of excellence and beauty, bred on the land for over two centuries—struggled to save their owners. My mother owned such a horse. I have attempted to reveal his bravery and large-heartedness in both Aztec's and Shambhala's characters. The more I read about the Trakehners, the more I felt that they were the true heroes of the trek. Undeterred by race, creed, or nationality, they hauled everyone across the ice, including Russian and Polish prisoners of war and any Jews or Romanies who had survived the Nazis.

The horses weren't interested in cultural differences, nor did they care about political beliefs. Surely many Germans who sympathized with Hitler were on that trek, but many others, like my grandparents, did not. It didn't matter to the horses. They focused on survival. Sadly, only twenty-seven mares, two stallions and seven foals of the herd of 1,200 warm-blooded thoroughbreds from the famous Trakehner Horse Farm in Trakehnen made it safely to the West. The rest perished along the way—eaten, stolen, or shot in cold blood by Russian soldiers whose leader, Josef Stalin, had given orders to annihilate anything German.

I hope what I have written helps the reader understand the turmoil of those final winter months during World War II. As my research unfolded, I realized that I had to write a love story—one that was set in this tumultuous time and gave expression to the agony and inspiration that lovers from different ethnic backgrounds experienced. I wanted to include their triumphs and tragedies as well as those of their families. And how could I leave out the horses, whose determination on the trek was the purest expression of courage and love? I also wanted to write a novel for readers who might be unfamiliar with this corner of history, for whom it might be tempting to lump all Germans together without sympathy for individual lives and a multitude of circumstances.

Having said that, I must confess that despite countless hours of research and writing, the book often seemed to take on a life of its own. For months, I lived in the emotional world of people forced to gather their lives in boxes and flee. Many nights, I encountered ghosts hovering by my bedside, their silent voices imploring me to bring their story to paper. I am a writer, but I have also dedicated many years of my life to the healing arts, for which

I rely on my intuition and spiritual insight. However, for this book, my intention was to stay grounded in factual details. The ghosts came anyway.

In my dreams, they urged me to look directly into the faces of starving women dragging their children through the snow. I saw babies frozen to death in carriages and old men weeping at the thought of leaving their land. I heard the whine of bombers, the blasts of artillery and guns, and I watched horses fall on bloodstained fields of ice. Each time I awoke, I found myself feeling more obligated to remember, a moral responsibility to those who never dared to speak of their ordeal because they were German. I wanted to give a voice to those who could not talk about their vanished land because the memories were just too painful.

I began to understand my grandmother and her dream to return home to East Prussia, the land of golden amber and green forests. She knew her dream would remain unfulfilled for as long as she lived. She would never stand by the sparkling Guja Lake and watch the swallows soar against the sapphire-colored sky. Nor would she look again at her house on the hill, nor open the heavy oak door to the foyer. Perhaps her loss is justified where the corpses of genocide are piled high. But does the judgment thus decreed, "Germans deserve every awful thing they got," lessen her loss? I think not.

I hope that readers will not think I am diminishing the ungodly cruelty of the Holocaust. I am profoundly aware of the atrocities committed by Germans against Jews and others who were forced into death camps and murdered. While researching the camps, I must say I felt my own life force dwindle. I felt a sense of shame and terror in my own German bones. Still, at the risk of being condemned, I want to say that the people of East Prussia also were victims.

My grandmother has been dead a long time, but from her unseen place of refuge I still hear her whisper: "Tell the story so that others may know what happened. Tell it so that people remember and have compassion for anyone killed in hatred, prejudice, and war. Tell it for the Jews, the Germans, the Romanies—every slain tribe and forgotten soul, and for any unjustly slaughtered animal in the history of humanity. Tell it so that healing may happen in all hearts."

I have done what she asked, to the best of my ability.

PART I

Manya

OCTOBER 1944

EAST PRUSSIA

ONE

A flock of common cranes swooped low across the Angerapp River, announcing the arrival of dawn. Their cries echoed through the willow trees that swayed like weary sentinels on the marshy banks.

From her perch on a flat, moss-covered stone, Manya von Falken watched the cranes lift into a pale, watery sunrise. She'd been sitting at the river's edge since just after midnight, when she'd awakened from the dream. Images had lodged in her mind like splinters—Russian soldiers breaking down the front door of her house, her parents dead in a pool of blood on the parquet floor of the winter garden.

Unable to sleep or shake her sense of dread, she had risen from her bed, gotten dressed, and made her way through the frosty air to the stables and her beloved stallion, Aztec. He had grown used to her nightly visits and pricked up his ears the moment she unlatched the gate to his stall.

"I had the dream again," she whispered anxiously, burying her face in his silky opalescent mane.

He nuzzled her shoulder as she lifted his saddle onto his back. She sighed and leaned her cheek against his warm flank before pulling the girth buckle tight. Outside the stable, she mounted him, and together they rode though the courtyard and down the grassy hill toward the river, the beat of her heart slowly adjusting to the rhythm of his gait.

Now the blackness of night had receded, but the fog still clung to the riverbank that had always been her refuge.

When Manya was little, her father had brought her here, holding her tightly on his lap as Fidelio, his bay Trakehner gelding, cantered down the embankment. Her father had taught her to listen to the calls of rosefinches and warblers while she fished for trout, pike, and eel. In the sacred call of the birds, she heard the spirits of her ancestors, felt their presence in the rustle of the leaves. And never once had she been afraid.

But everything was changing.

For the past weeks, even the forest creatures acted strangely, as if they smelled danger. What else could explain the disappearance of the otters from the riverbanks? They were the happy-go-lucky freebooters of nature, always ready for a bit of fun. It had been months since she'd watched them toboggan down the slippery incline, their front paws tucked beneath their chests. And she missed them.

If only I could forget the dream, she thought, but the sound of imagined gunfire still echoed in her head.

Last evening, she and her father had listened to Radio Beromünster, broadcasting from Switzerland. The newscaster had reported that the Russians were advancing on East Prussia. It was just a matter of weeks before the German army would be forced to retreat, leaving the province undefended.

For months, rumors had been spreading through the surrounding villages that the Russians were ruthless. Their orders were simple. Women were to be raped; men shot or sent to Siberian labor camps. Their rallying cry was simple, too. No mercy for Germans. Germans were evil. They had invaded Russia and slaughtered the innocent. Now they would be punished.

In the bigger towns to the east, such as Angerburg and Insterburg, officials swore that German troops were holding the Red Army at bay. But Manya trusted the foreign news reports and the rumors whispered in the villages. Germany was not as invincible as Hitler proclaimed. Every night, Russian planes were bombing the larger towns and cities. Everyone knew the drone of a Russian bomber. And anyone with two eyes could see that there were fewer German aircraft in the sky.

Aztec's shrill neigh snapped her out of her thoughts.

"Just a few more minutes, boy," she called, brushing away the dew that had gathered on the fine twill fabric of her jodhpurs.

Aztec pricked up his ears. Wisps of steam escaped from his muzzle. When she did not come, he lowered his head and began to nibble at the damp grass.

This mad world doesn't deserve such a quiet river, she thought as she leaned toward the water, the ends of her pale hair spreading like silky threads in the river's current.

She didn't care that her hair was getting wet. She loved the feel of the cold prickling against her scalp. Had a fisherman passed by just then, he could easily have mistaken her for a river goddess. He would have seen the otherworldliness in her eyes, gray with a translucent hint of lavender, and noticed her serious and observant expression, out of place on one so young.

She lifted her hair from the water and wrung out the dripping strands with what her mother called "farmer's hands." *I wish my hands were like Mother's*, she thought sadly.

Her mother had fine-boned, aristocratic hands, an expression of who she was, a sculptress, while Manya's hands were as big-knuckled as a man's. Manya let out a sigh. She was well aware that her hands did not match her slender frame and delicate features. They were the clearest reminder of the awkwardness that never left her, except when they held Aztec's reins. Then, her fingers became supple and confident, responding to the slightest twitch of his head. And when she rode Aztec, she felt strong, happy, even graceful.

She watched the dew shimmer on the green needles of a cypress tree. If only she were less clumsy, her mother would not snap at her so often when she bumped into the edge of the dining room table. Or when her butter knife slipped out of her fingers and clattered to the floor.

Aztec nickered again.

"The otters won't be coming today," she said, standing up and smoothing back her hair.

Aztec pawed at a hard, muddy ridge, letting Manya know he was ready to move on. She reached for the tanned deerskin bridle, woven expertly by Blacksmith Helling.

She couldn't remember a time when Helling wasn't in charge of the family's horses, ensuring they were impeccably shod and that their bits fit perfectly in their mouths. Helling's reputation reached far beyond their Guja estate and the surrounding villages. Over an hour's ride away in Nemmersdorf, where Helling lived with his wife, Karin, and their daughters, Maritza and Zarah, he was much loved and respected.

Manya shivered. The chill of the morning had awakened a hunger inside her, for food, surely, but also for the comfort of the blacksmith's home.

I'll go to Nemmersdorf, she thought, pulling herself into the saddle and nudging Aztec forward. It was a bit of a ride, but maybe Karin had baked an apple strudel. If not, Karin would surely fry an egg for her in butter.

Manya smiled to herself. It would be a treat to relax in Karin's kitchen, away from the deep bouts of depression that often struck her mother and filled their home with gloom.

Tugging gently at the reins, she trotted Aztec through tall, wrought iron gates and left the safety of her family's estate, descending the hill into the countryside. She glanced at the family crest decorating the entrance, a symbol she associated with her father's power and strength of character, and felt a pang of sadness. The baron's toughness wavered only for her mother.

But Manya understood why. She herself could hardly bear to see her mother retreat to the drawing room, where, for hours, she would play Chopin's "Nocturne in E-flat Major." It hurt to hear her mother starting and stopping and starting again, her fingers beating the sad and beautiful melody into the keys, reminding Manya that there was nothing she could do to comfort her mother.

The veil of clouds was lifting. Blacksmith Helling would already be on his way to the estate in the second-hand Opel her father had given him. She sighed. It was so very different at the Hellings' home. There, she laughed with ease.

Smiling, she remembered how hard she'd practiced her waltz steps with Maritza, the eldest daughter. Perhaps, this morning, they'd sit by the fire and chat. At least she wouldn't think about the dream. Best of all, she'd see Helling's eleven-year-old daughter, Zarah, a wisp of a girl, delicate and small for her age, but ever so lively. And Zarah adored Aztec as much as Manya did.

Her thoughts drifted back to the first time she had given Zarah a knee-up on a horse. Blacksmith Helling had been with them in the meadow that day.

"Fräulein Manya," he had said, grinning broadly as Zarah's giggles bubbled up to the sky. "Teach my daughter to ride as well as you do, and I'll teach you everything I know about hunting and fishing."

Manya had been asking him to teach her his hunting tricks since she was a young girl, so the offer felt like a triumph.

Just three years old at the time, Zarah proved to be a natural in the saddle. At first, she had ridden one of the gentle mares from the von Falken stables. Later, when Zarah had mastered her seat and learned how to keep her heels down while cantering, Manya allowed her to ride Aztec. She had been astonished to see their rapport, how fast Zarah responded to Aztec, and how quickly he trusted her sensitive hands and sweet nature.

And, true to his word, Helling taught Manya the secrets of the forests, the rivers, and the creatures that lived in each. He taught her how to gut deer without flinching, how to tie off the entrails. If he shot two wild boars, he always lifted the smaller carcass onto her shoulders and made her carry it through the forest to the horses. She never complained, even though the stench nearly knocked her over.

At first, she was afraid her father would argue against such unwomanly behavior, but with no male heirs to take over the estate, he was only too happy to see her acquire the skills needed to live off the land she would one day inherit.

And she loved Helling. He taught her how to build fires for warmth and for signaling, how to eat when the hunt brought no fish or fowl, where to find berries, greens, and mushrooms. When the rivers and the lakes froze, he taught her to read the markings on the white ice like words on the pages of a holy book.

Two years ago, on her eighteenth birthday, he took her down to the Angerapp River. Lighting his pipe, he motioned for her to sit with him on the moss-soft bank. "You have earned the right to know the most important secret," he'd said. "The will to survive in the elements will always summon the means."

He gave her a knife he had forged and honed, its handle carved from the horn of a stag they had hunted the year before, shaped to fit perfectly in her hand. She wore it now, tucked into her belt.

A breeze touched her face, bringing with it the scent of freshly turned soil. The women would soon be in the potato fields, digging up the precious sustenance they hoped would see them through the coming winter.

She longed to be worthy of the land where her family had lived for centuries. She had always thought she would grow old here, farm, and raise horses. But now, how could they stay?

Pulling her collar tighter against the chilly air, she cantered on, gathering the warmth that came with the midmorning sun. Finally, she saw the bridge that crossed the Angerapp River onto Nemmersdorf's oak-lined *Reichschaussee*. She slowed Aztec to a walk, surprised to see the ground so churned up.

She sniffed the air and smelled gunpowder and iron. *Something is terribly wrong*, she thought, urging Aztec over the bridge, away from the main road and onto a path that ran through the forest toward Nemmersdorf village.

A quiver ran through Aztec's neck.

"What is it, boy?" Manya murmured, gripping the handle of her hunting knife.

Aztec shook his mane and turned to look at her, his eyes shiny with the fear she'd felt ever since she went to find him in the stables this morning. She nudged him on with her heels, but he wouldn't budge. So she dismounted and led him off the path, deeper into the forest.

"Stay here," she whispered, stroking his muzzle. She thought for a moment and decided not to risk tying him to a tree. If a stranger found him, he would surely steal him. If she left him untied, he could always run.

"I'll be back, boy," she said. And set off.

TWO

Nemmersdorf village was a short distance to the north. As Manya scrambled through brambles and branches, she strained to hear the familiar sounds of the women calling to each other as they walked to the fields.

The air grew thick with smoke as she made her way to the old road lined by a grove of oaks that led from Nemmersdorf to Gumbinnen town.

She stopped.

Four Russian tanks were parked on the shoulder of the road. She could see movement in the village. Another tank rolled down the hill and into the village, crushing a cow too scared to move. The animal bellowed in pain before it fell silent. Soldiers with submachine guns and bayonets leaped down from the moving tank and fanned out into the streets.

Manya heard sharp blasts and looked toward the church. Beyond it, in Farmer Naujok's field, men were lined up. One by one, they jerked and fell as bullets ripped into their backs.

I've got to get out of here, thought Manya, her heart beating against her chest. But then a more urgent thought struck her. She had to get to Blacksmith Helling's house.

Cautiously, she moved along the edge of the forest toward Helling's stone cottage, with its clay pots full of red geraniums and rosemary at the gate. She heard a low moan and saw the tortured face of Ilse Sommer, the baker's wife. Her naked body had been stretched wide across the entrance to Blacksmith Helling's barn, her hands and feet nailed to the wooden frame like the crucifix that hung above the altar in the town chapel.

In the road in front of the cottage, three soldiers were standing over Karin and Maritza. Sweet Maritza was naked, too, and covering her breasts while her mother sobbed and pleaded for their lives.

"*Frau komm!*" the soldiers shouted. "Woman, come!"

The men surrounded Maritza, some of them laughing and jostling her hands away with the ends of their rifles so that others could fondle her breasts.

"Please!" cried Karin, scratching the face of a Russian soldier who had unbuttoned his pants. "*Nimm mich!* Take me!"

Maritza screamed. Karin lunged sideways to protect her, but the men grinned and shoved Maritza to the ground.

"*Schweine!*" Karin shouted over and over again. "Pigs!"

Another soldier with a wide nose and blank eyes pulled out his gun. Grunting in Russian, he grabbed Karin's face, forced the barrel into her mouth and pulled the trigger.

The men turned to Maritza, unbuckling their belts and thrusting themselves between Maritza's thighs. She struggled to fend them off, but soon, her long, blond braids turned red, and finally, her cries faded. In the street, an injured goose was hopping back and forth, honking woefully. Its wing was soaked in blood and it kept falling over. *Zarah's pet goose*, thought Manya, tears stinging her eyes. *Where is Zarah? Where is she?*

Manya's head began to spin. A stream of bile escaped her throat, landing on a dark square of earth beneath her feet. She raised her eyes to keep from fainting, but her knees buckled and she felt the sky fall down around her. Only then did the noise in her head stop.

THREE

*M*ajor Yuri Golitsin strode through the village, his high black boots clicking against the cobblestones. He was short and powerfully built. The tailored breeches and khaki tunic he wore stood in stark contrast to the shabby uniforms of his men.

"Kill everyone," he called out calmly, straightening the visor on his head. "There must be no survivors. Stalin's orders."

He glanced at his right shoulder. *After this mission, General Zhukov will know my name*, he thought. *And I'll add another gold star to my uniform.*

He passed a stone cottage and looked into the window, where he glimpsed a small, red-haired girl. Their eyes locked before she vanished, leaving him to stare at his own reflection in the glass, the wide cheekbones of his Slavic forefathers, the slate-gray eyes, calculating and magnetic beneath a thick black brow. He was handsome in a dark way. Many women had told him so. They also said that his gaze unnerved them, and that they never knew what he was thinking.

At first, his own men were deceived by his good looks. Since he rarely spoke with anger, they assumed he was weak, unable to make decisions. They even taunted him behind his back.

"Pretty boy," they sang. "Don't go into the showers alone."

But they soon discovered that Golitsin was anything but weak. He heard and saw everything. His sight was remarkable. He could see an index finger tremble on a trigger in battle. If the finger belonged to one of his soldiers, the punishment was severe. If it belonged to a German, the man was dead. His extraordinary ability to detect the slightest motion, whether on a snowy landscape, in the dark, or at great distance, had earned him the name Hawk Eye.

He was proud to say that he could find a stinking Kraut wherever one might be hiding. His hatred of them was so bitter, he gladly spread it like a disease among his soldiers.

The night before, he had prepared his troops, saying, "You must savor the smell of German blood. All Germans are pigs. Dangerous pigs. To kill one is to honor Russia. To kill many is to honor God."

"But must we kill children, too?" one weary soldier had asked.

"The Germans showed no mercy to us," Golitsin snapped, flecks of spittle showering the man.

Heads had nodded all around. His men hadn't forgotten the Nazi murders of hundreds of thousands of innocent Ukrainians.

And he would never forget the siege of Leningrad, where his own sweet sister Olga had starved to death because of the Germans. The time for Russia's revenge had come.

"In the name of your own dead countrymen," he said in a cold, flat voice, "slaughter the bastards. Cut off their balls. Fuck every woman who looks good to you. Even those who don't. Take what you want." His eyes narrowed. "I warn you, though. The ambush on Nemmersdorf must not fail."

His men had laughed raucously, but they did not miss the threat. Their laughter soon faded into nervous silence.

"This is the first time our Russian boots will touch German soil," he told them. "We will surprise our enemy before the morning fog lifts, roll over them with our tanks. Every German must die."

In the morning, Golitsin had awoken from his dreams with a rare smile. Joseph Stalin himself had pinned the Supreme Military Victory Medal on his army jacket. Ah, yes, and he had seen his name printed on the marbled pages of a history book bound in brown calf's leather.

A hand grenade exploded behind him, the spray of smoke propelling him on. He had done his job well. And his soldiers were doing theirs. He continued to survey the grounds. Where women and children lay dying, he called to the nearest soldier to finish them off, closing his mind to the victims' screams. His heart belonged to Russia. And this was an eye for an eye.

"Major, do you want her?"

Golitsin turned toward the voice.

"You can have her first if you like," grinned a soldier pointing to a girl with pale blond braids, lying on the ground near a pot of geraniums. A few yards away, an older woman lay dead in the yellowed grass.

Golitsin shook his head no.

He didn't want to fuck a farm girl. He wanted something else—an aristocrat. He smiled when he thought of the leaflets the Red Army had dropped from planes, calling for revenge on the flaxen-haired German witches.

But fucking women wasn't enough to satisfy him. He had ambitions larger than momentary pleasure. Somewhere a woman was screaming. He turned and scanned the village. On the path before him, an injured goose lay honking in the dirt. *Poor bird*, he thought, crushing its head with his boot heel. *You're better off dead.*

A slight movement in the nearby foliage caught his eye. Who was hiding there? A man? A child?

Slinking through the trees, he stepped onto a grassy trail that circled the village. Within seconds, he spotted a woman lying on the ground, partially hidden in the bushes.

He reached for her hair, and snapped her head back, dragging her to her feet and pushing her up against the trunk of a poplar tree. Her head lolled onto her slender shoulder and her mouth fell open, revealing a row of perfect white teeth.

By God! This woman was more than he could have hoped for. Even half conscious, she was splendid, her skin unblemished, her hair like white gold. And so much of it! As he waited for her to come to, his gaze traveled over her gray riding pants, stained at the knees with moss. He noticed her vest, too, closely fastened with ornate silver buttons bearing a family crest. It surprised him to see an elegant woman wearing such masculine clothing. He'd always thought that the female aristocracy wore frilly dresses, cut low to expose their white bosoms.

All the same, her womanly shape was unmistakable. He wanted to see more. Holding her firmly against the tree, he tore off the top three buttons of her vest and blouse and was quickly rewarded by the sight of high, round breasts. A surge of arousal passed through him. This was the woman. He squeezed the muscular mounds of her backside, and ran his hand down her long legs that ended in exquisitely crafted riding boots.

He looked her over again. She was taller than he was. He didn't like that. But in the end it wouldn't matter because he'd bring her to her knees.

He had fantasized a thousand times about raping this kind of woman. The rough ground in this forest wasn't a posh featherbed, but so what? He didn't have time to wait for a mansion. This girl was too fine. He'd fuck her right here, in the dirt.

Her lashes fluttered open. For a moment, he was shocked by the fierce and intelligent glare she shot back into his eyes. She tried to wriggle away, but he shoved his hand between her legs. He not only wanted to enjoy this, he wanted to hurt her, too.

He felt her twitch and then, unexpectedly, she struck, bringing her knee sharply into his groin.

He let out a groan and shoved her into the tree. "Bitch!" he spat. "You think you're smart? You think that will help you, you fucking German witch?"

Loathing filled her face. He could barely contain his fury. Why wasn't she afraid? He had expected a compliant victim, one who begged him for mercy. Why wasn't she cowering? He wanted that satisfaction. Of course, he could shoot her in an instant. But no, he'd fuck her first. *Careful now*, he thought, when she fixed his eyes with another direct stare.

Suddenly, she let out a whistle, much like the shriek of the snowy owls he'd heard in Siberia.

Who is she calling, he thought as he covered her mouth with his hand, smashing his palm against her perfect teeth. Had she tricked him? She squirmed and stared over his shoulder. He twisted around to look too.

A huge blur, mighty, black, and swift, came into focus.

Panic melted into awe as Golitsin beheld a horse charging straight for him. The animal halted abruptly and reared.

Golitsin could hardly breathe. All his life he had been enraptured by the image of such a stallion. He knew plenty about horses. As a boy he'd worked alongside his father on a nobleman's estate outside St. Petersburg. From his earliest days, he'd loved to see the horses gallop past, hear the rap of their hooves as they set out on the hunt with their wealthy owners. And *this* was a Trakehner stallion. A thoroughbred from the famous Trakehnen estate, the so-called "City of Horses" where stallions lived like kings. He could see himself on a horse like that, riding through the towns of his beloved homeland after they won the war. People would wave at him and know he'd risked his life for his country.

The horse dropped, pounding the earth with his hooves, and reared again. Golitsin spotted the mark on the stallion's right hindquarter right away. The single elk antler seared into the flesh—the original brand mark of Trakehnen.

The woman stemmed her boots into the dirt. The horse reared again and Golitsin stumbled sideways, giving the woman time to withdraw a hunting knife from her belt and plunge the blade into his right arm. With precision she cut into muscle, holding firm and steady, slicing from his shoulder to the underside of his arm, all the way to his wrist.

"You fucking cunt!"

Roaring more in surprise than pain, he tried to stem the flow of blood with his good hand, but there was no stopping it. In desperation, he wrenched his pistol from its holster, blood sticky on his fingers, and aimed straight at her heart. The woman stared, waiting for the blast, but he had no time to pull the trigger. A hoof slammed into his head, and he crumpled to the ground.

Golitsin stirred. Someone was shaking him.

"Major Golitsin. Wake up!"

His head was spinning in blackness. He tried to stand, but he couldn't find his legs.

"Shit," said a faraway voice, "he's covered in blood. Quick! Tie a tourniquet around his arm!"

"What the hell happened to him?" said another. "Somebody cut him open like a sausage!"

"Had to be a good German knife to cut that clean. These Germans have the best goddamn knives. Wait! What's this?"

Golitsin could feel rough hands on his skull.

"Oh man, what a lump. This isn't going to be good when he wakes up."

A band was pulled taut around Golitsin's bicep. He felt himself being lifted up, felt his life force returning as he was heaved across broad shoulders. His head ached. Mother of God. Now he remembered. The woman, the horse. Where the hell were they? He opened his eyes and blinked.

"Put me down!" he barked.

"Major, sir, you're badly hurt," countered the soldier who was carrying him.

"Goddamn it! Put me down! I can walk by myself!"

The soldier hurried to comply, setting him on the ground and letting him find his balance.

He composed himself and began to walk. His men stood by, ready to catch him, but he strode forward, making a show of strength even as humiliation descended upon him in full force.

He felt faint from the loss of blood, but even more so from the dizzying shame of failure. These men had found him unconscious and bleeding.

He had failed to carry out his own orders. He had let a woman get away.

I must kill them, he thought. He reached for his pistol. *Shit!* His gun must have fallen from his hand when the horse knocked him to the ground. Another wave of nausea hit him. *Good God!* His arm was butchered. The woman. She could have been his prize.

He imagined what his superiors would say. Gone was the Medal of Honor. Gone the rise in military rank that would enable him to say good-bye to mediocrity.

The star on his shoulder board was split in two sad halves, destroyed, as was his hope of becoming a general. His arm hung by his side. He couldn't feel his fingers. His throat tightened.

He wanted to cry. But no, he would pull himself together. If he could survive this, nothing would stop him. He could still prove himself. He wasn't that old. When his arm healed, he'd fight again. His superiors would forgive this small indiscretion.

He began to walk more quickly. He wouldn't give up. He would advance into the city of Berlin with his army and fight, and after the invasion, he'd come out a hero. He could still do it.

He stopped in the village square, steadying himself against a cart. Blood had congealed like pudding on the cobblestones and stuck to his boot soles.

"Attention soldiers!" he cried, forcing himself to stand tall. "Have you done what we came to do?"

"Yes sir!" shouted his men.

"Good! Then stay here and hold off the enemy while I return to field command headquarters to report our success." He turned to the soldier who had helped him. "Lieutenant, you're in charge until I return."

When he reached the nearest tank parked on the *Reichschaussee*, he mustered his last bit of willpower and, with his good arm, pulled himself up next to the driver waiting in the hatch.

His eyes skimmed the butchered corpses and traveled to the edge of the forest where he had encountered the woman. He felt a cold calm in his chest now. He would hunt her down. She couldn't live far away. After all, she'd come on horseback. When the final order came to roll into Trakehnen, Angerburg, and the rest of East Prussia, he would find her. And he would kill her. But first, she would suffer. He'd make sure of it. A burning pain shot through his wrist, doubling him over. He vomited a mouthful of bile onto the dirty tank floor and quickly covered it up with his boot. Had the driver noticed? He glanced sideways. No, thank God. He straightened up again.

As for the stallion, he'd track him down too. The horse was extraordinary. He'd never seen another horse like that one. Regal and black, with a mane like polished opals. He'd never kill that horse. Trakehner bloodlines were pure gold. No, he'd take the stallion back to Russia. And once he had him on his farm, he'd build one of the finest stables in the land.

The tourniquet on his arm bit into his flesh. He shifted in the hard seat and peered through the mud-splattered windshield.

The driver beside him grabbed the steering sticks, and the tank engine began to whir, *chunk, chunk, chunk-a-chunk.* The sound reminded him of hoofbeats. He could picture the stallion, black as the Bering Strait in winter, the fancy girl in the saddle, her legs spread wide.

"That bitch will not survive this war," he muttered as the growling flywheels gathered speed and the tank rolled toward the Prussian-Polish border.

FOUR

All morning Helling had been sweating before the forge he'd built on the von Falken estate, heating and reheating metal, hammering away at the rounded shape of a horseshoe. Usually his work absorbed him, but for the past few weeks he had been distracted. From all over the countryside, from Trakehnen, Insterburg, and the surrounding villages, troubling rumors were circulating about the German army and its inability to hold the front. He picked up a piece of red-hot iron with his tongs, set it down on the anvil, and pounded it with his hammer. He had dedicated his life in service of Baron Fritz von Falken's prized Trakehners, spending his week living in a small room next to his forge and driving home to Karin and his daughters on Friday night. Proper horseshoes were critical to the horses' well-being, but he didn't know how much longer he and his family would be able to stay in East Prussia.

He'd begun to worry about leaving Karin and his daughters alone. His Karin. He was already forty when Karin agreed to marry him twenty-two years ago. She had just turned twenty-six, and it still surprised him that a woman so young and beautiful would have fallen in love with him. But Karin had said that his gentleness of soul had won her over, and whether he was truly that gentle or not, she still welcomed him into their bed with the force of a love he only hoped to match.

He wondered, too, what would happen to his Gypsy friend, Andras Karas, and his clan. Andras was a master blacksmith, a magician with metal. Helling had learned much from him.

Holding one of Karas's fine hammers, he thought about the decades that had passed since they'd first met. Helling, five feet nine and stout, was hardly a delicate man. Yet, he felt intimidated when he looked up at Karas's enormous bear of a frame. At first it was Karas's attitude, not his size, that had unnerved Helling.

A brooder, Karas was easily moved to anger. His coal-black eyes flashed suspiciously at anyone who didn't belong to his clan. It was true that Gypsies were distrustful of those they called *gadje*—outsiders—but Karas was more distrustful than most. It had taken Helling years, and a great deal of nerve, to ask if he could pay him for an apprenticeship.

"Do you honestly believe the skills and secrets of my ancestors are for sale?" Karas had asked scornfully, his broad chest thrusting forward.

Helling's cheeks had burned under Karas's disparaging gaze. He felt rebuked for the sin of simply asking.

So, when Karas unexpectedly sent his son, Joshi, as an emissary to offer the opportunity, Helling almost refused out of pride.

Helling had always liked the curious boy who stood beside his father when wares and cash exchanged hands. Joshi's inquisitive eyes studied every customer. He could tell if a potential purchaser would pay a fair price. He knew instantly if a smile was false. He was smart, and beneath his assessing gaze, Helling sensed an intuitive soul.

He remembered the exact day Joshi had walked into his workshop and said, "Blacksmith Helling, I think I can work something out for you—with my father, that is. But it will have to be a bartering proposition."

"I really have nothing to barter," Helling had scoffed.

"Yes you do. If you teach me how to hunt, my father will show you his metalworking tricks."

Helling had stared at the boy, thinking he was being cocky, but Joshi had carried on. "Manya tells me you're teaching her. She already knows more about baiting hooks and tracking deer than I do. Please," he begged, "I want to learn too."

"You can always come with us, Joshi," Helling answered quietly. "You don't have to pay me."

"No. I don't want to be a tagalong. Fair is fair. I discussed it with Father this afternoon." He ventured a conspiring smile. "Just say 'yes,' Blacksmith Helling, and tomorrow you'll be making horseshoes as light as the wind and as strong as mountains."

And so it was.

The next day Joshi brought Helling and Andras Karas together. A man of his word, Karas taught Helling how to make the best forges, swages, and horseshoes, even tools that had no names and could never be duplicated by others.

My goodness, thought Helling, glancing at the flames spitting sparks in the fire. *What a long time ago that was. Manya is a woman, almost twenty-one. And Joshi?* Helling scratched his head. *He must be twenty-four. Surely, he has finished his studies in Sweden by now. Has Manya heard from him lately? I must remember to ask.*

Helling stopped hammering and was about to wipe away the sweat from the front of his blue overalls when he heard the clattering of hooves. He looked up sharply. Who would race across the cobblestones like that? What if the horse slipped? Broken bones were ugly on horses. And where in God's name was Manya?

Lately, he worried about her all the time. The countryside was full of German military transports. They plowed across the land with little respect for crops or animals. Nevertheless, Manya ventured out every morning on Aztec to inspect the estate and talk to the farmhands. It frightened him to think of her riding among rough soldiers and inexperienced boys carrying machine guns and shouting, *"Sieg Heil!"*

"The German army has already lost if it needs children to fight the war," he muttered to himself.

He rose, went to the open doorway, and looked out.

"What on earth?" he gasped. The thunderous noise was coming from Aztec's hooves. "Whoa!" he exclaimed. "What is it?" He grabbed Aztec's reins and saw Manya's blanched face.

"Nemmersdorf," she said, her knees nearly giving way as she slid out of the saddle. "I've just come from there. Everyone is—"

She started to shake and sob.

"Why are you crying, child? What's wrong?"

Manya raised her tear-streaked face to his. The anguish in her eyes froze his heart. "What happened? Tell me!"

Manya's voice was a crippled whisper.

"Everyone is—is—dead. Russian soldiers—they came early this morning like savages. They shot, they—oh no, they—Karin, she tried to protect Maritza, but—"

He heard the words catch in her throat.

"No one escaped. No one. I couldn't help them. Oh God, I'm so sorry I couldn't help them."

Helling gripped Manya's shoulders. "You must be mistaken," he said.

Just this morning, he had held his beloved Karin in his arms beneath the eiderdown in their four-poster bed, her blond hair loose upon her shoulders. She had talked of her plans for the day, saying she was going to make a fresh apple pie with Zarah and Maritza. Later, in her lilac dressing gown, she had kissed him good-bye at the door, the scent of soap on her skin. No, it couldn't be.

"I don't believe you," Helling cried. "I must go and see for myself."

"You can't," she said. "The Russians are there."

He noticed her torn jacket and the ripped blouse beneath it. And her hands, why were they stained with blood?

"What did they do to you, child?" he asked, horror on his tongue.

"One of the Russians found me. He—he tried to—but I got away." She laid her hand on Aztec's neck. "If it weren't for Aztec, I'd be dead."

Not far away, Helling heard whispering. Dazed, he turned to look. The von Falkens' cook, Ursula, and the old stable master, Schwitkowski, were standing in the courtyard, their eyes full of concern.

"There's been an ambush," sobbed Manya, waving them closer. "The Russians—"

Ursula ran over to hold her.

Helling felt his knees buckle, but his old friend Schwitkowski caught him, settled him on the bench outside his workshop, and was now holding him within frail arms. A sob from the depths of his soul rose over the tops of the red silos toward Karin and his girls.

FIVE

When she opened the front door of her beloved home and stepped into the foyer, Manya heard the sad notes of Chopin's etude, *Tristesse*. From where she stood, she could see her mother at the Steinway in the drawing room, her mother's left hand moving in a languid one-two, one-two over the keys while her right hand filled the house with Chopin's plaintive melody.

Pausing to steady herself, Manya glanced at her own hands. The Russian's blood had dried in the creases between her knuckles. A new terror welled up in her throat. They would all die like Karin and Maritza. She thought of her troubling dream. How soon would the Russians be at their gate? Was it a matter of hours, days, weeks? What if her father refused to listen to her?

In the drawing room, her father was writing at his rosewood desk near the window overlooking the lake. Behind him was the large Victorian birdcage that was home to her mother's blue and white parakeets. She hesitated when she glanced at her mother, whose eyes were lost in a dream of her own, her hands moving over the keys.

Manya swallowed, her mouth turning bone-dry as she thought about Helling and Karin, Zarah and Maritza. I mustn't upset Mother, she told herself, or Father will be impossible to talk to.

For as long as Manya could remember, her father had been protective of his wife, shielding her from even mildly upsetting news. Growing up, Manya soon learned that her mother was plagued with bouts of depression. An even-tempered man, Baron von Falken would have given his life to keep his wife happy. And he tried hard, indulging her every whim, giving her space to paint, sculpt, and make music, while releasing her from any arduous work that would have been the duty of most wives overlooking an estate as large as theirs. But whatever he did, his wife still fell prey to terrifying mood swings, and he lived in dread that she might harm herself.

Hearing the soft thud of Manya's boots on the carpet, the baron glanced up.

"Were you out fishing this morning, my dear?" he smiled, when she reached his desk. "Have you brought supper?" His smile quickly faded when he saw her blood-streaked sleeve, and he rose from his chair. "What happened?"

"Papa," she said in a low voice, and broke into tears.

The baron's eyes shifted toward his wife. "Oh my child," he murmured, opening the terrace door and motioning her into the brisk afternoon air. "What is it?"

She spoke quickly, recounting all she had witnessed that morning. "I'm so scared, Papa," she said when she'd caught her breath. "We've talked about leaving. I know you think we should stay, but after what happened this morning, there's no question."

The baron shook his head. His face had grown chalky and pale. He placed a shaky hand on the balcony railing to steady himself and gazed toward the stables.

"Oh God," he whispered. "Poor Helling."

"Papa?" she said, taking his arm, her voice rising in frustration. "Are you listening to me? We must leave. *Now.* At once."

Her father moved his gaze back to hers, his strong face suddenly worn and tired.

"It's impossible," he told her flatly.

The words filled her heart with anger. "Papa, please! We'll all die! Helling's family is *dead.*"

The baron's upper lip ticked. "Just yesterday a Nazi official from Angerburg came to see me," he hissed. "One of Governor Erich Koch's underlings."

He dropped his voice to a whisper and glanced into the garden, making sure no one besides his daughter could hear. "I told him we must begin transporting our people to safety." He pointed out over the railing, panic filling his eyes. "I asked him why our women and children have been prohibited from leaving for the west when the Russians are right on our doorstep. I told him they won't think twice about killing young children. They'll shoot our horses. They'll eat them."

"What did he say?" Manya asked.

"He screamed at me and warned me never to question the *Führer.* I've never encountered such fanaticism. He told me emphatically that if I attempt to take my family and flee East Prussia, I'll be considered a traitor to the German Reich, and we'll all be shot."

"You can't listen to him," she insisted. "Winter is coming. We have to leave before the cold sets in. Blacksmith Helling says it's going to be a harsh winter. If we don't leave soon, we'll never get out in time!"

Once again her father shook his head no. "Any attempt at packing up wagons will reach Governor Koch's ears." His gaze turned to the horizon. "There are spies everywhere. The people who work on the estate respect us. They would help us prepare, but I can't leave them to fend for themselves. I am responsible for their well-being. Besides, there are those who still think Hitler will win this war, and if we flee, we are showing the enemy that Germany is weak."

"Papa, look at me!" cried Manya. She grabbed at the rip in her blouse.

Her father averted his eyes, but she took hold of his arm. "Germany *is* crumbling! Our neighbors are fleeing. On farms further east, I saw cattle roaming wild with distended udders, sheep with dirty, unshorn coats. *It's because their owners are gone.* We should be gone too!"

She took a panicked breath and tried to even her tone. "Our coachman tells me that despite Nazi orders, many wagons have left Insterburg, Goldap, and the surrounding villages. Our neighbors see the handwriting on the wall. Why don't we, Papa? Herr Schwitkowski says that on the horse farm in Trakehnen, the wagons are set to leave."

"That can't be true!" exclaimed the baron. "They know it's forbidden."

"They don't care! They're ready. Their wagons are hidden in the woods. Everyone knows the Nazis should have given evacuation orders weeks ago."

Her father shrugged helplessly, and she choked back a sob. "Millions of people, *children*, will be slaughtered! Our Trakehner horses too! Don't you see, Papa? Hitler doesn't care about us."

"Keep your voice down," her father hissed, glancing into the drawing room. The baroness had stopped playing the Chopin melody and was idly running her fingers over the piano keys. "Let me think about this. I don't want to upset her. She can't cope with the thought of leaving Guja. Besides, one wrong move and the Nazis will shoot every one of us."

In the harsh afternoon light, Manya saw how the war had aged him beyond his sixty years. Always powerful and decisive, he was now haggard and too thin.

"Papa," she wept. "The Russians will shoot you, but Mother and I will be raped to death. Ursula too. Believe me, after this morning, I know."

Her father tightened his jaw, and her heart sank. She sighed as he stepped back into the drawing room, motioning for her to follow him.

Exhaustion had settled over her. She sat down instead on the terrace bench and stared into the garden. Her mother was now playing *Dark Eyes*, a haunting melody she had learned many years ago from Joshi's mother, Vavara. Even before the Nazi regime, it had been frowned upon for Gypsies to enter an upstanding citizen's home, but her mother had cared little for people's opinions. Deaf to the warnings of friends and townsfolk, she had welcomed Vavara into the drawing room.

The baroness came to rely on the singing lessons Vavara gave her. When the voices of the two women filled the room, Manya felt her mother's depression fade into contentment. Now, as she leaned her head against the brick wall, Manya let the familiar song transport her back to the past.

It was after her mother's first singing lesson with Vavara that she'd met Vavara's son, Joshi. She remembered the moment exactly. Her mother and Vavara were having coffee and cake. Bored with their chatter, she had wandered into the garden, where, to her surprise, she spotted a black-haired boy, no more than eleven, whittling a piece of wood under the willow tree beside the veranda.

"Who are you?" she asked.

The boy had looked up at her. His eyes, green as a mallard's feather, were so direct they took her breath away.

"Joshi Karas," he said, laying down his knife. "Vavara's my mum."

Every lesson after that, she found him sitting in the same spot, waiting. An only child, she looked forward to his company. While their mothers made music, she and Joshi climbed apple trees, peered into sparrows' nests or played hide and seek in the branches. On colder days, they spent their time in the stables, chattering away, grooming the horses.

One spring afternoon a couple of years after their first meeting, while she was walking down the garden path, she saw Joshi running toward her past the beds of purple irises. Breathless, he handed her a rough piece of amber. "For you," he said. "East Prussian gold. I found it myself by the Baltic Sea on the beach near Kahlberg. Look! It even has a butterfly inside. My mum says butterflies are a symbol of change."

"It's beautiful," she murmured, holding it up to the light. "But why are you giving it to me?"

He laughed. "Because you're my best friend."

When he was not around, Manya felt lonely, especially when her mother spiraled into one of her dark moods. She shuddered to think of the many times she'd found her mother disheveled, sitting on a stool in her art studio, mindlessly kneading a piece of clay.

"Go away, child," her mother would groan.

A raven cawed overhead. Manya's gaze traveled to the willow tree where she had first met Joshi.

"I wish you were with me now," she whispered.

SIX

*F*aded birch leaves tumbled past Manya's bedroom window. Again she hadn't slept. Over and over she heard the Russian soldier shouting, "*Ukas Stalin!*" Stalin's orders! Time and again she saw him shove his pistol into Karin's mouth and pull the trigger. Heard Maritza's screams. She could hardly bear to think about what might have happened to little Zarah. One week had passed since the Nemmersdorf ambush and only five days since the Germans had forced the Russians to retreat.

Restless, she rose, dressed, and went to the stables. She passed beneath the stone archway engraved with her family's coat of arms—a red and gold helmet decorated with an elk antler and a buffalo horn. As soon as she stepped into the entranceway leading to the stalls, Shambhala, her Trakehner mare that was pregnant with Aztec's foal, whinnied softly.

"Hello pretty lady," Manya crooned, stopping to stroke the mare's tender pink muzzle.

Shambhala's soulful eyes sought hers, and she felt a sudden pang of fear for her sweet mare whose mane lay like silver against her sleek neck. Shambhala's bloodlines could be traced back as far as 1732, when King Frederick William I of Prussia had established a royal stud farm. Her beauty, highlighted by a coat of sleek hair that gleamed like moonlight, was born from of a long line of Arabian thoroughbred horses, and her endurance stemmed from careful breeding with the hardy East Prussian *Schweiken* pony.

The von Falkens, too, had been breeders for generations; their Trakehner horses had even won ribbons at the English Derby races. Shambhala had come from the famous Braunsberg horse farm. Manya remembered spending long days at auctions there while her father bid on mares. She remembered evenings, too, sitting at his knee, when he would delight her with stories about Trakehners.

"Elegant, fast, and smart," he would boast. "Winners. Remember this, Manya, a Trakehner will give you its heart and soul, its life, even."

Shambhala nuzzled her hand, looking for a piece of sugar. Manya's throat tightened. What would the Russians do if they got hold of her mare? Shoot her? Most likely. Frightened by the thought, she turned away and went to fetch Aztec's tack.

Twenty minutes later, she and Aztec were cantering along the edge of the meadow, close to the woods. The autumn leaves were falling, turning the ground into a russet carpet. *In a few weeks winter will be here*, she thought. *Ice will fill the rivers.*

Aztec shook his head, breaking into an easy gallop. She relaxed in the saddle, her thoughts going back to the day Aztec had first high-stepped through the estate gates. He'd held his tail high like an opalescent plume, and she'd thought he was the most magnificent creature she'd ever laid eyes on. Figuring he'd been brought to the farm to cover a broodmare, she had assumed he would be taken away again. But that night when she had gone to the stables to help Schwitkowski, she found Aztec in a stall near the back entrance.

"Be careful," Schwitkowski had warned, his wild gray hair framing a weathered gaze. "He's been beaten. Look at him. All whip wounds and scabs. Rears and kicks and bites like the devil."

To her astonishment, she discovered that her father had bought Aztec from her Uncle Egon, her mother's brother. The war had just begun and, ever a schemer, Egon had enlisted in the army, hoping to make his fortune. In the meantime, he'd sold Aztec to pay off a bad gambling debt. She'd seen right away that Aztec was a full-bred Trakehner. He was branded with the single elk antler, but somehow her uncle was never able to produce the proper papers.

Manya, however, didn't care about the papers. Aztec was a prize with or without them. She visited Aztec every day, but for weeks he turned away when she came close.

"Look at me," she would plead in a gentle voice, trying to entice him with a cube of sugar or a carrot.

One morning, it seemed he'd had enough of being lonely, and he turned his gaze to her.

From that day on, their bond grew. Within a month, she was able to saddle him and ride him in the courtyard. She communicated with him gently, using her hands and knees and the tender nuances of her voice. Soon, their awareness of each other grew into a full-blown partnership in which each readily intuited what the other wanted. Together they became champions, winning ribbons and medals in the best horse shows in Georgenburg, Angerburg, even Königsberg.

She glanced at the sun. It was early yet. She hadn't said a word to anyone before leaving home, but she and Aztec were on their way to Nemmersdorf to look for Zarah. Two days after the massacre, the German army had pushed the Russians out of the village, so she felt safe enough to ride there. Helling had gone to Nemmersdorf to bury his family. Searching the bodies lined up in rows across the field, he found only Karin and Maritza—no Zarah. For days, he scoured the woods, but she had vanished. Finally, believing she was dead, he gave up. Somehow, though, Manya believed she was still alive.

Just as she was about to cross the Angerapp Bridge, a German army tank pulled up alongside her. Three soldiers, no older than sixteen, poked their heads out of the hatch.

"Miss," one of them called. "Do you have any cigarettes?"

"Sorry," Manya replied. "But I have a flask of coffee. Would you like some?"

The oldest, a boy with warm hazel eyes, accepted her offer. Looking straight at her, he said, "Miss, you really should get out of here. Many people are fleeing on foot, on horseback, and on bicycles. You're too pretty. If the Russians catch you they'll—"

She cut him off. "But tell me, do we stand a chance?"

The boy took a long swill of coffee before wiping his mouth with the back of his sleeve and handing the flask on to his comrades.

"Miss," he said in a low voice. "I'm going to tell you straight. I don't care who kills me for it. We're hanging on by the skin of our teeth. We've been promised reinforcements, but we've never seen any. The Führer talks about a killer war machine, and some infallible strategy." He laughed bitterly. "I haven't seen either. He says he *wants* the Russians to invade East Prussia so the *Wehrmacht* can annihilate them. It's a joke. There are millions of Russian soldiers, and only a handful of us. And now they have a new tank, a T-34. I tell you, our goose is cooked. They'll surround us from all sides, burn us, bomb us, whatever. Trust me. Don't wait. Try to get to Danzig or one of the seaports on the coast. Get on a ship that's headed for Kiel or Lübeck, someplace like that. Whatever you do, get going."

He took the empty flask from the last boy and handed it to her, thanking her for the coffee before closing the hatch. The tank rattled off. *How awful,* she thought with a heavy sigh, *to see boys in oversized helmets heading to the front.*

In the sky, two swans arched their wings toward the morning sun. Aztec began to canter. She leaned forward in the saddle.

"If only *you* had wings, Aztec," she murmured.

Finally, they entered the forest near Nemmersdorf. For two hours they walked beneath pine and birch and larch listening for voices or the sounds of snapping twigs. Nudging Aztec with her heels, she was just about to turn him toward a patch of bilberry shrubs when she saw something move behind a larch tree. Uneasy, she pulled her shotgun from its sling and aimed the barrel at the tree. To her surprise, Aztec let out a friendly whinny.

"Zarah," whispered Manya, but she didn't trust anything. What if there were soldiers in these woods? Keeping the gun cocked, she waited, her eyes fixed on the tree. A pale hand darted out from behind the trunk. "Who's there?" she called softly. "Come out." Aztec took a few steps forward, the trusting rumble of his neigh making her feel a little more secure. "Zarah?"

SEVEN

In a tent set up for disciplinary action, Golitsin stood in front of his superiors, his head bowed, his bladder bursting with terror. The brigade colonel who had listened to his earlier report on the Nemmersdorf attack sat stone-faced in a corner, while another officer, known for his torture and execution tactics, reprimanded Golitsin in a harsh, scratchy voice.

"Damn imbecile!" the officer shouted. "Who told you to return to field command headquarters?"

Golitsin wanted to say that he thought he'd done the right thing by reporting back after the ambush, but he knew better.

"You should have stayed in Nemmersdorf and maintained our position against those German dogs," the officer continued. "You stupid coward."

The officer stepped from behind a makeshift table and approached Golitsin with a threatening smile. "Where's your pistol, Major Golitsin?"

Golitsin felt his heart skip a beat. Losing a pistol was a serious offense. In his mind he saw the pistol lying somewhere on the ground in the woods near the village.

"Sir, I—I'm not sure. I believe it's in my—"

"You believe?" his interrogator snapped. "You're lying. You've lost it. Some German got the better of you. You think we can't see? Your arm is in shreds."

The officer spat on the ground. "Maybe you hid it in your underwear, eh?"

Golitsin's throat contracted but he had no spit to swallow.

"Get up on that table, Major," hissed the officer. "Let's see if your short legs can support you up there."

The sarcasm in the man's voice made Golitsin tremble. It reminded him of his father's voice, belittling and nasty.

"But then, short men don't have so far to fall. Isn't that right?"

Golitsin nodded and climbed on the rickety table, trying hard to maintain his balance while the pain of his infected wound exploded into his neck and shoulder.

"Take off your cap. Your belt too."

Memories of beatings flashed before Golitsin's eyes, filling his armpits with a cold sweat. For a second, the man in front of him was his father, preparing to whip him senseless with a belt.

"Now, take off your pants and your underwear. Let's see if we can find your pistol." The officer let out a loud guffaw.

Golitsin's knees were shaking, but he managed to pull down his khaki trousers.

"It's not there, is it," said the officer.

Golitsin shook his head.

"Did you know that it is a major offense to lose a weapon presented to you by Mother Russia?"

"Yes sir," mumbled Golitsin.

"Well then," said the officer, "you also know that you're not fit to lead a battalion. You've disgraced our army, our guard. You left your men in jeopardy, and now the Germans have regained what your men risked their lives for. So, in the name of the Russian Soviet Federative Socialist Republic, I sentence you to death."

The officer drew his sidearm and aimed it straight at Golitsin's face.

Blackness descended over Golitsin. *One single gunshot*, he thought, *and it will be over.*

He wasn't sure how long he stood trembling on the table, but when he opened his eyes, a pool of urine had formed at his feet.

"I've decided to let you live," he heard the officer say. "Now get down. Yes. You screwed up the mission, but you still have excellent eyes. We're going to use them. Believe me."

Relief rushed over Golitsin. Losing consciousness, he fell.

He didn't know how long he'd lain there in his shame when he felt cold water splashing against his face.

"Wake up," he heard the officer say. "Your actions have cost you your stars and stripes. You are no longer a major. Now get up off your ass and thank God that I'm allowing you to live. Wipe up this piss. Then, go to the barracks for some clothes and have the doctor change that stinking bandage."

Golitsin reached for the uniform on the floor, but the officer kicked at his hand.

"No way, soldier. You've forfeited these army breeches. You'll have to walk through the camp naked until you find something to wear."

Golitsin looked up. His arm throbbed. But, from deep inside his chest, he felt a surge of comforting anger. He'd show them, goddamn it! He would.

EIGHT

Aztec rounded the larch. There, crouched in the brambles, was Zarah, her bare feet bruised and bleeding, her tattered blue dress streaked with stains.

"Sweetheart," cried Manya, with a happy rush of relief.

She wanted to jump from her saddle and wrap her arms around Zarah, yet something told her to move slowly.

Zarah lifted her head and stared. Her face was a chalk-white mask and her glazed eyes held a faraway look, as though she'd never seen Manya before.

"It's all right, love," murmured Manya, lowering her gun.

But before Manya could dismount, Zarah caught sight of the gun. With her face twisted in terror, Zarah turned and ran toward an oak tree and scampered up the knotted trunk like a frightened squirrel.

Manya saw Zarah press her tiny body into a big, dark hollow. *How did she know that hollow was there*, Manya wondered, fixing her eyes on the tree. *Is that where she has been hiding? Poor baby.*

Urging Aztec forward, she rode close to the tree. "Don't be afraid, love," she called softly, looking up. "It's me, Manya."

Zarah's frightened eyes peered from her hiding place and traveled down toward Manya, her small, white-knuckled hands clinging to the rough edge of bark as if it were the only place of refuge left in the world. She did not smile, nor did she speak.

Moving slowly, Manya dropped the reins and rose in the stirrups, stretching out her arms.

"Come, sweetheart," she called. "I'll catch you."

But Zarah stayed where she was, her expression utterly blank.

"Zarah, can you hear me?"

Uncertain, Manya waited. Seconds later, Aztec let out a soft neigh.

Zarah's eyes flickered. Trembling, she inched her way out of the hollow. Clutching the bark of the tree, she slid into Manya's arms, her skin smelling of wild animals, dirt, and decay.

They sat in the saddle under the green canopy of trees, Manya stroking Zarah's hair and talking in soothing tones. At times, Zarah would twist around to stare at her, but she did not speak. No matter what Manya said, Zarah Helling would not utter one word. Finally, Manya took the reins.

"We're going to Guja now, Zarah, to see your Papa. He'll be so happy to have you back in his arms."

<hr />

On her twenty-first birthday, two weeks after she found Zarah, Manya woke with the same tangle of doubt and fatigue she had felt upon falling asleep. Maybe her father was right. Maybe they should stay. If they disobeyed orders and fled, they'd be shot anyway. Her mind drifted back to her Russian attacker. She could still feel his cold eyes on her skin. She shuddered, knowing full well what would happen if the soldiers got hold of her again. The clatter of dishes rose from downstairs. Pushing away her troubled thoughts, she kicked off the duvet.

No matter how depressed the baroness might be, she loved birthday celebrations and never forgot to place a wreath of violets and white chrysanthemums on the breakfast table. She always brought out the Meissen porcelain, too, and the antique silver cutlery and the gifts.

Two years earlier, Manya's father had surprised her with a custom-made Stübben saddle. The previous year, he gave her a buttery tanned bridle. Overcome with eagerness to see what gifts awaited her, Manya pulled her dressing gown on and hurried down the stairs to the glass-enclosed winter garden.

Usually her father was the first to greet her, but this morning she saw only her mother, who smiled from her seat at the breakfast table.

"Happy birthday, *Liebchen*," she said. "I have a different gift for you today." She set a buttered *Semmel* roll on Manya's plate. "Until now, your father gave you presents meant for tomboys, but at twenty-one, you're a woman."

Manya blushed. Her mother was not usually so direct. She sat down in her chair and watched her mother retrieve a small silver box from her cardigan pocket.

"Open it," urged the baroness, holding the gift across the table.

Manya took it and lifted the lid. Inside was a gold ring set with a large amber cabochon carved and polished into a glowing oval. Two diamonds sparkled on either side of the honey-colored resin.

"It's beautiful!" exclaimed Manya, her heart quickening with pleasure. "I love it. It's just like your amber cabochon, except for the diamonds."

The baroness smiled and set down her teacup.

"It *is* my stone, dear," she said. "The jeweler in Angerburg added my diamond studs when he sized it for your finger. I told him it was time you wore some jewelry. As you know, Guja means 'jewel' in Spanish. The Spanish Crusaders called our land *Joya* because it is the most beautiful place on earth." Her mother gazed at the ring. "The amber cabochon means so much to me. I've worn it for nearly fifteen years. Vavara Karas gave it to me."

Manya glanced up with surprise. "Joshi's mum?"

The baroness swallowed. "There's a story. I was never sure how to tell it, but now I feel it's important to share things with you—before it's too late, I mean."

Manya felt a chill settle on her skin.

"I'm ill," said the baroness. "How can I explain? Some call it a madness in my family. When it comes, I feel like a glass wall descends between me and the rest of the world. It's a loneliness I can barely describe to you. My grandmother had it, and my mother too, even though she was so full of life. But you, child, have escaped this curse, and for that I thank God."

The baroness pressed her hands to her eyes. "I've wanted to tell you this for a long time, but I never had the courage. When you were a baby, your grandmother Omi shot herself through the heart. Manya, I went crazy. I tore out my hair and hid in the closets of this house. No one would talk to me about it, except to say that it was an accident. But I knew it wasn't. No one spoke the truth to me until I met Vavara. She wasn't afraid of my demons or my grief. One day, she gave me her ring, saying that the amber was precious, that it held life and would protect me from evil spirits. She said it would bring my mother to me in dreams, and it has."

The baroness blinked and laid her hand on Manya's cheek.

"But now *you* need protection." She paused and looked at Manya, her eyes clear. "I warn you, though, the amber really does evoke dreams.

The dead may visit you, but don't be afraid. They won't harm you. Listen to them."

She took Manya's hand in hers and gazed through the window to the lawn sloping down from the veranda to the lake. The morning light that filtered through the beveled glass made her look much younger than her fifty-one years. She cleared her throat and continued, "There's something else I want to say. I haven't been a good mother."

Manya moved to reassure her, but the baroness placed a finger on her lips. "No, let me speak. I love you," she said, her gray eyes softening. "And I admire you. I want you to know that."

Suddenly, Manya felt shy, but she was so hungry for her mother's words that she could not look away.

"I've been cold," her mother confessed regretfully. "Even cruel at times. I'm so sorry. Please forgive me. I can't change the years. Nevertheless, I keep hoping that perhaps in some way, my mothering, though far from good, has made you a stronger woman, yes? Please say that it has."

Manya eyes filled with tears. She slipped the ring on her finger, her mother's words echoing inside her. Leaning forward, she kissed her mother gently on both cheeks. Though they would never again speak of it, a new understanding blossomed between them and filled the room with warmth. When her mother had finished her tea, she rose from the table and laid her hand on Manya's shoulder. "I'm sorry to say that Blacksmith Helling won't be coming to the winter garden today. He wanted to wish you happy birthday, but he's afraid to leave Zarah. Perhaps you'll go and see him later?"

Outside, a raven pecked at the window.

"I'm coming, Meister Eckhart, my feathered pet," her mother cooed. She took a crust of bread from the table, opened the door, and went into the garden, bending down to let the tame bird eat from her hand.

Manya looked at the wreath of white chrysanthemums cradling her plate. She thought of Helling. Ever since she was a child he'd brought gifts on her birthday: a carved toy, a special knife, a fishing rod or a spear, and always one of Karin's homemade strudels. In the weeks since Nemmersdorf, she had often sat with him in his workshop just to keep him company. Usually they spent hours in silence. Rarely, they talked. A few times, he mentioned Karin and Maritza, almost by mistake, and Manya winced to see the pain in his eyes.

She remembered how he had cried with happiness when she'd ridden into the courtyard with Zarah, but in the weeks that followed, his despair had increased. No matter how hard he tried, he couldn't make Zarah speak. Nor would Zarah let him close. In fact, she rarely even looked at him, spending most of her time huddled under a saddle in the stable, or curled up like a rag doll on a bale of hay near the horses. She ate less than a sparrow, and he'd given up trying to persuade her, because he couldn't bear the terror that loomed in her eyes when he raised the spoon to her lips.

In the past he had been a talkative man, cracking jokes with the stable hands and maids, but he hardly spoke now.

"What can I do to make my daughter talk?" he would ask Manya, his face creasing hopelessly.

She tried to soothe him, but she didn't know either. Even the doctor from Angerburg who came to see Zarah told them he couldn't help. All he could say was that she had left her voice behind in Nemmersdorf.

Manya held the ring up to the sunlight. Bubbles of trapped air floated in the yellow amber. She shook her head, blew out the candle, and made a wish. "Please," she whispered, "keep us safe and help my darling Zarah heal."

NINE

By early December the Russians were bombing Memel, Tilsit, and Ragnit. Their flares illuminated the night, crisscrossing the sky like flashes of lightning. From her bedroom window, Manya could see the empty stork nests on the stable roof. The storks had fled after Nemmersdorf. Others were fleeing now, too. The countryside was full of refugees, people who waited outside the gates of the estate every night before pressing on to the west at dawn. They came from Lithuania, Latvia, Estonia, and Poland, and with them they brought tales of atrocities committed by Stalin's troops. It seemed to Manya that the stream of frightened faces pouring past the estate was never-ending. Everyone needed food and a place to rest. The kitchen staff and the stable hands were always busy, bustling about to help the travelers.

On one of those cold, hectic mornings, Manya found her mother staring at the refugees from her studio window.

"I wish they'd all go away," the baroness said, disdainfully.

Manya wanted to yell at her, to tell her that they should be out on the trail, too, that they would surely die if they stayed. But she bit her tongue and joined Ursula in the kitchen, where the company was happier.

She stopped in the doorway to study the roll of fat at the back of Ursula's neck and watched the cook heft a wooden spoon through an enormous cauldron on the stove. The air was thick with the smell of potato soup simmering with bacon and onions.

"Don't just stand there, child," scolded Ursula. "Stir the second pot so we can get some food down to those poor souls." She lifted a dishrag to her damp forehead before picking up a tray of buns from the marble pastry counter. "On second thought, take these down to the gate."

Helling shivered. God, it was cold. Or maybe he was just tired. He watched Schwitkowski carry a bucket of grain into Aztec's stall.

"How the hell am I going to break the news to Manya?" he asked in a low whisper.

"I don't know," Schwitkowski muttered. "She'd rather shoot Aztec than let the army recruit him. There's nothing we can do. The Nazis know he's here."

Helling bent over to pick up Aztec's hoof.

"Why can't you go lame, old boy?"

"What are you two talking about?" Helling heard Manya ask in a sharp voice from Shambhala's stall.

"Damn," he muttered. He hadn't thought she could hear him.

A hard lump squeezed his throat. *I can't stand any more heartbreak*, he thought. *Still, I have to tell her.*

With dread, he listened to her footsteps coming down the hall. When she reached Aztec's stall, he straightened up and forced himself to hold her gaze.

"Aztec has been drafted," he said softly. "Officials sent a letter yesterday to all the horse breeders in the district. He must be in Angerburg Square tomorrow for inspection. If we don't comply, the Nazis will raid the stables, and if any other suitable horses are found, they'll take them."

"They can't do that!" she snapped. "Papa will lock the gates."

"They can, my dear, and they will. They have our records. They know our herd. Yesterday, Ulrich the stable hand saw a fellow snooping around the stalls. When Ulrich approached him and asked what he was doing, the man told him to shut up. He even threatened to take Ulrich to the police."

Helling sighed. It was early yet, but he felt so spent. "The *Wehrmacht* is desperate. They need horses. They're even recruiting thirteen-year-old boys for the front. Yesterday in Goldap, my friend's youngest son was ordered to show up in uniform. The Russians are too close and the German army is too weak."

"Why hasn't Governor Koch issued evacuation orders?" she asked angrily. "It's murder! Only women, children, and old people remain now! Are we supposed to fight the Russians?"

"Koch is a fanatic who has sold his soul to the Führer. He believes that

East Prussia will not fall. Anyone who says otherwise will be shot or hung. Yesterday, on my way to Goldap, I saw a man dangling from a tree, and 'traitor' was painted on his back. Koch says that Hitler has a *Wunderwaffe*, a superweapon capable of annihilating the entire Red Army." He scratched his head and sighed. "It makes you wonder, doesn't it? Why would Hitler need a few horses?"

"But Aztec can't be a workhorse!" cried Manya. "Uncle Egon's beatings have made him scared of strangers. He'll bolt and kick, and they'll beat him more." She was sobbing now.

"Aztec is a well-trained stallion," Helling said, but he heard himself falter, and he cast his eyes down as if to redirect the lie he was about to tell. "He'll do what is required of him. Besides, the German cavalry treats horses well. Let me take him for you, Manya. It will break your heart to see him go."

"No! Do something, please," she begged. "Don't let this happen."

He watched her grab Schwitkowski's frail arm in desperation.

"Herr Schwitkowski. You know horses. You'll find a way!"

But Schwitkowski just shook his old gray head.

TEN

*M*anya did not leave Aztec's stall that morning. She lay on his back, watching a gray mouse scuttle back and forth across the straw-strewn floor.

"How can you be drafted?" she asked, her tears darkening Aztec's withers.

Toward midday, she heard a voice calling her name. "Your mother said I would find you here. I see nothing's changed. You're still in love with the old boy. Have you taken to sleeping with him now?"

"Joshi!" She sat up, startled to see the man who had slipped into the stall so unexpectedly.

Gathering herself, she pushed her hair out of her face.

"Oh my God," she whispered. "How did you get to Guja? Did you take a boat from Sweden? I can't believe it. Is it safe for you to be here?"

"Hang on a minute," he said. "You're the one who looks like she's been crying. Maybe I should be asking the questions?" He was smiling, but his eyes were filled with concern. "What's wrong?"

He reached out his hand to her. She took it and slid from Aztec's back.

He moved to catch her, his arms encircling her waist. Her heart beat against her chest. Why did she feel so clumsy all of a sudden? They had known each other for half of their lives, for God's sake. She'd always been poised in his presence, but now the nearness of him was unsettling. The familiar scent of cardamom on his clothes made her feel dizzy. And somehow, knowing that her face was puffy and red made her feel self-conscious, too.

"I'm—ach—oh, excuse me." Her gaze slid from his chest up to his face, taking in the dark green of his eyes and the familiar scar that marked his left eyebrow. It had been a year since she'd seen him last, and she was startled by the changes. He had filled out. He was muscular, broad. His chin was stronger, too, and his expression, once so boyish and uncertain, was self-assured. It belonged to a man used to making decisions. And his gaze. Her cheeks grew hot under the warmth of it.

"I—" she stammered.

She didn't know what to say. Not even about Aztec. All she could do was take in Joshi's good looks, his glossy black hair falling across his forehead. She saw his eyes flicker over the curve of her neck, saw them linger in the hollow of her throat. He was looking at her differently, too. She pulled away, nervously smoothing down the creases in her jacket. He smiled, and in his eyes she saw a certain tenderness that made her heart leap again.

"When are you going to tell me what happened?" he asked, taking her hand lightly. "Shall we go sit on the bench in the orchard and talk?"

Manya shook her head and felt another wave of tears roll down her cheeks.

"I can't leave Aztec. They're taking him away tomorrow."

She told him about the Nazis and the threats. He listened quietly, but she saw his eyes grow fierce.

"Don't cry," he whispered. "I know how to make him lame. When must you show him?"

"Tomorrow, late morning."

"Then we'd better get to work." He laughed softly. "We're going to have him hobbling like an old man!"

"How?" she asked, her troubled eyes seeking his.

"Watch," he said.

Talking in a low voice, he approached Aztec and plucked three strands of hair from the stallion's tail, which he tied together carefully and looped around Aztec's front left fetlock in a tight knot.

"It'll take twelve hours before the blood circulation is cut off but by then he'll start limping. In the morning, you should see the full effects. It's not pretty. However, once you remove the tourniquet, he'll walk normally again."

Manya felt a rush of hope. "That's so clever," she said, her voice full of awe.

"It's a Romani horse trader's trick. They can make another seller's horse look bad if they manage to get to it without anyone noticing." Suddenly, his eyes grew troubled. "I wish I knew some other trick that could help us now. False documents won't stop the Nazis anymore."

"What are you saying?"

Now his dark eyes sought hers. "Listen, I came here because I wanted to make sure you were all right. Father is scared. He knows that the papers claiming we have Aryan blood won't hold water, so he wants me to get the clan to Sweden. I owe it to him to try."

He saw a flash of fear pass through Manya's eyes and tenderly brushed a piece of straw from her hair. "No one is safe any longer. Everywhere, Jews and Romanies are being exterminated. I know this because my friend in Sweden works with the resistance. Germany is a nightmare. Outside our borders, the enemy is preparing for slaughter. Inside, the Nazis are already doing it."

"I know," she said. "Even Papa was told he'd be shot if he didn't obey orders."

Joshi leaned against the wall as if to brace himself.

"There's more. You've heard of the work camps, Manya, the concentration camps. They're killing people there, too."

"I have heard," she said, shifting uncomfortably. "And yet, here in Guja, life goes on in such an oddly normal way. I carry on with my daily chores, doing and doing, because I'm so afraid to speak out. And even if I could, who would hear me? I always thought I'd do the right thing, but I don't know. Maybe I'm just a coward."

Her eyes met his, begging for understanding. "I'm scared that if I say something, I'll die. I've heard horrible things, Joshi. Just yesterday, a woman who was fleeing from farther east, near the Polish border, came to the house. She told us she'd been in the forest near her home gathering firewood when four Russian soldiers found her and raped her."

Joshi's lip twitched. Manya wanted to reach out and still it, but she felt frozen.

"I'm frightened too," he said. "I know it was crazy to come back. Every day, I bargain with God. I tell Him that I'll work hard to save lives if He'll just save my family." He gave a bitter laugh. "But there's no haggling with Him."

She wished she could tell him that everything would turn out all right, but she didn't believe it and he would see straight through the lie.

"I really need to go," he said, placing a finger under her chin and tilting her face upward.

Once more, she felt a fluttering inside like butterfly wings beating against her chest. Embarrassed, she avoided his eyes, her gaze falling instead on the same small, jagged scar that cut though his eyebrow. It had been there for as long as she could remember, and somehow this comforted her.

"I think my father's afraid of dying," he said suddenly, interrupting her thoughts.

Manya laid a hand on his arm.

"Maybe he wants to make peace with you after all this time," she said tenderly. "In your letters, you told me how angry he was that you chose medicine over the clan."

A troubled look crossed his face.

"I'll never make my father understand. I struggle with the two sides of myself, too. On one hand, I'm proud of our traditions. I've seen Romani remedies cure illnesses and I respect my Aunt Vadoma's abilities as a healer."

"What does the other side of you say?" she asked, gently.

Joshi spoke slowly, as if he were weighing each word.

"I just can't accept that carrying a mole's foot will lower a fever or save a life. I believe in science. I chose to study medicine because I wanted to know how the body works and why an herbal remedy is successful, not as a magic potion, but as a substance."

He paused to glance at a shaft of sunlight pouring in through the high rectangular window above Aztec's stall.

He looks so serious, she thought, *so dedicated to his work even though it has cost him his father's respect.*

"I've missed you," she blurted out suddenly. As soon as she'd spoken the words, a rush of embarrassment rose to her cheeks. Gathering herself quickly, she added, "I mean, I've missed our talks."

"Me too," he smiled.

He bent over to check Aztec's leg, and she thought about how easily conversation flowed between them, how she never felt bored in his presence. He'd always been interested in learning. As children, they'd read many books in her father's library, from Goethe's *Faust* to Rilke's *Stories of God*, spending hours talking when they'd finished.

But it was her mother who had awakened Joshi's passion for medicine. One day her mother had given him a book on human anatomy. Within weeks he was rattling off the Latin names for every muscle and body part. His gift for learning so impressed Manya's mother that she arranged for him to be schooled by Manya's tutors.

Manya remembered how angry Joshi's father, Andras, known also as "Black Andras," had become when he had learned of the offer. Although he permitted his son to be educated, he never spoke to the baroness again.

"I have to go," Joshi said. He patted Aztec's neck. "Walk like a cripple old boy. Make them think you're ready for the glue factory."

He turned to Manya. "When you show him tomorrow, confuse him with your heels and hands. Make him stumble. Run the circle so the lame leg is outside and the inspectors see it from the stand. Before you go, throw talcum powder on his coat to take away the sheen. Tatty up his tail so he looks like a nag."

She felt the panic rising. "Oh God, I hope I can do this."

"You can," he smiled reassuringly, and kissed her cheek. "I'll see you soon, I hope."

She heard the latch on the gate click, and he was gone.

⚜

The following morning, she reached the stables just after dawn to find Schwitkowski waiting for her.

"Here's your glorious Trakehner!" he grinned, rubbing a handful of talc into Aztec's coat.

Helling was matting up Aztec's tail.

"The old boy is actually lame," he said cheerfully.

It was the first time Manya had seen Helling smile since Nemmersdorf.

"Thank goodness," she murmured, swinging herself into the saddle. "Maybe, with a bit of luck, we can pull this off."

She and Aztec left the courtyard and limped along the road to Angerburg, arriving at the inspection site around midmorning.

Just after she signed in, a commanding shout pierced the air. "Fräulein von Falken, bring your stallion forward."

By now Aztec could barely walk. His fetlock was painfully swollen, and he was trying hard not to put weight on his leg.

"Trot! Canter!" came the sharp order. "Turn a figure eight."

Manya jerked the reins in one direction, while leaning her body in the other. Unable to make the quick turn, Aztec nearly fell.

"What's wrong with you, Fräulein?" shouted the inspector. "My staff tells me you're a top equestrian, yet you're riding that stallion like a bumbling idiot! Come over here now!"

Manya obeyed.

The major stepped off the platform, the swastika on his armband a terrifying reminder of what might happen if he discovered the string. Bending over, he ran his fingers across Aztec's joint. Manya's heart pounded at the walls of her chest. *Surely now*, she thought.

Instead the major stood up.

"Pull yourself together, girl!" he commanded. "You're riding for Germany, for the Führer! Now canter! And do it properly!"

But Aztec could only hobble.

Disgusted, the major waved her away.

"You should be ashamed of yourself," he snorted angrily. "He must have been a wonderful stallion at one time, but he's a disaster now. Go away so I can carry on with my business."

Shaking with fear, not even daring to let out her breath, Manya left the square. She was eager to cut the thread, but she wasn't taking any chances. Finally, several miles outside of town, she led Aztec to a stream so he could rest and drink. There, she cut away the binding strands with her knife and massaged his fetlock to ease the swelling. After twenty minutes, the swelling eased.

Swinging herself back into the saddle, she gazed across the narrow band of glittering water, past the small farmsteads towards Joshi's camp, which lay between Angerburg and Guja. She wished she could ride there and tell him the good news. However, he needed time with his family, and she was not one to intrude.

Tomorrow, she thought. *Tomorrow, I'll visit the camp.*

But now, she would go home. Helling and Schwitkowski would be waiting.

ELEVEN

The next day, a squall from the north shrouded the countryside in snow, coating the trees alabaster white. Unhappy that her visit to the Karas camp was delayed, Manya went to the stables to ask if anyone might still be going to Angerburg.

Ulrich, the stable hand, said he had a sick sister in town and that he would be going no matter how bad the weather. He promised to stop by the camp and tell Joshi that Aztec had been spared.

Manya thanked him and went to Shambhala's stall, where Helling was checking her horseshoes.

"We've got some time on our hands, with this weather," he said quietly, slipping his nail clincher into his apron and straightening up to look at her. "I want to talk to you about something. Can we meet this afternoon?"

"Of course," she smiled. Picking up a can of saddle soap, she walked past the stall of the other mare, Topsie, and toward the tack room.

Helling watched her disappear. He was worried. More and more, he feared for her life, and for Zarah's. He no longer cared if he died, but he had responsibilities. He had to take care of Zarah, Manya, and her parents. Everywhere he went, people were talking about the Nemmersdorf massacre. How long would it be until the same thing happened in Guja? His eyes welled up as he thought about his surviving daughter. She had escaped from Nemmersdorf with her life, but her voice was gone, as was her soul. She hardly slept. Neither did he. After the ambush, he'd returned to the familiar stone cottage he had once called home, but every time he lay down on the bed he had shared with Karin, he imagined what the Russian soldiers had done to his wife and daughter, how they had left his precious family to die like dogs. After two days he had left the cottage, knowing he would never go back.

He had settled into his room beside the forge, and when Zarah arrived, he had made a bed for her. But she never stayed there. At night, he'd find her on a bale of hay beside Shambhala. He'd wait for sleep to calm her restless limbs, but it rarely did. The minute her eyes closed, a strangled howl filled her little chest, piercing him with grief.

"It's all right," he'd croon. "I'm here."

But she never looked at him. Even worse, she cringed from his touch, her cold little hand seeking Shambhala's muzzle.

He sighed and picked up his toolbox.

"At least she has you, old girl," he murmured to the mare.

That afternoon, as promised, Manya came to his room. They sat down at the table, where he told her of his mounting fears. The time had come to plan the route that would take them west to Danzig, on the Baltic coast. They discussed which wagon they would take from the coach house, choosing one they had used to haul hay. It was light, yet big enough to hold the baroness and the baron, Helling, Manya, and Zarah. Helling agreed to take measurements in the next days and build a frame. He would get a tarpaulin in Goldap to make a cover.

"Once we are on our way, you'll have to ride Aztec," said Helling. "We'll hitch Shambhala and Topsie, to the wagon. They'll do the hauling. If we don't hit any delays, we'll be able to bring Shambhala to safety before she has her foal."

Taking pen and paper, Manya began to make a list of supplies: bread, biscuits, a wheel of Tilsit cheese, smoked ham and eel, goose fat, and dried fruit, plus oats and hay for the horses.

As she wrote, Helling watched the light from his lamp illuminate the tiny dimple in her chin. *She dresses like a tomboy*, he thought fondly, *and has no idea how pretty she is. She's kind, too, if a bit stubborn. Hopefully the war won't take her and she'll find happiness, maybe even a good man, if there are any left.*

"We need fur-lined coats, wool blankets, down comforters, medical supplies, extra tarpaulins," she recited, continuing to focus on her list.

Helling's mind wandered back to the early years. He remembered her as a child playing near the carp pond in the garden, her lanky arms reaching out over the mossy water for frogs. Holding half a dozen in one hand, she would line them up in a row on her arm and chatter away, as though they were her closest friends.

His Karin had loved her too. And oh, how his girls had enjoyed playing dress-up with her when the baroness had brought Manya to stay with his family. His family? Ach, he could hardly bear the memories. He sighed. Karin's warm lips would never melt the snowflakes on his moustache again. He'd never again see Maritza picking marsh marigolds by the lake. If only he could cut away those memories as cleanly as he carved a horse's hoof.

"Blacksmith Helling, are you listening?" Manya's voice jarred him back to the present.

He forced himself to concentrate.

"Yes. The horses will need attention along the way. I'll make sure my toolbox is in order. And I'll handle the provision list as well." He glanced at his watch. "I need to take a break now, though, and check on Zarah. I'm not sure where she's gone."

"I'll help you look," offered Manya, gathering up the maps and placing them in a crate beneath the table.

"Thank you," he said, relieved. "I'm worried. She's been disappearing on and off all day. Ursula says she went to the kitchen for some soup. At least that's a change. But it's too cold for her to be outside. I need to find her."

"She's probably in the barn with Shambhala," said Manya. "Earlier this morning, I saw her walking toward the shed. I'll check there."

Slipping into her coat, Manya headed down the snowy garden path toward the shed. Once her playhouse, it now stored apples and potatoes.

"Zarah?" she called softly as she opened the creaky door. "Are you here?"

The lid on the apple bin slammed shut with a loud bang. Zarah stood in front of it, motionless.

"What are you doing?" asked Manya, stepping forward and gently taking hold of Zarah's shoulders.

Zarah pointed to the bin, a large, knee-high trough that ran along the side wall. Two big tears rolled over her hollow cheeks and trickled onto her lips. She licked them away, anxiously looking at Manya as if she had a secret she was afraid to share.

"It's all right," said Manya, staring into Zarah's glassy eyes. "You can trust me. Will you show me what's inside?"

Slowly, Zara raised the lid.

At first Manya saw only mounds of apples, but when the apples moved, she jumped back in fright.

"Rats!" She pulled at Zarah's arm. "Come away."

But Zarah wasn't scared. Bending forward, she scooped off the top layer of fruit, revealing the face of a woman with skin as white as eggshells.

"Oh my God!" cried Manya. "Who are you?"

TWELVE

"*R*eport me to the authorities if you want," the haggard woman whispered, climbing up from the apple bin. Terror filled her copper-colored eyes. "I can't run anymore."

"There are no authorities here," Manya said, the note of alarm in her voice softening. She stretched out her hand. "Let me help you."

The woman's bony shoulders shook as she took hold of Manya's hand, her neck so corded and thin she could barely lift her head. Still, she managed to climb out of the bin. Once her feet were on the floor, Manya and Zarah sat her down on an old toy chest in the corner. Zarah fumbled to twist open the flask of soup she'd taken from the kitchen.

"Can you tell us your name?" Manya asked after Zarah offered the woman a sip of soup.

"Lillian," the woman answered faintly as she plucked a dry leaf from her frayed coat cuff. "Lillian Goltz. My husband is Max Goltz."

"You mean the horse breeder? I met him at a fair in Insterburg some years ago. My father was looking to buy one of his Trakehners. He is very tall, right?"

"Yes," Lillian smiled sadly. "And very bald." Her eyes searched Manya's. "I saw you there, too. You're the baron's daughter. You had a friend, a dark-haired boy from the Karas clan."

Suddenly, the woman looked down and blurted out, "They killed Max."

"Who?" asked Manya, alarmed.

"The Gestapo. But it was me they really wanted. I'm—" Again she glanced down at the floor. "I'm a Jew. Someone in our town must have known." She took a sharp breath. "Max would still be alive if it weren't for me. *Ach Gott*, if only we had never met." She choked back a sob, her dirty fingers clutching Manya's arm. "Please don't turn me in."

Manya eyed Lillian's disheveled hair. "How did you get here?" she asked, confused.

A frantic look rose in Lillian's eyes. "I thought I would lose my mind in that cramped space."

"What space are you talking about?" Manya asked gently.

"The space that Max built behind our cellar wall." Lillian covered her face with her hands, her muffled words falling out between the creases. "Max told me to hide when he heard them coming. At first they talked. Then I heard a shot. One single shot. Now I hear it over and over again."

She let out a long, sorrowful sob. "His blood soaked through the floorboards onto my hands. I was terrified. God forgive me. I didn't go to him. I don't know how long I was there. A day, maybe two. When I finally crept upstairs, he was dead. They had smeared the words 'Jewish Filth' on my walls. I left the house and hid in the forest. I stole potatoes from the fields. Yesterday, though, my stomach hurt so bad, I thought I was going to die."

Her words dissolved into a drawn-out sigh, and she strained to look at Manya. "I came because I know you're good people. Max always said Baron von Falken was a man of honor." She laid her hand on Zarah's arm. "And this sweet child found me and helped me hide."

"Good Lord," murmured Manya, trying to think. "What am I going to do?"

"I'll leave."

"No you won't," Manya said firmly. "I have an idea." She turned to Zarah. "We're going to take Lillian to my room. But no one must know. Do you hear?"

Baroness von Falken held a ladle above a big iron kettle of potato soup. Ursula had decided to get some fresh air and, leaving the baroness at the stove for once, she had taken her latest batch of soup to the hungry refugees waiting by the estate gates. Manya watched Ursula waddle toward the gate from the kitchen window, where she was kneading a loaf of rye bread with linseed oil.

In the courtyard, the baron and Helling were attending to the rising influx of wagons with broken axles and bent wheels, a by-product of the overused roads and rutted fields they had to cross.

Pausing for a moment, the baron wiped the grease off his hands. At the edge of their fields, he could see a line of German tanks, *Jagdpanzers*. He shook his head angrily. Rumors were circulating that many high-ranking officials had abandoned their posts and were secretly transporting their families out of East Prussia. But he dared not ask anybody in Angerburg about these matters. Authorities no longer welcomed questions, and anyone who doubted the outcome of the war was either thrown into jail or shot.

Military personnel who often stopped by the estate for food and provisions had informed him that the major roads were blocked now with tanks, soldiers, and convoys of trucks. The countryside, they said, was in total chaos. Some army divisions were still heading north and east to form lines of defense, but others, fully aware of what was coming, moved west, hoping to dodge the imminent battles they knew would be lost. As he thought of the sullen men he'd seen with machine guns, the fearful boys whose faces were shadowed by steel helmets, the baron wondered how it would all end.

He shoved his dirty rag back into his pocket and walked into the kitchen, where his wife was talking to Manya.

"Shall I ask Ulrich to bring more potatoes from the shed?" he called.

"Yes, thank you," answered the baroness. "Ursula's pot must be nearly empty by now, and this one won't last long."

When he was out of earshot, she turned back to Manya, her brow furrowing. "Has the Karas clan left?"

Manya glanced at her mother suspiciously. Unable to read her mother's face, she replied, "The stable hands tell me they're still there."

The baroness nodded quietly and began to ladle the creamy broth into a metal bucket. Lifting her knee against the inside hem of her skirt, she felt the weight of several silver coins she had sewn into the lining—monies earned from the sale of her sculptures, now kept safe for emergencies. She dipped her ladle back into the kettle and leaned toward Manya.

"I have some money for Vavara," she whispered, gazing through the window at the horizon with somber eyes. "Who could take it to her? One of the stable hands, perhaps?"

"No, let me go," Manya offered eagerly, wiping the flour off her hands.

The baroness paused. Raising one sharp eyebrow, she cast a knowing look over her daughter.

"But what about the weather?" she said. "And the roads? They're full of strangers. Aren't you being a bit bold?"

Manya blushed. "It has warmed up outside," she said, looking away. "I can ride near the forest. I'll be careful."

After being cooped up for days, Aztec was eager to run. They cantered along the edge of the forest, taking care to stay hidden in the shadows. For the time being, everything was quiet, and she loosened Aztec's reins.

Snow rose in gusts under his legs, filling the air with glittering flakes. They cantered past the Guja forest, which was draped in strings of pearly ice, and passed several hamlets of five or six cottages where fishermen's nets hung in frozen gardens. A few lonely dogs barked in the doorways.

Half an hour later, she saw thin scarves of smoke rising from the Karas camp. Slowing Aztec to a trot, she turned onto a trail that ran along the Angerapp River.

Ahead, on the bank of the river, two women wearing wide flowered skirts were scrubbing sheets in a big metal tub. They wore yellow headscarves, and the older woman managed to keep a pipe between her teeth while she worked. They waved at her, their bare hands chafed and red from the cold.

In the weeds to her right, an empty beer keg lay on its side. The words *Schwalben Hof*—Swallow Farm—had been painted on its circular belly. It marked the entrance to the settlement. The familiar smells of wood smoke, wild garlic, and herbs drew her forward. She smiled to herself, realizing she'd never been to the camp when there wasn't a pot of stew on the stove.

Near the edge of the encampment, she caught sight of a sturdy mare with gorgeous tufts on her lower legs. The mare snorted.

"You're a good guard dog, Tsura," laughed Manya.

Within seconds, a young man waved from behind an upturned cart, the large metal cufflinks in his jacket sparkling in the sunlight.

"Hello Harman," she smiled.

"Mistress von Falken," he called to her teasingly. "Is it Big Man Karas's son, Joshi, who brings you here? Or is it Karas's wife?"

The mention of Joshi's name made her blush.

"His wife, sir," she replied, relieved to see Vavara's curvy figure coming down the muddy path.

"Manya, my dear," scolded Vavara. "You shouldn't be out riding alone. All the same, I'm happy you're here. Come, you must be thirsty." She looked at the watchman. "Harman, please fetch some water and hay for Aztec. And make sure you rub him down with a towel."

Manya slid out of the saddle and let Vavara take her hand.

Vavara scanned the line of trees that shadowed the carved wooden caravans. "I never know if we are being watched," she whispered. "Lately, I feel invisible eyes burning holes into my back."

"I didn't see anything suspicious when I rode up to the camp," Manya assured her. "And certainly no strangers."

"They may not be here today, but we've seen tracks. The massacres occur after dark. Has Joshi told you that we are leaving?"

She turned her worried gaze toward her caravan. "He's in there, now, giving Sofia a violin lesson." Her whisper became even softer. "He wants to teach her to read and write as well, but no one knows. It would raise hell among those who don't trust books, most of all Andras." She sighed. "I'm so happy to have Joshi back, even though he risked his life to get here."

"I can only imagine," said Manya. "I've missed him too. But tell me, how are he and his father getting on?"

"Not good," said Vavara, with sad resignation. "They fight."

She gave a little shrug and tilted her head. Her husband could be difficult, but Vavara knew his anger emerged from loyalty to the clan. Even if she disagreed with Andras about Joshi, Vavara deeply understood him. She looked at Manya's curious eyes and knew that no matter how much she trusted Manya, the girl was too young to fully understand. She smiled inwardly: *And like me, the girl is too devoted to my son.*

"Ah, but what if Joshi can bring us all safely to Sweden?" Vavara said. She fingered the snail shell amulet that hung at her throat. "He must have told you we've been waiting for him. That's why we didn't leave sooner." She shook her head. "I argued with Andras to let Joshi stay where it's safe. But I just couldn't persuade him, and the truth is, I wanted to see my son walk up that path one more time."

"I understand," said Manya.

Vavara was silent for a long moment.

"Sometimes I think Joshi was born under another star. Andras and I love our life. We'll never sleep in a house. I'll always hang my laundry on a pine branch to dry. Beat my rugs clean in the wind. But Joshi is different."

"Don't say such things," protested Manya.

"No," countered Vavara. "It's true. And I'm to blame because I always wanted a different life for him. I persuaded Andras to let your teachers tutor Joshi when he was young. I defended his decision to study medicine in Sweden."

She lifted her face to the sky, her eyes searching for something beyond the clouds. "I hope Joshi finds where he belongs. But enough of this talk now. Come. You need something to drink."

At the campfire stove, she poured Manya a mug of sweet black coffee. "Here, love," she said. "Drink it while it's hot. And forgive me for talking about family problems." She shivered and pulled her red woolen shawl around her shoulders before gazing down at her worn velvet skirt. "I used to be more elegant," she murmured, "but it's dangerous to go into town now. Besides, the seamstress won't serve me anymore. And lately, I—I've had the strangest premonition. One that comes to me repeatedly in my dreams."

"What is it?" asked Manya, leaning forward uneasily.

Vavara hesitated. "I dream I'm running toward someone. I don't know who, and as I run, I fall. When I look up, an owl is staring me in the eyes." She swallowed. "Owls mean death."

"It's only a dream," said Manya, touching her shoulder. "Try not to let it trouble you." She raised the mug to her lips, hoping the warm, sweet liquid would soften the lump in her throat.

Vavara touched the ring on Manya's finger and smiled.

"Mother told me how kind you were to her years ago," acknowledged Manya. "She told me about Omi, too, and how she hoped the amber would protect me. She wanted me to give you something." Manya reached into her pocket for a small leather pouch with the coins the baroness had sent along and pressed it into Vavara's palm. "With love to you from her."

Vavara rolled the leather between her fingers, the coins clinking softly.

"So thoughtful," she murmured. "She's like a sister to me. She trusted me and let me into your house when no one else would." Vavara smiled tenderly. "Sometimes I think she wishes she were like me, unconfined by so many rules, but she's a true East Prussian."

Manya was quiet. In her heart she wished her mother were more like Vavara, so open and easy to talk to.

Vavara seemed to read her thoughts. "She difficult, I know, but she loves you." Taking Manya's hand, Vavara led her up the rickety steps into her caravan, perched on its oversized wheels.

Inside, the air smelled of cloves and sage. Joshi was sitting on a three-legged stool, reading to Sofia, who clung to his every word. When he saw

Manya in the doorway he stood up quickly, and a warm smile spread over his face—a smile she returned. Vavara stepped aside, her eyes intently surveying them both.

"Why don't you stay for supper, Manya?" she said. "We're having a christening this evening for Harman's new baby. Joshi can take Tsura and accompany you home after the celebration." She paused. "But dear, I don't want your parents to worry."

"Mother knows where I am," said Manya. "I told her I might be late. But what about Andras? Won't my presence upset him?"

"He'll be fine. I'll tell him that it's a thank-you for the gift you brought." She turned to Sofia. "Darling, would you go and peel the potatoes? Joshi, you and Manya fetch some cooking water. But hurry. You'll find the bucket under the wagon."

⁓⚹⁓

Joshi and Manya walked alongside the Angerapp River. Where a narrow tributary flowed into a half-frozen pond, they spotted an otter ambling through the reeds.

"I haven't seen an otter for months," whispered Manya. "Do you remember when Father brought me one as a pet?"

Joshi laughed. "Your beloved Ingo, who used to swim in your bathtub and cuddle up on your pillow when he was still sopping wet."

"Yes." She chuckled at the memory. "And one day he vanished. Remember how we searched his favorite hideouts? The chicken coop, where the farmhand always rolled an egg to him? The cowshed, where the milk was his constant temptation? We whistled and called, but he was nowhere to be found."

Joshi touched her shoulder. "You were so upset. You couldn't stop crying. And then, a few days later, we thought we heard him. We ran down the hill toward the lake. I think it was March because the ground was wet with spring melt and your shoes got stuck in the mud. You were so impatient, you kicked them off and left them behind."

"Yes," murmured Manya, meeting Joshi's gaze. "We waited in the bulrushes at the edge of the lake for two solid hours. My stockings were soaked!"

He smiled.

"We were ready to give up, but just then we heard his high-pitched whistle. And there he was, standing on his hind legs, chattering away to a lady otter."

"Remember his funny expression that seemed to say, 'Sorry, but love calls'?" laughed Manya.

"Until it didn't." Joshi's laughter mingled with hers. "I remember when he showed up at the bay windows of the study, whimpering so beseechingly that the math tutor let us go outside and get him."

"And that very night, he was back on my pillow."

They walked on, listening to the run of the river under the ice.

"What are you thinking about?" asked Manya, sensing a change in him.

"We're packing up tomorrow," he said with a shrug. "Father wants us to leave for Sweden, but I don't know how we'll make it."

Manya nodded. "Listen, I came this afternoon to give your mother some money. But I brought something for you, too." She stopped beside a willow tree with wide, sweeping branches. "Blacksmith Helling and I have been preparing for the trek westward, too. We've established a route to Danzig. Even though we haven't yet persuaded Papa to leave, we're planning on going to Schleswig-Holstein. We have cousins there, and I'm hoping they'll take us in until the war is over and we can get on our feet again."

Joshi began chopping a hole in the ice for his bucket. "Leave as soon as you can," he said.

"Papa won't leave before Christmas, if he leaves at all. Especially now that the front appears quiet."

"Not quiet, *sinister*," corrected Joshi, laying down his ax and dropping the bucket into the water. "I keep wondering what the Russians are planning. Some people are fooled by the stillness, but I urge you, Manya, go, before it's too late." His voice trailed off. "If it isn't already."

He pulled up the bucket and watched a shard of ice circling on the water's surface. "My father believes I can get the clan to safety, but wherever we go, we'll be hunted. So far we've been lucky. If we could get to Sweden, my friend Ragnar would protect us. But, honestly, I don't know how we're going to do it. There are no ferries running anymore, and even if there were, they wouldn't take us."

Tears filled Manya's eyes. "Then hide. Go deeper into the forest. Find some caves."

"Ah, you should join us," Joshi smiled, his eyes lighting up briefly. "He touched her arm. "What were you going to give me?"

"This." She pulled a folded piece of paper from her pocket and handed it to him. "I don't know what's going to happen either, but if we do leave, this will be our route. We'll take shelter with horse breeders and family along the way. And we'll definitely be stopping at the Trakehner farm in Braunsberg. Once we're there, we'll know whether we can follow the road west, or whether we'll have to cross the Frisches Haff lagoon. Our decision will depend on how far the Russians have advanced and whether the lagoon freezes over or not."

Joshi tucked the map inside the breast pocket of his jacket. He could not bring himself to voice his misgivings, so he remained silent. Manya was hopeful, but he didn't think for a minute that she—or his clan, for that matter—would get past Danzig. The Soviets were no fools. They would surround Braunsberg, Danzig, and every major port on all sides, leaving the Baltic Sea as the only escape route. If they were lucky, Manya and her family might board a refugee ship, but no ship would transport the horses.

He knew Manya better than she knew herself. Their friendship had seen many childhood winters. He admired her persistent streak, but he knew how easily it could lead her into danger. She loved Aztec and Shambhala beyond reason. If she couldn't get them past Danzig, she would never leave her horses in enemy hands. She'd stay with them until the bitter end.

"Let's go back," he urged, taking her arm. "The sun has already dropped behind the trees. My mother will skin my hide if we don't hurry."

They arrived to find a small group of men tuning violins, guitars, and an oboe. Joshi pointed to a graceful harp, carved and painted with leaves and birds.

"Sometimes they bury the old beauty," he said, "in case the Nazis come around. But tonight she'll be singing."

Near the fire, Joshi's Aunt Vadoma and two other old women were kneading bits of fried bacon into dough to make the savory bread *bokoli*, which Manya loved. A group of children were pushing an empty wheelbarrow in the narrow spaces between the caravans. Two coal-eyed boys ran up to greet Manya, asking whether she had brought any presents.

"Not this time," she shrugged apologetically, watching the boys scamper off.

The children liked her. Over the years she had brought them toys, colored pencils, and chocolate. The women liked her too, perhaps because she brought butter, *Semmel* rolls, and bottles of Slivovitz brandy especially for them whenever she came.

The men were more reserved, but there had been times when they drank and joked in front of her. Tonight, though, everyone was subdued, as if they were afraid the outside world might hear.

Still, pinecones burned on the fire, their clean fragrance mixing with the smell of roasted hare, garlic, and rosemary.

Just past the first caravan, Manya and Joshi saw Karas standing like a king in the center of the circle, hands planted on his hips. A long wisp of hair poked out from beneath his wide-brimmed felt hat. With a start, Manya noticed that it was gray. She had always thought of him as young and unchanging. As he stared into the fire, he lifted a veined hand to brush the hair behind his ear. It was a nervous gesture, vulnerable in its own way, and it touched Manya, giving her the courage to greet him with a nod. But he turned away.

"Grouchy old man," Joshi muttered.

Karas knew he was scowling, but he couldn't help it. He didn't like seeing the von Falken girl with his son. She wasn't a bad person, but she was a *gadji*.

The wind blew, stirring the ash in the fire and sending pins of embers through the air. He thought about his clan. It had never been large, thirty-nine people at most. In the last year, though, several members had gone out to their usual work and had not returned. Word came back that the women had been charged with spreading diseases and thrown into prison, while the men, arrested for no reason, had been sent to a work camp near Danzig. Whenever he thought of them, his heart hardened to lead.

He often wondered why he was still alive. He was lucky to have the forged Aryan documents that kept the Gestapo at bay. But this stroke of luck was also a burden. Guilt weighed on him. Why had he been spared and not his people? From beneath hooded lids, he watched Joshi pour water into a charred pot, the von Falken girl right beside him. He loved Joshi. But it angered him that his own son could not commit to Romani law, that he had defied everything to earn a *gadje* medical degree.

"You make me ashamed," he had told Joshi just last evening. "My closest friends are dead because of the *gadje*. Yet you, a chief's son, deliberately choose an outsider's life. I was weak. I let you have tutoring with that girl, but I *never* thought you'd go to university. I was tough on everyone except you, and now I pay the price."

"Even Romanies need to read fake documents that say they have Aryan blood," Joshi had snapped back. "What would have happened if I hadn't helped you sign those papers? You'd be dead. And don't talk to me about studying medicine, because no matter what you think, your good luck charms can't heal the sick!"

Karas glanced up from the fire. Joshi and the girl were standing in the snow-dappled grass now. He cursed and turned to see Vavara glaring at him from her cooking station.

"I told you earlier to put your opinions aside," she hissed, slamming the pot cover on the stove. "Now, give it a rest. It's not much to ask after all the baroness has given us."

"What did you say, woman?" He was so angry he could have hit something. "You care too much about the *gadje*. Look what your son has turned into. A *gadje* lover, a *gadje* doctor."

Vavara moved close to him so the others would not hear and he would not be shamed.

"I told you to leave it alone tonight," she growled. "Now stop grumbling. You have other responsibilities."

Wiping specks of soup from her shawl, she walked away.

He watched the swing of her green velvet hem, the resolute stance of her shoulders. Overhead a bird whistled. And then, in spite of himself, he smiled. She had a way with him and he didn't like fighting with her. She was too damn beautiful. But more than anyone, she understood him.

"All right," he called after her. "But I'll need warm water and almond oil for the baby. And tell Harman and his wife to bring the talisman they chose to protect his spirit."

THIRTEEN

"*O*n the name of our clan, I baptize you, Shandor," Karas intoned. "May you be proud and loyal to the Romani way of life."

Safe within his blanket, the baby stared up at Karas with wide eyes. Karas, too, seemed enthralled. For once, his stern countenance had softened. He even cooed as he placed the infant in his mother's arms.

Manya and Joshi stood under the branches of a tall fir tree. Manya was curious to see more, so she inched a little closer. Dika, the baby's mother, had plaited her hair into two thick braids that hung down on either side of her face. She wore no jewelry and was missing a bottom tooth, but she looked radiant in her beaded vermilion shawl. With every movement, the beads would catch the light, setting her shoulders aglow. When Karas kissed the talisman, she lifted one of her dark plaits and brushed the baby's cheek.

"What's she doing?" whispered Manya.

"She's giving him his secret name," Joshi murmured into her ear. "Only she and her son will know it."

Manya looked up at him and smiled, kindling a warmth that ran up his spine. Was she feeling it too? He moved toward her, but suddenly he wasn't sure. Apart from a slight tipping of her hip, she stood motionless, almost passive. He paused; clasping his hands together, he stepped back.

"The secret name is used to confuse the spirits so that the child's true identity is not revealed."

"So you have a secret name too?" she asked, her face full of curiosity.

He nodded.

"And I mustn't know it, right?"

He paused again, half hoping to suppress a sudden compulsion to tell her. It wasn't as if he believed in such superstitions. And they had never kept secrets from each other.

"It's—"

"No, don't tell me," she broke in swiftly, placing a gloved finger on his lips.

They gazed at each other. Then, quite suddenly, she stepped farther into the shadow of the tree, where no one could see them, and kissed him on the lips.

He stared at her in astonishment. He had always assumed their friendship was, for her at least, just that—friendship, nothing more. He wanted to ask her how long she had felt this way or if it was just a whim, but the moment was lost when his father's voice boomed a final blessing over the baby and old Mrs. Florian, the clan harpist, began to pluck at her strings with long red fingernails.

Manya felt shy. She had just kissed him. And now he was staring at her with a look of disbelief. She wished she could disappear.

"I'm sorry," she murmured, her cheeks burning. "I don't know what I was thinking."

Laughing, he steered her toward the trestle table where Vavara was carving a roasted hare. When she was done, she filled their plates and called for Sofia to bring the salt and herbs.

"I saved seats for you," Sofia smiled, pointing toward two stools beside a row of candleholders hollowed out of raw potatoes.

In honor of his firstborn son, Harman opened two wicker-bound jugs of fruit wine. Manya drank deeply from the glass he offered her, enjoying the warmth of the alcohol as it spread through her limbs. She wasn't drunk, but she became aware of a deep restlessness inside her.

The singers began with ballads—old songs, raw and melancholy until dinner was finished. Then the pace grew lively. The oboist played notes in counterpoint to the twanging sounds of a zither, while the drummer beat a syncopated rhythm.

Near the fire, a group of men and women had started to dance, among them a striking woman with a mane of russet-red hair whom Manya recognized. Nuri had always liked Joshi, and while she was polite to Manya, she had made no secret about her feelings.

The women stomped black leather boots into the frozen ground as if they were calling the earth to bind them to it, their fingers opening and closing like fans as their arms reached toward the starlit sky.

I'll never be able to dance like them, Manya thought, noticing that Nuri was an especially good dancer. Her long skirt, held at the waist by a willow-bark belt, billowed about her legs like a purple cloud.

Someone called to Joshi to play the violin. Children beat on overturned buckets, cheering him on. Taking a violin from one of the musicians, Nuri whirled toward Joshi.

"Play for us," she laughed, handing him the violin and bowing at the waist.

Manya's hands clenched when she saw the swell of Nuri's breasts above her low-cut velvet bodice. She wanted to push Nuri away from Joshi, but there was something between them that was not hers to touch. *I won't ever be part of that*, she thought, feeling a sharp sting of jealousy.

Joshi's fingers swooped across the strings in chromatic runs. And Nuri spun around him, her eyes never leaving his face, her hips mimicking every tilt of his shoulders.

"Son," Manya heard a cracked voice shout. "Play the 'Romani Orphan Song!'"

Joshi's grandfather Besnik was seated nearby. His glasses were strapped together by bits of wire and perched low on his nose. "Today I woke up wanting to die," he wheezed. "Empty because the angst was eating at my bones. But now, hearing you, I want to kiss the ground."

Joshi bowed to him and the tempo slowed into a soulful melody that spoke of separation. Soon the melody rose again, becoming light and gay. Manya saw Vavara and Sofia walking toward her, past the older women who sat with their hands folded on their stomachs. Vavara's eyes were full of pride as she gazed at her son.

"Papa Besnik taught Joshi how to play that style," she said, sidling up to Manya. "Watch how he rolls off the strings."

"It took him years to get the hang of it," Sofia chimed in. "One day I'll play like that." She gazed adoringly at her brother. "He's going to teach me."

Manya smiled and bent down until her face was level with Sofia's. "I'm sure he will. He told me today that you have a talent for the violin."

Sofia giggled bashfully. Two coins had been fastened into her copper-colored hair. They flashed like gold sparks in the dark.

Vavara nudged her on. "Come, your father's wine glass is empty."

With no one to distract her, Manya's gaze fell back on Joshi. Nuri was still dancing with him, and with each sensual twist of her body, Manya felt more invisible. How could she have kissed him? Of course he had laughed.

Now, she couldn't bear to think of her foolishness. Her mother was right. She was too sporty to be graceful. She took another sip of wine but could barely swallow. *I don't need this*, she thought. She walked away and settled herself near Vavara's caravan.

A strand of hair had fallen into her eyes. She brushed it away and gazed at her hands before tucking them under her legs. *My hands are too big*, she thought. *I'm just not the feminine type*. Her mind wandered to other men she'd known, suitors from aristocratic families. They were nice enough, but none of them had been interested in mucking out stalls or wading through the river with her. They wanted her to go to parties in dresses and pearls, and when it became clear that she wasn't interested, they had stopped calling.

But Joshi had always been different. He liked what she liked—riding, hunting, music, books. Although they were lively competitors, they also discussed everything, both of them holding their own in every conversation. But what Manya loved most about Joshi was that he made her laugh.

Her eyes wandered back to the fire. Nuri was still dancing, but another man was playing the violin now. She heard a footstep and felt Joshi behind her, his chest pressing against her back. "Where were you going so soon?" he teased, as he encircled her waist. She caught her breath in a wave of relief.

"I didn't want to get in the way of you and Nuri," she said, spitting out Nuri's name.

"Nuri is only a friend," he said, in a voice hoarse and tender.

She trembled as his hands caressed her face, her throat. "It's you I care about."

Taking her hand, he led her to a copse of fir trees at the edge of the camp, where moonlight fell between the trees. With a swiftness that surprised her, he pressed his lips against hers and parted them with the soft edge of his tongue. She yielded with desire for the soft urgency of his mouth and the warmth of his body.

"You might be quicker at love than me," he murmured with a mischievous grin, pulling her close.

She reached up to touch his face.

"Is this where we—?" she asked, her shyness returning.

His eyes opened wide and a soft laugh escaped him. "Does it matter? Do you want to go somewhere else?"

"No. It's only—well—the ground is cold, but—"

Her glance, so uncertain and endearing, brought forth a feeling of protectiveness in him.

"Don't worry," he smiled. "I'll fix that."

He disappeared into the shadowy light, leaving Manya with a flutter in her belly—only this time she knew what it was. She leaned against the mossy trunk of a fir and closed her eyes, her senses taking in the sounds from the campfire—pieces of poems, the half bars of a love song, the light tinkle of glasses—all carried to her on the wind.

A twig snapped. Joshi had returned with two blankets, an ebony polecat fur and a white ermine. She smiled in recognition. She had similar blankets at home, treasures of hunting expeditions with Helling. She helped him spread the furs on the ground, and when he drew her down, she felt as if she were sinking into a cloud of dandelion fluff.

At first he held her, keenly aware of her breath against his throat, the weight of her hand on his chest. The warmth of her limbs stirred him, and he began to caress her, his fingers following every contour and line of her body as if she were a treasure.

She was beautiful. Her legs were so long. And her hands. They had always been too big for her willowy arms, but they were surprisingly tender. His breath caught in his throat as her hands slid over him.

He pushed himself up onto his elbow to look at her. The moon had shed some of its light on her face and throat, forming soft pools in the hollows behind her collarbones. He kissed her there and raised his eyes to hers. She smiled and urged him on.

He unbuttoned her jacket and her blouse, letting her pale white breasts fill his palms. Opening his mouth, he leaned toward the ovals of her nipples, warming them with his breath.

She shivered and raised her head, and he saw that despite the newness of it all she was daring herself to go on. He kissed her again. Taking her hand, he guided her fingers toward his belt, bidding her to unbuckle it as he unbuckled hers. When she did not pull back, he slid her jodhpurs over her hips, stroking her inner thighs with his thumbs.

Her breath quickened, and her lips began to move over his face, engulfing him with tenderness, her tongue soft as a moth's wing on his skin. Taking her time, she loosened his shirt, her fingers meeting each juncture of button and skin with a circular caress.

He drew the ermine over them and kneeled between her thighs, his mouth sliding over the curve in her belly to the tangle of hair below. A low groan escaped her. He sensed her suppressing the sounds that might travel to the fireside and reveal their presence. But he didn't care. He was already lost to the outside world.

A screaming whine split the night air. There was movement in the camp, shadows twisting through the trees, people shouting for children to take shelter in the caravans and douse the lights.

Manya's body tensed. "It's a Russian bomber," she said. "I know the sound."

He drew her close as if to protect her. She shuddered, waiting for the sound of the plane to die away. Finally, it faded. She heard him exhale, but when he spoke there was a strong note of hopelessness in his voice.

"We're doomed," he said. "There's no future for us, Manya. We won't get out of this war alive." He turned her face to his. "You know that, too. That's the reason you wanted to make love tonight, isn't it? You're afraid we won't see each other again."

"No. I wanted to because I—"

"But we may never be together again after tonight," he said.

She cupped his face in her hands. "Please don't say that. Have you no faith?"

When he did not answer, she sat up, gripped his shoulder, and locked eyes with him. She ran her fingers through his hair, caressing his face. "Let the bombs fall," she whispered. "Whatever happens, they won't take this from me. If what you say is true, if I never see you again, then I want this moment."

He sought her mouth, felt her skin, porous and warm, as if she were emptying herself into him and absorbing him at the same time.

His body began to burn and he moved toward her, molding himself to her and meeting the upward arch of her hips. As soon as he entered her, she cried out his name.

"I'm sorry," he moaned, pulling back. "I was too quick. I'm hurting you."

"Don't say that," she whispered. "At least I know I'm alive." And wrapping her legs around him, she drew him to her once more.

She found his rhythm right away, as if their flesh were bound together by an invisible thread. Bliss spread through her body, traveling to her throat and arching toward the sky in a wild animal roar. Somewhere inside, she understood. This was her cry to the Almighty.

"I love you," Joshi whispered when his breathing had slowed.

She smiled and closed her eyes. "I've always loved you."

They lay together in silence, breathing each other's scent. When the moon floated over them, he saw her lift her hand to the sky as if she were asking fate for mercy.

"We have to go," he whispered, with a pang of concern. "Your parents will worry."

"I know," she murmured. And she drew him close one more time.

The camp was quiet when they left, the embers of the fire giving off the last remnants of warmth. They cantered close to woods, ducking under pine branches heavy with snow. When they passed the lake near Guja, they turned onto the road that led to the von Falken estate. Tsura fell in step beside Aztec. Joshi took Manya's hand. They rode in silence until they came to the gates at the entrance to the von Falkens' courtyard.

"I want to see you tomorrow," said Joshi. Manya looked at him, her eyes hopeful. "I'll come at dawn before we begin packing up the caravans." He flashed her a crooked smile. "But remember, I like my coffee black and sweet."

Blowing her a kiss, he cantered off into the night, Tsura's hooves churning up the snow. A few flakes landed on Manya's cheek, stinging strangely like a cold, unbidden farewell.

FOURTEEN

*W*hen Manya rode into the courtyard, she was surprised to see light pouring from nearly every window of the house. *Everyone should be in bed*, she thought as she led Aztec to his stall.

She settled him and sprinted across the courtyard, pushing open the front door. Ursula was waiting for her in the foyer, her plump body shuffling back and forth across the parquet floor in well-worn, brown leather oxfords, her hands pulling at her apron.

"They've taken the baron!" she sobbed.

"Who took him?" cried Manya, dread filling her heart.

"The Gestapo. They came this evening. Your parents were having dinner. I had just served the pumpkin soup. The men didn't knock. They opened the door and marched into the dining room. Dragged your father from his chair. 'Traitor!' they shouted. Your father was calm. He asked why they were calling him that. One of the men pulled out his pistol. 'Admit it, Baron,' he yelled, and hit your father across his temple. Oh, Manya, there was blood everywhere! It sprayed across your mother's white linen tablecloth."

She wiped a shaky hand across her forehead as if to banish the memory. "They bound your father's arms and took him away. It was shameless," she cried.

Ursula moved closer to Manya and gripped her collar with her reddened hands. "And now your mother won't speak. Every time I go into the music room, she tells me to leave. I don't know what to do. She keeps playing those sad songs she and Vavara used to sing."

She pressed her wet cheek to Manya's and began to wail.

"Calm yourself, please," urged Manya, freeing her collar from Ursula's grip. "What did the men say? On what pretext did they take Father?"

She glanced at the ceiling with sudden alarm. Her bedroom was just above the foyer. If someone found out about Lillian, they would all be killed. Her mind raced. "Did they search the house?" she asked, her voice cracking with fear.

"Every room!" cried Ursula. "They said they were looking for proof!"

"Proof of what?"

"I don't know. Your father told me to stay in the kitchen. Oh child, your father is such a good man. He makes sure we all have clothes and food, coals for the stove."

"Please," said Manya, taking Ursula's hand, "try to remember what you heard."

"I heard them say he was going to Gestapo headquarters in Angerburg."

"What else?"

"They said something about Count von Stauffenberg and the assassination attempt on the Führer in July. They think your father was involved." Ursula began to shake. "He wasn't connected to that, was he, Manya?"

"No," said Manya, but suddenly she wasn't so sure.

"They mentioned the name of the general who used to visit your father."

"General Köstring?" asked Manya, incredulously. She knew him well. He had come to dinner often, seeking her father's advice after Hitler forced him to become head of the Eastern Troops. Although her father had never mentioned the assassination plot, Manya knew that Köstring was friendly with von Stauffenberg.

One night, while sipping brandy, Köstring had mentioned that things would change after the twentieth of July. Thinking that the war might be ending, her father had shared the general's news with Helling and a few of his workers. Now it dawned on Manya that perhaps one of those same workers had gone to the police and accused her father of being an accomplice. Her heart raced on. "What else did you hear?"

"They called your mother a Gypsy lover and told her it was a crime to associate with untouchables. Oh, how they shouted! They threatened to arrest her as well, but your father begged them to leave her alone."

Dazed, Manya turned from Ursula and headed up the stairs.

Ursula followed. "Your father said *he* was the one who let the Karas family into his house. Your mother held herself together. She even took them through the rooms, but when the car drove away, she fell apart."

From the banister, Manya stared into Ursula's eyes.

"Did you see them when they left?" she asked.

"No, I only heard scuffling up and down the stairs. The door slammed, and they were gone."

"Make yourself some tea, Ursula. I'll be right back."

Manya raced up the staircase. What if they had found Lillian? She had been careless. She should have hidden Lillian in a safer place, but where? The woman needed shelter.

Her hands shook as she turned the brass doorknob. Her bedroom had been ransacked. She stumbled across the contents of her dresser to her closet and tore open the door. Jodhpurs, muddy boots, dirty towels, blankets, coats, even underwear lay in a tangled pile, almost to the ceiling.

"Lillian. Are you here?" she cried.

"Manya?" a muffled voice cried back.

Moments later, Lillian crawled out from under the pile, her face ashen. "It was all I had time to do when I heard the ruckus downstairs. Thank God they didn't rummage through this heap. I don't think they were looking for Jews tonight."

"They took my father," said Manya, her relief mixed with dread. "Who knows if they'll be back. You must remain hidden." After she recounted what Ursula had told her, she hastened back down the stairs to the drawing room, where her mother sat hunched over the piano, her elbows on the keys.

"Get out," the baroness said in a listless voice. "You should have been home earlier to help us. Now he's probably dead, and it's your fault."

Manya drew back from the venom in her mother's words, but as she watched the baroness staring coldly at her sheet music, she felt an equally cold rage rise up inside her.

"You had better pull yourself together," she said, anger spilling into her voice. "We have some decisions to make. Now."

"I'm not leaving Guja," her mother spat. "If that's what you think!"

"First, we're going to get Papa back," said Manya, her words hammering the air. "After that we *will* leave Guja. If the Russians don't kill us, the Gestapo will, and I refuse to die because of you." She walked across the room to the piano and slammed her palm on the sleek mahogany surface. "The Russians will rape us all! Ursula, you, and me. And not just one man. Fifty men! They won't give a damn about you or your feelings."

She paused. She had overstepped a boundary, but she couldn't stop. "Everyone coddles you because of your so-called demons. The world is full of living demons now. And we're all suffering, Mother."

No one had ever addressed her mother in such a brutally frank manner. And clearly her mother was not happy. Her eyes smoldered, and she banged her fists against the keys. Manya flinched but found herself leaning even closer.

"Do you hear me, Mother?" she hissed. "I'm tired of your demons."

A resounding slap knocked Manya nearly to the floor.

"You insolent girl!" shouted the baroness, her voice dangerous and high-pitched. "How dare you speak to me like that?"

Manya caught herself on the piano bench and glared at her mother. With deliberate steps, she stomped out of the room. She wished she could focus, but her mind was a blur. Everything seemed unreal, even the scent of her own skin, musky now from lovemaking. She had come home ready to sink into blissful dreams. Instead she had stepped into a nightmare.

I mustn't cry, she thought, sitting down on a chair in the foyer. *I must think clearly and devise a plan to get Papa back.*

She swallowed and pressed her hands against her temples. How long would the Gestapo hold him for questioning? Would they ever let him go? With every passing day the danger in Guja was mounting.

Her thoughts flew to Joshi. Tomorrow, when he came, she would make him tell her exactly where the clan was going. At least she'd know where he was.

The grandfather clock in the foyer ticked on, eroding the night hours. Her mind raced ahead. Should she go to the Gestapo and plead her father's case? To whom could she turn for help? After turning the questions over in her mind, she closed her eyes and drifted into a fitful sleep.

Almost instantly, a dream washed over her. It was brief, but it left her with a sense of clarity. In it, she saw her Omi step from the photo her mother kept in the winter garden. "Leave," Omi urged, but the voice, which sounded so much like that of her mother, was obscured by the sound of hooves.

FIFTEEN

The morning sun rose steadily through the dawn mist beyond the foyer windows. Still Manya sat by the staircase, hoping the phone would ring or the front door would open. But her father didn't call, and Joshi never came. Something had happened to him, too. She was sure of it.

At noon, the baroness came down the steps and into the foyer dressed in the gray tweed suit she usually wore when she accompanied her husband into town. Her ash-blond hair was swept back into a tight chignon. On her lapel she wore a diamanté fly brooch with wings that trembled every time she moved.

"Get out of that filthy riding garb, child, and put on something decent," she ordered. "We're going to Angerburg to inquire about Father. You will drive."

An hour later they were in the baron's shiny black Mercedes, parked outside the municipal building that had been set up as Gestapo headquarters.

"You go in, Manya," directed the baroness, staring straight ahead. "I'm so angry I could kill someone."

Manya stepped out of the car and walked toward the austere municipal building, her elegant beige trousers flapping against her legs in the wind. Her mother had said they were unladylike, but the trousers gave her confidence. Never a slave to fashion, she simply wore what suited her. However, inside the building, her brashness dwindled. The stony-faced officials were curt and unfriendly. They gave her no information. Exasperated, she approached an officer who was stationed in front of a door that never seemed to open.

"Excuse me, can you just tell me if Baron von Falken is here? And if he is alive?"

The officer looked her up and down.

"Please," she murmured. "My mother's waiting in the car. She's sick with worry."

"Are you his daughter?"

"Yes."

"All right, then. As far as I know, your father is being interrogated by one of our head officers this afternoon. But I can tell you this much. If they find out he's even remotely connected to von Stauffenberg, he will pay the consequences. Your father was a fool to consort with criminals."

He paused to pick at a tooth, letting his eyes slowly slide over her body. When he took his hand out of his mouth, he gave her a wet, lascivious smile. "But what about you, young lady? I hope you're not a fool, because you're a perfect Aryan specimen. Have you produced any babies for the Third Reich yet?" He let out a nasty chuckle. "I'd be happy to oblige, although you dress a bit too manly for my taste. But who knows?"

Disgusted by his aggressiveness, Manya hurried down the corridor and out the door. Back in the car, she gripped the steering wheel. "He's alive, Mother," she said, catching her breath. "That's all I know. We just have to wait."

In the dank basement of the Gestapo headquarters, Baron von Falken sat in a ladder-back chair. His hands were tied together, his long fingers swollen thick from the biting cord. The officers had used whips and truncheons on his ribs and legs, hoping to get a confession. Each time before they beat him, they forced his head between his knees and tied his hands to his ankles.

"Baron," he would hear one of them sneer, "Tell us what you know and we'll loosen the bonds."

He was nauseated and had been afraid that if he vomited, he would choke to death, so he fought to control the impulse. Once in a while his tormentors went away, but never long enough for him to sleep.

Now he'd been alone for twenty minutes since the last round. He wondered if the next set of beatings would kill him. He guessed it was nearly four o'clock in the afternoon, but he had no way of looking at his pocket watch.

The door opened again.

"*Ach Du lieber Gott*," he murmured, breathing heavily. "Oh, good Lord."

He wished they'd just finish him off, but interrogations didn't happen that way. They went on and on, breaking a man down even if he were innocent.

"Baron von Falken, do you recognize me?"

The baron raised his swollen face and saw a neatly dressed officer with light blue eyes staring at him.

"No, I'm sorry. I—"

The officer's voice fell to a whisper.

"Baron, years ago when I was a bellboy at the Park Hotel in Königsberg, I helped carry your wife's bronze statues to an exhibition. You were so kind; you treated me like a man—not a servant. You tipped me with a gold coin. It was the most generous tip I'd ever been given."

Reaching into his pocket, the officer pulled out a coin and waved it in front of the baron's nose. "I still carry it with me for good luck." He leaned closer, and the baron could smell the coffee on his breath. "I've read your file. I believe you're innocent. And since I'm the one who decides, I'm letting you go. But after this, I can't promise you a moment's safety."

Manya and the baroness watched the chaos in the street. Refugees were pushing in different directions, dragging along children and suitcases. When a young woman carrying a puppy stopped to rest beside their car, Manya rolled down her window.

"Where are you headed?" she asked.

"Home," smiled the woman. "If I keep walking, I will be home in three days."

"What do you mean? Are you going back east?"

"Yes. The army told us it was safe to return. Everything's been quiet lately. No bombs, no gunfire. The Russians are backing off."

The woman cradled the puppy against her shoulder as if it were a baby and waved good-bye.

"I don't believe it for one moment," said Manya, turning to her mother. "Something else is going on. I guarantee you, the Russians are getting ready to attack."

"You always think the worst."

Manya was about to respond when she heard a loud honk. To her left, a lorry rolled through the crowded street.

"Dirty Gypsies!" a white-whiskered man yelled from the sidewalk. "Conniving Jews! It's time they got rid of you. Now you'll work for Germany. No more feeding off the nation like parasites."

The lorry, fitted in the back with wooden slats, should have been transporting livestock. Instead, Manya was horrified to see forty or fifty people, crushed together. When the lorry braked, they tried to stay upright, but with nothing to hold on to, they tumbled forward. Two young mothers were fighting to lift their babies out of the mass of bodies, but they could barely move.

"Oh, my God!" cried Manya. "Stop!"

But the lorry rolled on, the tires spraying up plumes of muck. Manya stared at the blur of faces rushing by. *Was that Sofia? Oh God.* She could swear she saw the girl's coppery hair.

⚜

Darkness had fallen by the time her father, accompanied by an officer, limped down the station's steps and into the street. Her mother gasped when she saw his battered face.

"Can you drive, child?" she asked Manya anxiously. "I want to sit with Father in the backseat."

Manya nodded, but she was only half listening. Her ears still roared with the sound of the lorry's blasting horn. Feeling numb, she stepped out of the car and took her father's arm. He gripped her hand tightly.

"Thank you, officer," she heard him say. "You're a good man."

The officer's face softened.

"Sir," she asked. "Where are they sending the prisoners? I saw a lorry pass about an hour ago."

The officer looked from Manya to the baron. "Why are you concerned about Jews and Gypsies? They're filth!" His eyes narrowed.

"Manya," her father said nervously. "He's done all he can. Get back in the car."

"Tell your daughter to be careful, sir. You are already on the blacklist. Any further questions will cost you your lives. Good night." He turned on his heels and walked away.

Her father drew her closer. He was trembling and weak. She could smell the blood and sweat and urine on his clothes.

As she drove along the pockmarked road, Manya's mind spun. What kind of world was it where an aristocrat who'd had the good fortune of being able to tip well could go free, but a child like Sofia might now be crammed in a lorry like an animal? What had happened to her, to Vavara and Joshi?

"I think I saw Sofia in that lorry full of prisoners," Manya finally blurted out to her parents. "But it was so crowded."

Her father's voice cracked. "I heard them talking inside. They made a raid on the Karas camp. I am not sure who survived, but if Sofia is among those prisoners, they are planning to send them to Stutthof, a forced labor camp near Danzig."

PART II

Joshi

DECEMBER 1944

SIXTEEN

Joshi rode back to the camp across the fluorescent fields of snow. Manya's kiss tingled on his lips. German army units were probably nearby, but he couldn't resist whooping at the moon.

"Listen, you lonely old ball floating up there among the stars. I have something to tell you. Manya loves me."

He grinned and opened his mouth to catch a falling snowflake, imagining it melting on Manya's sweet lips. Never had he felt so hungry for a woman, never so full with one. He closed his eyes, remembering the sheen of Manya's skin. Another shiver of delight ran through him, and once more he broke into song.

He had never really been in love. During his university years in Sweden, he'd had numerous sexual encounters. Eager to learn the art of lovemaking, he enjoyed discovering what pleased a woman. Yet, no matter how intriguing or beautiful the women were, he always felt that something was missing. Not so much in them as in himself. It was as if some essential part of him stayed hidden, remote. And it made him feel lonely.

Sometimes he blamed himself for this inability to love completely. Usually, though, it was his father's voice that stopped him, those urgent, unswerving threats that had left their mark on his mind. When Joshi was a teenager, his father used to sit him down on a log and yank at his ear.

"Listen up, boy," he'd say. "Certain things will take the life from you. The worst is a gadji woman. If you give yourself to one, you will lose your connection to your people. You will lose your soul. A gadji will pollute it and make you dirty." It was always at this point that his father's eyes would bore into his own. "And if that happens," his father would continue, "you'll be exiled from the clan."

Joshi hadn't believed those words, and yet it was astounding how often they haunted him. Especially when he was making love to a woman. But tonight with Manya—. *Why didn't I see it before*, he wondered. *She always had my heart. All that time.*

He leaned back and laid his head on Tsura's rump, letting himself remember the softness of Manya's sighs, the moans of her pleasure.

The sharp yip of a timber wolf broke his reverie. He sat up. Somewhere deep in the forest, another wolf was howling a response. Tsura, usually so intent on plodding home, stopped short to shake the wet snowflakes from her mane. He dug his heels into her side, urging her along the river bend, and she started forward again. The camp was just ahead.

He cocked his head, listening for any sounds that might reassure him—a guitar, a voice, the clink of a bottle. Nothing—only the thud of Tsura's hooves against the compacted snow.

Another howl floated through the trees. *Those wolves are too close for Mama's liking*, he thought. *She'll say they're carrying the dead in their jaws.*

He tied Tsura to her hitching post and hurried along the rutted path to the caravans. The fire had burned out. Through the trees, he could see cold strings of smoke hovering over the ashes. Several dark shapes lay still in the moonlit snow. He began to run, his heart pounding with dread.

Near his family's wagon, he tripped, his boot tip catching the curved neck of Lala Florian's harp. He fell hard, his hands smashing into a torso. His father lay dead in the snow.

A cry caught in his throat. He turned his head from side to side, struggling to comprehend, yet not wanting to believe. Less than a yard away, beneath a wagon pan box full of cooking utensils, was his mother, her vacant eyes fixed on her husband, her frozen hands clawing at the ground. Joshi stumbled over to kneel beside her. A single bullet had entered the center of her forehead, leaving only a bloodless hole.

Swastika signs leered at him. Black paint had been sloshed on in haste and was dripping like blood down the sides of his family's caravan. Not far away, Harman and Dika slumped over the steps of their caravan. Shandor was now a frozen bundle at their feet. The older children were dead, too. They lay in the snow beside upended buckets, their arms stretched out like wings.

His heart stopped. *Sofia.* But she wasn't among them.

"Sofia, are you here?" he cried. "Sofia!"

His knees began to shake, and he crouched down beside his mother to stop himself from falling. He stared at her lifeless face and began to sob.

How could they do this to you, most gentle of souls? He lifted her up and placed her next to his father, whose features were clear and stern, his prominent jaw defiant, even in death. Were those papers in his hands? Joshi pulled them from his grasp, the bloodstained edges flapping in the wind.

"Oh Father," he wept. "Papers can't stop massacres. They can't turn Gypsies into Aryans." He cradled Andras in his arms, rocking back and forth. "I'm so sorry. I should have been here with you."

As the grief rose in him, so did the rage. He wanted to lash out, to kill those who had killed his own.

"Why do you want us to be like you?" he cried, pounding his fist into the snow. "Even the worst of us has never been among the worst of you."

But his words were caught in the snow-covered branches overhead. And with every sob, he became aware of a sinking helplessness. There was no recourse, no retribution. His happiness with Manya was colorless now, too. He cursed himself. If he hadn't lingered with her, he would have been here with his family. He might have been able to do something.

Gathering himself, he went inside the caravan. The oil lamp was still flickering on the table, the tiny flame throwing shadowy fingers onto the flowered wallpaper. He stared at the familiar objects: the worn deck of cards his father used to stick in the children's bicycle spokes to make them laugh, the two sooty champagne flutes that had sat on the corner table for years, Sofia's quilt neatly folded on the three-legged stool. His grief changed to resolve. His parents would be buried with dignity. At least that was something he could do.

Inside his parents' cupboard, he found a clean shirt and his father's favorite silver-studded trousers. From a dresser drawer he gathered his mother's beaded purple shawl along with the family's silver snuffbox, which contained some loose pearls. Outside, he filled a bucket with clean water. Gently, he bathed and dressed his father.

"I wish you well on this last journey," he said as if his father could hear. He looked at his mother. "Mama," he whispered, "the wolves have stopped howling. Perhaps that means Sofia is alive."

He prepared the bodies of his parents, and rose to count the corpses. Twenty-two. Sofia and Nuri were not among them. Since the ground had not yet frozen, he found a pickaxe and shovel and began to dig, determined to bury his clan before daybreak. He lifted the pickaxe and pounded and chipped and tore at the earth until his muscles burned.

When he had dug a shallow trough, he began with his grandfather. The old man's withered bones seemed to weigh less than a twig in the forest. He wept when he saw dry breadcrumbs fall out of his Aunt Vadoma's skirt pockets. Until the end, she had believed they would protect her against evil.

He buried his mother and father last. Holding his hands out over his father's body, he poured his strength into his father's spirit, hoping it would help his father take flight. "Father," he said, "you never betrayed your own. I did. Forgive my vanities, please. Do not condemn me. I need your blessing now, your fearlessness too, if I am to carry on."

Bending over, he kissed his father's hand and carefully removed two pearls from the snuffbox. He plugged Andras's nostrils in the old way meant to prevent evil from entering a dead man's body. He did the same for his mother, and when he was done, he covered his parents and the rest of his clan with shovels of wet dirt, broken grass, and snow. Finally, he took a can of petrol and doused the caravans, setting fire to every one. No outsider would touch what belonged to the clan.

The morning sun rose, barely penetrating the low clouds. Joshi's eyes moved painfully in their sockets. Rising, he wondered what to do next.

He noticed a bow beside a broken carriage tongue. It lay on the ground like an arm. Beside it was his violin, unharmed. He picked up the instrument and rubbed the fingerboard clean. Wasn't it just yesterday he'd taught Sofia a melody on these strings? Where would the SS have taken her? He had searched everywhere, but she was nowhere to be found. Trying to block the unthinkable from his mind, he closed his eyes, bowed his head, and asked the heavens for some kind of direction.

A twig snapped. He turned toward the sound and, to his surprise, saw a stag standing motionless at the edge of the encampment. A strange feeling came over him.

"Whose spirit are you?" he whispered, trying to make eye contact. "What have you come to tell me?" But the stag bolted, and once more he was alone.

He needed to formulate a plan, to find Sofia. He breathed in the cold air, forcing himself to think. Where would they have taken her? To Angerburg? Rastenburg? He wished he knew where they detained people before sending them off to the labor camps.

He was sure she was alive, and he tried to imagine how she was feeling. It only made sense that she would be with Nuri.

His eyes fell on his mother's grave. He felt a stirring inside. Rising to his feet, he tucked the violin under his chin. After tuning it carefully, he swept the bow across the strings, drawing out his mother's favorite song, "Dark eyes, dark eyes, calling me to a faraway land . . ."

So absorbed was he in the music that he missed Tsura's soft, cautionary neigh, nor did he see the two uniformed strangers who had entered the camp's outer border.

"By damn, there's one left," the younger officer said. "I thought we got all the dirty buggers last night." He reached for his pistol and, cocking the trigger, aimed the barrel at Joshi's head.

"Stop," he called. "Immediately."

Joshi spun around. He saw the black boots, the swastikas on the sleeves. He knew he should run. If he somersaulted sideways and bolted, he might dodge their bullets and make it into the forest. They'd never find him in the brush-covered ravine.

But in that split second, another thought entered his mind. What if these men could take him to Sofia? Was that what the stag had tried to tell him?

"Put your hands up," ordered the older officer, approaching Joshi and shoving the gun barrel into his stomach. "Where did you learn to play like that?"

The violin slipped from Joshi's hand and hit the ground with a dull thud. He hoped it hadn't splintered, but he was afraid to look.

The officer repeated the question.

"Tell me, where did you learn to play like that?"

Joshi hesitated. Was this some kind of trap? "I learned as a child. From my grandfather, but mostly from my mother." He glanced at his mother's grave.

The officer nodded almost imperceptibly. "You play well, Gypsy. It's not often one hears the music of the soul." He bent down to pick up the fallen violin. "Here," he said, handing the instrument to Joshi. "Take it with you. They'll want you to play it where you're going. Now let's move."

The officers led him to a jeep behind the copse of trees where he and Manya had made love. He sat in front and the young officer sat behind him, holding a gun to his head. Running his fingers over the violin's strings, he thought about Tsura. She was like a devoted dog, reliable and trustworthy. He hoped someone would find her so she would not starve.

They stopped in Nordenburg, a small town just north of Guja where several men were guarding the doors to the school's gymnasium. He was ordered into the building. Inside, the hall smelled of mold and piss. Everywhere, people were huddled in clusters, some of them sitting on mats, others leaning against the walls.

He scanned the room for Sofia and saw her standing near a window, staring at the cold sky. Nuri was on the floor beside her, dozing, her purple skirt spread over her bent knees. Joshi felt a rush of relief. No bruises. No blood. He hurried across the hall, stepping over bodies and knapsacks, and gathered Sofia into his arms.

"I knew you would come," she whispered, her topaz eyes filling with tears. "But Mama and Papa—"

"I know," murmured Joshi, holding her tight. "I saw what happened."

Nuri rose unsteadily to her feet. Her eyes were blackened from lack of sleep and smudged eyeliner, her cheeks splattered with mud.

"They got you too," she wept, pulling at the broken string of pearls that dangled from her hair. "But why did they take Sofia and me? Why didn't they shoot us?"

"They must have their reasons," he answered softly, trying to suppress the quaking in his voice. "But if we stick together, we'll get through this."

It was a lie. For the moment, though, it was the only thing he could think of.

No one came to give them food or water. Occasionally a child would cry, or someone would whisper a complaint, but most of the time the hall was quiet.

Joshi's thoughts became erratic. He couldn't stop the shaking in the pit of his stomach. *Where would the SS take them*, he wondered. He imagined all the ways the Nazis could kill him. He had seen the look on the young officer's face. It was cold, completely disconnected, as if the man's heart and mind functioned separately. Looking into the man's eyes, Joshi had understood how utterly worthless he had become.

He thought about the gray-haired older officer who had asked where he learned to play the violin. At least he had an appreciation of music. Joshi was thankful for that, not so much because it had saved his life but because it gave him hope that wherever they were going, there might be other officers like him.

Sofia stirred uncomfortably. "I'm so hungry," she whimpered.

The woman beside her pulled a small loaf of chocolate-covered marzipan from her coat pocket and offered Sofia a piece.

Thanking her, Joshi wondered what had made her bring the marzipan. What made people grab certain items when guns were pressed hard into their kidneys? He curled his fingers around the neck of his violin. *Others are probably wondering the same about me*, he thought.

The gymnasium door opened with a bang. Half a dozen guards marched in, holding machine guns.

"Out, vermin!" the first one shouted.

SEVENTEEN

For three days, the lorry barely stopped moving. When it did, it was to gather more prisoners along the way. Rain, sharp and gray as pencil lead, fell in cold, bleak sheets. There was no place to sit in the cramped space. Helpless, he watched the more feeble prisoners fighting for balance. One by one they fell, and each time the lorry braked, the other prisoners could not avoid stepping on them. Finally their cries trailed off, dying away inside them. The guards never bothered to remove their bodies, letting them lie half frozen in the filth.

On the second day, the guards pulled over to hand out a few loaves of rye bread. Joshi stuffed the dry piece they gave him into his mouth, devouring it hungrily, but as soon as he swallowed he was overcome with revulsion. His hands reeked of piss and shit. With no sanitation facilities, no toilet stops along the way, the prisoners had been forced to relieve themselves right where they stood.

He held Sofia close, trying to keep her warm. From a conversation between the driver and a guard, he had gathered that they were being taken to Stutthof, a labor camp some 20 miles east of Danzig. He had heard of the place. Ragnar, his Swedish friend and mentor, had traveled there long before the war, when it had been a holiday destination. *What is it now*, he wondered grimly.

"Tell me a story," Sofia whispered, looking up at him with baleful eyes.

Joshi glanced at Nuri. She was huddled against the side of the lorry, tears falling over her dirt-streaked face. He looked back at Sofia and felt a strangling in his throat.

"I'm not sure I can talk right now."

But Sofia was insistent. She tugged at his wrist and pushed her face into his jacket. "All right," he said, finally giving in. "What story do you want to hear?"

"Tell me about the day you saved the boy on the runaway horse."

He nodded quietly. He remembered it exactly. It was how his dream to study medicine had come true. But now there was no joy in it. Still, he didn't have the heart to deny Sofia.

"It was summer. You were just a wee thing. Our clan used to travel to Göteborg because the Swedish farmers loved Papa's horseshoes and tools. We would go north of the city to visit other clans, but mainly to pass by the summer residence of a shipping magnate named Ragnar Malmberg. Ragnar had horses on his estate, and his son Olaf and I used to ride out together. Olaf's mount was a former racehorse, totally unpredictable. One day, while we were trotting back to the barn along the rhododendron path, his horse got spooked."

"What happened?" asked Sofia breathlessly, as she always did.

"Olaf fell out of the saddle, but his foot got trapped in the stirrup. He couldn't free himself, and his horse began to gallop, dragging him over the ground."

"Could he have been killed?" asked Sofia, wide-eyed.

"For sure," Joshi nodded. "Anyway, Papa and Ragnar were outside the barn. They could see us. Papa kept shouting for me to do something. Instinct took over, I guess, and I whipped my horse forward. I managed to catch up to Olaf's runaway horse, grab the reins, and yank his head back."

"He stopped?"

Joshi nodded.

"What about Olaf?"

"I jumped off my horse and pulled his foot out of the stirrup. His head was bleeding badly, but he was alive. We rushed him to the hospital, where I watched the doctor stitch the wound."

Joshi remembered his fascination with the procedure—the deadening, the needle, the neat line of stitches. The next day, Ragnar had visited the caravan, saying that he wanted to repay Joshi for saving Olaf's life.

"You can have anything you want," Ragnar had said.

Joshi had hesitated before blurting out his wish: "I want to study medicine."

His mother, who was offering Ragnar coffee, nearly dropped her tray. It was the moment in which Joshi realized his destiny could change. His mother's eyes had flashed back and forth between him and the Swede. In them, Joshi saw the deep, hard questions he knew he would have to answer.

"If that's your wish," Ragnar said sincerely, "then I will fulfill it, and if your parents agree, you can live with us. I'll see to it that you stay in Sweden and attend the university in Göteborg."

The lorry bounced forward.

Joshi held tight to Sofia, his eyes settling on the gray mist that hung over the distant hills. That day had heralded the beginning of a deep friendship with Ragnar. However, it was also the start of countless violent arguments between Joshi and his father; arguments in which Andras repeatedly accused him of bringing shame to the clan.

In the end, it was Vavara who urged him to follow his soul's vocation. "I'll handle your Papa," she'd said.

Late that summer when the clan returned to Angerburg, Joshi stayed behind with the Malmbergs. His father did not force him to come along, but he was angry, and he rode off in the horse cart without a word of farewell.

Joshi had adjusted quickly to life in Sweden. Ragnar's close circle of friends included university professors who gave their time to coach him. In Germany, Romanies were banned from universities, but on his first try, he passed the entrance exam and was accepted into one of Sweden's most prestigious schools, the University of Göteborg. Even in Sweden, Ragnar had needed to pull strings with politicians and embassy contacts to make sure Joshi's papers were approved. But he'd always called Joshi his "other son," and there was nothing he wouldn't do for him. The previous year, Joshi had graduated with a degree in medicine, and he had been working for one of Ragnar's friends in a small clinic not far from the university.

As the war progressed and Joshi traveled back and forth between Sweden and East Prussia, Ragnar's concern grew. "Be careful," he warned. "I've heard stories from ship captains here in Göteborg. They tell me Jews and Romanies are being sent to forced labor camps. Conditions are abominable. The camps are often built near sewage grounds. People are dying of typhus and starvation. Don't get caught, Joshi. I can't help you in Germany."

The lorry honked and braked sharply. Through the slats Joshi could see a massive gate, embellished with metal grillwork and a medieval turret.

Beside it stood a neat, two-story, red brick building, immaculately land-scaped and resembling a hotel. The building was flanked on each side by well-kept barracks painted dove gray.

"That must be the SS garrison," Joshi whispered to Nuri.

The forest was so close and quiet that he could hear the murmur of the wind through the branches.

Nuri squeezed his hand. "Maybe we're in luck. This place doesn't look so bad."

"I wouldn't count on it," he murmured, glancing up. "There's a machine gun in that turret pointing straight at us."

The back of the lorry was yanked open. A guard began to poke at the prisoners with a long stick.

"*Raus!*" he shouted. "Everyone out!"

Joshi kissed the top of Sofia's head before lifting her off the truck. "Do as they say, sweetheart," he whispered.

She smiled bravely, but when she heard the loud bark of a dog, she clutched at his hand. Moments later, on their left, the door to a brick guardhouse opened. Three German Shepherds bounded out, snarling and straining at their leashes.

Sofia and Nuri were pulled into a separate line of women.

"*Marsch!*" barked another voice. "March!"

Joshi fell in line with the men, moving along a cobblestone walkway that led through the iron gate and onto a field. A row of shabby buildings under a single, common roof lined the field's edge. *The prisoners' barracks,* he thought, with a sinking feeling.

He turned to look for Sofia and Nuri and saw them in a column of women to his left, being directed by a female warden. The warden was lithe and muscular, pretty, too, in a hardened sort of way, with red lips and flawless white skin. *She decides who lives and who dies,* he thought, staring at her thick auburn ponytail, which was held in place by a white pearl clasp.

The warden had lined up her prisoners in front of a roofless barrack. Sofia stood as still as a tree in the forest, fear in her eyes.

Joshi watched the warden saunter past the male guards, a noticeable swing in her hips. Smoothing down her skirt, held at her narrow waist by a wide black belt, she looked fiercely at her captives, her voice quiet but severe.

"You will follow the rules or you will die. Work is your life now, so get used to it." She paused to take in the faces. "You there," she called to Nuri. "Can you sew?"

Nuri nodded.

"Good. You will be sent to the stocking darners' *Kommando*. Is she your daughter?" she asked, pointing the whip at Sofia.

Nuri was too afraid to answer, but her eyes darted toward Joshi.

Curious, the warden followed her gaze. "Ah," she murmured. "He must be your husband. Or your lover." Taking her time, she scrutinized Joshi's face, then let her eyes slowly roam over his shoulders and chest and down, stopping at his crotch. He felt a chill in the pit of his stomach.

Suddenly he felt a sharp blow on the side of his head, and with a yelp he pressed his hand to his right ear. Blood seeped onto his collar.

"Stop daydreaming and get a move on," snapped a guard.

He tried to hold back a scream that rose from the depths of his soul. The voices around him had become muffled. *My eardrum's ruptured*, he thought. The pain spread and a wave of dizziness washed over him, but he didn't dare sit down and risk another hit from the guard—or a gunshot.

He walked on through a door and into a room that contained a mountain of shoes so high it nearly touched the ceiling. The heavy smell of old leather and sour sweat swelled in the air. His eyes moved over several stray loafers, a brown shoe with a tear in one seam, a child's dress boot.

"Take them off," ordered a fat guard waving a leather-bound cudgel over the prisoners' feet. "You won't need shoes here." He snickered. "In Stutthof, clogs are the fashion."

Joshi threw the leather boots Ragnar had given him onto the pile, dreading the unknown fate that lay in store for him and for every newly barefoot man who shuffled out of the room.

Against the far wall, behind a table, sat a clerk who was busy jotting down the personal data of each prisoner. Soon it was Joshi's turn to be questioned.

"Nationality?" the clerk asked.

Joshi hesitated.

"German—Romani."

The clerk looked up. Joshi was surprised to see serial numbers stamped across the breast pocket of the man's suit. *You're a prisoner too*, Joshi thought.

"Is that a violin you're carrying? Can you play it?"

Joshi nodded, remembering the officer who had arrested him.

"Yes."

"Then slide it under the table. They're always looking for musicians. If they like your music, they'll feed you extra. Now move on."

The violin disappeared. Joshi was hustled back out into a muddy field, where he waited with what seemed like hundreds of other prisoners, all of whom had arrived that day. He learned that many had come from camps in Latvia, but most had traveled from a camp in southern Poland called Auschwitz. The Germans, afraid of the advancing Russian army, had begun to evacuate thousands of prisoners from there to Stutthof.

"I hoped it would be better here," said a man beside him, "but I can smell death already." With dark rings under his eyes that purpled his face, he looked at Joshi. "You had better take care of your ear. If that doesn't get you, something will. Typhus, dysentery, work, beatings."

Joshi shuddered. His feet burned from the cold, and his ear was swelling. In this filth, his condition would deteriorate into mastoiditis, which would eventually enter his brain and kill him. He took a deep breath. *Keep your wits about you*, he thought. *Don't let them see you panic.*

Another shout and he and the others were herded into yet another hut.

"Strip!" a raspy voice commanded. "Hang your things through the wire loops on the hooks over there. Keep your belts. Nothing else. Place all personal belongings on this pile here. *Schnell!* Quickly!"

Joshi started to undress, pausing to finger his leather jacket one last time. Like the boots, Ragnar had bought the jacket for him on the day he'd finished medical school.

"Hurry up!" said the officer, poking him with his pistol. "You have exactly two minutes. I'm counting."

Documents, photos, jewelry, and cash landed in a heap on the dirty floor. Those who had already been in a camp had nothing to add. Others simply trembled with shock. An aging, bow-legged man in front of Joshi begged to keep his wedding ring.

"I can't take it off!" he cried. "My knuckles are too big."

"Come here," said the officer, reaching into his pocket for a knife. "I'll help you."

The officer grabbed the man's finger and sliced it off. Ring and finger fell to the floor.

Blood spurted from the man's hand, dripping onto his genitals. The man's face was blank with shock, and his body trembled.

"I'm going to take your belt," Joshi said softly. He reached for the belt dangling from the old man's good hand and looped it around an arthritic wrist, pulling it tight.

"This will stop the bleeding," he said in a low voice, but the old man was already crumbling to the floor.

A pair of rough hands pulled Joshi away from the man and toward a stool, where a barber began dragging a dull razor over his head. The blade attacked his chest, too, scraping away until only angry skin and bleeding nicks remained.

"For hygienic purposes," the barber muttered with a bored smile. "Stops the lice. Now get up. It's time to bathe."

Another door opened. Joshi was given a piece of cracked soap and shoved into a room full of showerheads. He stopped short, holding his breath, waiting for the icy water to shock his body, but when the stream came it was just a faint trickle on his head. He sighed. For some reason, the water reminded him he was still alive.

Within minutes, someone hauled him out of the shower, splashing him with a pail of disinfectant. As the liquid stung his body, he thought of Manya and their lovemaking. He was shocked that such images could run through his mind in this awful place. Still, she was there. Hoping to preserve something of her, he covered his genitals with his hands, but the disinfectant was already burning the skin and stealing the memory.

Now he waited in air so raw it tore at his muscles, until a man handed him a pair of gray and blue striped cotton pants, a thin jacket of the same material, and a round beret. The wooden sabots, or *Klumpen*, that he shoved on his bare feet were streaked with someone else's blood.

"You're a number now," an SS officer grinned, shoving a strip of cloth into his hand. "Memorize it."

The cloth was imprinted with a serial number and a black triangle bearing the letter Z, *Zigeuner*, Gypsy.

Beside him a skinny man who looked like he'd come from another camp whispered, "You better watch your back. Your kind get beaten even worse than us Jews."

A bugle sounded from inside the turret, and a group of musicians assembled near the main gate. As the gate swung open they began to play, announcing the return of the prisoners who had worked outside the camp.

They filed into the square, bodies doubled over from exhaustion, dirt molded to their suffering faces. Last came a cart filled with the men who had not survived the day, their corpses bobbing up and down with every jolt, their lifeless arms dangling over the sides. Two skeletal men lugged the awful load like beasts.

"*Achtung!*" shouted an officer. "*Mützen!* Hats!"

Joshi shifted his gaze back to the sea of people stretching across the field. In one remarkable, unanimous gesture, the prisoners all raised their right hands to their caps, as if saluting.

"*Ab!* Off!" shouted the officer.

Every cap came off, striking the thigh of the inmate who had been wearing it.

"Line up according to height!" the officer commanded.

A tall man with stubbly red hair and freckled skin ambled up to Joshi and took his place behind him.

"I'm Ben," he said with a small smile. "I can see you're new. Listen, I've learned a few tricks and I always try to pass them on. Obey rules to avoid beatings. Do what they tell you. Beatings kill quicker than anything else. Enough for now," he said, turning away. "They can't catch us talking. I'll fill you in later. Most likely you'll be in Block Two, because you're in my column."

Hundreds of female prisoners stood on the far side of the quadrant. Joshi looked for Sofia, but he couldn't find her in the crowd. He prayed that she had been spared. Children and old people were probably of little value to Stutthof's labor force, but maybe the Gestapo had kept her alive for some reason. He could only hope.

The prisoners were called to the canteen for supper. Someone handed him a dirty, dented bowl, half full of rust-colored broth made from rotten vegetables, and gritty with what he was sure was sand. Instead of a spoon, he was given a small piece of hard bread.

"Don't gobble the bread," warned Ben, falling into the seat next to Joshi. "Suck on it so it lasts. And drink the hot bog water. At least it's been boiled. Fresh water is contaminated. It'll give you the runs."

Joshi nodded in thanks and took a sip of the soup.

"Tastes like piss," he said.

Ben smiled grimly.

When they had finished eating, Joshi followed Ben into a barrack where rows of three-tiered bunks lined the walls. Inmates were dragging pallets of rotten straw into the middle of the floor.

"Four to a pallet," said Ben, pointing to a spot that was less drafty. "And four to a blanket. The old-timers have the top bunks. No one likes the middle or lower ones because the shit drips down." Seeing the disgust on Joshi's face, he flashed him a half grin. "Look, this place is no amusement park. You have to decide right now if you want to survive. You're a big man. So they're going to notice you and work you like an ox. And if you haven't figured it out already, this place is run by *kapos*. They're prisoners, too, except generally they're the worst kind. The camp heads choose them as supervisors, and they'll kill to stay on top.

"Sometimes, weird little things will make you laugh," Ben went on. "And the only way to get through is to remember someone you want to live for." He blinked as though he were going over a list in his head. "Shave every day—with a piece of glass, if you have to. It'll make your face look healthier. And for God's sake don't limp when you get blisters. They'll shoot you if they think you're no more use to them. Now get some sleep. You'll get a backbreaking baptism tomorrow. That's the one thing you can count on."

Joshi crawled under a blanket that smelled of vomit, piss, and shit. Despite the pounding in his head, he fell asleep among the many men pressed together like herrings in a barrel.

⚜

He woke with a start. Someone had entered the room and was lighting a lantern. It was Esser, the overseer.

"Wake up, you lazy shits," he bellowed, kicking the men onto their backs. "I want music! Where's that Russian prisoner who plays the accordion?"

Not far from Joshi a young man with enormous black eyes sat up and coughed.

"There you are," grinned Esser, dragging the man to a stool near the door. "Sit here while I get your instrument."

He disappeared inside his cubicle, only to return moments later with an accordion, which he shoved into the man's shaking hands.

"Play," he ordered. The prisoner obeyed, pushing and pulling on the bellows until a sad little polka had emerged. Esser's dark eyes surveyed the dimly lit room. "Whoever dances for me will get a piece of bread."

Joshi looked on in horror. There was no lack of hungry volunteers. The first was a skinny teenage boy whose knobby knees and pathetic skeleton dance nearly broke Joshi's heart.

"No good!" cried Esser, kicking the boy away. A few more men stepped up, none of whom performed to Esser's liking. After twenty minutes, he became impatient with the Russian accordion player and boxed his ears. "Stop," he hollered. "Your music is shit! They can't dance to your songs."

All at once, his gaze fell on Joshi.

"You there," he said with a mean smile. "Aren't you the Gypsy who arrived today? The clerk told me you play the violin. Get up while I fetch one!" He let out a harsh laugh. "I'm the king of instruments, aren't I, boys?"

Ben shot Joshi a concerned look.

"The man is a maniac," he whispered. "Rumor has it he killed his own mother."

Joshi nodded and crawled over to the stool. Moments later, Esser returned with a violin.

"The man who owned it is dead now," he laughed, handing it to Joshi. "But you'll make it come alive, I'm sure."

As Joshi touched the strings of the polished instrument, he was filled with memories of his mother, his father, and Manya. A fierce pulse ran through his fingers. He drew the bow across the strings, and the romantic notes of *The Blue Danube* waltz spilled into the stale air. Rising sweet and sad, the waltz seeped into the room and the tired men around him.

When Joshi had finished, Esser applauded.

"Bravo! You earned the bread tonight."

He threw the crust at Joshi's feet.

Joshi grabbed it. For the first time in his life, he felt a terrible greed. He wanted to swallow the bread whole, hide it from the others' sight. His eyes sharpened themselves against the figures in the room. Looking up, he saw Ben's sallow eyes crying out for food, and his newfound miserliness softened. Silently, he ripped off a piece and handed it to Ben.

Lowering his eyes in shame, Ben snatched it and stuffed it into his mouth.

EIGHTEEN

Joshi's first assignment was in the sand pit with Ben. They spent their days hauling carts of sand from the dunes near the sea to an enormous pit on the other side of the forest.

Word soon spread to the camp authorities that Joshi was a talented violinist. In the evenings, he performed with the "orchestra." For hours he stood on the shoddy platform, his feet frozen with cold, his fingers aching on the strings. For hours he forced himself to play, but no matter how hard he tried, he simply could not shake the thought that his father was raging in his grave. Andras would never have entertained Nazis. He would have first chosen death.

One evening, while Joshi was performing, four inmates were marched past him to the gallows, two of them Romanies from Auschwitz who had tried to escape. He knew they'd been crazy to attempt it. Still, he envied their courage. As he watched them limp across the field, he felt ashamed. Unlike him, they had remained true to their Romani beliefs. They had chosen to die rather than live like dogs.

His fingers stiffened when he saw the gallows plank hovering above the ground. How could he continue playing when he wanted to kill the officer in charge, strangle him with his hands? But he played when the gallows executioner tightened the noose around the first man's neck and when the plank was pulled away. And he played when he saw the man choke and urinate down the front of his filthy uniform.

He willed his fingers to move faster, playing whatever came to him— mazurkas, waltzes, hymns—anything to drown the roaring in his ears.

He watched the man's legs dangle above the warped circle of mud, and he understood why camp musicians often committed suicide. They couldn't stand to hear their songs mingle with the moans of death.

When the four hangings were over, it was the women's turn. From his corner on the platform, Joshi watched the hard-faced warden organize races to determine which women were fit enough to work the next day and which were not. Snapping a tasseled whip, she ordered them to hike up their skirts. Terrified, they obeyed. Slowly she went down the line, her red lips twisted into a mean smile, her cold eyes studying their legs with calculated deliberation. She chose the thinnest women first. Pulling them out one by one, she forced them to run races until they collapsed in the snow. The losers were dragged away and shot.

Joshi closed his eyes, hoping to find some redeeming quality in the music he played. He chose familiar melodies that he hoped would let the men and women remember who they once were and where they had come from. Something that might comfort them. Yet thoughts of Sofia tortured him. He had not seen her in days.

Two evenings after the hangings, Joshi and Ben were among a group of prisoners walking along the path that led from the sand pit back to camp. Exhausted and covered in grit, they followed the guard in charge. Halfway to the camp, the guard veered left into the forest. *Maybe we're going to be shot*, he thought. Too tired to care, he trudged on after the guard, keeping his eyes on the ground. Ten minutes later, the guard hollered for them to stop. Joshi glanced up to see a tidy brick cottage with a white picket fence.

"Shit," whispered Ben, his breath coming in quick, shallow gasps. "I hate this goddamn place."

"What happens here?" asked Joshi, fear snaking through his chest.

"It's a brothel," croaked Ben. "It's where the fucking SS take the most beautiful female prisoners."

"What?" said Joshi, staring at the curtained windows.

But there was no time to talk.

"Hurry up," the guard shouted, kicking at the shins of the first prisoners in line and pointing to a huge pile of logs stacked near the far wall of the cottage. "Chop those logs into firewood." He walked up to Joshi and hit him on the arm with his whip. "You," he said. "Go around the back into the kitchen. Take out the trash and the empty bottles. *Schnell!* Quickly!"

Joshi hurried to the back of the cottage. Cautiously he entered. The delicious smells of bacon grease, cigarettes, and brandy nearly unhinged him. The stove was still hot, and the warmth seeped over his calves and thighs like a bath.

Across the room, near the pantry, stood a woman in a long crimson dressing gown. A saffron-colored turban was wrapped around her head. He cleared his throat politely to let her know he was there. When she turned, he sucked in his breath.

"Nuri?" he whispered in disbelief.

A muffled cry escaped her lips and she stepped toward him, the dim light from a wall sconce accentuating her rouged cheekbones and red painted lips. "Joshi," she whispered, drawing her eyes away from him. "They had me pretend there was a campfire in the living room and they made me dance for them. They didn't touch me, but they gave me a little food." Her eyes filled with self-loathing. "Hunger makes us do unimaginable things."

"I know," Joshi said quietly.

"One night, one of the SS officers demanded more."

"Did he hurt you?" asked Joshi softly.

"No," she said, with a shake of her head. Her turban had slipped a bit, revealing her bald scalp. Joshi's heart ached. Never had he seen Nuri so vulnerable, so sad. "He didn't rape me," she said, "if that's what you mean. I did it for some bread and cherry marmalade, and a rabbit-fur vest to wear under my uniform when I'm at camp. His name is Klawan." She sighed. "It's strange, but I think he cares for me."

"I know him," Joshi murmured. "A short, plump officer. Likes music. Stands close to the platform whenever I play."

"Yes, that's him." A faint smell of musk and lemon emanated from her skin. As if reading his thoughts, she said, "I'm allowed to bathe here. It's a boon because it keeps the lice away. And now that there's typhus in the women's block, I'm scared. Everywhere, women are coming down with fever. They're shoved off to the sanitary ward, but they just lie on the cement floor until they die."

"What about Sofia?" Joshi asked anxiously.

"She's been luckier than most. The female prisoners take care of her. They try to keep her away from the warden in charge, the one who whips our naked backsides if we leave even a wrinkle on those piss-stained blankets. We call her the 'Prophetess of Doom' because she tells us every day that we're going to die. I call her 'the bitch.' She had it in for me from day one. Tried to send me on the *Strumpfstopfkommando*—the stocking darners' commando."

"What's that?" he asked.

Nuri stared at him hard.

"It's a wagon hitched to a locomotive, and it collects women who say they know how to sew. The poor things are given knitting needles and told they'll be darning socks for the German army. They volunteer because they think they'll be better off in a subcamp away from Stutthof, but it's all a lie. They don't sew a stitch." She exhaled, and Joshi could smell the cigarette ash on her breath. "The wagon is the new gas chamber. It just circles the camp. They closed the old one in December. Too many people, I guess. I was supposed to get on board, but I managed to get my name struck from the list by volunteering to clean the toilets. When the warden found out, she took to beating me. On the first night you played the violin, she dragged me to the punishment block and made me strip. I stood naked in the snow, holding two heavy bricks in my outstretched arms while she threw buckets of ice water over my head." Nuri looked away. "She asked if you and I were lovers."

Joshi hung his head. It was all so surreal. He wanted to stay in the warmth with Nuri and forget the world outside, but he knew he had to go. Reaching out, he touched the back of her hand, hoping she would stop talking for a moment, but she carried on.

"It was she who sent me here to be their whore," she said, looking at her red nails. "She wants to humiliate me." She snorted, "At least I'm alive. That's one up on her." Suddenly the cords in Nuri's thin neck tightened. "You better watch her, Joshi. I've seen the way she looks at you. The devil is in her eyes. They say she uses prisoners for sex games."

Joshi's gut clenched at the thought of the warden's perversions. He hated the way she looked at him.

"I'd better go," he said quickly. "The guard outside will be looking for me."

"Just one minute more," she begged. "Oh, the comfort of feeling safe with someone, of not being afraid to speak what comes to mind." She took his hand in hers and kissed it. "To know that you know me as I was before."

She straightened her shoulders, and a hopeful glimmer appeared in her eyes. "Klawan tells me that the Russians are preparing for their final attack. He says they'll advance toward Berlin as soon as the ground freezes. He promises to get me out of here. I tell you one thing, Joshi. If he does, I'm taking Sofia with me. I'll do whatever he wants."

Color pierced her cheeks and she gazed up at the rafters, hoping in vain that Joshi might not see her shame. "If we all get out, I mean—the three of us—"

She paused as if she were searching for words, her eyes tracing the beams down to a far corner in the room, away from Joshi.

With a sudden breath, she looked straight at him. Her voice was pleading when she spoke, full of love. "I want us all to be together. To live as a clan once more. Could we do that, Joshi?" She exhaled and her chest fell. "Or am I polluted now that I've slept with Nazis?"

Joshi took her face in his hands.

"You'll never be polluted, Nuri. You're not to blame for any of this."

He kissed her cheek tenderly.

Squeezing his hand, she turned toward a cupboard and took out a pack of cigarettes. "Take these," she whispered. "They'll come in handy if you need to bribe someone. Here's some bread, too, and a bit of hard cheese. Hide it in your pockets. Don't let them catch you or they'll kill me."

"Thank you, dear Nuri," said Joshi, stooping to gather up the garbage as she unlatched the door. When he stepped outside, he heard her say, "There's a hole in the hornbeam tree by the fence. Check it when you pass this way. If I escape from Stutthof with Sofia, I'll leave a note. I'll leave food for you, too, whenever I get the chance. God be with you."

Joshi looked up at the clouds thickening in the sky and sighed, "That's if God remembers who we are."

NINETEEN

In the days that followed, when he played the violin for the steely-eyed Nazis in the square, the warm classical melodies they requested turned to ice in his fingers. Still, he played. Often, he felt completely lifeless, yet somehow the music pulled him through. Without his captors knowing it, he would let the genius of his teachers, his grandfather and mother, rise in him to embellish a musical passage with a soulful spark or a sustained quarter note.

In those rare moments, he felt he was still in control of something, that he could still glimpse his life as it once was.

The harshness of the camp returned in the mornings, when he stood in line to use the single washroom. There were days he never got in, and on the days he did, water trickled so slowly from the pipe that he was able to gather only a handful. Soon, grime burrowed into every pore. At breakfast he choked down a cup of bitter corn coffee with a thin slice of bread baked from sawdust and rancid flour, hardly enough to stem the ache of hunger, let alone fortify him for a day of hard labor. And his ear had swollen. Pus seeped out and had formed an ugly crust. *My ear will kill me before any hard labor will*, he thought.

The job site was a two-mile walk from camp, and the work was humiliating. All day, he, Ben, and their fellow inmates filled wagons with sand and hauled the wagons over broken railway tracks to a deep pit.

Since the tracks were uneven, the cars often derailed, which fueled the kapos' wrath. Nearly every day, Joshi felt the sting of leather biting into his flesh and heard the word *Schwein*—pig—resound in his head.

He and Ben worked with several older men who were familiar with the task but had grown so weak they could barely stand. One morning, as Joshi waited to pull his heavy load onto the slippery tracks, the wagon in front of him rolled backward, threatening to crush an older man who had lost his footing. Joshi lunged forward to help.

"You all right?" he said as he helped the man to his feet.

"I just want to die," the man muttered.

"Back in line, you dogs!" shouted the kapo, his whip cutting into the old man's neck. Joshi felt sick. He stumbled back on his own clogs, a stabbing pain shooting from his toes up through his arches and ankles until, unable to bear it, he sank to his knees.

"Shoot me," he muttered, inhaling a mouthful of sand. "Put an end to this goddamn misery."

A hand jerked at the back of his uniform. "Get up," hissed Ben. "The kapo is watching. He'll beat the hell out of you. And I don't have the strength to lift you. So *get up!*"

Joshi slowly stood up and brushed himself off. The kapo nodded and moved ahead. A sob rose up in Joshi's throat.

"All right, my friend," murmured Ben. "You've had your first and hopefully last cry in this hellhole. Now move your ass. It's Christmas Eve and you've forgotten already. We only have to work half a day. Come on, man. I've been watching your ear. There's pus coming from it. You need your strength."

"I need something for the infection," muttered Joshi. "If my ear festers any longer, the infection will go into the bone." He drew in a breath. "All I can say is, fuck that son of a bitch who hit me. If I meet him on the other side, he'll lose both ears!"

"That's the spirit," grinned Ben. "Better to be mad than sorry for yourself." He brushed the sand off his hands and peered around the cart. "Come on, you smelly dog. We'll figure out how to get you some medicine. I heard that the nurse in the sick bay likes to think he's a doctor. He gets his kicks out of injecting prisoners with phenol."

Joshi took a step forward. He'd always been lucky. But he had taken so much for granted, especially his dream to go to medical school. That, too, had happened thanks to others: Baroness von Falken and Ragnar had done everything possible to help him. And there was Manya. Always a friend, she had given him whatever he asked for, including her heart. But had he ever really said thank you?

He strained to push his cart forward. *I've grabbed whatever I could from life*, he thought, *without giving back. Here I am a doctor, yet I've never cared about people the way Ben does.*

He glanced at Ben, who was struggling to lift a sand-filled shovel into the cart, and wondered: *Would I have risked my life to help him?* He wasn't sure. A rush of shame hit him, and he shoved his cart hard across the rails.

Beside him a whip snapped.

"Stop!" the kapo hollered. "We're going back to camp. You can rest your lazy backsides for half a day. By the way, Merry Christmas."

Joshi caught Ben's eye, and for the first time since he had arrived in Stutthof, he smiled.

On the way back, they stopped at the cottage so the head kapo could speak to someone inside. Joshi looked up at the hornbeam tree, wondering if Nuri had left a bit of cheese or bread, but with a second guard so close behind him, he couldn't check the hollow.

"I bet he's going to make an appointment," Ben hissed. "Kapos with special privileges are allowed to use the women on certain occasions. They have to pay a few *Reichsmarks*, but the SS think they control us better when they have sex."

"How do you know all this?" asked Joshi, studying Ben's face.

Ben was silent. Only after the column had moved forward and they were deep in the forest did he speak.

"From my beautiful Rivka," he said in a raspy whisper. "My girlfriend. The officers took her to the brothel. Another woman who was there told me that they gang-raped her. She tried to run, but they sent the dogs after her."

He cleared his throat as if he were trying to clear the memory. "They brought her back and paraded her body in the square. She was so badly mauled; you couldn't tell whether she was a man or a woman. They said that's what would happen to us if we ran."

He wiped his eyes with the back of his hand. "For a while I pretended it wasn't her."

"I'm so sorry," Joshi whispered.

"Yeah," said Ben, looking up at the barren trees. "I know."

The *Himmler Allee,* a wide cobblestone drive, cut straight through the camp. At the end were the gas chamber, the crematorium, and the gallows. On Sunday afternoons and holidays, SS officers who wanted a break would allow prisoners to congregate in the *Allee,* and it gave Joshi and Ben the opportunity to learn any news that had filtered into the camp.

That Sunday, they stood near the main entrance known as the "Death Gate." Joshi had not seen Sofia for days. Nor had he seen Nuri among the growing number of female prisoners.

Listening to the soft voices of his fellow inmates, he thought about Sofia. When she was a baby, he had often picked her up and cuddled her, ignoring the Romani custom that forbade a man from touching an unbaptized child. He tried to banish the doubt that was now poisoning his mind. What if his disregard for clan customs had actually brought Sofia to this? He shook his head. No, that was superstitious nonsense.

But what if?

He tugged at his throbbing ear and felt a tap on his shoulder. Glancing to his left he saw Klawan, the officer who was sleeping with Nuri.

"Gypsy," Klawan said, his tone flat. "You're an excellent musician. I always enjoy listening to you. I know it's Sunday, but Kommandant Hoppe wants you to play at the Christmas carol service tonight."

Ben edged closer.

"Excuse me, Officer," he said, removing his cap respectfully. "But I'm afraid my friend is losing his gift."

"What do you mean?" frowned Klawan, jangling a large ring of keys.

"Well, sir, he's got a stinking ear infection, and frankly, he's going deaf. He needs some salve or alcohol, something to ward off the germs. Can you help?"

Klawan regarded Ben for a long moment. Then he gave a barely perceptible nod and turned back to Joshi, "I don't know what Kommandant Hoppe will want you to play. A few Christmas carols for sure, maybe something classical. Just make sure you show up on stage tonight." He walked away, leaving behind a faint smell of sausage and aftershave.

"Jesus, Ben," whispered Joshi. "What gave you the nerve to ask?"

"I don't know," shrugged Ben. "I've heard people say he disagrees with SS tactics, but he's afraid to speak up, so he keeps to himself. Well, not altogether. You know he takes care of the rabbit hutches behind the barracks. That's why he has all those keys. Apparently, he discusses his veterinary problems with a Lithuanian prisoner, a doctor assigned to the typhus ward. He wasn't going to kick my teeth in, so I figured I could ask. Maybe he has access to medication. Anyway, we'll see."

That evening, Joshi stepped onto the wooden stage with three other musicians who had been chosen to play in the Christmas ensemble. A fir tree decorated with shiny red and gold ornaments shimmered in the center of the square. Joshi stared at it. *How dare these butchers insult us with such beauty*, he thought. *How dare they make us play their damned carols?*

An oboist, accompanied by two cellists, began *Stille Nacht*, Silent Night. For the second verse, Joshi swept his bow across the strings. The notes spilled into the cold night air, Joshi's violin vibrating like a sweet and lonely soprano.

As he played, he looked over the crowd, his eyes seeking those of his sister. He followed the camp searchlight sweeping back and forth over the sad faces. There! To his relief, the light illuminated the face of Sofia, who stood in the far corner near the crematorium, her eyes fixed on his.

She's alive, he thought. *Alive!* He shifted his gaze to the line of female wardens standing guard. The one Nuri had called the bitch cocked her head sideways to stare at him, her lips sliding into a half sneer, half smile.

He realized that the look he and Sofia had shared had not escaped the warden. Sensing danger, he averted his gaze.

When the speeches were over, he stepped down from the stage, only too happy to get away from the warden's hard, inquisitive eyes.

"Good show, my friend," murmured Ben, falling in step beside him. "And guess what? Klawan came through. Look what he brought."

He slipped a vial of boracic ointment into Joshi's hand, along with a small bottle of alcohol.

"Maybe there's a God after all," whispered Joshi. "Thank you so much, Ben."

"It was nothing. I just hope it helps."

The pain in Joshi's ear began to ease that same evening, but he could tell that the rupture had left him partially deaf. As he lay on the barrack floor taking in the sour odor of unwashed flesh, he heard a nearby prisoner sigh, "Another day and we made it through."

It sounded almost like a prayer. Joshi had a prayer too. He wanted to dream. In the past few days, he had dreamed of food—hot buttered bread, tender meat chunks swimming in savory paprika goulash, and sweet, black coffee. He loved his dreams. They were the only mercies in Stutthof, and they fulfilled his most primitive desire: to eat.

That night, however, no food appeared. Instead he dreamed he was flying high above the camp in a body that was light and clean and free. In the distance, where the sandy shore ran beside the Baltic Sea, a group of people was following a flock of cranes westward. He recognized Manya and called her name, his heart pounding with excitement. She was walking backward, looking up at a lagging bird when suddenly it swooped to the ground and landed beside her boot, turning the sand into ice and changing itself into Aztec. Afraid that Aztec would slip, she began to tug at his reins.

He rushed forward on the wind to help her, but when he looked down, he saw that he was naked, his legs just skin and bones. Manya didn't know him anymore. Swinging herself onto the stallion, she cantered off.

"Wake up," he heard Ben say.

Joshi groaned and opened his eyes.

"Sorry," whispered Ben, "but you were shouting for someone, and I was afraid you'd wake Esser."

Joshi lay still, trying to hold on to the dream.

"So, who's Manya?" asked Ben.

"Along with my sister, she's my reason for living."

"*Mazel tov*," whispered Ben, flashing him a smile. "I see you're getting the hang of survival. Good. Now I can go back to sleep."

"Wait," said Joshi, pushing himself up on his elbows. "I want to ask you something. What's your reason?"

Ben fell silent, as if he were deciding whether to answer or not.

"You know," he said after a long moment, "I don't really like talking about it. But you're my friend, so—"

He paused as if to gather the threads of his story.

"The night the Gestapo came to the house, Rivka was having dinner with us. They took her, my parents, my brother Samuel, and me. Mama died in the train on the way here. When we arrived in Stutthof, the SS officers split us up. I came to this barrack, and Papa and Samuel were placed in a barrack several doors down. On the fourth morning, there was an early bugle call. I was half asleep, and instead of following the other prisoners, I went to the washroom. I didn't realize that Papa and Samuel and the others were being taken to the forest. I was trying to get a handful of water from the pipe when I heard the gunshots. Later, I was one of those forced to dig a pit for the bodies. Papa and Samuel had both been shot in the back of the head."

A search beam filtered through the cracks in the wall, casting a ghastly glow on the valleys beneath Ben's eyes. "I'm telling you this because, like you, I have a sister. Only they didn't get her. She was at a friend's house when they came. She and I had made a pact when we first heard about the camps. We decided that if we were ever separated and if we survived the war, we'd meet in a certain place. I don't know where she is, but I believe she's still alive. If I ever get out of here, I'm going to find her at the harbor in Husum, in Schleswig-Holstein."

"Why Husum?" asked Joshi.

Ben closed his eyes as if he were willing a memory.

"Well, when we were kids, our parents took us there for summer holidays. We used to visit a little diner famous for its shrimp sandwiches. Everybody knew the place. There was a lone elm tree growing up out of the sidewalk. My sister and I would climb it and pretend we were sailors."

He blinked, his eyes focusing on Joshi in the dark. "Whoever gets to Husum first will wait for the other by the elm tree every Sunday at three o'clock. That's the plan. That's what I'm living for." He sighed. "Now you know. Let's go back to sleep."

TWENTY

$\mathcal{N}$ot far away, in the female wardens' quarters, Elisabeth Martens let out a frustrated groan and turned over on her mattress. She couldn't stop thinking about the Gypsy. He had intrigued her from the start. His talent with the violin, yes. But his eyes. She hated the fact that she found him attractive, and so she cursed him, too. But if he was afraid when she tried to stare him down, he didn't show it. And Elisabeth, who had been in charge of discipline in the women's unit for over a year, knew intimately the nuances of fear.

She had noticed him the day he arrived, and after the selection process, she had sneaked a look at the men's ledger for his name. Joshi Karas.

The fact that he was a doctor had stunned her. She was appalled that a Swedish university would educate a dirty Gypsy. Still, as much as she tried, she couldn't stop thinking about him.

Officers could choose any prisoner they wanted for their sexual needs. They even had their own whorehouse. However, those privileges did not apply to female wardens. Still, Elisabeth had her ways. She knew how to engage female prisoners for her own enjoyment. But a man from the barracks? That would take some planning.

While she secretly admired the Gypsy's good looks, his aloofness had also earned her contempt. She wanted to smother the sparks that flew from his fingers when he played the violin. She pulled her hot water bottle onto her stomach, the warmth hardly comforting her. When she was a child, she had longed to become an opera singer. Her father had paid for lessons with the best voice teachers in Berlin. But she never got the parts she wanted.

Auditioning time and again, she had even slept with one of the conductors who might have helped her step on the stage of the *Deutsches Opernhaus Berlin*, but it was only after she bedded a handsome Nazi official that her life changed and her struggle to be a singer ended.

He had flattered her with sweets and jewelry, telling her she was beautiful and smarter than any opera singer. Finally, he had persuaded her to give up her dream and join the party.

"Himmler is recruiting Germany's best women for important positions," he told her one night after they had made love. "And you, my dear, will be greatly rewarded."

After she joined the Nazi party, she was sent to Ravensbrück for overseer training, where she thrived. Excelling in political science, she also discovered that she had a keen gift for marksmanship and organization. But then she discovered that a whip in her hand was the tool she had been waiting for. Whenever she struck, the whip became a stream of light unleashing her frustration and anger at a God who had given her a love of singing, but no talent.

She had been promoted to Stutthof in 1944, when it became the final destination for prisoners from Auschwitz and other camps. She had gladly accepted the job as *Aufseherin*—overseer of the women's block. The prisoners addressed her as Frau Aufseherin. She knew that behind her back they called her the Prophetess of Doom, but what did she care. The truth was, every prisoner in the camp would die eventually.

It wasn't difficult to persuade female prisoners to come to her room. She only had to offer them a slice of sausage or a piece of buttered bread and they would do whatever she wanted with their mouths and delicate fingers.

She chose only the prettiest girls. When they arrived, she allowed them to bathe in the large earthenware bowl in the corner of her bathroom. Never, ever, were they to use her tub. That was where she relaxed after they had pleased her.

Once they were naked and she saw them teetering on the edge of uncertainty, she would pour a few drops of sweet lavender into their water. Handing them a sponge, she told them to wash, smiling reassuringly when the tears of relief fell down their cheeks, and watching until all the filth had run off their breasts and thighs.

After they had toweled dry, she led them into her sitting room, where she offered them a slice of ham or a piece of chocolate, explaining that it was now their turn to make her happy. If they did, they would get more food. If not, she couldn't promise to keep them alive another day. Hunger and self-preservation always drove them to perform exquisitely.

Until this point, she had never dared to involve a male prisoner in her secret trysts. If caught, she would have been punished more severely than if she had shot a prisoner in cold blood. A prisoner's life had little value, but a German overseer's honor was a different matter.

What would his skin feel like on hers? *Too dangerous, even for me,* she thought, pulling her eiderdown up to her chin. No, she just wanted to watch him when he was aroused. But how? She sat up and drew her knees to her chest, pondering the question.

⚜

By mid-January, Joshi guessed that Germany was losing the war because the guards had turned increasingly savage, handing out beatings and withholding food rationings for even the most minor offenses.

Since he was over six feet tall, he had to be even more alert, more careful not to draw attention to himself. The flesh on his bones had withered, and what he feared most now was a beating. The slightest blow would tear through his skin. He had watched gangrene eat the flesh of too many men.

One morning, while he and the other inmates were making the beds, Esser appeared and ordered them to report to Kommandant Hoppe after breakfast. Executions had become more frequent since the beginning of the year, and Joshi was certain their turn had come. *We've come as far as we could*, he thought. *Of course they won't leave any of us alive.*

A secret chapel had been set up in a storeroom near the barracks, presided over by a Pomeranian priest who had been a resistance fighter. Word soon got out that he would be performing last rites.

Although Joshi hated the gadjo religion, he liked the feisty little priest, whose Latin chants were meant for a God Joshi didn't trust. On the rare days he went, the musty space seemed to fill with clarity and light. He sensed a presence there, one that was loving and undeniably peaceful.

That morning, as he stooped to enter the tiny room, he was overcome with regret. How could he meet his death without one more day with Manya? One more hour, at least, near the river where he had lain with her against the moss? Turning inward, he grieved for the loss of his parents. For Sofia, too.

The priest never had anything to offer, no wine, no wafer, but he squeezed between the men, pretending to give communion, bidding them to open their mouths, and touching their lips with his liver-spotted hand.

"Take this as the blood of Christ," he would say, "and may His peace abide in you."

Joshi never expected anything to enter his mouth, and so, that morning, when he felt the weight of a single raisin on his tongue, he could hardly believe it. His eyes flew open and he chewed the wrinkled fruit, its syrupy sweetness making his gums tingle. He chewed slowly, trying to recall some forgotten piece of life, something that would let him go to his death singing.

He felt the priest press a hand against his chest, soothing his aching heart. "Don't be afraid," he said. "He who loses his life shall find it. The body may suffer, but the spirit is free. So when death comes, be at peace."

Joshi bowed his head, hoping against his deepening despair that he might know such freedom, such peace.

The priest returned to the front of the room.

"Friends," he said, "I know you think your lives are lost. Nothing I say can protect you from our captors' will. The prayers we offer God may not influence Him, or change our destinies. Still, through prayer we remember the beauty of each and every soul, ours included. So hold fast to it."

The priest's sincerity ran so deep. Joshi looked into his face and their eyes met. *Where on earth did you find raisins*, Joshi wondered. As if he'd heard the question, the priest's lips spread into a wide, knowing smile.

"God shows His love through miracles," he said. "Some are big, some are small. But they are still miracles."

The priest coughed. Dry sputum rattled in his chest. The service was over.

"All right," said Ben with a shake of his head. "I guess it's time to line up on the Himmler Allee."

⚜

Kommandant Hoppe paced in front of them, his black, steel-tipped boots crunching the snow, his gun in his gloved right hand. He clearly enjoyed lording over the men, yet this morning his voice was strangely pleading.

"I'm looking for volunteers," he said. "Men who can use a welding torch and mold scrap metal into engine parts. Raise your hands if you're able. It will mean that you leave for Elbing tomorrow morning to work at the Ferdinand Schichau shipyard."

Ben nudged Joshi. "They're not going to kill us after all. I was close to shitting my already shit-stained pants," he whispered, with a nervous laugh.

But Joshi couldn't crack a smile. He still felt death gripping his soul.

Ben nudged him again. "Didn't you say your father was a metal craftsman and that he taught you the trade?"

"I did," answered Joshi, his tongue dry as cotton. "But I don't know if I can pull off a job on my own. I've worked only under him."

"Raise your hand, for God's sake! Get out of this rat hole. Go where you won't be wading knee-deep through sand and dead bodies. And where you might find a latrine that's not full of shit."

"I can't leave Sofia," Joshi said firmly.

"You won't save her by staying here," hissed Benjamin. "Go!"

In a trance, Joshi lifted his arm. The kommandant stared at him.

"You, Gypsy? You can weld?" Sarcasm laced his words. "You must be a man of many talents, eh? Aren't you a doctor too?"

Joshi felt an inner quickening.

"Yes," he replied.

"All right, then," said Hoppe, striding toward him. "You'll look after the men who are going to Elbing. Their health will be your responsibility. But don't forget, work comes first."

"Cursed German," murmured Joshi, glancing at Ben. "I sure hope I'm not making a mistake."

At the opposite end of the square, Elisabeth Martens was in the process of selecting female prisoners for the same assignment. She had been appointed as women's overseer at the shipyard in Elbing, an unexpected promotion.

"Only the healthiest women," she told her assistant. "No walking skeletons. We don't want the citizens of Elbing to know what goes on in Stutthof. Fourteen-hour shifts on the assembly line will be the norm, so make sure their fingers are nimble and strong."

Her gaze softened briefly as it landed on a delicate, hazel-eyed woman who was standing in the long line of anxious prisoners. A few days earlier, Elisabeth had caught her drawing on a scrap of paper with slivers of burnt wood. Drawing was a serious crime in Stutthof, punishable by death, but when Elisabeth saw the woman's artistry, she let her go. That night, however, she called the woman to her room, gave her a bath, and fed her. While the woman drank honeyed milk and ate warm buttered bread, Elisabeth talked to her about art. Nothing else.

"That one will come," she said, flicking her whip in the prisoner's direction and turning to her assistant. "Her name is Gesa Rosenthal. Make sure you tick her on the list."

She let out a contented sigh. She'd see to it that Gesa's duties would not be too strenuous. She'd appoint Gesa to be her helper there—have her tend to the Schichau ledger, and perhaps manage the laundry room. Light work, easy on the girl's delicate hands. They had more important work to do. They'd be busy painting portraits. Elisabeth smiled smugly. She was ever so curious to see the various ways Gesa would portray her.

She looked down the Himmler Allee and saw the Gypsy standing in line. Smiling, she rubbed her hands together in the cold.

Early the next morning, those destined for Elbing were called back to the Himmler Allee and ordered to strip naked. The guards took their time distributing civilian clothing to the shivering prisoners, throwing pants, jackets, shirts, and socks into the lines without any regard for size or height. Joshi looked at the small woolen jacket he'd been tossed. It was meant for a young boy. Next to him, a Russian prisoner who stood just higher than Joshi's waist started to laugh.

"I'm sorry," the prisoner chuckled in his strange accent, "but you won't get your fist into that sleeve! Here, let's exchange." He handed Joshi the jacket he was holding.

Joshi paused. Tears came to his eyes as he stared at the dwarflike man with strong arms and heavy eyelids that folded halfway over his gray eyes. The man looked back at him and smiled through cracked lips.

"This is my jacket," said Joshi, stroking the stained leather and pressing his nose to the quilted silk lining that still smelled of wood smoke. "Some are big and some are small," he murmured.

"A big man like you deserves his jacket back," the Russian said.

But Joshi hadn't meant the jacket. He was remembering what the priest had said the day before about miracles. And this one threaded him to his past, restoring a piece of his old identity. And he was grateful.

On the other side of the courtyard, the women were undergoing the same humiliating ordeal. Gesa stood naked on the cobblestones trying to avoid eye contact with the guards who were leering at her through the barbed-wire fence.

"Here," she heard a voice say. "Wear these."

Turning, she saw the predator-like eyes of the Prophetess of Doom sweep over her goose-fleshed skin. She quickly grabbed the wool gabardine skirt and black sweater the warden was holding. She thought about what her fellow inmates said when they heard she'd been called to the warden's room. They had warned her about what might be coming next. She had come through that first encounter unscathed, but she suddenly wished she had a pair of underwear—although she knew underwear wouldn't keep her safe.

Joshi fidgeted and glanced toward the barracks. Where the hell was Ben? The lorries were about to depart for Elbing, and he hadn't had a chance to say good-bye. Just as he was contemplating stepping out of line, he saw Ben limping past the canteen, sucking on a broken icicle.

"There you are," Joshi said when Ben drew close. "I thought I'd miss you."

Ben looked as if he'd been hoping Joshi wouldn't see him.

"What's wrong?" asked Joshi. "Why are you limping like that?"

Looking defeated, Ben rolled up his left pant leg.

"Shit!" cried Joshi. "Your ankles and legs are swollen."

"Yeah," Ben said with a tired smile. "The good news is my legs look fat. The bad news is I'm starving."

"Don't try to be funny with me. You've got edema. Your kidneys are going." Joshi's voice grew urgent. "Listen! Go to Klawan. Get some salt."

He reached into his jacket and passed Ben six of the cigarettes Nuri had given him. "Use these to get whatever else you need. They're as good as gold here."

"Thanks," said Ben, slipping them into his pocket. He shoved the last chip of icicle into his mouth and swallowed it greedily. "I tell you, I'm so thirsty, I'd sell my soul for a beer."

"I'll buy you one in Husum someday," said Joshi. "But don't drink too much now, or you'll bloat."

Snow was falling in hard little flakes.

"It's getting colder," Ben murmured, looking up at the sky. "If this keeps up, the ground will freeze. Maybe the Red Army will get here after all."

"Ben." Joshi hoped his voice did not betray his fear. "Please get the salt. And if they liberate Stutthof, will you keep an eye out for Sofia?"

Ben gripped Joshi's hands.

"Of course, my friend," he nodded. "Of course."

TWENTY-ONE

A golden ribbon of light laced the horizon, throwing a spray of saffron-colored threads across the rolling dunes that curved toward the frozen inlet of the Frisches Haff lagoon. The sun was just rising over a row of beech trees, setting ablaze the remaining leaves. Joshi sniffed the fresh salt air in wonder.

From where he stood, he could see that the road was packed with refugees traveling west. A railway worker in Stutthof had told him that millions of people were fleeing East Prussia now. Many were trying to cross the lagoon to reach the narrow spit of coastland called Frische Nehrung, hoping it would lead them west. Others were heading to Danzig and Pillau, the main ports. All points of exit, the man had said, were bedlam.

If the refugees were lucky, thought Joshi, *they might be one step ahead of the Russian army.* He hoped to God that Manya was already safe.

In Stutthof, Manya had appeared in his dreams nearly every night, her hair falling across his face, her body as real as those of the prisoners beside him on the barrack floor. He could almost taste her lips, feel the pulse of her wrists against his skin. Those were good dreams because he could rest in them for as long as they lasted. But always, he would awaken in the chill night darkness and feel the ache of her absence.

His thoughts traveled back to a summer day, years before, when he, Manya, and Blacksmith Helling had gone riding. A storm was about to break, and a bird, startled by a flash of lightning, had whirled into the sulfurous sky, cawing like an angry gull. Manya, who prided herself on recognizing birds, had been the first to identify it as a goshawk.

She'd explained how in medieval Europe, goshawks were prized as the most tenacious of all falconry hawks. He'd lost himself in her excitement, in the violet light of her eyes. Never had he known anyone to take such pleasure in birds and animals, even worms. And that day, when she had stretched out her arms to mirror the goshawk's grace, he had seen just how fiercely she loved life.

It comforted him now to pretend that she was beside him, talking in her familiar way. He didn't know whether the Russians had broken through the front lines into Guja, or if she had already fled. But he hoped that she would have the tenacity to find a way out.

He thought of their last day together and the piece of paper she had given him—the one that marked her escape route. His fingers trembled as he unbuttoned his jacket and fished through the sleet-soaked lining. He pulled it out, his stomach knotting as he touched the soggy sheet of paper. There was the route, written in her looping handwriting. She had drawn it with a dark lead pencil: Guja, Dönhofstädt, then the bigger towns of Schippenbeil and Bartenstein, and on through the tiny village of Klein Stegen to Rödersdorf, Braunsberg and finally Danzig. He knew the route well. His clan had traveled it many times in summer on their way to Sweden. As children, he and Manya had visited Braunsberg. They'd even stayed at the horse farm famous for its Trakehner mares. He pressed his lips to the paper.

Shaking with excitement, he looked around for the Russian who had been kind enough to swap jackets. He found him huddled into a space between two prisoners' legs. Joshi caught his eye and waved him over.

Small as the Russian man was, he was able to ferret his way under the armpits of the other inmates.

"Everything all right?" he asked when he reached Joshi.

"Yes, I—I told you that this was my jacket," Joshi stammered. "Thank you again. It feels good to have it back. I found a—" He started to take out the piece of paper, but then he stopped himself.

"We haven't really met," he said, grasping the Russian's wiry arm. "Not that names mean anything here, but I'm Joshi Karas."

"Leonid Petrov," smiled the prisoner. He pointed toward Gothic church spires rising in the distance. "That's Elbing. We're getting close. I've been there before."

Seeing Joshi's surprise, he explained, "I'm a mechanic. The Germans captured me a few months back while I was on a mission near the front. I ended up in Stutthof. When the SS found out I spoke German and knew a thing or two about engines, they sent me to Elbing. Later, they transferred me to Danzig, where I worked as a welder, refurbishing U-boats." He pointed to his scarred eyelids. "Welding burns," he said. "Prisoners don't count for much, so they never supplied us with goggles."

"Why did they move you around?" asked Joshi.

Leonid shrugged.

"I don't know. They're crazy. I was in the Danzig shipyard when a small cutter carrying U-boat parts mysteriously sank one night. They called it sabotage. Then came the beatings and executions. Even some of the German workers were shot. That caused an uproar in the shipyard—in the whole city, actually. It got so bad, they sent us back to Stutthof. Luckily that was only a stopover for me." He pointed to a huge administrative building that stood along the waterfront. "We're here. That's the Schichau shipyard." A wrought iron gate opened and the lorry drove through, stopping with a loud honk.

"Stick close," Leonid murmured as they jumped off. "I know my way around." His eyes darted sideways. "I just hope we don't attract attention with you being so tall and me such a dwarf."

But no one took any notice of them, except Elisabeth Martens, who was sitting in the passenger seat of the women's transport vehicle, stroking a brown leather suitcase perched on her lap. As her fingers curled around the suitcase handle, she smiled and thought about the violin inside.

When the Gypsy had disappeared into the processing line, she reached for her purse and removed a small makeup bag. Gazing into the rearview mirror, she applied a dab of Vaseline to her lips. Deep red wouldn't do today, even though it set off her auburn hair. She needed to make a clean impression on the chief administrator. After all, he had the power to assign her a decent place to live.

She passed her tongue over her lips before pouting at the mirror. A low chuckle escaped her. Oh, what those lips had done to the SS officer in Stutthof last night, the one who guarded the prisoners' valuables. She'd gone to see him with a simple request. At first, he'd refused her.

"Come on," she had murmured, unbuttoning his fly. "No one will know. I just want a violin. Easy for a powerful man like you." She had laughed seductively.

The officer had laughed too, no longer resisting when she lowered her head.

TWENTY-TWO

*A*ssigned to the U-boat repair facility, Joshi and Leonid spent their days assembling heavy steel plates for submarine hulls and welding pipe fittings, flanges, valves, and hatches. When they weren't toiling in the sweltering heat of the smithy workshop, they worked in the dank cold, repairing warships, tugboats, minesweepers—any vessel that had been hauled onto a slipway.

Schichau was not much better than Stutthof. Food rations consisted of a bowl of thin turnip soup, a slice of bread and sausage, and, if they were lucky, a spoonful of mashed potato—not nearly enough to sustain hard laborers working fourteen-hour shifts. The men had grown desperate. Whenever a boat was hauled out of the water, they would grab the pilchards spilling from the bilges with their bare hands and shove the wriggling fish into their mouths while the guards howled with laughter.

At night, when Joshi finally made it to the barrack, he would see how the men were doing. Each night it was the same: oozing boils and untreated wounds, hacking coughs and diarrhea. The most dreaded symptom, however, was the spiking fever that signaled the onset of typhus.

When the angry red skin blotches appeared, the men would tug at his sleeves and beg him to do something. But without soap, disinfectant, or even an aspirin, he had no way to treat them. Their helplessness weighed heavily on his mind. But there wasn't much he could do except try to reduce fevers with rags he had boiled on a stove near his workstation during the day.

He scraped up ashes, too, from the bottom of the stove and made them into a charcoal paste, which he fed to men suffering from diarrhea. It wasn't a proper remedy, but at least his patients felt cared for.

One day, while he was at his workstation pounding rivets, his hand slipped and caught the rough edge of a metal sheet. Although it wasn't a serious wound, it wouldn't stop bleeding, so he went out into the courtyard to ask the guard for a strip of cloth.

"You lazy dog!" the man barked at him. "I bet you never worked a day in your life until now. Eh? You're big, but you're stupid and soft! What purpose could a dog like you possibly serve in life?"

Joshi said nothing, hoping the guard would finish his tirade and give him what he needed.

"Answer me, or I'll give you a beating you won't live long enough to forget."

Joshi was past caring. Still, he took the threat seriously.

"I am a doctor," he admitted softly.

"A what?" sniggered the guard, butting him hard in the stomach with his rifle. "A liar is more like it."

A surge of anger swept over Joshi. What did this jackass know about his life? He balled his fists, preparing to strike the man.

"Leave him alone, guard!" he heard a woman shout. "You want to turn Elbing into another Danzig episode? Go back to your post before I report you."

Joshi whipped around, startled to see the auburn-haired warden from Stutthof. She stood a yard away, so close he could smell the sweet scent of lavender on her skin. Suddenly he felt his body go cold, as if the blood had left his head. Resisting the urge to faint, he forced himself to look at her, aware of the flat expression in her eyes.

Murmuring a quick thank you, he turned to go.

"Wait, Gypsy," she commanded, enunciating every syllable. "Take this for your cut."

She handed him a clean lace handkerchief. "You were lucky this time, but now you owe me. You wouldn't want me telling the authorities that you were going to hit that guard, would you?"

"No," Joshi answered, He had never seen eyes like hers before. They were the dark blue of veins just below the skin.

"Good," she said, her mouth twitching. She sauntered off, leaving him to stare at her swaying hips and the deep square imprints her heels left in the snow.

Elisabeth could hardly believe the unexpected turn of events. How dumb men were. So quick to yield to a woman who made them cower.

"Soon," she hummed to herself. "I'll have the Gypsy where I want him."

Just a week ago she had met with the workers' administrator, who had promised her a small, ground-floor apartment outside the shipyard complex on Schichau Street. The basement below her flat was to be used as housing for the female prisoners. She was to oversee them and make sure they were locked up after work, a job that would make Gesa's nightly visits undetectable.

Two days after the guard incident, Elisabeth stopped by the Gypsy's workstation. She found him sweeping up ashes.

"Gypsy," she said, walking up to him and ignoring the little Russian who was sorting screws in the corner. "I see you're still using my handkerchief. I hope your hand is better, because I need someone to secure the women's housing area and carry out some repairs in my living quarters."

The Gypsy stopped his sweeping to look at her, the green of his eyes contracting and aloof. She swallowed. "That line of work is not my forte," he murmured. "I'm sure you can find someone else, someone more skilled at carpentry."

She felt the urge to shoot him on the spot. How insolent, after she had saved the dirty dog from a beating, after she had given him her clean, white handkerchief.

"Gypsy," she snapped. "You *will* report to the main entrance this evening, after work. Is that clear?"

"Yes," he said, looking over her head.

"Good. Then we understand each other."

"That woman makes my flesh crawl," Leonid whispered later that afternoon as he accompanied Joshi to the gate. "I'll take the son of a bitch guard any day. At least I know what I'm up against."

"I wish you were going instead of me," murmured Joshi.

"Very funny," said Leonid. Pausing for a second, he added, "Just be careful."

Ten minutes later, Joshi was walking alongside an armed watchman, past houses and shops and pubs. Music trickled into the dusky street, as did bursts of laughter. Was it possible that people still laughed? He sniffed at the air. The smell of curried sausage and beer made his stomach clench.

He imagined what it would be like to be free and to walk home for supper hip against hip with Manya, her head resting on his shoulder. The thought brought an unexpected smile to his face. He would find her again, and he would hold her, if not in this world, then in the next.

He looked up at the buildings. Behind the lace curtains, he imagined couples moving to embrace each other. His pulse beat faster. Oh, to hold her like that again, but on clean, soft sheets.

The watchman coughed, bringing him back to reality. "We're here," he said. "Go ring the bell."

Elisabeth had been waiting for the buzzer. When it rang, she tucked her pistol under her belt and a picked up a small toolbox she had stolen from Stutthof.

"It's a good thing you came, Gypsy," she said, opening her door with a smile. "You don't ever want to cross me." She handed him the box. "Now, first things first. Come and fix the basement door padlock."

She led him down the hallway to the door and casually leaned against the wall to watch him while he worked. When he was finished, she jangled her keys.

"My living quarters, remember?"

"Yes," he said quietly, turning to face her.

By God, he's tall, she thought, feeling nervous. She took out her gun and motioned for him to walk back through the hallway. When they reached her flat, she turned the doorknob and prodded him into the narrow foyer with the barrel of her pistol. The smell of freshly brewed coffee hung heavy in the air. She smiled to herself. She'd prepared it on purpose.

"Come here," she said, leading him into her kitchen. "Start with those cupboards, and board up that broken window. I don't like the cold wind whipping through."

She poured a cup of coffee and saw him eye it longingly. *Good*, she thought. *Just as I anticipated.*

He caught himself quickly and picked up a nail. Moving a little closer, she blew the steam from her cup in his direction, watched him close his eyes. *There you go. Savor the aroma.* She saw a muscle twitch in his cheek.

He hammered nails into the window frame. *By God*, she thought, *your hands are beautiful.*

When he was done, she poured another cup. "Here," she said. "Have a sip for your trouble. There's sugar in that dish. Take as much as you like."

She paused, waiting for him to register her offer. At first he hesitated, but she could see that he was eager. When he accepted, she knew she had found a weakness.

He placed his lips on the white porcelain rim and took a sip.

"Tomorrow evening, when you return," she said, forcing a hard tremor into her voice, "you'll do what must be done in my living room. Yes?"

He nodded his head quietly.

Suddenly she felt uneasy. The apartment seemed strangely foreign and lonely to her now. Had she gone too far? She tried to choke back her doubt.

She glanced at the Gypsy's soft, green eyes. Tired as he was, his pleasure at the cup in his hands seemed so complete. Her eyes ran over his broad shoulders and slim hips as she remembered how he looked when she had first seen him in the yard. For a moment, she wanted to be in his arms. To trace her fingers across his face, over the little nick in his eyebrow. She wanted to tell him how scared she was of the advancing Russians; to have *him* tell her everything would be all right. No man like him had ever held her before.

He looked up and caught her eye. She stopped. There, in his gaze, was that terrible indifference she'd seen on so many men's faces throughout her life. Her eyes fell from his.

What had she been thinking? This was not a man. This was a Gypsy *dog*. He would probably throw a curse on her. She exhaled sharply. She had a responsibility to her race, to the Nazi party. She had to remember that he was just like a dog. And dogs should behave for their masters.

Tomorrow when he returned, she'd give him more coffee. Some bread, too, and a slice of spiced ham. Gypsies liked spices. And he was just a Gypsy. Nothing more. That was something she had to keep in mind. Always.

Her eyes moved over his body once more, and she swallowed hard to block the rising attraction. *That was a weakness on my part*, she thought. *It won't happen again.* Straightening her shoulders, she pointed to the door and told him to get moving. Weaknesses made her angry. Luckily, though, anger always restored her sense of self.

⸎

Joshi had little time to reflect on his encounter with the warden. One of the officers had left a package of medicine on his bunk with instructions to contain the typhus and dysentery that were spreading through the shipyard.

Joshi asked Leonid to help him set up a sick ward at the far end of the prisoners' quarters. Even with medicine, he could do only so much. The diseases were rooted in filth. He needed hot water, clean bedding, and fresh food. The truth was, every inch of skin, every stitch of clothing, every bed and building had to be disinfected.

"If we could just get rid of the lice," groaned Leonid, shaking out a filthy blanket. "I spend all my spare time squashing the buggers between my thumbnails, but they always come back."

Joshi gave a resigned sigh. "Yeah, the SS don't need guns or gas now. Typhus does the job."

Leonid chuckled derisively. "I must confess, though, I like to see them running scared when there's another epidemic. I bet they're bathing ten times a day."

Joshi grimaced. "What I wouldn't give for just one bath."

"Forget it. That won't happen. Now, let's get some sleep. Müller, the head mechanic, informed me that we are working on the docks tomorrow. It'll be colder than a welder's ass."

TWENTY-THREE

*J*oseph Müller had fallen into despair. The conditions his workers endured were barbaric. Almost no food, no warm clothes, no breaks. What further angered him was that, as a German employee, he was forbidden to befriend any of the prisoners. A mechanic himself, he had grown to respect the skills of many who had passed through his shop. In this latest group, he had come to rely on Joshi, the tall Gypsy, and Leonid, the Russian dwarf, for more complicated tasks. Production in his unit had gone up since they arrived, earning him a small raise.

To thank them, he would leave small stashes of food in his coat pocket. And every day around noon, he'd call one of them over. "Is it lunchtime yet? Would you check my watch, please? It's in my coat."

When they looked, they would find an extra pumpernickel sandwich, a biscuit, or a piece of fruit.

This morning, however, he was wearing his heavy workman's jacket because he had orders to take his crew to the docks. The temperature had dropped below freezing overnight, and as he prepared his toolbox, he pretended not to notice the Gypsy and the Russian stuffing their shirts with empty cement bags. The docks would be frigid, and he was not about to deprive them of that extra bit of warmth.

As soon as he and his workmen were ready, they headed down to the drafty hangar to start work on the hull of a destroyer. Damaged by artillery fire, the ship had arrived at the dock for emergency repairs the day before. Because it was engaged in providing cover fire for evacuation maneuvers, it was due to sail out again the very next morning. Müller thought it was madness to rush the job, but the German naval fleet was desperately short of vessels, and he'd been informed that repairs were to be carried out speedily, or else.

Before they could repair the hull, however, the men had to scrape away the calcified barnacles, a slow and difficult process requiring acid and chisels. For men who were just skin and bones, it was exhausting. They stood on high scaffolding working their way from bow to stern, scraping and hammering at the crusty shells until their fingers bled.

Often the weight of the cement bags they wore threw them off balance. Whenever Müller saw a slime-covered clog miss a step, he would hold his breath and hope for the best. By midafternoon, he had completed the engine check, so he started working at the ship's stern, dissembling the damaged propeller. The Russian was the first to inch up beside him.

"Can you hold this metal shaft while I check the prop blades?" Müller asked.

"Sure," said the Russian, reaching out over the boat's stern with his free hand, but as he grabbed the shaft, a look of horror crossed his face. "Herr Müller," he cried. "My—my fingers—I can't hold it. Help!"

The shaft slipped from his hand, falling into the water below with a splash.

"What the hell?" shouted a guard. "Are you trying to sabotage us, prisoner? Get your useless ass down here."

By this time, the Gypsy had come up on the other side of the hull. He was watching the Russian closely.

Müller waited while the frightened Russian slid down the scaffolding. The beating started immediately.

He hurried down the scaffolding, his boots landing on the dock with a bang. "For heaven's sake, stop!" he shouted when he saw the cudgel come crashing down on the Russian's head. "He's my best worker. I'll find the part. The water isn't deep here. You don't have to kill a good man for such a small mistake!"

Ignoring the guards, he pulled the Russian to his feet.

"Hang on to me," he said. Draping the Russian's arm over his shoulder, he settled him on the dock and turned back to the guards. "Don't you dare lay another finger on this man. If that ship doesn't sail tomorrow, it'll be your goddamn fault."

The water was frigid when Müller entered it, but he was still on the shallow end of the inclined plane. Luckily the shaft was only a yard beneath the surface, and he was able to retrieve it in less than a minute. Holding it high in the air for all to see, he glared at the guards.

"All right," he shouted. "Let's get back to work."

He pointed at the Russian. "You take a break." To the Gypsy, he added, "Come and look after him, please."

⁓❧⁓

That afternoon, when they returned to the workshop, Müller drew Joshi and Leonid aside.

"I'm so sick of what's happening here," he hissed, his messy gray hair sticking up in tufts. "Listen," he whispered, "I'm going to break you two out for an evening to have dinner with my wife and myself at our home." He looked away. "You'll die if you don't get a bath and a good meal."

"Your home?" Joshi was dumbfounded. He could hardly imagine what it would be like to sit at a table and eat a meal prepared by a woman's hands. "Please, sir," he murmured. "You're not teasing us, are you?"

"No. But I'll have to bring you back, or I'll be in big trouble." Seeing Leonid's worried expression, he laughed softly. "Don't worry, I've done it before. I have my own arrangement with these jackanapes." He searched their faces. "So, you'll come?"

⁓❧⁓

Later that evening, the watchman took Joshi back to the warden's apartment. To Joshi's surprise, a young woman answered the knock. He saw straightaway that she was a prisoner because she wore a kerchief over her shorn head. Unlike other prisoners, though, she did not appear to be one of the walking dead. Her eyes, bright hazel in color, were kind and full of light, and when she smiled at him, he felt a welcoming safety in their depths.

"I'm Gesa," she said, taking his hand. "Miss Overseer is waiting for you."

He sensed a warning at the edge of her words.

"Address her only as that," she instructed. "She doesn't want any of us asking her name."

She ushered Joshi through the narrow hallway, past the kitchen and into the living room. The warden was seated in an armchair, studying a thick ledger. Resting on a nearby easel was an unfinished portrait of her, and Joshi could tell that the artist had used pastel colors to make her look soft and beautiful.

In a nook to his right was a bed, covered in green velvet. Gold pillows were neatly stacked against the headboard. A loveseat and a lacquered armoire in need of repair had found their place beneath a row of broken shelves on the wall to his left. A folding screen with swans and nude cherubs stood next to a gramophone player. Wagner, he thought, straining to hear a man's rich tenor coming out of the horn-shaped speaker.

He cleared his throat.

"Good evening, Miss Overseer."

The warden leaned forward, the neckline of her blouse revealing an unseemly amount of cleavage.

"You've come to do the jobs, eh?" She spoke almost coquettishly, and the pout of her lips made Joshi deeply uncomfortable. "Well, you can see that a man is needed here."

Waving her left hand toward the armoire, she put her right hand on the pistol that lay next to her thigh. "So, what are you waiting for? Get to work."

Joshi pulled out the loveseat and began to reassemble the shelves while Gesa went to the easel. As he glued and hammered, he tried to make out the lyrics of the arias that were playing on the gramophone, but the nerve damage in his ear had taken its toll. The tones had lost their crispness, and all of the voices were muffled. He'd been working for about an hour when the warden stood up and sent the ledger crashing to the floor.

"Gypsy," she said, flinging the word at him. "You stink to high heaven! Crack open that window so I don't puke."

Alarmed, he went to the window. Glancing at Gesa, he saw a tremor of fear run through her delicate hands.

"Don't you ever shower at the shipyard?" the warden railed at him.

"No," he answered, looking at her. "I haven't had the chance."

"Well then, next time, Gesa will show you where you can bathe." She paused before adding, "By that I mean your whole body."

A familiar queasiness rose in the pit of his stomach.

"Carry on," the warden sneered. "I'll be in the kitchen."

"What does she want from me?" he whispered when the warden had left.

"I don't know, exactly," Gesa breathed. "But I'm sure it's more than just repairing broken shelves. I know from other prisoners that she has certain fetishes. It's best to do whatever she asks." Gesa's eyes were unwavering as she looked at him. "It's about staying alive."

Joshi shot her a sideways glance.

"Does she make you do anything besides painting?"

He felt as if he were suffocating.

"No. I've only painted her in different poses, with various costumes and expressions. I do what I can to capture the softer side of her soul on the canvas, but she's cold-blooded."

She sighed and bowed her head, touching her pale lips to her paint-stained fingertips.

He swallowed. He had been walking through a wasteland of cadavers and unholy sights for too long not to be enthralled by her beauty. He understood why the warden wanted to be near her. Who wouldn't? She was serene and delicate, beautiful even without hair.

A clattering noise in the kitchen made him jump. Gesa grabbed a brush and glanced at the door. The warden entered the room carrying a tray with two slices of dark bread and ham and two sugarcoated biscuits, all neatly arranged on a saucer. Joshi's stomach leaped.

"I see you're nearly done with the shelves, Gypsy." The warden's eyes narrowed into slits. "But before you go, can you tell me who wrote the opera we're listening to?"

"Wagner," replied Joshi.

"Very good," she smirked. "One more question. If you answer correctly, I'll give you one of these sandwiches."

Joshi held his breath. He was so hungry, and the tray was poised right under his nose.

"What was Wagner trying to express through his music?"

She spoke amiably now. This could only mean that she was at her most dangerous.

"I—I don't know, Miss Overseer," he mumbled.

He never had liked Wagner's macho fanfares, but it would have been stupid to answer glibly.

The warden laughed, pursing her lips like a schoolteacher.

"Well, let me tell you. His philosophy can be summed up in one little phrase." She put down the tray and fixed her steely eyes on him. "Sex and death."

With her gaze trained on him, she stepped to the bed and reached beneath it. "You didn't answer the question," she said, pulling out the violin. "But don't worry, you'll have another chance. Play for me tonight, and you'll eat."

She handed Joshi the instrument.

He stared at the beautifully polished maple top and lightly antiqued golden varnish.

Whose fingers touched your fingerboard before, he wondered. *Who drew the bow? And where are you now? Rotting in a field somewhere?*

"Gypsy," barked the warden. "Don't you care about the piece of paper wedged between the strings? I put it there for you. Go ahead. Look at it. It's one of Gesa's masterpieces. I'm sure you'll like it."

He touched it and noticed that it was fine-grade drawing paper.

"Go on," urged the warden. "Pull it out."

He obeyed, wondering with trepidation what she was up to as he unfolded the paper. There staring at him was a portrait of Sofia. Her face had shrunk around large, scared eyes. His hands began to shake.

He looked at Gesa. Ashamed, her shoulders sagged and she turned away.

The warden's lips turned up at the corners.

"Sofia is her name, I believe?"

Joshi swallowed hard and nodded.

"She's still alive," said the warden, her voice carrying triumph. "However, I hear there's typhus in her barrack. All the prisoners who look after her are either too weak now or they're dead. Ah well, that's how it goes." She glanced at her watch with a bored expression. "Hmmm—but I do call Kommandant Hoppe every evening to discuss business."

"What are you saying?" asked Joshi.

She looked at him, her eyes flickering dangerously now.

"I can put in a good word for her. But you will have to pay for that kindness."

He looked at the drawing and gently traced the curve of Sofia's cheek. His mother used to touch Sofia's face with such tenderness, he thought, wanting to cry. He swallowed, remembering how protected Sofia had once been, how loved by them all. Gathering himself, he placed the portrait on the table where he could see it and picked up the bow and played.

At first it was difficult. There were no songs left inside him. Still, he did what he had to do, pulling notes from the violin until they turned into buoys floating on the sea of emptiness inside him.

When he had finished, the warden clapped.

"You may go now," she said, waving him away. "Oh yes—and take a biscuit and one of those sandwiches. It's the weekend, Gypsy, but remember, I expect you back on Monday."

Gesa led him to the door. Tears stained her cheeks.

"I'm so sorry," she whispered. "I feel as though I've betrayed you, but I had no idea why she wanted Sofia's portrait. She had me do it while we were still in Stutthof."

"It's not your fault," he murmured. "She used you to get to me."

"God knows what else she has in mind," murmured Gesa. She locked eyes with Joshi, a look so earnest that he caught his breath. "There's something else," she said. "I have a baby boy."

The words came out in a rushed whisper as she searched his face with her hazel eyes. "The warden doesn't know. He was born in Stutthof before Christmas. He's our youngest prisoner. My friends in the basement watch him while I'm here."

She closed her eyes, and Joshi could see the love unspooling inside her before she abruptly turned away.

TWENTY-FOUR

A week later, Müller led Joshi and Leonid through the curving shadows of the shipyard, past the piers and supply sheds. Moonlight fell through the clouds, spiraling in wide silver swaths across the water.

When they reached the fence that marked the shipyard's perimeter, Müller paused and ran his hand along the edge, counting the diamonds of interlocking wire until he found the opening he had cut out months before. It blended perfectly into the monotonous acres of fencing. Bending over, he showed Joshi and Leonid where to peel back the wire and squeeze through.

"That's the patrol guard over there," he whispered. "As I told you, he and I have an agreement. Basically, I pay him off, but here's what we do. When he takes a pee, we go." He gave them a crooked grin. "Do you still want to do this?"

"Yes," Joshi replied, assuming an air of calm he didn't feel.

"All right then. We're on."

Müller signaled for the two men to drop down on all fours, and, in a haze of nervousness, they crawled through the wire. Seconds later, they were scuttling along a dark alley.

Nearby, on a street of red brick row houses, Müller's front door was distinguished by a cheerful wooden gnome holding a blue beer stein.

Liesel, his wife, a chubby woman with warm, toffee-colored eyes, opened the door as soon as they reached the top step.

"Come in," she said, and ushered them into the living room, where she bid them to sit down on a sofa covered with a sheet. She looked at them apologetically, "I'm sorry, but others before you had lice. Please, have an almond cookie and a small glass of milk. I'd like to give you more, but you mustn't overeat or you'll be sick. And I promise that you will have a warm bath."

Herr Müller was staring into the fireplace. "We do this because of our son," he said, pointing to a picture on the fireplace mantle of a young man in his army uniform. His name was Uli." His voice cracked with sadness. "Uli died at the front two years ago. Liesel and I want to believe that someone was kind to him at the end."

Liesel patted his shoulder. "Let's not talk about that now, Joseph," she murmured. "We'll never stop thinking about him, it's true, but I want these boys to have a good time tonight. I imagine the best thing we could do is let them have their baths. And dinner. A bit of brandy wouldn't hurt either, right?" She winked at Leonid. "You shall go first." Taking his arm, she led him toward a narrow hallway.

Twenty minutes later it was Joshi's turn. His shame deepened when he stepped into the steaming clear water and watched foul black dirt slide from his skin. Carefully, he scrubbed his back with the long-handled brush and freshly cut piece of red disinfectant soap Liesel had left beside the tub, relishing the hot water that fell abundantly from the tap.

Later, when he was toweling himself dry, he heard a knock and opened the door a crack to find Liesel before him, holding out fresh clothes. The moment they touched his skin, he felt as if he were remembering a part of himself, the man who prided himself on his looks and what he wore.

They gathered for supper in the dining room. Although Joshi was starving, he could eat only a few mouthfuls.

"Frau Müller—" he said apologetically.

"Please, call me Liesel."

"Liesel," he smiled. "A few months ago I would have polished off a dozen of your delicious bratwurst, but my stomach has shrunk to nothing."

"Well, when the war is over, you'll come back." Her voice was soothing, her nod motherly. "Then you'll be able to eat again, and I'll prepare a feast."

She rose to clear the table, refusing any help her guests offered. Later, she returned with a glass decanter full of brandy.

"Are you married, Joshi?" she asked as she poured a bit into his snifter. "With your good looks, the girls must fall at your feet."

Joshi rubbed his hand over his shorn head.

"Maybe, if I had more hair," he laughed.

"Don't let him fool you," said Leonid. "He *has* a girlfriend, and from what I gather she's beautiful." He chuckled. "But maybe you can find *me* a wife, Liesel. One as sweet as you."

Leaning back in his chair, Joshi sipped his brandy. *One day*, he thought, *when I find Manya, I'll bring her here to meet Liesel. They remind me of each other, both so straightforward and lively.* He blinked, realizing with a start that certain things he'd once taken for granted had suddenly acquired a new poignancy. The clink of Liesel's teaspoon against her saucer, the creak of Leonid's chair, the softness of the pale blue cloth napkin in his lap made him ache for something he never had, but all of a sudden wanted: a home.

They talked for a while longer. When Liesel had cleared away the last of the glasses, she went to the dining room sideboard and opened a drawer. "I want you to take this," she said, laying a pocketknife on the table in front of Joshi. "It's from my son's collection. It's a Solingen."

Müller looked at her in surprise, but she pretended not to notice. "The blade is razor sharp. Joseph tells me you're a doctor, so I thought you could use it for cutting bandages, even for surgical procedures if you have to. There's one for you too, Leonid," she said returning to drawer. "This one's a Sauter, and it has a corkscrew."

Joshi let the tears run down his face as he examined his gift, the ache growing stronger. "Thank you," he murmured.

"It's time, Liesel," said Müller, rising from his chair. "As much as we'd like Joshi and Leonid to stay, we don't want any trouble."

She nodded and led them to the door.

Joshi held her in his arms and lifted her off her feet like he had once lifted his mother.

"I don't want to leave," he laughed, setting a flustered Liesel back on her polished oak floor. "You've spoiled us so much."

Smiling, Liesel laid a hand on his cheek. "In the name of my Uli," she said. "My home is forever open to you."

Outside, Joshi fell in step beside Leonid and Müller, reliving the evening as he walked: the heartfelt conversations, the laughter, and the beautiful food. So lost was he in thought that he failed to notice the sign for Schichau Street. Everything inside him froze. The warden was standing outside her building, only fifteen feet away, smoking a cigarette. With each puff, the burning tip lit up her sharp profile. A cold dread surged up his spine.

"We're in trouble, Herr Müller," he whispered.

"Don't worry," said Müller. "The warden's seen me with prisoners before."

"Walk ahead," warned Joshi. "She's out to get me."

But it was too late. The warden's voice whipped through the night air.

"Gypsy, is that you?" Joshi's step faltered. "Why, it *is* you. Stop, or I'll shoot!"

"Shoot?" cried Müller. "There's no need for that, Miss Martens. He's with me."

"Well, he damned well shouldn't be!"

She pulled her pistol from her belt and aimed it at Müller's belly.

"For heaven's sake," said Müller, trying to control the shake in his voice. "Put that gun away. We're going back to the shipyard."

He took a step toward her, but when she cocked the trigger, he stopped.

"I don't care where he's headed or who he's with," she spat. "He's not supposed to be anywhere without an armed guard. Take the dwarf back. I'll see to this one myself."

Müller turned to Joshi, unsure what to do next.

"Please go," murmured Joshi.

"I am going to have Müller shot for taking prisoners without authorization," the warden barked, pushing Joshi into the living room where Gesa sat sketching.

Joshi studied the warden's hard blue eyes. He'd have to think fast and lie well, because there was no compassion there.

"Herr Müller only cares about winning the war," he said. "He's dedicated to the Reich."

He was making it up, but it sounded plausible. He went on. "He knows that if we have food and clean clothes, we give better service and production goes up."

Suddenly his tone turned bitter, but he could not help himself. "How do *you* expect us to work, Miss Overseer, when we're always starving?"

"You insolent dog," the warden hissed. "How dare you speak to me like that? You have an errant mouth, you know? Don't you realize there are thousands of you? If I say the word, Müller will be executed, and you along with him."

"Then why am I here?" he asked. He was floating now, beyond fear.

"Because I *want* you here." She moved to the gramophone and gave the handle a hard crank. "Ach, damn you. I need music to settle my nerves. You've upset me so."

She lifted the needle and placed it on the spinning turntable. A woman's voice crooned the words to "Lili Marleen": "Underneath the lantern / By the barrack gate / Darling I remember / The way you used to wait . . ."

Elisabeth wasn't really upset, but she wanted a drink. She went to the armoire for a bottle of cherry brandy and poured herself a glass, enjoying the burn of the alcohol on her tongue as she studied her two prisoners.

Gesa had stopped painting. Her hands lay folded in her lap, but Elisabeth could see the quiver of fear at the base of her throat. *Good*, she thought, turning her gaze toward the Gypsy. He stood close to Gesa, his face veiled with contempt. Yet she was pleased to see a trace of fear in his eyes.

How many times had she imagined seeing Gesa naked with the Gypsy? He was a handsome specimen, more so now that he was clean. Desire curled hot between her legs.

"Gesa," she said softly. "Now that Müller has given our friend here a bath, I'd like a painting. You're good at nudes, aren't you? Unbutton his shirt, and undo his overalls, so that I may see him."

Gesa looked up, her eyes registering shock.

"No, Miss Overseer! Please, it isn't right. Just his face. That's enough."

"Don't contradict my orders," Elisabeth snapped, but she caught herself and a false sweetness brightened her voice. "You might change your mind, Gesa. I heard a baby whimpering today. I followed the sound into the basement. And guess what I found? A little boy." She let out a mocking laugh. "Funny, he looks like you. Such big eyes." She saw Gesa's face go white. Her body seemed to shrivel on her stool. "Secrets, Gesa," she hissed, "are never silent when people are hungry."

"Joshi," Gesa whispered, turning toward him. "Please, help me. I must do as she asks."

Joshi stared at the warden as Gesa approached him, unhooked the links of his overalls and let them fall to the floor. An unfamiliar dizziness overtook him as she unbuttoned the chambray shirt Liesel had given him.

"Lie down on the carpet," said the warden. "Gesa, take off his pants and his shoes."

"I'll do it," said Joshi, wishing he hadn't left Liesel's knife in his jacket pocket. He would have been only too happy to gouge out the sick bitch's cold eyes. Once he was naked, he lay down on the floor.

Gesa twisted sideways to avoid looking at him, but the warden gripped her shoulders and turned her back.

"Draw, Gesa!" she barked. "Or else."

Gesa picked up her pencils, pens, and chalk and began to draw, shutting off her revulsion by pouring herself into the contours and lines of Joshi's body. He lay on his side, completely still except for his thumb, which quivered back and forth across a pale pink flower petal on the rose-patterned carpet.

The warden was pacing like a drill sergeant. Gesa dared not look at her. Joshi had closed his eyes, and Gesa thought she could see shame pouring through his veined lids.

When Gesa finished her drawing, the warden stepped behind her. Gesa sat motionless. A hot, dry hand slid under her thin blouse and pinched her nipples, which were raw from nursing. Gesa looked down to see a few drops of milk seep through the cotton.

She could smell the warden's desire, dangerous, like the ocean before a storm.

The warden began to sing along to the music. "Darling I'd caress you / And press you to my heart." Her voice had grown hoarse with excitement. "You know what I'd like you to do now, Gesa, don't you?"

Gesa shook her head numbly. "No," she whispered.

"Oh yes, you do. Pretend the Gypsy is the father of your baby. Lie with him—naked—do I need to explain any further?"

Gesa looked up at the warden, hoping to find a way out.

"Well?" spat the warden. "Do I hear a baby crying?"

A surge of panic drove Gesa to slide off the stool. She moved toward Joshi.

"Take off your clothes," the warden commanded.

Gesa trembled, dreading the inevitable.

"Come on. I don't like waiting."

Something inside Gesa gathered nerve, and she removed her blouse and her skirt. Joshi was sweating. She knelt beside him. Embarrassed, he pulled away. Gently, she placed her lips against his left his ear, which was lovely and not grotesquely swollen like his right.

"You remember the golden rule at Stutthof?" she murmured. Joshi let out a muffled groan.

"Find someone to live for?" he heard himself whisper.

"We'll save your sister," Gesa said. "And my son."

She drew her lips down over his belly, her tongue soft against Joshi's skin. When she pressed her body against his, he felt as though he were nailed to the floor, but spinning. Desire and terror rolled into each other like drops of water. His eyes now sought Gesa's tender gaze and he climaxed, whispering her name.

"May God have mercy on us," she said when his trembling had subsided.

"There is no God," he murmured.

The warden had slipped behind the screen, her pistol forgotten on the table. He could hear her breath coming in short gasps.

"I'm going to shoot her," he whispered.

Gesa pressed her hand hard against his chest. "No," she murmured. "Her guard will shoot us."

Moments later, the warden stepped out from behind the screen. Pretending nothing had happened, she smoothed back her hair, picked up the gun, and tucked it under her belt.

"Please get dressed," she said, leaning over her bed to switch on the wireless.

The newscaster's voice crackled through the room. "Citizens of the German Reich. We have learned that the Soviet army is planning further attacks against the eastern front. But do not be afraid. Believe. Fight. Win. The Führer's call is our sacred order."

What a load of bullshit, thought Joshi, his body shivering as pulled on his overalls. Sacred order? The eastern front was lost. The Russians would win. He felt sick to his stomach. He thought of Manya, the joy on her face when the first wild swans returned to Guja in spring. She'd never see them again. And her smile, her tender affection and the way she trusted him, especially on the night they had made love. He froze, the events of the evening plunging him into a vile and inescapable pit. No amount of water would ever cleanse him of this foul breach in his soul. He would never touch Manya again. Worse, he could never escape the fact that as much as he tried not to, he had taken pleasure in Gesa's body.

The warden moved across the room.

"It's time," she said.

Her eyes gleamed. She opened the door and whistled to the guard. "You there, take this dog back to the shipyard. By the way," she said, smiling at Joshi. "Your sister is still alive. I'll see to it that she gets some extra food. Would you like that?"

Joshi felt the knife in his pocket. *I should slit your fucking throat*, he thought. Instead he nodded and stepped toward the guard.

"Good," said the warden. Gesa was standing behind her. "Come here, girl," she murmured, pulling Gesa close. "One more thing, Gypsy. If life means as much to you as it does to this devoted mother, you'll continue to do exactly as I say. So I expect you back here tomorrow."

On the street, the guard prodded him with his gun.

"You're lucky to have a job at Miss Marten's apartment," he said. "Gets you out of the shipyard, eh?"

TWENTY-FIVE

Every night for two weeks, Joshi was escorted to the warden's apartment. Gesa waited for him in the living room, her eyes full of shame as they undressed. One night, after he had returned to the barrack, a guard came in and confirmed what Müller had told him would soon happen. "Everybody out!" he hollered. "We're evacuating!"

Joshi and Leonid tumbled from their bunks and rounded up their scant possessions, throwing them into knapsacks Müller had given each of them. Then they waited at the shipyard entrance in the predawn cold.

The area behind the gate had filled with beeping lorries. Headlights cut through the darkness.

"I wonder where we're going," said Joshi.

An hour later he felt a tug on his jacket sleeve and turned to see Gesa's lovely face.

"We're going back to Stutthof," she said breathlessly. "From there, they'll send us to an undisclosed destination."

"How do you know?"

"I overheard Miss Overseer talking to an officer from Schichau last night. The Russians have advanced quickly. They're nearly here in Elbing, and the SS are scared. They don't know what to do with us."

"Why can't they just leave us to find our own way out of this mess?"

"They don't want the enemy to discover what they've been doing with people like us. And they still think they might win the war."

"They're all crazy," muttered Joshi.

Gesa glanced toward the gate. "I don't have much time. Miss Overseer knows I'm talking to you. She's over there."

Joshi followed Gesa's gaze. Sure enough, the warden was watching them. Her head was still cocked indifferently, her lips pursed. But now, in the hard blades of the headlights of SS jeeps and lorries, she looked like a stunned bird. Without lipstick, her mouth was cracked and dry, and her hair, normally so sleek, was disheveled as though she too had not had time to prepare for the journey. She stared at Joshi without blinking, the circles beneath her eyes growing darker.

Joshi stared back with hatred. Night after night, the sick bitch had watched him and Gesa debase themselves on the floor. Night after night, he had thought of ways to kill her.

"She's been nice for the last few hours," said Gesa. "She keeps pleading with me, saying, 'If the Russians come, you'll tell them I've been good to you, won't you?'"

"Her kind always asks you to do something for them after they've killed off a piece of your soul," Joshi muttered.

"I think she's scared of what they'll do to her if they catch her," Gesa whispered. "The officer who came last night after you left gave a gruesome account of what's happening in villages. Everywhere, the Russians are raping women and girls, even eighty-year-old grandmothers. The men and boys are rounded up and shot or sent to labor camps in Siberia."

Joshi shook his head sadly. "They're taking their revenge."

Gesa squeezed his hand. "I want to show you something." She stepped close to Joshi and unbuttoned her coat to reveal a bundle slung low across her chest. "My son, Elias," she whispered. "He's alive because of you. The warden kept her promise not to harm him."

Joshi could scarcely breathe as he looked at the perfect little face. The baby stared back at him before breaking into a toothless smile. Unprepared for the rush of emotion, Joshi felt his heart crack open. Tears rolled down his cheeks despite his struggle to stop them.

"I'm not sure if we'll see each other in Stutthof," said Gesa. She was suddenly shy. "Even so, I—I was wondering, would you be his godfather?"

"Me? Why that's—that's such an honor," stammered Joshi, choking on his words. "But there's so little I can do for him here."

"Oh, don't say that!" Gesa cried softly. "I'll never be able to thank you enough."

Joshi reached out to touch the baby's cheek. A tiny hand curled around his finger.

"He's an old soul," Joshi murmured, looking into the black center of Elias's eyes.

"Yes," she smiled. "But so are you."

Joshi pulled his finger from the baby's trusting grip. Opening his knapsack, he rummaged until he found a packet of biscuits Herr Müller had given him. He handed them to Gesa.

"A gift for my godson."

"Thank you," she whispered, withdrawing one of the buttery wafers and stuffing it into her mouth. She chewed hard and fast, and then, lowering her head, she placed her lips on Elias's lips and passed her saliva into his eager mouth. When Elias had finished swallowing, she looked up at Joshi with thankful eyes. "My milk is drying up. These biscuits will keep him going for a while."

The loud crank of engines startled them. Over the racket, they could hear the warden's shrill voice calling for Gesa.

"I must go," she said, slipping toward the crowd. "Good luck." Suddenly, she turned back. "Wait! I almost forgot."

She pressed a folded piece of paper into his hand. "Sofia's portrait," she whispered. "I stole it this morning."

Moments later she vanished into the crowd, but as Joshi climbed onto the lorry and found his place among the other men, he could still smell the faintly sweet scent of the baby's breath.

***

The lorry started up and rolled toward Stutthof. News had spread that they were all to be part of a forced march. No one knew what that meant, or where the march would take them, but there was a new sense of hope. Some men were too tired to believe that anything good could happen. Others began to plan their escape. The guards, worried about their own safety, held tight to their rifles and said nothing.

Joshi too was quiet. He watched darkness lift itself from the earth and make way for the dawn. The cold air hurt his skin. He pulled up his collar, the bitter memories of Schichau filling him with shame and confusion.

The sun broke over the horizon, tingeing a low spit of cloud strawberry red. He thought of Manya. *Does she see the same sun?* he wondered. *The same cloud? Is she alive?* His longing to know where she was ebbed as quickly as it had risen, recoiling into an ache. What if they actually found each other? He didn't even know how he felt about her anymore. And if there still were anything between them, he'd have to tell her the truth about Gesa and those moments when he had drifted into a horrible pleasure.

Artillery fire vibrated in the distance. Beside him, two prisoners, drunk on the idea of freedom, were trying to figure out the date.

"January 24, 1945," said Joshi.

"How do you know that?" Leonid asked, surprised.

"The warden had a calendar in her apartment. And, believe me, I counted the days."

PART III

Manya

AND

Joshi

JANUARY 1945

On New Year's Day, the baron gave his remaining geese and pigs to the farmhands. Then he called a meeting in the drawing room with the baroness, Manya, Helling, Schwitkowski, and Ursula.

The light from the candle on the shelf beside him danced over their grave faces. "I've made a mistake," he said in a strained voice. "We should have left Guja weeks ago."

His eyes swept over the mounted antlers of stags hunted on his land, the framed photographs, the bronze otter his wife had sculpted, and the furniture that had known the touch of so many generations. He forced himself to continue. "I'm ashamed to say that I did not flee because I was afraid of the Nazis, afraid of leaving my friends and everything I love."

"Have you changed your mind?" asked Helling.

The baron nodded. "The SS has been lying to us. Soviet troops are already on the Polish and Lithuanian borders."

He rubbed his temples as if to gather his thoughts. "They're hell-bent on vengeance. Our own *Gauleiter*, Erich Koch, ordered the slaughter of thousands in the Ukraine and sent more than eight thousand children to a death camp."

Casting a worried glance at Helling, he went on. "What they did in Nemmersdorf was only the beginning. We cannot expect kindness in East Prussia."

The baron waited for his words to sink in before continuing. "The Russians have been quiet over the past few weeks. We've been fooled by their silence, and by Hitler. The German army is spread too thin. It won't withstand a major attack."

Schwitkowski raised his hand.

"Excuse me, Herr Baron, but how do you know all this?"

"I overheard several officers while I was being questioned at Gestapo headquarters in Angerburg. The attack could happen tomorrow. It could be in several weeks. Nobody knows." His gaze took in their anxious faces. "I must ask a difficult question—do you want to flee or stay? You alone must search your hearts for the answer. You can come with us, but the trek will be difficult. I don't know whether we'll make it. We can't take the car because the roads are packed. We can't go by train because the railroad tracks have been destroyed. Horses are our only hope."

He looked at Manya.

"I'm sorry, child. I should have listened to you. Your judgment was better than mine. And I thank you and Blacksmith Helling for making preparations in spite of me." He looked to his wife for support, but she was stroking the smooth head of the bronze otter she had cast in honor of Ingo. "So, my friends, what will you do?"

Minutes passed in silence as gazes met only the floor. Finally, Schwitkowski and Ursula exchanged a look. Clearing his throat, Schwitkowski folded his calloused hands in front of him.

"I speak for both of us, sir, when I say we wish to stay." Ursula nodded, the gray bun on her head bobbing with the movement. "We're too old, Herr Baron," Schwitkowski said quietly. "This is our home, our land. We won't be forced from it." He shrugged his thin shoulders. "Perhaps the Russians will show mercy after all and we can take care of things until you return."

The baroness floated forward and took Schwitkowski's hand. "I think that's a fine idea," she told him. "I'm certain we'll be home before you even miss us." She turned to the baron. "Isn't that so, darling?"

Manya tried to catch her father's eye, but he ignored her, moving to take his wife in his arm.

"Of course it is, my love," he cooed over her head. "We'll be back before the first daffodils bloom."

─── ⚜ ───

That evening, Manya and her mother and father sat in the dining room. She traced her finger along the edge of the pale blue silk upholstery on her chair cushion and tried to commit the room to memory: the oil painting of Aztec, the silver teapot that never quite matched the brass candlesticks, the china cabinet with the beveled glass door that creaked when it opened.

How many times had she reached inside it for her favorite cobalt blue Meissen teacup?

She heard a cork pop. Her father poured champagne into three crystal flutes.

"Now we see the temporary nature of possessions," he murmured. "God is asking that everything familiar be returned to Him." He lifted his glass. "*Zum Wohl*," he said quietly. "To health. I hope He finds us worthy of living."

Manya could hardly taste the champagne, nor could she eat her favorite dish, *Königsberger Klöpse*—meatballs in white sauce with capers. She stared out the window at the willow tree where Joshi had waited for her so many years ago. She'd lost her appetite after her father had told her that the Karas clan had been murdered and the camp burned to the ground.

TWENTY-SEVEN

*Y*uri Golitsin sat in his tent poring over a military map of Germany. *And a damn good map it is*, he thought to himself. It outlined every river, border, and town, right down to the smallest village.

He reached for a mug of watery coffee, gasping as pain shot from his right shoulder to his thumb and index finger.

"Goddamn it," he whispered, waiting for the pain to subside.

Since the injury, he never knew what kind of pain would strike. Sometimes his arm went numb. Sometimes his fingers felt like they were being scraped raw to the bone with a hot iron file. But the shame of his failure at Nemmersdorf stung even more. He lifted the cup to his lips, watching the involuntary twitch of his fingers.

When he found the blond, he would get his revenge. And he *would* find her. Ah, the ways he would torture her. Last night, he had imagined her in a fancy dining room serving him strong German coffee laced with brandy and cream. He'd forced her to kneel, and after unbuttoning his trousers, he had made her press her lips along the full length of his cock. But that was nothing. When she was through, he'd nailed her tongue to the heavy mahogany table, relishing every scream, every streak of blood on the white blond mane of hair cascading over the table's edge.

He took another sip of his awful army coffee. A few drops spilled on the map.

"Goddamn it!" he murmured again.

He glanced at his arm. Two months ago she had cut him, and his hand still looked like a gnarled and clumsy stump of wood. Still, he had to admit that the doctor had done a damn good job sewing him up.

The son of a bitch had strapped him to a table and poured vodka down his throat. After rubbing iodine on his oozing flesh, the doctor had stitched the wound together with regular sewing thread, paying little heed to his cries.

In the days following the surgery, he had taught himself to operate a machine gun with his left hand. It had been awkward at first, and he felt stupid. Nevertheless, he had persevered and succeeded. His comrades had even changed his nickname from "Hawkeye" to "Rubber Gunny."

He didn't care what they called him. His mind was focused on one thing—regaining the respect he deserved.

The German girl had set him back. But he had guts and brains. Maybe he would never be a marshal like his hero, Georgy Zhukov, but he could still find honor. He smiled. If nothing else, he would be known as the Soviet Army's most valiant one-armed soldier.

He'd already earned back his lieutenant's uniform. Two weeks earlier, in a brilliant stroke of luck, he and three other soldiers had captured a German pilot. He'd been the one to spot the plane, a Messerschmitt Bf 109, and he'd been the one to bring it down intact. Now the Russian army planned to send it back into the air. When they did, the Germans would be fooled into thinking it was one of their own.

In the pilot's belongings, he'd found a Knight's Cross and knew he'd snared an ace. That was when he realized he was on a winning streak. Since he spoke some German, his commander brought him in to help with the interrogation, but the pilot wouldn't talk. Even Golitsin had to admire the man. What a resolute bastard! He'd broken his eyeteeth gnawing on the end of a wooden stool. No matter what they tried, that pilot stayed mum.

Golitsin, however, wasn't about to let the advantageous situation slip from his grasp.

"Sir," he'd said, addressing his commander. "Give me the prisoner for two days."

"How the hell are you going to extract information from this man?" the commander had asked. "He's not a talker."

"Herring, sir. Salted Kandalaksha herring. And no water. In two days, he'll tell us everything."

Sure enough, two days later, the pilot was screaming through foam-flecked lips.

"Water! For God's sake, give me water."

Taking a tin cup, Golitsin poured a few drops over the man's fingers. "You talk, you get."

By the third day, the pilot could take no more. He had been throwing up for most of the night and was begging to be shot. Golitsin agreed to grant his last wish if he would divulge information. Weeping, the pilot admitted that he had hidden several secret military maps in the cockpit of his plane. That was how Golitsin got hold of the one he was now studying.

And then, another stroke of luck.

The previous week, General Chernyakhovsky had arrived from the Belarusian front to help organize the final assault against the East Prussian border and what remained of the German army. Within hours, Golitsin was ordered to appear before him.

Chernyakhovsky had looked him up and down several times before fixing his gaze. Golitsin sensed that the general was testing his mettle. Staring back at Chernyakhovsky, he held firm to the thought, *I am loyal to the cause. Please. Use me.*

After a minute, Chernyakhovsky nodded, as though he'd heard.

"Your efforts are to be commended, Golitsin. The documents you confiscated from the German pilot, along with your interrogation report, have helped us compile detailed information about Berlin and the German defenses constructed there. For that, I am promoting you to lieutenant and decorating you with a Fighting Merits medal."

Golitsin had nearly wept with gratitude. After that, he was sure that Chernyakhovsky saw him as a protégé. The general had even asked him to sit in on an important meeting.

"This is the plan for the final attack," Chernyakhovsky had said when everyone was gathered in the tent. "When the ground is completely frozen in January, we will march into East Prussia. We will surround the major port cities of Königsberg, Elbing, and Danzig. If the enemy tries to escape across the Baltic Sea, submarines and aircraft bombers will make certain they drown. We will move through all of Prussia, Poland, and Pomerania, across the Vistula and Oder rivers and into Berlin. Marshal Zhukov is determined to take the capital before the first of May."

At the mention of Zhukov's name, Golitsin had caught his breath. If only that German girl hadn't ruined his chances. He might have ridden into Berlin on a T-34 tank, and Marshal Zhukov might have chosen him to raise the Soviet flag on the roof of the Reichstag.

"Lieutenant Golitsin, are you listening?" Chernyakhovsky had looked straight at him.

"Yes, sir!" Golitsin answered, snapping to attention.

The general pointed to several of the commanding officers. "You, gentlemen, will lead our battalions through Ebenrode and Trakehnen, Gumbinnen and Insterburg, into East Prussia."

Upon hearing Trakehnen, Golitsin had wanted to shout, "You idiot! Those men don't know the first thing about horses." But he had enough sense to keep quiet.

Chernyakhovsky continued, his clear brown eyes fixing on the officer in charge of Golitsin's battalion.

"You, Koslov, will cross the East Prussian border a bit further south and drive your forces into Angerburg and the surrounding areas. Your orders are to instill terror into the heart of every town." He turned to the group, a knowing smile creeping over his lips. "I think your men could use, ahh—" He cleared his throat. "A little pleasure?"

Laughter had erupted in the tent, and when it had died down, Chernyakhovsky looked at Koslov once more. "I want Lieutenant Golitsin to head up your reconnaissance team. Send him out after the ground freezes." Pointing at Golitsin, he simply said, "Prove yourself."

Now Golitsin took another sip of tasteless coffee. He'd been studying the map for hours. He knew the enemy's terrain inside out. Smiling, he fingered the small pouch he kept hidden beneath his belt. Inside was a lock of his dead grandmother's hair. He'd never admit it to a soul, but he was superstitious.

He thought about his grandmother. Born with the second sight, she had predicted many things, most of which had come true. He remembered crying at her kitchen table one day after his father had beaten him so hard he'd pissed blood. He was only ten. The czar had just been overthrown, and Lenin was the leader of the Bolsheviks. She had brought him a bowl of borscht and had set her gray-green eyes on him with a stare so hard it scared him. Raising her warm hand to his face, she had pinched his eyebrows and said, "I'm sorry your sweet Mama died giving birth to you and that your father blames you for it. But one day you'll show him who's boss. Eyebrows that grow together like yours mean fame and fortune. So think greatness, Yuri. Think of our country's future."

He glanced at the map. Ebenrode caught his eye. Trakehnen lay right below it. He picked up a ruler, measuring the distance. So close—twenty miles at most. He drained his mug and smacked his lips. He wasn't leading the Red Army into the city of Berlin. All the same, he'd make sure that these smaller villages were decimated. His mind kept circling back to the German girl. It was just a matter of time—days, actually—until his battalion moved in on her territory.

As the baron had feared, the baroness stared at him with her haunted eyes and demanded they stay until the end. Something about her spells terrified him, and he felt a familiar frustration as he tried to piece together the right words. "I won't leave without you," he pleaded. "But right now, we're in danger. All of us."

"We've heard no news from the front," the baroness countered.

"I know, but it won't be long now," he answered. And he was right.

During the second week of January, the Russians broke through the borders of Lithuania and Poland. Explosions shook the ground, rattling the windowpanes. From refugees who passed by the estate, they learned that the Red Army was only twenty miles away.

In the kitchen, the baron saw Ursula sitting at the table sipping a cup of coffee, her head bowed toward Lillian Goltz. They were deep in conversation. At first he had been furious when Manya told him she'd hidden Lillian in her room, but when he learned that the fugitive hiding in his house was the wife of the famous horse breeder Max Goltz, he asked Manya to take him to her right away.

The baron had sat on the edge of Manya's bed, and after much persuasion, Lillian had opened up. To the baron's horror, he learned that his wife's brother, Egon, had been involved in Max Goltz's murder. When the hunt for Jews began four years earlier, Egon had come to Lillian's door, threatening to inform the Gestapo about her unless Max paid him off. When Max informed Egon that the market for horses had dropped and he didn't have any funds, Egon demanded their best stallion.

"And so Max gave Aztec to Egon as payment," said Lillian. Turning to Manya, she added, "Max and I had four more years together, but in the end the Gestapo found out. I'm not here to claim Aztec, child. I heard he was on your farm and I knew he was in good hands. But after Max was murdered, I was hiding in the forest with nowhere to go, so I came here." She choked. "Aztec is my last link to Max."

"What a terrible ordeal, Frau Goltz," sighed the baron, burning with shame and anger. Rising from the bed, he'd laid a hand on her shoulder. "You have my word that we will make every effort to ensure your safety."

Now he strode into the kitchen. "Frau Goltz," he said. "I'm sorry to interrupt, but I've decided that we're leaving Guja at midnight. If you still want to come with us, I'll ask Manya to give you some warm clothes."

⚜

Helling had outfitted their largest wagon, once used to haul hay bales, with benches and bins, and had built a frame to which he had secured a waterproof tarp. He and Ursula had packed enough supplies to last the two weeks it would take them to reach the Frisches Haff and travel on to Danzig. The baron and baroness sat numbly beside Zarah, who clung nervously to Manya's mohair blanket, the night veiling the dull fear in her eyes.

Up front, Helling and Lillian shared the reins, their breath crystallizing in the frigid air.

Manya settled into her saddle astride Aztec. Helling nodded and shook the reins. Except for the jostling of the wagon wheels and the low crunch of the horses' hooves against the snow, they passed in silence through what was left of the forest that had graced their land for over three hundred years. The German military had chopped down whatever tree they needed—oak, birch, pine—leaving a graveyard of branches and tree stumps.

At the far edge of the estate, near the Angerapp River, the baron asked Helling to stop. Pale moonlight glinted on the river stones.

"Good-bye, dear river," he said, and urged Helling on.

⚜

For three days, they traveled over heavily congested roads from Guja to Dönhofstädt and on to the village of Klein Leunenburg. At Schippenbeil, they joined a line of refugees snaking from village to village and town to town like a forsaken many-limbed beast, littering the snowy landscape with their waste and their baggage and their dead.

Manya and her family stopped only for short periods, either to eat or to relieve themselves. There was no time to give her muscles, sore from so many hours in the saddle, a chance to recover.

On the second morning, they had broken briefly from the column, stopping at an estate in the hope of finding a cup of coffee. When no one answered their knock, they had entered the house. Six or seven people were rummaging through the kitchen, taking what little remained in the well-looted cabinets. One of them held up an egg before cracking it on the edge of a table and pouring the raw yolk into his mouth.

The rest of the house had been alarmingly quiet. Sensing that something was amiss, Manya and Lillian moved through the living room and into the hallway, where they dared to open a bedroom door. In the semi-darkness they found a woman, a man, and three young children, lying side by side in a four-poster bed, white as alabaster.

Manya stared at the bodies and asked herself whether suicide was a kinder fate than facing the enemy, and right there and then, she had thought that perhaps it was.

Stepping to the side of the bed, she had closed the father's eyelids while Lillian drew the quilt over the children's tender faces. On the dead man's nightstand, she'd found a tiny silver pillbox containing two cyanide tablets.

"Let's take them with us," urged Lillian, following Manya's gaze. "I would have gladly swallowed one when Max was killed."

Nodding sadly, Manya had slipped the pillbox into her coat pocket. Lillian locked eyes with her.

"Make sure your mother doesn't see those," she said.

"I know," Manya sighed.

Now, on the fourth morning, they were stopped outside the town of Schippenbeil, at the edge of the Alle River. The bridge that led into the town had been closed to civilian wagons—only *Jagdpanzers*—German tanks—and military vehicles could pass.

Manya shivered, shifting anxiously in her saddle, her nerves worn thin by the delay. The air, sharp and icy, stung her eyes. Behind her, the shrieks of Soviet rocket launchers were growing louder. With each explosion, screams erupted from the column of refugees. Next to her, a husband and wife, each carrying a child, abandoned their cart and fled into the woods bordering the river.

Jagdpanzers rumbled past with broken gun turrets and cracked windshields. *They're allowed to flee and we must wait,* she thought with rage as another, louder blast shook the earth.

This time Aztec recoiled. Helling hopped out of the wagon to steady Topsie and Shambhala. He looked to Manya, fear etched in his face.

"By the sound of things, the Russians are less than a mile away!" he called.

Manya nodded and leaned into Aztec's mane.

"Steady, boy," she whispered, but she was shaking.

Lillian sat in the front of the wagon, holding the reins. Her woolen cap was pulled down over her brow, almost meeting the jade green scarf covering her chin. Only her eyes were visible. They watched the world like a hawk.

Lillian's quiet authority had grown in the short time they had been on the trek. Somehow the chaos had made her stronger, more present, and the death wish that had so fiercely marked her face on the day Manya found her hiding in the apple bin was gone. In its place was a new confidence, fortified by the ease with which she handled the wagon. Helling and the baron had both recognized her ability, and they often asked her to drive so they could slide into the back and sleep.

"How's Mother doing?" Manya called over the noise.

Lillian shifted uneasily in the trestle, exchanging a look with Helling as he climbed back in.

"She's still demanding we turn around," Lillian said. "Won't eat a thing, either. Your father is looking after her as best he can."

Manya stood up in her stirrups and peered into the wagon. Zarah lay curled up on a bundle of hay, sucking her thumb and staring into space. She had not spoken a word since the day Manya found her in the forest.

The baroness sat beside her, stoic and erect. A few strands of her ash-blonde hair had loosened from the coiled braid at the nape of her neck, and they fluttered like lost threads in the wind.

"You!" a soldier called to Manya from the side of the bridge. "The Russians will be here any minute. Leave your horses and your wagon. Cross the bridge on foot. We're going to blow it up in a few minutes. You'll be trapped on this side."

Manya squinted at him through tired eyes. A strange drumming filled her head.

"Leave my horses?" she asked. "Here? To die?"

"Go," he commanded.

She was startled to see a gap behind the row of dilapidated panzers crossing the bridge. Could she and Lillian pull into that space? Would the army shoot at them? Her heart began to pound.

"Let's go, Lillian!" she hollered, pointing to the opening.

Lillian understood. She slapped the reins hard and the wagon jounced forward through the deep snow ruts.

The soldiers directing traffic began to yell for them to stay back, but

Manya and Lillian ignored their orders. The horses, tired too of standing in the cold for so long, pricked up their ears and started to pull the wagon, skidding over the bridge. A shot rang out behind them. She dug her heels into Aztec's sides. She heard Lillian urging Shambhala and Topsie forward. Schippenbeil became a blur as they raced past the church and the town buildings. Twenty minutes later, they reached the snow-covered fields outside the town and finally slowed the pace.

Manya saw both relief and astonishment on Lillian's face. She knew what Lillian was thinking, for she was thinking it, too. *We could have died back there at the bridge, with the Russians so close. Why did fate choose us to remain among the living?* But Manya couldn't think of an answer.

They continued through slush and mud, afraid to stop. Carts stood by the roadside, their owners unable to push on because of broken axles, sick horses, or the plain heartbreak of leaving home. Some people still believed that the invading army would be merciful. Others, too weary to care, sat by the side of the road, hunched over and hopeless, resigned to their fates.

The more Manya saw, the more infuriated she became at the indifference Germany's leaders had shown to her people. Clearly, proper evacuation plans had never been in place. Koch, who called himself governor, had left his people to die. But it took energy to be angry, and Manya had little left. Besides, her fingers burned from holding the reins, and her toes, frozen in the tips of her boots, felt as if they might be turning black.

She noticed a woman walking beside her, carrying an infant. Snow clung to the young woman's hair.

When Manya's shadow fell over the baby, the woman raised her eyes.

"Spare any food, miss?" she asked vacantly.

Manya had heard the question a thousand times since leaving Guja, and each time the answer grew easier. "I'm sorry," she murmured, shaken by the hollow tone in the woman's voice.

She glanced at the woman's chafed hands, realizing with a gasp that the baby was ash-blue. Dead. *Oh God, have mercy*, she thought.

TWENTY-EIGHT

"What the hell are you doing?" Golitsin heard his comrade Afanasiv shout. "You're a lieutenant, for God's sake. Control yourself!"

Flushed with shame, Golitsin searched for words to explain himself.

"This is her room, Afanasiv. The one who butchered my arm slept in this bed!"

Moments before Afanasiv had walked through the door, Golitsin had been striking every object in the room with his riding crop, shattering a vase and china figurines and ripping apart books and clothes.

"I can't believe I missed her," he panted, catching his breath.

His eyes flew around the room. Beside the ottoman he spotted a trash can stuffed with a jacket and a pair of jodhpurs. He yanked them out and kicked the can. The jacket was missing the three top buttons, but he recognized the crest on the remaining button right away. The jodhpurs, too, were familiar. Now she was gone. He threw the clothes on the floor and stomped on the silver crest. Again he heard Afanasiv's voice.

"Stop, Golitsin!"

A bitter wave of disappointment swept over him. How could he have lost control of himself like this? He barely remembered grabbing the riding crop from the windowsill, but he had whipped everything in sight: lamps, curtains, pillows. He'd gone mad at the sight of the girl's personal things on the vanity table and had swept the crop back and forth across the surface until the perfume bottles and mirrors smashed on the floor. Afanasiv gripped his arm and shoved him down on the bed, the feathers from the duvet spraying into the room.

"Such goddamned bad timing," Golitsin sputtered. "If only we'd come sooner."

It had taken entirely too long for their battalion to move into German territory. Golitsin had wanted to cross the border much earlier, but Commander Koslov had refused to budge until the final order to attack came through. Rain had kept the ground soggy for weeks, and the tanks had not been able to roll in until the twelfth of January. Golitsin's platoon had battled fiercely before finally breaking through the enemy trenches along the forests north of Angerburg.

Early this morning, Koslov had sent him, Afanasiv, and four other soldiers on a recon mission to Guja. Strategically positioned on a hill, Guja had been a stronghold against Russia during World War I, and Koslov wasn't taking any chances. "The Germans must be overtaken," Koslov had screamed. "Let us not repeat the shame of World War I, when five hundred of our countrymen fell in battle at Guja." His eyes scanned the troops. "The Germans won't be so lucky this time."

Camouflaged in white sheepskins, Golitsin and the others had crept across the snowy expanse of the lake, but when they arrived in Guja, they found that all of the Krauts had fled.

"But I'm still the best tracker in the Russian army. I swear I'll find you," Golitsin muttered.

"What?" Afanasiv asked.

Golitsin didn't answer. He was thinking about that very morning, when he and his comrades discovered the manor on the hill. They had smashed in the front door. To his surprise, right inside the foyer he had come face to face with the girl's portrait. She was not from Trakehnen, as he had first suspected, but she was an aristocrat nonetheless. Her name, Manya von Falken, was engraved on the shiny silver frame.

He had raced up the stairs, flinging open every door until he found her room. A leather photograph album lay open on her nightstand. Most of the pictures were missing, but she had left a few, as if to tease him. Those images of her on the stallion. He hated her strong, jutting jaw, her inquisitive eyes, and the wisps of white blond hair that fell across her confident smile.

He shifted uncomfortably on the bed and saw Afanasiv drumming his fingers against the mattress. Downstairs he could hear the men guffawing and singing and breaking glass. They would be looting whatever they could find before the main troops arrived. But the one thing he wanted was gone.

"What's wrong with you, Golitsin?" Afanasiv's voice was insistent. "Have you lost your senses?"

Golitsin glanced at his comrade. Clearly, he needed to explain himself.

The man was his only friend. A recon pilot, Afanasiv had been shot down by the Germans near the Romeinte forest a short while back. Somehow he'd managed to make his way to the Russian front, where he'd wound up in Golitsin's unit. When Koslov discovered that he was a sharpshooter, he refused to send him back to the air force, assigning him instead to ground recon. Golitsin and Afanasiv had shared a tent and become friendly. Although he was a loner, Golitsin enjoyed Afanasiv's company. The man was smart. He never mocked anyone.

Golitsin felt a hot prickle of embarrassment under his cheeks. What must Afanasiv be thinking of him? He felt a sudden need to confess, to relieve himself of the weight brought on by his shameful encounter with the girl. Slowly, he recounted his story. Afanasiv listened, and Golitsin, mistaking the other man's silence for sympathy, told him everything. When he finished, Afanasiv gave him a disparaging look.

"That girl was just defending herself," he said. "You, however, failed to carry out your mission in Nemmersdorf. And now you blame her?" Afanasiv shook his head. "That aside, what really concerns me is your lack of self-control. I hate to think what might happen in a dangerous situation. You'll put my life at risk."

"I will not," Golitsin shot back. "First and foremost I am a soldier."

Afanasiv gave him a worried look.

"I need to trust you when we're on a mission. I'm not willing to die at your hands." Afanasiv waited for further words of reassurance from Golitsin. When none came, he decided not to press the issue. His unit needed Golitsin, but he would have to keep an eye on him. He rose and clapped Golitsin on the back.

"Come on," he said. "Let's get something to eat before Commander Koslov and the battalions arrive. We've sent word. They'll be here shortly. Also, just to let you know, I'm concerned about the woman I found hiding in the kitchen. She says she's the cook. She's so scared, all she does is mumble the estate owner's name."

Golitsin rose. He was on the verge of telling Afanasiv to shoot her when Afanasiv said, "I've ordered the men downstairs to leave her alone. She'll be swept up in the surge when the main troops come. They'll rape her, fat or not. In fact, the fatter they are, the more our soldiers want them." He kicked at a pile of feathers that had gathered on the floor. "And to think she looks like my own mother."

Golitsin went over to the window. A hungry cow was bellowing in the garden. Near the open stable door, two stray dogs were sniffing at a pile of horse manure. *Probably the stallion's*, he thought.

"All right, let's go," he said, pulling himself together.

He shoved a photograph of the girl into his pocket and turned to follow Afanasiv out the door. There was little chance of finding her now. Millions of Germans were running from them. And run they should. Just yesterday morning, he had caught one of the propaganda fliers floating down from the sky over his encampment. It read: "Soldiers of the Red Army, the blonde beast belongs to you. Kill her!"

The blonde beast was a double entendre for German women, as well as Germany itself. Golitsin's jaw tightened. It wasn't enough to chase the Germans westward, he thought. They need to be chased to their graves.

He fingered the photograph in his pocket. The girl would die with or without him. The advancing Red Army was all-powerful now. It would squash every living thing on the way to Berlin.

He followed the winding stairs back to the foyer, stopping abruptly on the bottom step. From her portrait, the girl stared straight at him.

"To hell with you," he said, and spit, hitting between her eyes.

Lillian had been driving the wagon all day over muddy fields and roads hollowed out with potholes. At dusk she veered away from the column and pulled the horses to an abrupt stop. Manya, who was riding behind the wagon, trotted up to the trestle to see what had happened.

"Please take the reins, Helling," she heard Lillian say in a tone that was clipped and shaky. "I can't drive anymore."

Helling's eyebrows knitted in concern. He patted Lillian's hand.

"Yes, please rest. I should have offered to drive long ago, but you were handling the wagon like a charioteer." Lillian tried to smile, yet Manya noticed with a start that Lillian's eyes had welled up. Suddenly, Lillian, who had been so brave for the entire hellish journey, erupted into tears.

"I'm sorry," Lillian cried, jumping up from her seat and climbing into the back of the wagon. "I'm so sorry."

Helling and Manya looked at each other in shock, their eyes following Lillian as she moved past the baron.

"Herr Helling," said the baron, after he had settled a blanket over Lillian's shoulders and joined the blacksmith in the front seat of the wagon. "Do you know where we are?"

Still dazed with concern for Lillian, Helling shook his head.

"We're at the Goltz horse farm," the baron said.

It took Helling a moment, but then it dawned on him. "How could I have been so thoughtless?" he whispered. "Of course, Lillian's home is just beyond that forest."

Manya pushed her heels down in the stirrups, hoping to ease the burn in her calves. Darkness had wrapped the chimneys of Bartenstein in veils of blue, and the church steeple was now a stark and lonely arrow in the sky. She glanced at Helling's wind-chapped face. It was hard on him to see Lillian so distressed. He kept looking over his shoulder at her, but since her teary outburst, she had fallen silent.

"Perhaps we should find a place to stop for the night," Manya called to him.

At the sound of Manya's voice, Lillian rocked forward and pointed.

"There's a road just up ahead to the right," she said, her voice hollow and spent. "We can sleep there."

Aztec began to tug at the bit, pulling toward a copse of snow-covered birch trees. Manya raised her eyebrows at Helling.

"Looks like he knows where he's going."

"Horses never forget the way home," he replied softly.

Lillian looked up, her eyes glassy and sad.

"There is no more home," she murmured. "It burned to the ground." She gave no further explanation, and Helling dared not ask. Instead, he followed Aztec's shift in direction, and, with a shake of the reins, he broke from the crowded column of refugees. The wagon lurched onto a path that led to a clearing at the edge of the woods. Lillian climbed back into the trestle and squeezed in beside the baron.

"This forest belonged to us," she said, in a shaky voice. "Max and I spent hours walking through it." She pointed to a fenced-in field. "We used to run our best Trakehner mares there." Her eyes filled with tears again. "Ach—it's no good, this. Let's stop. I'll get the horse feed."

Helling brought Topsie and Shambhala to a halt and Manya dismounted from Aztec, hitching him to the back of the wagon and removing his saddle.

"How's your back, old boy?" she asked.

He nickered softly.

With a towel, she wiped him down while Helling and the baron set about building a fire. When the fire was lit, the baron cut a chunk of bacon and set it sizzling in a cast-iron pot before adding potatoes, dried rosemary, and a handful of snow. The rich scent nearly made Manya swoon. They hadn't had a decent meal in days, and the bacon smelled like home. With her mouth watering, she sat down on a tree stump and waited for the stew to boil.

Helling offered the first scoop to the baroness, but she raised her hand and looked away.

"No thank you," she murmured. "I'm not hungry."

"Darling, but you must eat," the baron pressed tenderly. "You missed dinner last night."

Manya let out a sigh of frustration. Her parents were such children. She rose and grabbed the bowl of stew from Helling and set it on her mother's lap.

"Eat," she said, refusing to move until her mother took a bite.

Helling's eyes met her own and he gently shook his head as if to say, don't let your mother get to you, especially now. As Manya watched him dish out the rest of the stew with calloused hands, she thought about how she had come to rely on him. Aside from Joshi, he was the only one who understood what she had been through with the baroness.

After they had finished supper, they gathered their pillows and blankets and lay down in the wagon. Sleep never came easy. Each night became a copy of the one before: hopelessness stretching into dawn, along with the sound of bombs and gunfire.

Manya settled beside Zarah, stroking her hair until, blessedly, the little girl fell asleep. The baroness lay next to her husband, mumbling to herself in the darkness. "We never should have left Guja. Never, never, never."

"*Liebchen*, be strong," the baron whispered. "We'll go home as soon as we can."

Finally her mother's ramblings ceased and her father's breathing became deeper, as did Helling's and Lillian's. Manya wished she could escape into a similar slumber, but the itchy straw beneath her offered little comfort from the disturbing images that spun through her mind. She was tired of falling asleep to the sounds of refugees crying, tired of the bombs that seemed closer than ever. As she closed her eyes, she thought she heard Joshi's voice mingling with the wind, calling her name. She refused to believe that he had been murdered with the rest of his clan, but on nights like this, she wondered if she was being as stubborn and foolish as her mother. Finally, fatigue won out and she drifted into sleep.

※

Manya woke to Lillian shaking her shoulder.

"Come with me," Lillian whispered.

"It's too cold," Manya groaned, wrapping her hands around her knees.

"I know," said Lillian. "But I want to show you something, and I don't want to wake the others."

Wearily, Manya rose to follow her. There was no need to dress. She had only one outfit anyway and her boots were still on her feet. Quietly, they left the wagon, and she followed Lillian toward a stream that gurgled under a thick crust of ice. They walked along the embankment for a few minutes until they came to a fir tree. Lillian looked down at the gnarled roots. "This was my favorite tree," she said, her breath white on the silvery chill of the morning air. "I wanted us to come here because I have a present for you, something I've been meaning to give you for a while but couldn't." She reached into her coat pocket and pulled out a thick, dirt-streaked envelope, pressing it between her palms. "These are Aztec's documents. They certify him as a pedigree Trakehner. I kept them hidden in my blouse the whole time I was running, even at your house. I didn't want your uncle to find them. I didn't want anyone to find them. They are the last pieces of Max I have."

She coughed and straightened her back. "But this morning, before dawn, I made a decision." She handed Manya the envelope. "I want you to have them."

Manya felt a rush of lightheadedness. "No, Lillian. Aztec belongs to you."

Lillian's face grew stern. "Don't deny me this pleasure," she said, hugging herself from the cold. "I want to do this. Please."

"Are you sure?" whispered Manya, feeling an upsurge of happiness. "Do you realize what this means?"

"Yes," Lillian smiled. "It means Aztec can sire his own bloodline. It's obvious he was born in Trakehnen because he is branded with the single antler. However, when Max bought him at the yearly auction, we became his private owners and took him to Königsberg, where he passed state inspection. These papers are stamped with the official seal that allows him to stand as a stud."

Manya drew her breath in.

"And Shambhala's foal will be guaranteed Trakehner papers in the West," Manya said. "We can start a breeding establishment. Lillian, I don't know what to say."

"Really, dear," Lillian murmured kindly, "you don't have to say anything. You risked your life when you took me in. You shared your room, your clothes, everything with a total stranger—a Jew."

A bird was hopping up the trunk of the tree, tilting its gray head from side to side as if it were listening. Lillian saw it first and smiled.

"It's time," she said, hooking her arm through Manya's. "The others will be wondering where we are."

As they retraced their steps under the glossy gray sky, Lillian grew quiet, and Manya knew she was saying a silent farewell to the land that had once been her home.

When they arrived, the others were packing up the blankets. Helling was trying to patch the wagon's fraying tarpaulin.

"Where did you two go?" he asked, his brow furrowing.

A quiet smile touched the edges of Lillian's mouth.

"We were taking care of women's business," she replied. "Why? Were you worried?"

Helling cocked his head sideways to look at her, the color rising in his cheeks.

"Not—not really," he stammered. "Ach, never mind. Are you going to drive? Or should I?"

TWENTY-NINE

As soon as the transport lorry passed through the "Death Gate" in Stutthof, Joshi and Leonid noticed an unusual buzz of optimism. Everywhere prisoners were whispering that the camp was breaking up. This new hope stood in sharp contrast to the SS officers' somber faces. Curiously, they did not shout out any orders, even when the lorry pulled in. Instead, the arriving prisoners were told to forget about check-in procedures and return to their barracks.

Joshi ran along the worn cobblestone path, past the guardhouse and the commandant's villa, until he reached his barrack.

"Ben," he called, shoving the door open. "Are you here?"

A man who was no more than a living skeleton pointed to a bunk. "He's not doing well. He's got the sores."

Joshi found Ben curled up in the fetal position, shivering.

"Hey Ben, it's me," he said softly, stroking the curve of Ben's emaciated back.

"My God," mumbled Ben, rolling his glazed eyes sideways. "You made it back?"

"Yes," said Joshi, leaning closer. "May I look at your sores?"

Ben gave him a tired nod. Joshi drew back the blanket and began to palpate the swollen bumps on Ben's ribs.

"What the hell are those things?" croaked Ben.

"Embedded boils that won't burst, and yours are the size of chicken eggs," Joshi said. "It's an infection called phlegmon."

"Not too good, huh?" wheezed Ben.

"No. I'll have to lance them. Are you up for that?"

"Yeah," murmured Ben. "Just don't send me to the infirmary."

"Still stubborn, eh?" said Joshi. "That's a good thing." He took off his coat. "All right, let's do it. But I have to warn you. It'll hurt and stink like hell." He reached into his knapsack and pulled out Liesel's knife. "Brace yourself," he said. Gripping the knife, he cut through Ben's skin.

Ben cried out only once. After that he bit his lip, forcing himself to lie still. The procedure took less than twenty minutes, and when Joshi was finished, he gave Ben a wry smile.

"You look like you have fish gills now, with all those slits."

"I smell like a rotting fish, too," groaned Ben, turning to look at his friend.

Joshi pulled the warden's lace handkerchief out of his knapsack and wiped the sweat from Ben's brow. He hated the thing, but it was useful.

"Once the incisions drain, those boils will heal. Rest now."

The tension ebbed from Ben's face, but Joshi stayed close to him. At four in the morning, Esser stomped into the room.

"Everybody to the square!" he shouted. "Now!"

Scrambling to his feet, Joshi peered through the door. Hundreds of prisoners were filing onto the Himmler Allee. Leonid was pushing his way through the crowd toward the barrack.

"We're leaving Stutthof," he cried when he stumbled into the room. "Rumor has it we're marching west. Come on. Get your things. They want us to form columns." He paused to sniff the air. "Mother of God, what *is* that?"

"My friend," Joshi said, pointing to Ben. "We've got to help him."

Leonid peered into Ben's bunk.

"Jesus, he looks awful." He shook his head. "But if you think he can make it, let's go."

Together they lifted Ben off the mattress and set him down on the floor. Ben groaned.

"Stay quiet, Ben," Joshi said, shoving clogs on Ben's feet. "Walk! Think of your sister and how happy she'll be to see you in Husum."

A glimmer of hope flickered in Ben's half-dead eyes. Taking a breath, he jutted out his chin and walked as if his swollen ankles had just sprouted wings.

They gathered into nine columns, each consisting of nearly a thousand men wearing only the thin, striped uniforms they'd been issued at Stutthof. Joshi noticed that a few prisoners had managed to steal sweaters and jackets from the laundry room. One man had extras, and with the last precious packet of biscuits he'd brought from Schichau, Joshi bought Ben a coat.

At sunrise, SS *Unterscharführer* Reiss, the designated officer in charge of their column, bellowed, "March!"

The men surged forward through the gate and veered into the forest, past the whitewashed cottage where Nuri and Ben's girlfriend had been held captive. Joshi shuffled along the muddy path, thinking of Nuri and Sofia. What had they done with the female prisoners?

Ahead, a haze of light filtered through the branches of the hornbeam tree where Nuri had promised to leave him a message. His stomach seized. How could he check the hollow? As he racked his brain, he noticed a guard posted by the white picket fence. Gathering his nerve, he stepped up to the man.

"Sir," he said in pleading voice, "I can't hold my water. Could I just take a piss by this tree over here?" He eyed the officer's rifle. "I'm not going to run, I promise."

The guard growled at him.

"No pissing allowed, prisoner."

"Please," groaned Joshi. "I'll just be a minute."

The officer squinted at him.

"I remember you. You play the violin. All right, but make it snappy."

Joshi slipped behind the hornbeam tree, and as he dropped his trousers, he slid his hand into the hollow and pulled out a small package wrapped in brown paper. A note, rolled tightly like a cigarette and tied with a red string, had been pushed under the edge of the wrapping.

"Nuri," he whispered gratefully.

He unrolled the paper and read the words, written in Romani.

Jan 23. I hope you find this. Your sister is alive. I have an infection. The officer I mentioned has promised to take us to safety. I hope so. But whom can we trust anymore? Wear the red string for luck. I love you. N.

For a moment, he stared at Nuri's words. Then he stuffed the note and the package into his rucksack. When he rejoined the line, Leonid and Ben stared at him in astonishment.

"You've got chutzpah, my friend," Ben said weakly. "I wouldn't have risked that."

"Yes, you would," countered Joshi softly. "Especially if you thought you had a chance of finding something out about your sister."

"What do you mean?"

Joshi pointed over his shoulder.

"My friend Nuri left a message in the hollow of that tree."

Ben shot him an incredulous look.

"And?"

"All I know is that two days ago, she and Sofia were still alive."

⁕

The prisoners marched westward toward Danzig in large zigs and zags, covering nearly twenty-five miles the first day, the officers avoiding the main roads so as few people as possible would see them. They marched over winding country lanes, uphill and downhill, through valleys and forests and fields, until their feet bled.

It had been a long time since the men had seen anything of beauty, and they stared at the landscape of glinting brooks and frozen marshmallow-snow lakes. Some men, drunk with the notion of freedom, even laughed out loud.

However, as darkness fell, so too did their spirits. Many began to lag behind. Joshi and Leonid, barely able to drag their own feet, were nearly carrying Ben, whose already limited strength was rapidly diminishing.

"The first day is probably the hardest," muttered a thin, benevolent-looking man in the column.

"Yes," a young Pole chimed back. "Tomorrow will be easier. We'll get to Danzig. Surely they'll put us on a ship out of here."

A prisoner who had survived Auschwitz said, "You're deceiving yourselves."

That night they took shelter in an evacuated women's camp on the bank of the Vistula River. Conditions there were even worse than in Stutthof. Snow blew through the cracks in the walls, melting and mixing with the excrement on the floor.

In spite of it all, they settled down and Joshi summoned what little strength he had left to check on the weakest prisoners. Without a stethoscope, he could only kneel in front of an exposed chest and scrape off the lice, press his ear to the area, and listen. Most of the heartbeats were faint and erratic, their bodies succumbing to pneumonia, diphtheria, and typhus.

Men with frostbitten feet begged him for help, and when he bent down, he saw blisters green with gangrene. He tried to be encouraging, but in most cases, he knew it was hopeless. The infection would soon spread into their bodies and poison their blood.

Finally, exhausted, he dropped to the ground beside Ben and fell asleep. Dreams of Danzig's harbor, the magnet of hope, drew him into another world, where ships left the port for some safe place far, far away. He saw Manya and Aztec chasing a freighter over the ocean. Ben was riding behind her in the saddle. Sofia and his parents, Nuri, Gesa, Elias, and so many others were there, too. They surged forward into a circle of fire that the sea could not extinguish. He ran behind them but could not catch up.

He woke with a start. Ben's body had become a furnace. Quickly, he searched his rucksack for the small vial of aspirins he'd brought from Schichau. Mashing two in his palms, he made a paste with some snow and fed it to Ben.

The next morning, after a quick head count, Joshi and Leonid pulled Ben to his feet.

"I can't believe they're still counting us," Leonid muttered as he shoved his arm under Ben's elbow. "As if we matter to anyone!"

Joshi's legs ached. His shoulders were rubbed raw from the rucksack, yet he refused to throw it away. Though minimal, its contents were precious. The night before, when he had unwrapped the red string binding Nuri's package, he found a bit of cheese, a piece of bread, some goose lard, and ten cigarettes. Savoring the richness of the lard, he knotted the string around his wrist and thought about his clan. When he closed his eyes, he could almost see their beloved faces.

Now as he and Leonid carried Ben between them, a stiff wind arose, ushering in wet flakes of snow. Leonid tripped, and as he scrambled to keep hold of Ben, his face twisted into a pained grimace.

"What's wrong?" asked Joshi, leaning into the wind.

"That was a goddamn corpse!" Leonid yelled, looking over his shoulder "That's what the guards do when they ride to the back of the line on their bikes. They shoot the stragglers like dogs."

Leonid started to sob, tears making trails through the grime on his face. Joshi felt numb, too empty to speak.

Within an hour, more corpses appeared. The wind had lessened. Joshi looked back to see a crimson trail looping in circles across the snowy hills.

"My God," he whispered, nausea filling his stomach. "We are walking in circles!"

"Are we lost?" coughed Ben.

"Maybe," replied Joshi. "More likely, though, the SS doesn't want to stray too far from Danzig harbor, so they keep turning us around."

Ben squeezed Joshi's arm with feeble fingers. "I have to stop. I can't go on. Let me lag." He turned to look at a guard. "He'll finish me off. It'll be fast. Just a flash in the snow. So much easier for me and a damn sight lighter for you and Leonid."

"No," Joshi said, fury rising in his voice. "We haven't carried you this far for nothing. You're not giving up!"

On the third night, the column halted on a narrow street that ran through a village. It was bitter cold, but clear, and the stars shone high in the sky. Joshi's eyeballs hurt. He turned to look at the houses and saw faces staring out from windows. Officer Reiss walked down the line, ordering the prisoners to wait while he went to see whether they could spend the night in the village church.

"Maybe he's going to negotiate with God," Ben smiled weakly as Reiss disappeared inside the rectory.

There was a flurry of movement in the houses. Windows opened and loaves of bread fell through the air.

"Here," cried a woman tossing a loaf. "Catch!"

"Christ only knows where we are," exclaimed a man behind Joshi who caught the loaf, "but it must be a Kashubian village. Only Kashubs would be so kind."

Incredulous, Joshi turned to Ben.

"These people must know about us, about the camps."

"They do," said Ben. His voice shook under the strain of speaking. "There were Kashubs in Stutthof. Strong people. I knew a few. The Germans have never liked them because so many are resistance fighters."

A few minutes later, Reiss returned and the bread stopped falling. "Everyone into the church," he shouted, urging them past a small cemetery and into the sanctuary. Near the altar, beside a beautiful pipe organ, Joshi and Leonid settled Ben on the floor.

Joshi sat down beside Ben. Ugly, misshapen blotches had crept over Ben's skin. "Typhus," Joshi murmured, his breath catching in his throat. "Goddamn filthy marauder! You've finally caught up to us."

From his knapsack, Joshi withdrew his last aspirin and placed it on Ben's tongue. Ben's eyes glittered at him from inside hollow gray pits, the bones of his face shining like yellow seashells beneath his transparent skin.

"Swallow, Ben," said Joshi.

As the pill slid down Ben's throat, his eyes seemed to fix themselves on an invisible presence above the organ.

"Shalom, Rivka," he whispered through cracked lips. "It's my turn. I'm coming."

"Ben," murmured Joshi, shaking him gently. "What's your sister's name? How will I know her if I ever make it to Husum?"

But Ben didn't answer.

"Hang in there, Ben," pleaded Joshi. "The aspirin will work. I promise. Stay with me, please."

A hand touched his shoulder. The pull was gentle at first, but it became more insistent. He looked up, surprised to see the Pomeranian priest from Stutthof's storeroom chapel.

"Who should have to bear witness to such things?" the priest asked sadly. "But I promise you, your friend is at peace. You gave him that gift."

He stooped low to make the sign of the cross on Ben's forehead.

"He's a Jew," Joshi said, anger filling his voice.

"It doesn't matter. God's blessing goes with him whatever his religion." The priest looked into Joshi's eyes, his breath rattling in his lungs. "I heard you play the violin at Stutthof. You were so good. Can you play the organ too?"

"Not very well," Joshi frowned. "And I really don't feel like it now."

"I know, but—" The priest pointed toward the bone-colored organ keys with the same authoritative finger that had blessed Ben's forehead. "Play," he said. "For your friend." Straightening his shoulders, he pushed his way to the pulpit and began to pound it with both fists. "Friends!" he cried, his voice rising above the din. "Have you forgotten where you are? You are in a church! Be quiet and listen! We have music tonight."

He motioned for Joshi to stand.

Joshi thought of the sweet and precious raisin the priest had given him.

Surely the priest had risked his life to bring pleasure to others. He rose and sat down at the organ, where he picked out the notes of the first song that came to him. It was a Polish hymn, "Bogurodzica"—"Mother of God,"—and he wept.

From a pew in the rear of the church, a beautiful tenor joined him: "Mother of God, have mercy on us . . ."

After he had stopped playing, he noticed that some of the villagers had set up kettles of soup that smelled deliciously of fried bacon.

Leonid brought a bowl to him, but he waved it away. "You have to eat," said Leonid. "Ben would be furious if you gave up now."

I know, thought Joshi, accepting the soup and settling next to Ben. When he finished eating, he leaned over and kissed Ben's forehead. It was already turning cold.

"Rest," he whispered. "No one is after you now."

His gaze traveled into the sanctuary, where women were mingling among the prisoners, doling out cookies and biscuits. Some were even sewing tattered uniforms. As they carried out their kindnesses, they questioned the prisoners about Stutthof.

"My grandson was there. Do you know if he was in your column?" a wrinkled old woman asked Leonid, her eyes brimming with tears.

"How about my father?" inquired a young girl with long, amber-brown braids who had come to stand by the organ. She spelled out a long surname. "Do you know if he's alive?"

Joshi shook his head sadly.

"I'm so sorry, but we hardly knew anyone's last name." He glanced at Ben's body and felt a stab of shock. "I didn't even know my friend's last name. He was just a number and now he's—he's gone."

The older woman took hold of his arm. "Don't worry, love, God knows his name. We'll bury him for you."

Joshi looked at her frail shoulders, her missing front teeth.

"I can still wield a shovel, young man," she said, reading his mind. "My granddaughter will help me. We did it yesterday after the women from Stutthof left."

"Women?" Hope surged into Joshi's chest. "Please, grandmother, tell me—did you see my sister? She's thirteen with brown eyes, the color of topaz. Sofia is her name."

The woman shook her head. "No, I'm sorry. There were no young ones."

"Perhaps a tall, olive-skinned woman, Romani, like me?"

The woman shook her head again.

Joshi was desperate now.

"Maybe you noticed a tiny woman with delicate features? She would have had her baby with her."

The woman thought for a moment. Suddenly, her withered face filled with light.

"Yes," she said, breathlessly. "There was only one woman with a baby. One of the mothers from the village suckled him." She grinned. "Elias is his name. He sucked those tits dry! That baby's got a will, I tell you, and so does the mother. Such a sweet face—like an angel." Her voice fell to a whisper. "Are you the baby's father?"

Joshi smiled tenderly.

"No, I'm his godfather."

THIRTY

The sun rose, pouring light through the high church windows. With the sun came the sound of gunfire and cannon thunder. The guards marched through the aisles, shouting orders and dragging the tired prisoners out of the pews.

Leonid and Joshi pushed their way past the baptismal font. One of the guards, busy cleaning a bicycle, was asking Reiss where they were going. "Plans have changed," Reiss answered brusquely. "We're not headed toward Danzig or Pomerania anymore." He ran his hand over his greasy brown hair, and Joshi was surprised to see a ring of nervous sweat under the armpit of his uniform. "We have orders to march these prisoners up the coast," Reiss said, resting his hand on the bicycle seat and dropping his voice to a whisper. "Past Elbing and Braunsberg and into Palmnicken, where they'll be working the amber mines."

The guard twisted the pedal nervously. "But sir," he argued. "It's over sixty miles! We'll never get through. Civilians and military convoys will block our way. We'll be sitting ducks for the Russians. Surely it's best if we stay here, in this area, closer to Danzig and the ports."

"Who cares what you think is best?" Reiss snapped. "Have you lost all respect for the Führer? You will follow orders, or else!"

There had been no headcount when Joshi and Leonid stepped into the stinging daylight.

"They're becoming dangerously lax now that their own number might be up," snorted Leonid.

Outside the village, the line came to a stop beside a slushy river. Reiss was in a foul mood.

"We've been gracious enough to give you three piss breaks a day," he barked, waving his gun. "But today, you scumbags are only getting one. So you'd better do your stinking business now, because you won't have another chance."

Scowling, Reiss headed into the woods to relieve himself in private. He'd been gone for less than a minute when Joshi saw him come bounding back over shrubs and rocks, his pants twisted at his ankles, his genitals bouncing up and down in the cold air. "A Russian tank!" he screamed, his face a mask of fright.

A few moments later, a tank came crashing through the bushes. Reiss raced ahead of it, his naked legs carrying him to the riverbank, where, in panic, he became so tangled up in his trousers that he missed his footing and fell down the slope.

Joshi laughed out loud, surprising himself. But everyone else was laughing, too.

"Look!" Leonid grinned as the tank curved away into the distance. "That's not a Russian T-34. That's a German Panzer. Reiss is so scared of the Russians, he'd run from a cow."

Furious, Reiss scrambled up the embankment.

"Shut up!" he roared, "or I'll shoot every one of you."

Uplifted by the laughter, Joshi walked on. A word had entered his mind, and he played it over and over: *Escape.*

With every step, he felt a quickening. Escape was dangerous. He'd seen men shot as they attempted to dash out of the column. No, that wouldn't be the way. Still, something was daring him to do it.

He dug into his knapsack for a piece of bread. If he ate, he might be able to think. He knew the contents of his bag blindfolded, so when he touched an unfamiliar flimsy piece of cloth, he was taken aback. He pulled it out, and it fluttered in the icy wind. On the cloth he saw the yellow Star of David.

Ben's armband, thought Joshi. *I bet he slipped it into my bag before he—.* He drew his eyes away from the star to gaze at a thread of cloud, curling like a ghost above the barren treetops. Ben had told him that the Star of David was a symbol of protection, a shield against the enemy. His heart beat faster. Maybe something was about to change.

THIRTY-ONE

Snow fell in thick flakes, burying Shambhala's and Topsie's legs up to their hock joints. Quivering with exertion, the mares fought hard to keep their footing and pull the wagon forward. Manya rode beside them, her wrists aching with cold, her thighs bruised from clenching the saddle.

She slid her boots out of the stirrups to stretch her legs and heard the sound of tires skidding on ice. A German military lorry was coming straight toward them. She held her breath. The lorry passed with a loud *vroom*, shocking her face with an ice-cold splattering of slush. She pulled on Aztec's reins and, too tired to curse, stared at the driver.

"Manya, are you all right?" called Helling, when the roar of the motor had faded. She nodded. "Another six miles to Klein Stegen is what I reckon," he hollered over the wind. "And then we'll be at your cousin Hetta's. Can you make it?"

Again she nodded, but her legs felt like lead. She wished she were in the back of the wagon with the others. The snow was deep now, and she was still on Aztec. It was just too risky to hitch him to the wagon. In these slippery conditions, he might fall and break a leg.

She scanned the landscape. Bloated bodies lay scissored in the snow. Dead animals lined the roadside. Where was Joshi? Was he a corpse in the camp? On this road? She imagined all the ways he might have died, alone and comfortless, without anyone to care for him.

She tried to distract herself by remembering his face, but it was becoming more and more difficult. Wincing into the wind, she looked over the heads of starving and dying refugees.

The sheer mass of East Prussian families trekking west had created deadlocks on the narrow roads and bottlenecks at river crossings. On a good day, their wagon covered twelve miles or more, on a bad day only five. Today was a bad day.

As they rode on, she saw a lorry stopped on the shoulder of the road. Three soldiers were leaning out the back, waving the German flag.

"Turn back, people!" Manya heard them shout. "Go home. We're going to win the war! The Führer is sending bigger rockets. The *Wunderwaffe*—the miracle weapon is on its way."

"What?" cried Manya, her distress mounting. Some of the wagons were actually turning back, creating even more chaos.

"Keep going," her father shouted. "Those soldiers don't know what they're talking about. There is no miracle weapon. No one is going to help the Prussian people, least of all the Führer."

"Don't say that, Fritz," countered the baroness. "Maybe it's true." She hadn't spoken all day, but now her voice was clear as a bell. "Let's turn around too. I want to go home!"

"Hush, Mother," begged Manya. "Please."

"Don't tell me to hush!" her mother snapped angrily. "We *must* go back. What if Ursula forgets to feed my parakeets?"

The unnerving light in her mother's eyes terrified Manya.

"Please don't do this," she breathed. "There's no going back right now. Do you understand?"

But her mother shushed her again. "And what about Meister Eckhart and my horses? If I don't feed them, they'll die!"

Manya watched her father move toward his wife and lay his huge hands on her shrunken shoulders. He began to rub her neck. Manya took a sharp breath, trying to keep herself together. She could not bear to see them like that.

"Manya, come talk to me. Please," she heard Helling say. His voice shook. Gathering herself, she trotted up beside him.

"Your mother's horses," he said, his eyes wide with worry. "The skewbald Trakehners and the little gray mare, Bella. I shot them." He winced at the memory. "If she goes back, they won't be there. I had to do it before the Russians got hold of them. I didn't want them to suffer."

"I know," whispered Manya. "It's all right."

Lillian laid a hand on his shoulder. The tender gesture did not slip past Zarah, who stared at them with curiosity. She had fallen in love with Lillian, who was always fussing over her and telling her stories about ordinary people who were caring and heroic. Manya had been so caught up in the trek that she hadn't noticed. But now she could see that Zarah's brittle body had softened.

Manya opened the small leather pouch that was fastened to her belt and pulled out one of Ursula's marzipan candies. "Zarah, love," she said, holding it out. "Would you like a sweet?"

To her surprise, Zarah nodded and reached over the side of the wagon to grab the sticky treat, which she popped right into her mouth.

Manya laughed lightly. "You deserve to eat sweets like a princess—" Her voice broke off. In the distance was a narrow tower. "Look," she said, turning to her mother. "We've reached Cousin Hetta's."

⚜

"You're alive!" Hetta cried when she opened her front door. She rushed to embrace the baron and the baroness. "Oh God!" she clucked, grasping the baroness's chapped and filthy hands in her warm palms. "You're nothing but skin and bones." Her cheeks became flushed with worry. "What has this man Hitler done?" she said, before summoning a stable hand to care for the horses.

"Don't fret," she said when she saw the concerned look on Manya's and Helling's faces. "The horses will be safe with Hans."

But Helling wasn't taking any chances and went off with the boy.

Hetta took the baroness's hand. "Come, come, cousin dear, you need to eat."

They followed her into the front hall. The air smelled of sweat and straw and mud, and the living room and parlor were crowded with refugees. When they reached the kitchen, Hetta bustled between her old iron stove, the tin sink, and a kettle of soup that smelled deliciously of dill, onions, and potatoes. The baron settled his wife in a chair at Hetta's large wooden table and helped her remove her gloves. Manya glanced over the pots cluttering the tabletop at Lillian, who gave her a knowing look. Hetta also shot them a look as if to acknowledge how helpless and disturbed her cousin had become.

She reached into her cupboard, withdrew a wicker-bound bottle of Chianti, and poured the contents into a saucepan to which she added a stick of cinnamon and a handful of sugar. When her brew was hot, she poured it into teacups and passed the tray around. "Drink. Warm your bones."

Grateful, Manya took a sip, letting the sweet liquid run down the back of her throat.

"Hetta," she said. "Are you going to stay in Klein Stegen? I mean, when the Russians come?"

"I know I should leave," Hetta said quietly. "But I just can't abandon what I love." She returned to her soup pot. "I keep hoping the Russians will be kind and let me carry on in the old way. They need to eat too, don't they?" She tasted the soup and gave a nod of satisfaction. "Let's dish it out." She plunged the ladle back into the pot and began to fill the bowls she had set beside the stove.

"I understand why you want to stay," the baron murmured when Hetta served him. "Believe me, I do."

The baroness turned to him.

"You didn't have the courage to stay."

He blushed. "Hush, my love."

"Mother," said Manya, "Please. I don't want to hear this." *I've got to get out of here*, she thought, and stood up. Her mother's haunted eyes followed her as she left the kitchen and stepped into the hall, which smelled of soggy garments and sweat. She was surprised to hear laughter coming from the library. Curious, she opened the door. Inside, she found a group of children putting on a play.

Zarah lay on a heap of pillows in the middle of the room, clutching an apple, her soulful eyes taking everything in.

"She doesn't talk," giggled a little girl who was standing near the bookshelves, "so we chose her to be Snow White. She just took a bite of the apple, and now she's asleep."

Zarah closed her eyes.

"See?" said the little girl.

Manya smiled at Zarah's attempt to feign sleep, and after watching for a few more minutes, she went out and closed the door behind her.

When she returned to the kitchen, an officer in a frayed Wehrmacht field uniform was sitting at the table. He was handsome in a measured way, and she couldn't help notice that his blue eyes lit up with equal measures of interest and kindness when she crossed the room.

Acknowledging him with a shy nod, she went to sit beside her father, letting her head fall on his shoulder and giving his arm a squeeze.

The officer's name, she learned, was Hollberg, and he was a friend of Hetta's. As he and Hetta talked, it became evident that he was in charge of moving army supplies from ports on the Baltic to the front. However, when Hetta questioned him about the outcome of the war, he hesitated.

"Don't worry, Hartmut," she said quietly, passing the ladle to Lillian and stepping away from the stove. "Everyone in this kitchen is trustworthy. Speak."

"All right," he said. "I've been everywhere. All directions. It's only a matter of days before the ports are overrun by the enemy." He gazed at Manya. "Like you, millions are fleeing to the coast, but even if you make it, you might not get a passage out."

The baroness was sitting beside him, twisting her cup in her hands. Some of the wine spilled into her lap, but she made no effort to wipe it away. Instead she picked up her spoon and hit her saucer with a loud clink, catching the attention of all.

"Excuse me, Officer Hollberg," she said, her gray eyes narrowing as she turned her head to look at him. "I'm sorry to interrupt, but do you by any chance know my brother, Egon von Eberhardt?"

Manya's eyes darted to Lillian and then back to her mother.

The officer thought for a long moment.

"Madam, I—well—yes, I do. He was enlisted in a regiment that was under the command of a friend of mine." He cleared his throat nervously. "I'm so sorry to tell you, but everyone in his regiment was killed in combat near Königsberg. I only recognized his last name on the casualty list because it was the same as Hetta's."

The baroness shifted in her seat. Her vocal cords quivered. "*Fritzchen,*" she murmured to the baron. "We're going home now, of course. I must bury Egon and plant the forget-me-nots on his grave. As I do for all the other headstones in the forest." She patted his fingers and sighed. "I can see it all before my eyes."

"What do you see, Liebchen?" whispered the baron.

"Guja. Our house on the hill. The wild rosebushes along the path leading to the lake." She began to pluck at her eyebrows, pulling them away from the bone underneath. "You'll take me now, Fritzchen, won't you?"

"Father?" Manya whispered, alarmed.

The baron's face sagged. Tears spilled down his cheeks and onto his green hunting jacket. He would not meet Manya's eyes.

Dazed, she watched him gently take her mother's hands in his own.

"Manya, dearest," he said. "We can't go any farther."

"You can—" The words froze on her tongue.

The baron nodded.

"You won't survive," she cried.

"I'm sorry," he said. His voice had gone flat.

"Then I'm going back with you and mother."

The baron looked to Lillian.

"You must come with us, Manya," Lillian said gently.

Helling was checking Topsie's horseshoes when Manya entered the stable.

"All the clenches are in place now," he said when he noticed her standing behind the stall door. "A few were sticking out of Topsie's left front hoof, but I tapped them back in."

"Thank you, Herr Helling," she murmured. "I'll stay with the horses tonight. You go and get something to eat."

"Have you been crying?" he asked, straightening up.

"Mother and Father are going back to Guja." Her eyes filled up again.

He took off his cap and nodded, touching her shoulder gently when she passed by to enter Aztec's and Shambhala's stall. The horses stood side by side chewing on mouthfuls of hay. She placed her hands on the low hang of Shambhala's pregnant belly. A small movement against her palm made her heart jump with relief. She had seen too many mares miscarry on the trek, their full-grown foals falling dead to the ground.

"Not this foal," she prayed, pressing her cheek against Shambhala's warm neck.

"Miss von Falken, are you in here?"

Startled, she saw Officer Hollberg gazing at her over the stall door.

"May I speak to you?" he said. "I'm so sorry about what happened in the kitchen. If I had known, I would have withheld the information."

"It's not your fault," Manya reassured him. She rose and laid her hands on top of the stall door. "Mother hasn't been well for a long time."

Officer Hollberg leaned forward to pick a piece of straw from her hair. Manya drew back.

"Forgive me. It's just that—you're beautiful," he said quickly, color rushing to his cheeks. "I know I shouldn't be saying these things, but in times like these, honesty comes easy." He gave a nervous cough.

"I'm driving a lorry to Danzig tomorrow. I could take you with me. The others, too. Blacksmith Helling and his daughter, and Madam Lillian."

"I don't want to seem ungrateful," Manya said. She chose her words carefully. "Your offer is so generous, but I can't leave my horses." She turned to pet Aztec's ear. "They're Trakehners. They're doing everything they can to save us. I must do the same for them. I must get them to the West."

"But even if you get to Danzig, there's not a ship that will take them," he countered. "The Soviets will invade from the west as well."

"I have to find a way." With shock, she realized that she sounded just like her mother. She took a deep breath and held her head up. "Thank you, though."

Catching her hand, he pressed his lips to it. When he looked up, his blue eyes were bright with hope.

"If I survive this war, would there be a chance for someone like me?"

Turning her head away, she let her mind fill with the memory of Joshi.

"Forgive me yet again," the officer apologized, his tone growing cold. "For being so forward. Perhaps I am not someone you'd even consider?"

"It's not that at all," she whispered. "You are so kind. I'm sorry. It's just that—Sir, I wondered if you would be kind enough to tell me. Do you know about a camp called Stutthof?"

"Stutthof? Do you know someone there?" She saw him swallow in surprise. "That camp was evacuated a few days ago."

A surge of hope rippled through her. "Can you tell me anything else? Someone I know, a dear friend, might have been sent there."

"The army is not usually informed about these kinds of things," he said. "However, I passed several prisoner columns on the road."

She sensed that he was protecting her from what he'd seen.

His thumb moved nervously across the back of her hand, and she could see that he was troubled.

"The prisoners are in a bad way. Barely clothed. Emaciated. Some columns are moving westward. One or two are headed up the coast towards Braunsberg and Palmnicken."

She stared at him, trying to pin down the possibility his words held.

"Braunsberg," she whispered. "That's where we're going." Suddenly, her face felt hot.

He gazed at her. "Please know that I will help you anyway I can," he said, touching her fingertips. "I wish the best for you and your beautiful horses."

Manya watched him leave, his shoulders slightly stooped. *You are a kind man*, she thought, and lay down on the straw next to Shambhala.

She fell asleep quickly, traveling through a dream in which she saw Vavara walking in the snow dressed in a red cape. Joshi was following her, and he stopped near a poplar to gather something in his hand. When Manya drew closer, she saw that he was holding a snowy owl.

"Joshi, look away!" she shouted.

But before he could turn from the bird, it drew back, ready to peck his face.

She awoke to find herself holding on to Shambhala's tail, the long horsehairs twisted around the stones in her ring. She untangled the knots, and when her hand was free, she studied the amber cabochon. It glowed like red gold in the darkness. *Like a beating heart*, she thought.

⁂

After breakfast, Helling saddled Aztec and hitched the mares to the wagon.

Manya ran her hand along the buttons of her mother's coat, feeling a childish urge to lay her head against her mother's chest. Despite her mother's madness, her mother had loved her. And taught her so many things. "Mami," she whispered. "What a beautiful word. Thank you, Mami, for teaching me to see through your eyes, for showing me that all people are equal."

"I taught you your first bedtime prayer, too," her mother said with a playful smile. "And, I showed you where the first white lilacs bloomed in spring."

"Yes, Mami," Manya murmured sweetly. "You showed me where God lives in nature, and you did so much more. You know something? I've only ever called you Mother, and I love calling you Mami. Is that all right?"

"Yes," her mother said, smiling brightly.

The baron moved close to his wife and placed a reassuring arm around her shoulders, his curved hand white as porcelain. He looked so tall, so lonely.

"Papa, are you sure you can bear the weight of this?" Manya asked. "You can still come with us."

The baron lowered his eyes.

I must be strong, Manya thought. She removed from her pocket the pillbox containing the cyanide and slipped it into his hand, silently begging

God to pardon her. "If it becomes too much," she whispered, "take these. I couldn't bear to learn that either of you suffered."

He held her in his arms and she breathed in the familiar scent of bergamot, tobacco, and oak. "Whatever the future brings, your mother and I shall be buried in Guja," he sighed.

A sob rose from her belly, and her father whispered a line from their beloved "*Ostpreussianlied*": "Over your endless fields of light, the dawn breaks."

Aztec whinnied impatiently. The baron let her go. "Auf Wiedersehen, my angel," he said. "May the Lord guide and protect you."

THIRTY-TWO

*U*rsula moved toward the drawing room, her plump hands gripping the handles of her serving tray.

"Whatever you do," she mumbled to herself, "don't spill the coffee."

But she couldn't control the waves of fear whipping through her. When a few drops of coffee spilled out of the antique Meissen coffee pot and soiled the white doily, she froze, unsure of whether to return to the kitchen and wipe the tray or carry on. Wherever she went now, one of the Russians occupying the house might see her.

They had broken in that morning while she was still asleep on the narrow cot in the kitchen, the one she'd slept on ever since the von Falkens left. She thought she'd dreamed the splintering noise at the front door, the breaking of the windows in the hallway, but then she'd heard their voices, so loud and acutely foreign. Throwing off the warm eiderdown, she'd hidden in the broom closet. But one of them had found her. When he opened the closet door and yanked the mop out of her sweaty hands, she had screamed in terror. Speaking in Russian, he had motioned for her to come out.

She had screamed again, but when she noticed that his eyes were kind, she stopped.

She tried to explain that she was the cook and the caretaker of the estate, but two more soldiers had crashed through the kitchen door and tried to push her onto the cot. The merciful Russian had drawn his revolver and ordered them to stop.

"Why didn't I flee with you?" she whispered, glancing at the beautifully framed portraits hanging on the walls, faces of people she loved and trusted. She bit her lip to stop from crying.

But she knew the answer, and it was bitter. She had been stubborn.

She gripped the handles of the tray more tightly, summoning her courage. The squat Russian with the thick eyebrows had shouted for coffee before vanishing into the drawing room. He was the same one who had shot Schwitkowski. She'd seen the murder from the kitchen window earlier that afternoon. It had been swift. No talking, no shouting, just one bullet and a streak of blood as her beloved friend's gray head slid down the white stable wall.

She looked at the ceiling. If she were friendly and useful, if she cooked and cleaned for them, perhaps they wouldn't harm her.

"Oh Lord, don't forsake me," she begged.

Golitsin was alone in the drawing room. He had asked Afanasiv to take the other four men out of the room before they could touch anything. Eager to find a wine cellar, they had gone down the basement stairs, returning an hour later with champagne bottles and singing bawdy songs. Thankfully, they were napping now in the bedrooms upstairs.

He returned his attention to the drawing room. Fascinated by the simple elegance of the room and the objects it contained, he decided to do some snooping of his own.

An antique armoire caught his eye. It was dated 1729 and inlaid with swirling silver flowers. Turning a silk-tasseled key, he opened it. On the shelf inside, he found a mahogany box containing some of the finest German knives he had ever set eyes on. He lifted the lid and fingered the blades. Knives like these were every Russian soldier's dream, so sharp they could be used as shaving razors. One of the handles was made of polished buffalo horn and engraved with the name *von Falken*. He felt his stomach clench. Was this the knife that had sliced through his tendons and his military aspirations? He picked it up, feeling the weight of it. Then he slipped it into its leather sheath and tucked it under his belt.

A Steinway baby grand piano stood in the middle of the room. He walked over to it and banged the ivory keys, finding the discordant sounds strangely arousing. He remembered the girl's lily-white breasts, the pubic mound he had cupped in his hand. *I would have fucked her here*, he thought, feeling himself grow hard.

He moved on to the rosewood desk near the window and pulled out the drawers, filled with neat stacks of ledgers and documents. A few stray coins had been tossed into an old inkwell. Nothing of value. A walnut-stained birdcage, large enough for two parrots, stood near the terrace door. Stepping closer, he saw two blue and a white parakeets sitting on the perch. His presence sent them fluttering.

A clear cawing noise startled him. At the window, a bold and shiny raven pecked at the glass.

"Are you tame?" he asked, touching his fingers to the glass and whistling a little.

The bird tilted its head sideways to stare at him with fierce ebony eyes. Something in its decisive gaze made Golitsin feel apprehensive, almost sick inside. It looked straight through him, as if it knew the secret about his terrible judgment in Nemmersdorf. Had this same bird been watching from a tree in that village? Had it witnessed his incompetence?

Golitsin pushed his palms against his forehead to try and stem the obsessive thoughts. But he couldn't. He would always feel like a failure. In the honest kernel of his soul, he knew that the girl had outsmarted him and that the Trakehner stallion had acted more like a soldier than he had.

He'd replayed the scene over and over in his mind, but it always ended the same way. He'd been mesmerized, paralyzed by the sudden sight of the horse. And like a soldier who knew his opponent's weakness, the stallion had gotten the better of him.

Turning away from the raven's accusing stare, he strode across the room to the wall of leather-bound books, where a decanter full of port wine stood on the shelf. He wasn't actually on duty. He could have a drink before Commander Koslov and the battalion arrived.

He poured a glassful and sat down on a soft chair. The wooden armrests, carved in the shape of swans, felt cool to his touch. Oh, how he wished his babushka could be here to enjoy these luxuries. The smell of fermented grapes transported him back to her small flat in Leningrad. She had been ill with influenza and he had been caring for her. He remembered sitting in her kitchen, drinking a glass of homemade wine and listening to Joseph Stalin speak to the nation. The great man was urging younger men like himself to sign up for the People's Militia. Excited, he had rushed to her bedside and told her about his hope to join the air force or the army and become someone of whom she would be proud.

She'd listened to him quietly, her face white as moonstones, before reaching up with her bony fingers and drawing his face close to hers.

"Yuri," she wheezed, her breath sour as death. "Something is worrying me." Her voice had cracked. "I—"

He remembered his impatience at having to wait for her faded eyes to wander to the cheap orthodox icon in the corner shrine, an icon that no longer held sway in Stalin's Republic. She'd coughed, and a fleck of spittle had landed on his cheek.

"Horses," she whispered. "You must be careful around horses. They gallop alongside your reaper of death."

"Don't worry, Babushka, there's not a horse I can't handle." He patted her hand. "Now rest."

She'd tried to tell him something else, but he couldn't make sense of it. The next day she was dead.

She hadn't been far off the mark, though. The girl's stallion *had* nearly killed him. He twisted his glass in his hands and stared at the parakeets.

"Well," he muttered, as if the birds could understand, "I survived her prophecy, didn't I? Horses have no power over me anymore."

He took a sip of port, the alcohol warm on his tongue. Shaking doubt from his mind, he watched the afternoon shadows lengthen on the ceiling. When the room filled with twilight, he unbuttoned his breast pocket and pulled out the wallet and watch he had taken off the man he'd shot that afternoon. Why should the other soldiers get the goods when he'd done the work? The watch wasn't fancy but it ticked, and although the wallet smelled of horseshit, it contained a bit of German currency. He riffled through it and fished out a folded piece of paper.

He almost threw it on the floor, but then a bold loop of writing caught his eye. Curious, he smoothed the paper out across his thigh. By God, it belonged to the girl! He recognized her writing from the captions in the photo album on her nightstand. It had a strong vertical slant. His stomach began to burn.

At first it wasn't clear what she had written. But, slowly, he deciphered the scribbled names of towns and villages. Obviously the girl had left a copy for the old man, outlining her route to safety. He smiled bitterly, realizing with a sudden start that his luck regarding the girl might have changed.

The floorboards creaked under Ursula's feet. She whimpered before open-ing the drawing room door. *Only one Russian*, she thought when she saw Golitsin. The scary one, the one who had shot Schwitkowski.

"Coffee, sir," she said, resting the tray on an antique side table.

He took no notice of her. Instead, he rose and went to the birdcage, popping open the latch and ducking as the frightened birds whirled through the room.

"Stop!" Ursula cried when he pulled open the terrace door. A rush of cold air shocked her into action. "Those birds belong to the baroness!"

Flapping her arms into the air, she tried to catch the parakeets, but her movements only frightened them more.

"The soldiers will eat them when they get here, you silly woman," the Russian laughed in his crude, guttural German. "And you'll be the one boiling them in the soup. Better they're free."

Ursula began to cry, but her tears irritated the man. He opened the drawing room doors and shooed the birds out.

She grabbed his shoulder, but he spun around and slapped her. "You worthless German cunt," he snarled, and pulled her onto the terrace, slamming the doors behind him. She saw the baroness's parakeets whirling far above the hawthorn tree.

"Barbarian!" She broke free and ran down the path that led to the lake. Another pair of hands pushed her to the ground. Desperate, she sought the face of the Russian who had rescued her in the kitchen. But now it seemed as if hundreds of faces were leering at her, and his was not among them. She rose to her knees. So many boots. All of them muddy.

"Oh, Christ have mercy," she breathed. And fainted.

She woke to find a stranger was smothering her. He smelled of stale cigarettes and sweat. Around her there was laughter. In her womb was a hard, ruthless pumping. When the stranger stopped, another took his place. Her back ached against the wet ground, but in the sky, she saw a figure hovering in the air. *Why, that's me*, she thought.

She drifted toward the figure and floated above her beloved village of Guja, over shingled roofs and snow-covered gardens. Higher, until the pain in her womb ceased and her cries for help faded into a sigh.

Golitsin and Afanasiv were talking when Commander Koslov entered the drawing room. They rose to salute him.

"Good work, boys!" he said, nodding with approval. "Your information got us through this first maneuver unscathed. There were no casualties. Some of the other battalions have not been so lucky. There are still German units holding their own, and although they're tired, they fight like dogs."

Koslov's eyes lingered on the gold plaques and silver candlestick holders. "These people certainly lived in style, eh? But don't get too used to it. We're only here for a short time until reinforcements come through Goldap and Raudischken. Once they arrive, we're moving on."

He poured himself a cup of cold coffee and tipped the sugar from the sugar bowl into his mouth. "God almighty, that tastes good! We sure miss sweet things in the field, eh?" He belched and licked his lips. "I've told the men they can take what they like, women included. They found one poor bitch running toward the lake."

Afanasiv cleared his throat. He had seen the cook's dead body when he'd come up from the lake that afternoon. The sight had sickened him. "Sir," he said, "these crimes against German women are heinous. They must stop."

"Ah, come on man. Let it go," said Koslov. "Frankly, it isn't something I choose to participate in either, but our soldiers have been marching for months through a terrain of blood and guts. Let them have a little fun. They deserve it."

"Enough to rape a woman to death?" Afanasiv asked.

Koslov shrugged, but Afanasiv did not give up. "Sir," he said. "This kind of violence is out of control. All of us will be labeled rapists, whether we engage in the deed or not."

Koslov took another sip of coffee.

"Afanasiv, you think too much. Let's win the war first and worry about labels later, eh? Now, to more important matters. I have another mission for you two." He pulled a map from his overcoat and spread it out on the rosewood desk beside him. "It's not a tea party, but as you well know, reconnaissance is everything."

Golitsin stepped forward eagerly.

"Where are you sending us, Commander?"

"Into the Wolf's Lair. Well, not quite, but close to it. You'll set off as soon as I know exactly where our main troops are positioned." He trailed his index finger down the map, stopping at a village named Görlitz, some twenty miles south of Guja.

"What's the Wolf's Lair?" Golitsin asked.

"Hitler's headquarters. It lies camouflaged in the forest. Our sources tell us that trees are growing on the roofs of the buildings. Your mission is to find out everything you can about the surrounding area—access roads, airfields, and so forth. Don't try to enter, whatever you do. You'd be blown to smithereens by mines and guards."

Golitsin's heart raced and he felt light-headed with anticipation. Suppose he managed to capture Hitler?

THIRTY-THREE

"I think we did it," Joshi whispered, lifting his head up against the thick layer of straw that covered him and Leonid.

They had been hiding in the cold barn all night, hardly daring to breathe, but now, after an hour of silence, Joshi was almost certain the guards were gone.

"They didn't count one prisoner this morning," Leonid murmured. "Too scared of the enemy to spend the time."

Joshi began to dig his way through the pile of straw, squinting into the barn when he reached the edge. His body was porous to every sound, but there was none.

"We're safe, for the moment."

"Mother of God, it's cold," said Leonid, crawling up beside him. "My blood has turned to ice. And my stomach. It growled so much in the night, I thought for sure the guards would hear. All I could think of was that final *bang bang bang* of bullets."

"Yeah, we were lucky," Joshi agreed, spitting out a piece of straw. His lips were so numb he could hardly feel them.

Crawling forward, they moved to a corner in the barn where several bales of hay formed an alcove. When they had settled themselves, Leonid asked, "What gave *you* the nerve to escape? I feel like I just followed along!"

"I kept hearing Ben's voice. 'Escape. Escape.'" He shivered, his smile fading to a sad line. "You know, I think Ben chose to die because he knew as long as he was alive, we would never run without him."

"What should we do now?" asked Leonid. "We've got to keep moving, but where to? We don't even know where we are."

A sudden meow startled them, and a calico cat jumped down from a rafter. Purring, she began to wind her warm body around their ankles.

"We have to wait for darkness," Joshi said, leaning over to stroke the cat's head.

He closed his eyes to try to think, but in the absence of the groans and coughs he'd grown used to, his thoughts had too much space. What arose in him now was almost more frightening than the guns and guards. He shuddered, hunger biting at his stomach. Was he going to die in this empty barn? Freeze to death like a pile of cow dung on the floor? His bad ear hurt, too.

"What's the matter?" Leonid asked softly. The cat had settled on his lap, and he was scratching its ears.

"Silence," Joshi said. "It makes me think about things." He took a breath. "When I was a boy, my Aunt Vadoma, who was a seer, used to tell me that I'd face death before my time. She said I would be given the choice to live like a gadjo or die like a Romani. She swore that I would betray myself whatever I chose. She was right."

Leonid's glance was kind, but probing.

"Why do you say that?"

Joshi felt as if something inside him were coming undone, something big that he couldn't contain. He told Leonid about his life, about his choice to leave the clan and study medicine, about Manya being a gadji and the rift their friendship had caused between him and his father.

"I always broke the rules because I liked the gadje life." He swallowed. "But that's not the worst of it. I've done other things that would have had me banished from my clan forever."

"Like what?" asked Leonid.

"Like playing the violin in Stutthof."

"Don't be stupid. You had no choice."

"Yes, I did. No decent Romani would play music and look on while one of his brothers or sisters was led to the gallows. They'd die with them." He took another breath. "And all those nights when I went to the warden's flat. Do you know what I was doing?"

Leonid shook his head.

"I was playing the violin there too. And fucking."

"What?" Leonid exclaimed, his eyebrows shooting up in surprise.

"You remember the pretty prisoner, Gesa?"

"The girl who worked in the laundry? The artist?"

Joshi nodded. "Every night we were at the warden's house, Gesa painted portraits and I played the violin, and the warden made us fuck on the floor, right in front of her." He picked up a piece of straw and began to twist it between his fingers.

"The worst of it is, it felt good. What a bargain I struck. Sex for food. Sex for Sofia's life. Sex for my life, Gesa's life, her baby's life. I sold my goddamn soul for a cup of coffee and some ham and bread. I tell you, there isn't another Romani alive who would do that."

Leonid rubbed the knuckles of one hand across his brow, as if he were scanning his brain for something to say.

"Maybe it's different than you think," he said. "Maybe your father taught you how to be tough enough to survive Stutthof." He paused to chew on his lip. "Maybe fate led you to the warden for a reason. You're alive, aren't you? And maybe Sofia is, too, because of it."

Joshi smiled. When Leonid spoke, his accent often landed on the wrong syllable, which had the odd effect of giving more weight to his thoughts.

"And you're here with me, a gadjo," Leonid said. "So what? Maybe you're just an ordinary man. Who's to say what an ordinary man will do when he's starving or when he has a gun to his head. You judge yourself for some Romani rules you think you've broken. Well, sometimes you have to rewrite the rules, because none of them works anymore."

The cat stirred in Leonid's lap, and he blew on its fur before looking back at Joshi. "You have a destiny, my friend, if only for the next breath you take. To hell with the warden and the things she made you do. You're here now, aren't you? You can still dream about your gadji girl."

Joshi sat very still, turning Leonid's words over in his mind.

THIRTY-FOUR

Lillian's anger grew as she watched Manya ride through the columns of refugees like a warrior headed into battle, her long torso jutting sharply forward over Aztec's arched neck, her hair sticking out from beneath her fur cap in spiky tufts.

"She's possessed," Lillian murmured, her teeth chattering in the cold.

"All God, all devil," said Helling, pulling his cap down over his ears.

"Well, the devil side of her frightens me. I can't even talk to her anymore. And I felt we had grown so close."

"I try to remind myself that she just left her parents behind," Helling said. "But she's very ill-tempered."

"There's a meanness in the way she rides now," said Lillian, "as though she has no tolerance for anything, Aztec included. She's kicking more than she should. She's rough on his mouth, too, and I don't like it."

She had noticed the change in Manya shortly after leaving Klein Stegen. The girl had become tempestuous. This morning was no better. Impatient to move on, she had slashed at the mounting snowdrifts with her riding crop as if she could make them disappear.

"To hell with you," Lillian heard Manya shout when a cavalcade of military lorries forced her and Aztec off the road. "It's every man for himself now, right?" She spat at the ground. "Damn renegades leaving us here to fend for ourselves now that the war is lost."

Lillian was so intimidated by Manya that she dared not suggest a rest. She didn't want to be the object of Manya's fury. Finally, Helling called for a break.

"We've got to stop!" he yelled over the wind. "There's a village just off to the right."

"No," cried Manya. "I want to get to Braunsberg!"

Helling didn't have the strength or the inclination to engage in a shouting match.

"*You* may want to get to Braunsberg," he said, pulling up beside her, "but in case you haven't noticed, Topsie's limping. So, I'm telling you, we *are* stopping!"

Tugging at the slippery reins, he turned the wagon onto a side road that curved past a frozen pond and toward several cottages. However, when he went inside one of them to see if they could stay, he found the room packed. Refugees nursing black, frostbitten fingers sat crammed together on broken crates, while soldiers with missing limbs tore at their soiled bandages. *Volkssturm* fighters, nothing more than toothless old men drafted for the home-front army, lay on the slime-covered floors, rifles slung across their chests, eyes dull with resignation. Outside, the walls were splattered with mud, blood, and feces.

"We can't stay here," muttered Helling, hoisting himself back into the driver's seat. "We've got to carry on to Rödersdorf. I know a farmer there named Liedtke." Snow was whirling down in thick flakes, and the cold wind stung his bloodshot eyes and made his nose run.

"It's another four miles," he added, pulling out his handkerchief. "I'm sorry, Topsie, old girl. We should have stopped hours ago." He shot Manya a sour look. "Maybe you'll be a bit kinder when we're closer to Braunsberg. Eh?"

Manya did not reply. Without another word, Helling urged the horses on, while Lillian sat beside him, holding his silent daughter.

Everywhere Helling looked, he saw death. Charred wagons lay by the road, the passengers inside burned nearly to a cinder. To his right, on a sloping hill, two barefoot toddlers were crying for their mother, their spindly legs stumbling over a horse carcass that had stiffened in the snow. One whiskered grandfather, fearful of losing a little girl, had wrapped a rope around her waist and was dragging her behind him. Helling shuddered. He took one hand off the reins, thinking he should cover Zarah's eyes, but when he looked, her face was already hidden in Lillian's scarf.

⁂

The Liedtke farm lay in a wooded area just outside Rödersdorf. Farmer

Liedtke was a lean man with a curiously high tinge to his voice, but he was kind enough. He welcomed Helling with a handshake and the women with a shy smile, inviting them all to spend the night on the kitchen floor near the white enamel stove. Manya insisted on guarding the horses; Helling, whose tired knees were about to give way, did not refuse her offer.

Manya has her shotgun, he thought. *No one's going to pull a fast one on us here. Maybe she'll be in a better mood tomorrow if she has some solitude tonight.* Hoping he could talk with her in private, he said, "Let's tend to the horses, child, while Lillian and Zarah go inside."

She nodded curtly. When they were by themselves in the yard, he paused to watch her chock the wagon tires with some bricks she'd found in a pile beside the barn wall. It pained him to see her bent over, her lips blue and grim, the snow melting like teardrops on either side of her nose.

It's hard, he thought to himself, wishing he could comfort her. *Damn hard. I know, believe me. And though you're not the most agreeable, you're one brave girl.*

In the barn, he watched her hang up the harnesses and oil the leather with saddle soap while he poured oats into the feed buckets.

"Topsie's refusing her feed," he said, trying not to sound worried. "The trek may be too much for her. Trakehners don't often get hoof disease, but the old girl's been marching through slush for days. Haven't you, my sweet?" Taking a pick from his tool bag, he stooped to clean out Topsie's front left hoof. Manya came into the stall and started toweling Shambhala dry. In all their years together, Helling had never seen her so silent, so sulky. Unsure of what to do, he decided to keep on chatting, hoping that sooner or later she'd engage. Just one word would break the ice. "I removed Topsie's horseshoes two nights ago because I thought she'd be better off in the snow without them," he said. "What do you think?"

She shrugged.

He probed Topsie's fetlock. "Ah, girl," he murmured softly. "Now I see what's troubling you. Your tendon is inflamed. Let me see what I can do." Taking a jar from his box, he unscrewed the top and scooped out a gob of menthol-scented liniment. After rubbing it into the mare's joint, he rolled up his overalls and massaged some into his knees. "I don't think Topsie can get back on the road tomorrow," he said, straightening up slowly.

Manya, who had been standing with her back to him, whirled around.

"That's not an option," she barked, her tone harsh and blistering. "She *has* to."

Helling's eyebrows shot up in mute surprise. Ordinarily, he would have barked back and told her straight out that she was being impossible, but something in her eyes stopped him. Was it panic? He wasn't quite sure, but he'd never seen that in her before. *There's more to this*, he thought. *This is not just about her parents.*

His heart softened, but he kept his tone stern.

"We are all doing the best we can. The horses most of all. They are sacrificing body and soul to pull us through. So, you must understand. If Topsie is still limping tomorrow, we won't be going on."

She hardly seemed to hear him. He saw her mouth harden. Her eyes had turned distant and brooding again.

"We all need to rest," he continued. "You too, Manya."

"How can I rest?" she cried, snapping the towel she was holding like a whip in the air. "Rest may be good for you, but it's torture for me. I won't wait! We must leave for Braunsberg tomorrow."

Helling shook his head. "I don't understand you right now. You more than anyone should recognize the courage and heart these horses have shown. My God, they're risking their lives for us, girl."

He let out a frustrated sigh. Lately, talking was such a strain. Since the Nemmersdorf massacre he'd felt constantly cold, numb. Even the heat of a stove could not warm him. Every time he looked at Zarah, he wanted to creep away, to any place where he might forget.

He wished he could be silent and angry too. But he couldn't allow Manya to place Lillian, Zarah, and the horses at risk.

In the last day or two, he'd watched her yank at Aztec's reins. That, more than anything, shook him to the core. It wasn't like her to be tough on Aztec. For one terrifying moment he even wondered if she was cracking under the strain like her mother. No! That couldn't happen. Or could it?

He wiped his hand on his pant leg and ran it through his damp hair, the lingering smell of menthol catching in his nostrils. No. Something else was at work in her. Something complicated. Something she couldn't talk about.

He thought about Joshi. She hadn't spoken Joshi's name since she'd found out about the massacre of the Karas clan. Even then, he had known from the look on her face that she would not accept Joshi's death. And that he understood. She had told him that she was sure she'd seen Sofia in Angerburg, in a lorry headed to Stutthof.

It was far-fetched, but Stutthof was on their route. Was that why she was pushing to get there? He wouldn't put it past her. He shook his head.

They'd never get into that prison to save Sofia. He looked at the slope of Manya's slender shoulders, the towel dangling limply in her hand, and his eyes welled up with sympathy.

"Is there something you want to tell me?" he asked gently.

She looked at him, her eyes opening wide for a second. All at once, two dark parallel streaks ran down her cheeks, giving her away. He felt something sharp move under his heart. He was right. It was all too much for her. He opened his mouth to ask again, but she turned away and thrust her hands deep into her pockets.

"I'm tired, Manya," he said with a sigh. "My bones ache. I'm going inside to eat with Lillian and Zarah. I'll stay with the horses if you decide you want a break. Otherwise, I'll make sure you get some hot tea and supper."

Manya watched Helling hobble out of the barn. When the crunch of his boots on the snow had faded, she went into Aztec's stall and buried her face in his mane. Arching his neck, Aztec peered at her, his eyes inquisitive, his neigh friendly and forgiving.

She inhaled the earthy scent of his coat, still damp with sweat and snow. Taking off her gloves, she stared at her hands, ashamed at the hardness they had shown him over the past few days. How could she have yanked at his mouth when he was so constant, so unwavering in his struggle to get her through? How could he not hold a grudge after she had kicked the softest part of his flanks?

She closed her eyes, and as she listened to the soft flutter of his breath, she was overcome by a familiar feeling of dread, one that had often gripped her since her conversation with Officer Hollberg in the barn in Klein Stegen.

Initially, when he had told her about the prisoners marching up the coast toward Braunsberg, she'd been hopeful. But riding along roads paved with corpses, she began to see her optimism for what it was—fantasy. How could she have been so naive as to think she might find Joshi with his sister? How could Sofia even be alive, let alone with her brother? Why would God choose them above the many thousands who were lost? She knew it was wrong to push the horses past their breaking point when the odds were so small. Helling, Lillian, and Zarah were exhausted too. All the same, she couldn't stop herself. If only she'd confided in Helling, as she always did. But she was afraid even to speak Joshi's name.

She let her hand slide down Aztec's muzzle. Her muscles were so tired of holding up and holding on. Aztec sniffed at her palm, his tongue softly licking her skin as if he wanted to soothe her. Tears gathered behind her eyelids. Ach, how she hated those tears. They made her weak when she needed strength, mean when she needed comfort. *Pull yourself together*, she told herself. She recognized her mother's words, and in spite of herself, she smiled a little. Like it or not, the baroness's tough sayings did hold merit at times.

She planted a soft kiss on Aztec's muzzle. Leaving his stall, she walked out to the wagon to gather the things she needed for the night.

Half an hour later, she settled onto a bed of straw in the corner of Shambhala's and Topsie's stall. Wrapped in her mother's green mohair blanket, she hungrily ate the corned beef that Lillian had brought her from the kitchen. Dawn found her dozing against the wall. Somewhere at the dull edge of consciousness, she heard the jangle of a bridle being lifted off a hook. A lamp flickered in the barn. She opened her eyes.

Why was Shambhala whinnying? And Aztec? Stumbling to her feet, she grabbed her gun and left the stall. Aztec was in the corridor with his ears flat against his head, his teeth bared. A soldier, dressed in a uniform and three-quarter-length jackboots, was yanking at Aztec's curb chain to keep him from rearing.

"What are you doing?" Manya cried. "Let go of that horse immediately!"

"I have orders, Miss," the man growled. "We need horses. Especially Trakehners, for the cavalry. He can pull a canon where no vehicle can. I spotted him yesterday when you arrived, and I'm requisitioning him for the German army. You will get your payment later."

"Requisitioning?" shouted Manya. "That's nonsense. You're stealing him!"

"Too bad, Miss." The soldier's face was stubborn. "We're at war. The army has the right to take what it needs."

Manya's mind went numb. She opened her mouth to plead and felt blood beating against her skull. Lifting her gun, she aimed the barrel at the crease right between the man's eyes.

"Let him go, or you won't see daylight."

Her voice exuded danger, and the soldier, seeing that she was more than he had bargained for, blinked in surprise. Her finger curled around the trigger and she took a wider stance, preparing to shoot.

"Put the gun down there, sweetie," the soldier said, holding up his arms and addressing her as if she were a child.

For a split second, Manya hesitated. A resounding thud exploded through the barn, and the soldier fell to the ground, Aztec's reins slipping from his hand. Manya stared at the crumpled figure, shock spreading through her limbs as she lowered her gun. Had she shot him? She saw no blood. From what seemed like far, far away, she heard a voice saying, "God in heaven, I hope he's not dead."

Manya began to tremble. She blinked, trying to make her eyes focus. Helling stepped from the shadows just behind the soldier, holding a muck shovel in both hands. He was scowling.

"I couldn't sleep worrying about you. I sat on a chair in that damn kitchen keeping watch by the window, afraid you might do something stupid like ride off on your own, and when I saw this soldier sneak in here, I knew he was up to no good. So I followed him, grabbed this shovel, and I—"

Eyeing Manya's gun, he reached for Aztec's reins. "You weren't going to shoot him, were you?"

Manya stared at him, her heart stalling. "I think so."

Helling laid the shovel down and bent over to check the soldier's pulse.

"He's alive, but if his companions get wind of this they'll string us all up on the next tree." He glanced at her. "Stop staring at me as if you've lost your wits. Help me drag him into a stall."

Gathering herself, Manya lifted the soldier's feet while Helling grabbed his shoulders. When they'd covered the man with straw, Helling touched her elbow. "Get the horses ready," he said. "I'll wake Lillian and Zarah. We're leaving."

"What about Topsie?" Manya asked.

"Well, she hasn't got a choice, has she? We're dead if we stay here." He glowered at her. "We all needed rest, but you've got your wish now."

THIRTY-FIVE

Snow continued to fall as Joshi and Leonid made their way to Braunsberg. Although the journey was tiresome and tedious, they were grateful for the protection the snow offered against passing German militia. Two nights earlier, after their escape, they had broken into the barn's storage room and had found potatoes, which they had eaten, and bikes, which they had taken. Joshi's bike was too small, but it was far better than walking.

"What a funny sight you are," laughed Leonid when he first saw Joshi on the bicycle. "Don't knock out your teeth with your kneecaps."

Joshi grinned. "Stop making fun of me, dwarf. You can barely reach the pedals."

The laughter felt good, but it lasted only a short time before they were confronted with hundreds of sad-eyed civilians on the run. Abandoned prams stood in the snow, the faces of the dead babies inside covered with nothing but handkerchiefs. However small and shallow their graves might have been, the frozen ground would not have yielded to human hands.

At times the trail veered dangerously close to the front, and the noise of combat became a constant companion. Exploding bombs echoed around them, vibrating their teeth and ringing through their heads. Twice, explosions jettisoned them into ditches. Scrambling to their feet, they got back on the bikes.

"Just keep pedaling," Leonid would shout. "Maybe there'll be news of your girl in Braunsberg."

The following day, near dusk, they veered off into the forest, skirting encampments where soldiers stared into paltry fires. Threadbare and lethargic, the soldiers had somehow managed to defend a few pockets of

East Prussia, enabling thousands of civilians to flee toward the coast. But now, defeat gripped their shrunken faces.

"It's too risky here," Joshi whispered when they noticed an officer rallying a group of wounded men. "Come on, let's keep moving."

The pace was slow, and as they made their way along the crowded trail, Joshi heard other travelers talking. No one worried about spies anymore, and criticism was no longer whispered.

"This war had no purpose," grumbled a thin-faced man driving a small farm wagon.

"And we'll be branded as Nazis for it," his friend answered.

A woman wearing a black cloak and clutching a rosary leaned toward them from her wagon. "We women are already branded. And when we are all marked, you men won't be able to handle what happened to us." Her voice turned hollow and her dull eyes fell on Joshi. "Even young boys are being raped," she said softly, pressing her rosary to her lips and staring straight through him. "Oh God in heaven, my poor Johannes. Only fourteen. We tried to hide in the basement, but two Russians found us. Bad enough for a mother. But no son should have to share the same fate." She began to sob, and a woman wearing a red kerchief rose to sit beside her.

"All my life I heard God in the wind that blew across our lake," the woman told her. "I saw Him in the clouds." She began to cry too. "But God left us and now my home is gone, too, burned to the ground."

Enough, thought Joshi, pushing on. His head ached and his legs felt like they were on fire.

He passed thickets of willows shedding snow, and clusters of barren alders, and somehow the steady rotation of the bicycle's wheels soothed him, creating a musical note in his head. He began to sing aloud in Romani, ignoring the pain in his back and the soreness that had crept into his throat. He heard his mother's voice, too. *Mother, please be at peace*, he thought.

It was late afternoon when he and Leonid finally relaxed the pressure on their pedals.

"We must be close to Braunsberg," said Leonid, pointing to a church spire in the dwindling light.

"I was here as a boy with Manya and her father," Joshi said. His eyes searched the landscape until he saw an elegant gold Trakehner carved into a wooden sign.

"We're here," he said.

They turned down a side road, maneuvering through the slush. In the distance, they could hear guns and tanks along with the hiss of bombs. The air smelled heavily of smoke. A prickle of fear ran up his neck.

"Leonid?" he asked. "What if Manya never made it to the farm?"

THIRTY-SIX

Joshi and Leonid leaned their bikes against a tree in the courtyard of a large, gabled manor house.

I'm so tired, Joshi thought as he followed Leonid toward the front steps. His eyes fell on the heavy oak door through which he had once passed as a young boy with Manya, her father, and Blacksmith Helling. When he and Leonid reached the top step, he doubled over to catch his breath, rubbing his chapped fingers against his sore eyes. It hurt to breathe.

Noticing Joshi's distress, Leonid rapped the brass knocker against the door.

Joshi's gaze wandered down the courtyard path to a birch tree that stood among the poplars. He knew the tree well. He and Manya had picnicked in its shade during that spring visit. He remembered the sticky buns they had eaten and the impish way she'd pulled out her pocketknife, insisting they carve their initials into the tree's silvery bark.

That was over a decade ago.

Leonid knocked on the door again, harder this time. Suddenly the door swung open, creaking on its hinges.

Joshi straightened up and looked into the fearful face of Herr Thiele, the accountant. Once robust and spry, Herr Thiele now looked more like the thin wooden cane he carried.

Joshi cleared his throat. "Hello, sir," he said. "I'm—"

"Come in, come in," breathed Herr Thiele, stepping aside. Joshi nodded to Leonid and they shuffled into the house. The old man shut the door hastily. "The Russians will be here soon," he told them, stooping to peek through the keyhole. "Then it will all be over."

The marble floor, once polished to a fine gleam, was now matted with dirt. Cobwebs covered the ceiling. Joshi shivered in the draft that swept through the house.

"Sir," he said, speaking to the bald spot on the back of Herr Thiele's head. "We've met before. I came here once to buy a horse with—"

The man whipped around to face him.

"It's all so sad," he lamented angrily, not showing any sign of recognition. "Did you see? The stalls are empty. The horses, gone. All our color-coded mares, our gold medallion winners. Gone! They were like family to us."

Joshi shifted the weight on his feet, trying to stay focused. The pain behind his eyes was becoming unbearable.

"Only a few days ago," continued Herr Thiele, "in the middle of a blizzard, the administrator of this once beautiful estate, Dr. von Warburg, drove a hundred Trakehners through the village of Alt Passarge and over the Frisches Haff. I watched them leave in the snow," he said, licking his dry lips as he spoke. "Ach, I don't know if they made it. The army took all the horses that von Warburg left behind."

He shook his cane at the door. "And to think how often we begged *Gauleiter* Koch to let our Trakehners out before this happened. It's a sin. That man should burn in hell."

Joshi nodded. "Herr Thiele," he asked quietly, "did Baron von Falken's family stop here at any time during the last weeks?"

Herr Thiele tilted his head. "Baron von Falken," he repeated. "You mean the baron from Guja, eh? He bought a dappled mare for his daughter some years back."

"That's him," said Joshi. "Did they stop here?"

The old man shook his head from side to side as though he were counting the many comings and goings. "I've opened this door to many strangers and to many friends, but Baron von Falken was not among them," he finally said. "Nor his daughter."

Joshi felt as if he would faint.

Leonid moved closer.

"Are you all right?" he asked, patting Joshi on the back.

It was a kind gesture, but Joshi shrugged Leonid away. Straightening his shoulders, he looked at the old accountant. Maybe the man was not of sound mind.

No, thought Joshi. *I was hoping for the wrong thing.*

Herr Thiele glanced at Leonid, noticing him for the first time. "I was just making a hot toddy," he grunted. "You like pickled herring?"

Flustered, Leonid looked at Joshi and noticed that his face had become red and splotchy and his breath was coming hard. With concern he watched Joshi pull open the door and walk out into the fast-approaching darkness. He hesitated, wanting to follow him, but there were times when a man needed space. So, with a sigh, Leonid turned away and followed his host into the kitchen.

***

Joshi's temples throbbed as he walked along the courtyard path. Beads of sweat had gathered on his top lip, and he licked at them, his tongue dry as cotton.

He stopped beneath the birch tree, which stood like a lonely sentinel in the moonlight. His fingers searched the bark. Nothing. *Where are Manya's and my initials*, he wondered. *Where?*

"It was all so meaningless," he said to himself. "Worse than meaningless." Chills shot through his chest. Hugging himself, he let his legs give way and knelt in the snow, pressing his burning forehead into the soothing cold. Startled, an owl took flight, its shrill hoot sending sharp pains through his injured ear. "Get your ass up, Karas," he commanded himself. "Or you'll die here."

His body was on fire now. With a last bit of effort he made it to the stables, where he collapsed in the straw.

A thick sleep washed over him. Manya and Gesa and the warden flashed through his mind. Sometimes the warden's head appeared on Manya's beautiful naked body. At other times, she became Gesa, tearing at his eyes with her nails. He began to shake. Somewhere in the back of his mind, it dawned on him that he was sick. Now half awake, he vomited and wiped his mouth on his coat sleeve, the edge of a broken button scratching his lip.

For just a moment, he forced his eyes open and glimpsed at his arm. Dirty pink blotches spread across his skin like rotten mulberries. *Typhus*, he thought. It had hit him so fast.

THIRTY-SEVEN

"Miss von Falken," Herr Thiele said. "Please come in."

He ushered Manya, Helling, Lillian, and Zarah into the wood-paneled hallway, pressing his hand gently against Manya's back as she passed through the door. "And the baron and baroness, they are not with you?"

Manya felt tears fill her eyes and straightened her shoulders. "They're going back to Guja."

"Ach, I understand, child," he said, his breath coming in hoarse gasps. "Everything is falling to pieces, and your mother and father need to be on their land. Please, you must have something to eat and a good night's rest. Your parents would want that for you. Sleep wherever you find a bed."

Herr Thiele raised his watery eyes to look through the open door and into the courtyard. "No one is left here but me. They've fled across the Haff." He pointed his cane at Topsie and Shambhala. Their tired heads hung low to the ground. "But *you* mustn't do that, now. Your horses are exhausted. Besides, the ice is breaking up. That wagon will fall into the water."

Squinting into the gray chill, he gestured toward Aztec. "Now, that is an exquisite horse. Take him to the stallion's quarters. The mares will rest in the barn. Here in Braunsberg, we shall maintain horse etiquette until the end. There's plenty of space in the stable now. The army took our last horses weeks ago." His voice fell to a whisper. "I barely know day from night anymore. I heard from a factory worker who drove in from Palmnicken that the SS shot hundreds of prisoners on the beach there today. What has the world come to?"

Helling let out a deep sigh and looked to Manya.

"Come into the kitchen," said Herr Thiele. "You'll freeze to death in this hallway."

Quietly, Helling wrapped his arms around Lillian and Zarah. He turned to Manya. "Dear girl, if you have something to eat, perhaps you'll feel better."

She shook her head. "I want to take care of the horses,"

Her eyes welled up again. She opened the front door and ran down the steps to Aztec, her fingers fumbling to untie his reins.

After settling Shambhala and Topsie, Manya brought Aztec to the stallion's quarters. The stall doors were ajar and the air smelled of sour hay. From one of the stalls, she heard a rustling.

"Hello?" she whispered, her neck prickling with fear.

She reached for her gun. A man was in the second stall, stretched across the dirty straw. Nervous, she cocked her gun. If he tried to attack, she would shoot this time.

"Come forward, whoever you are. But I'm warning you, if you try to hurt me or steal my horse, I'll kill you."

The figure stirred. Aztec pricked his ears forward.

Stepping into the shadows, Manya inched toward the figure. As she moved, Aztec nickered.

She leveled her gun at the man's head. His shoulders were hunched as if they had been broken, his close-cropped skull wet with perspiration and dirt. The smell of vomit, urine, and excrement rose from his body, nearly choking her.

"Are you all right?" she asked, compassion replacing fear.

Feebly, the man turned his head. His smoky eyes were rimmed with broken veins. He tried to push himself to his knees.

"Joshi?" gasped Manya. She dropped down beside him. He was drooling, and little choking sounds were coming from his mouth. For a second she thought he recognized her, but when she set down the gun, the glint of it caught his eye, and he let his head fall back down on the straw.

"Kill me," he choked.

"Joshi! For God's sake, stop. Don't you know me?"

"I know you," he whispered. "But this time, you'd better kill me or I swear I'll kill you first."

He began to froth at the mouth.

She touched his hand. He was burning with fever, muttering names she didn't recognize. He called for Sofia, and his body grew agitated. His hands clawed at her face. "You bitch," he cried. "You stole my life."

"Please! Someone help!" screamed Manya. "Helling. Where are you?"

Cradling Joshi's head in her lap, she stroked his forehead, reeling in shock at the sight of him. Gaunt and decaying, his face was only a skull now. "What have they done to you?" she sobbed, wiping away the yeasty bile that had caked at the corners of his mouth.

His eyes flickered open, meeting her gaze with unexpected clarity. She felt her heart stop.

"Manya?" he asked, his voice barely a whisper. And then his lids closed.

She could hardly breathe as the shock settled into her bones. There was so little left of him. She pulled his withered body close, rocking him back and forth, and screamed out again for Helling.

***

Helling had taken his first sip of hot toddy when he thought he heard Manya calling his name. He looked at the thin little man at the other end of the table.

"I heard her, too," said Leonid, whom Helling, Lillian, and Zarah had met in Herr Thiele's kitchen. "I'll come with you."

They found Manya on the floor of a stall with an unconscious man in her arms.

"Joshi," Leonid gasped.

"Joshi?" Helling repeated, confused.

Manya looked up at Helling, tears streaking her pale cheeks. His heart jumped. "Hurry!" he cried, motioning to Leonid. "Let's get him inside."

When they reached the house, Lillian, Zarah, and Herr Thiele were waiting at the front door. Lillian opened it wide to let them in. Her eyes landed on Joshi as his limp form was lowered to a bench in the hallway. "Oh my heavens!" she exclaimed.

"Take him upstairs," Herr Thiele ordered. "Put him in the room at the end of the hall."

"We need a doctor," urged Manya.

Leonid coughed and began to wring his hands. It was Helling who noticed.

"What is it you want to say?" Helling asked, seeing the awful fright on the little man's face.

"Typhus," Leonid whispered. His hands shook as he bent forward to roll up Joshi's sleeve. "I think he has typhus."

Pointing to the rash on Joshi's arm, he went on, "These spots are a symptom. He's a doctor himself. He told me that there is no medicine to cure it, only hygiene and proper care."

Manya stared at Leonid.

"We're prisoners from Stutthof," he stammered, raising his panicked eyes to hers. "We've escaped. If you involve a doctor, he will surely report us. Please," he begged, "don't do that. I'll watch him. I'll bathe him. I'll never leave his room if you are afraid."

"Is he contagious?" asked Helling.

"Only if he still carries infected lice. We'll need to bathe him right away. The fever must have been in his system."

Manya willed herself to stay calm. Leaning over the bed, she took hold of Leonid's hands. "We won't turn you in," she assured him. "We're his friends too. I grew up with him."

Leonid's worried eyes brightened a little. "Are you Manya? The gadji girl?"

She nodded.

⚜

They brought Joshi to the room at the end of the upstairs hall, with windows shielded by heavy blue velvet curtains. In the middle of the room was a four-poster bed with a walnut headboard. Carved into the headboard was an angel whose hands were pressed to her breast. Wings as wide as swan's wings spread to the edges of the wood. Her eyes were kind and she gazed toward the pillows.

"Our guests say she sings at night," said Herr Thiele. "May she protect your friend."

"I'll stay with Manya and Joshi," said Lillian, gathering up pillows that lay on top of an old chest near the window. "We need fresh water to wash Joshi. Herr Thiele, would you fetch some?" She rolled up her sleeves and started to unbutton Joshi's jacket. "The rest of you, leave now. Manya and I must get to work."

As she and Manya gently rolled Joshi onto his right and left sides to remove his jacket and shirt, she saw Zarah standing in the doorway with

Leonid. "Dear little one," Lillian said, "will you bring us some soap and towels? A bit of broth, too, would be good."

She turned to Leonid. "Perhaps you'd fetch the dried ham that's in the food container on our wagon and help her boil it?"

She stooped to pull off Joshi's soggy boots and didn't see the flash of willingness that passed across Zarah's ashen face, nor did she notice the word "yes" forming on the child's lips.

$\mathcal{F}$or three days Joshi's fever refused to break. From her chair beside his bed, Manya sponged his limbs with lukewarm water and spoon-fed him drops of tea and broth. Often his hands shook so badly, she thought he was having seizures. But what distressed her most were the words he spit out, the vile curses she could barely stand to hear. He shouted at a woman he called the warden, terrible things, as if they had been lovers. *What in God's name happened*, she wondered.

Sometimes he plummeted into silence and she was sure he was dead. When that happened, she would press her ear to his chest and listen, praying for the erratic thump of his heart and crying with relief when she heard it.

Occasionally she would walk across the musty wooden floor and stand at the window, where she cracked open the heavy curtains to watch bombs falling on Braunsberg. The explosions had doubled in the last few days, but she was so exhausted that she merely returned to her chair and let the sound of sirens and flashes of light wash over her.

On the third night, Joshi's breath came in weak, painful rattles. She sat up in her chair, wide awake and certain he was going to die. Outside, the boom of heavy artillery rattled the windowpanes. Her eyes darted to the window, fearful that if the glass shattered, his spirit would be whisked away.

Around ten o'clock the bedroom door opened. Helling entered, carrying an oil lamp. The flame was merely a flicker. Light was a dangerous thing now. Enemy bombers circling above were drawn to it like vultures. Everywhere, people used blackout blinds, and if none were available, they nailed blankets over their windows.

"How is he?" Helling whispered.

Manya shook her head. The light from the lamp stretched up to the ceiling in long shadows, darkening the angel in the center of the headboard. She ran her fingers over the angel's chiseled wings. "We've been here for three nights, but the angel never sings." She gave a dry, sad laugh. "Perhaps Joshi has been cursing too much."

Helling sat down on a stool beside her and laid his calloused hand over her fingertips.

"I don't want to be the bearer of bad tidings," he said, his voice grave. "However, I must talk to you. This morning I rode Leonid's bicycle through Frauenburg to the Frisches Haff. Herr Thiele has been saying that the ice is melting and we won't be able to make it to the Nehrung and on to Danzig. I wanted to see for myself."

"We should have crossed the Haff days ago," Manya said, leaning forward and rubbing her eyes. "I've kept you back. I'm so sorry." She sighed and squeezed his hand. "Leave tomorrow, before the ice melts completely. Take Lillian, Zarah, and the horses before it's too late."

He blinked at her. "It's not the ice, child. I know large ice surfaces. Even if the water is knee-deep in some places, it quickly flows out between the cracks and thick ice always floats up again. Crossing the Frisches Haff will be treacherous, yes, but not impossible."

He sighed. "That's not the problem. I'm worried about the Russians. I expect their tanks to roll into the courtyard at any moment." He rubbed his swollen knee as though he were trying to soothe his worries. "Today I stopped into a café by the Haff. I talked with a German soldier there. He told me the Russians are on the city's doorstep. Only one or two miles away. He said that although the German soldiers are fighting to keep the escape routes over the ice open, it is only a matter of time, perhaps hours, before the Red Army breaks through the lines. Every minute we wait lessens our chance of getting out alive." He took a deep breath and turned his eyes to Manya. "Lillian and I have talked," he said quietly. "We're staying with you."

Manya folded her hands in her lap and stared out over the bed into the dark.

"The Russians would have caught up with Mami and Papa by now," she whispered emptily. Then, as if coming to, she turned to Helling. "You must go. The risk is too great."

He started to protest, but her eyes welled up with tears. "He's so sick," she said. "How could I possibly abandon him when he needs me most?" Her gaze followed the flickering shadows up the walls, past the water stains to the cornice molding over the window. She sighed. "I want to be with him no matter what."

She closed her eyes. "But I don't want you and Lillian and Zarah to do the same."

"I'll talk with Lillian about this," Helling said, standing up and groaning at his painful knees. "But first I should check on Leonid. He's been watching the horses all evening."

⚜

Sometime after midnight, Manya found herself on the brink of wakefulness and sleep. Although her eyes were closed, she sensed the weight of Joshi's head on the pillow, the draft from the fireplace behind her, and the curving outline of the angel's wings in the headboard. And far, far away, she heard a whisper.

"I've come for him."

"Leave us alone," she cried, pressing Joshi's hand against her chest.

"You're so weak, my love," she whispered. "Please stay with me." She lay her head on the edge of the bed and saw the angel drop her arms over Joshi's pillow and wrap long fingers around his shoulders.

"What bargain are you asking me to make with you?" Manya whispered.

The amber ring on her finger glowed like liquid light. *Vavara*, she thought. *Mami. Please help me.* She stared into the angel's eyes, which burned like amber too, and saw the angel's wings beating the air. "Please," she said. "You took Vavara and Mami. Let Joshi live and I promise to love him, no matter what."

"Why should he live when so many others have died?" asked the angel.

"Because I love him," said Manya, with a helpless shrug. And the angel smiled.

When Manya woke, she touched Joshi's cheek. The fever had broken.

⚜

In the afternoon, Joshi awoke, his eyes confused and dizzy. "I've been sick," he said.

Manya stroked the fuzzy bits of hair sprouting from his scalp, the ragged stubble on his cheeks. "Yes, you were, but you'll get better now."

He struggled to focus on his surroundings: the blue roses on the wallpaper, the heavy carved bureau at the foot of the bed. *How long have I been living in a nightmarish dream world*, he wondered.

"You had typhus," Manya said. "We weren't sure if you were going to make it."

"I remember now. It hit me in the stable." He leaned back and fixed his eyes on hers. "I dreamed I was dead and I heard you calling me."

She nodded and gazed at the angel.

His eyes followed her gaze and suddenly it came back to him—the camp, Ben, Gesa, and the warden. His heart seized. His parents, his clan had died when he was with Manya. He thought of Sofia. Oh God, had he lost her? His throat hardened.

"You must eat," Manya said, taking a biscuit from the plate on the nightstand. When he did not take it, she touched his brow. "Come on," she urged, placing the biscuit in his hand. She poured some cold tea into a cup. "You must drink, too."

He raised the biscuit to his lips with one pale hand and took a bite, while the other hand curved around the mug. After every bite he took a sip, but he could hardly swallow, so shrunken was his throat.

Manya reached out to refill the mug, her fingertips grazing his hand affectionately.

He pulled back unexpectedly, and she blinked in surprise. "What is it?" she asked, seeing a look of anguish pass over his face.

"Nothing," he murmured.

All at once, she felt uncertain. Beneath her sweater, tucked into her bra, she carried the piece of butterfly amber he had given her so many years before in Guja. She pulled it out and held it in her palm.

"I've kept it next to my heart since leaving home," she murmured. "It's bruised my skin, but it's been a constant reminder of you and of our—"

He closed his eyes, and she knew he did not want to hear the word "love."

A loud clatter in the courtyard below made her jump. She went to the window and drew back the curtain. Helling, Leonid, and Lillian were pushing the wagon into the barn. The wagon's iron tongue was dragging across the cobblestones and making an awful racket. Helling looked grim. He kept glancing up in her direction.

Manya opened the window. "Don't put the wagon away, Blacksmith Helling," she called. Joshi's fever has broken. We can all leave together!"

She closed the window and bent down to open the lid of the cedar chest, from which she pulled Joshi's clothes. Lillian had washed and ironed them.

"You must get dressed, Joshi," she said, returning to the bed and handing him a shirt. The Russians are almost here." She took his elbow. "Can you stand?"

He nodded and rose to his feet. With great effort he moved to pull the shirt over his head. As she hurried to smooth out the wrinkles, his face twisted into a dark mask. "I can dress myself," he said, pushing her hand away.

"I'm sorry," she said, taken aback. His tone had been harsh and his touch a bit too rough. She smoothed back her hair and decided to let it go. *He's alive*, she thought, her happiness returning. *Nothing else matters.*

Leonid was preparing a flask of hot coffee when Joshi shuffled into the kitchen beside Manya. As soon as Leonid saw him, he began speaking in Russian, a wide grin spreading across his face.

"Stop talking in tongues," Joshi said, smiling weakly. "Anyone would think you'd seen a ghost." He sniffed the air. "My God, but that coffee smells good. Would you pour some for me, Leonid, please?"

Leonid handed him a mug before pouring a cup for Manya.

When Joshi had taken a sip, he turned his exhausted face to Manya, his eyes blank. She couldn't bear to look at him, so deep was the fear gripping her belly.

Helling's voice in the courtyard outside gave her reason to turn toward the window.

"The wagon is ready," Manya said. "Lillian and Helling have hitched up the mares, and Aztec is saddled."

Zarah came into the kitchen bundled in her winter coat, clutching a handful of colored pencils and a stack of paper. Manya was startled by the change in her. Once lifeless and vacant, Zarah's eyes appeared focused now, alert. Manya looked her over more closely. The aura of tragedy still clung to her tiny frame, but it seemed that a part of her had come home.

"Have you been drawing?" asked Manya.

Zarah nodded.

"Did you get those crayons from the little girl in Klein Stegen after you played Snow White?"

Another nod.

Manya could hardly believe that Zarah had responded. She wanted to shout hallelujah, but the moment was delicate. Uncertain, she waited to see what would happen when Zarah saw Joshi. But it was he who broke the silence.

"Hello, Zarah," he said in a gentle voice.

Manya held her breath and saw a glimmer of a smile cross Zarah's face.

"We met a long time ago in your Papa's workshop in Guja," continued Joshi. "I was with Sofia, my sister."

Zarah cocked her head and blinked as though she remembered.

Joshi's eyes filled with tears.

Leonid, who was watching him closely, took hold of his arm. "Listen," he said. "I have something good to tell you. Sofia may still be alive. The Pomeranian priest from the camp was here last night. He's on the run. The guards were going to shoot him in Palmnicken, but somehow, like us, he escaped and found this place."

He shook his head. "You can imagine our surprise at seeing each other here in this kitchen. The priest told me that while he was on the march, he saw Klawan arrive in a car from Stutthof with an envelope for Officer Reiss. Before driving back, Klawan sought him out because he wanted to confess his sins and ask God for forgiveness. When the priest asked him what good deeds he'd done, Klawan mentioned that he'd tried to save Nuri and your sister."

"Is Sofia still with Nuri?" asked Joshi.

"He said he didn't know. Nuri was sick, and he doesn't know if she survived, but evidently Sofia ended up with the seamstress in Stutthof village."

"Where is the priest now?" asked Joshi, his forehead suddenly shiny with sweat.

"He left before dawn. He wanted to get to the church in Braunsberg because he thought the clergyman there could help him, but not before he came upstairs and said a prayer for you. Manya was asleep beside you, holding your hand."

The door to the foyer swung open.

"Get your coats!" Helling hollered. "We're leaving."

❧

Settling himself next to Leonid in the back of the wagon, Joshi watched

Manya take Aztec's reins from Helling's hands. "I have to find Sofia," he murmured.

Leonid nodded quietly. "You'll have a chance. Helling tells me that if we make it onto the Nehrung, there's only one road leading west. It passes straight through Stutthof."

"He knows?" asked Joshi.

"Yes, but he's scared that things might not go well for you, for all of us."

"I understand," said Joshi.

Herr Thiele limped out of the main barn, his cane tapping carefully against the icy path.

"Stay," he begged, when he reached the wagon. "The ice on the inlet will be more treacherous than the enemy. Over two hundred people died there this morning. Poor souls. At least here the walls will protect you."

He stooped low to run his hand over Aztec's hindquarter. "Poor stallion—ach!" he wept. "Germany's sins are too many. These horses have never offended a soul."

"Please don't worry, Herr Thiele," said Manya, tenderly patting his shoulder. She glanced at Joshi as if to reassure herself that he was still there. "I have faith," she said softly.

"I don't," Herr Thiele said, and tightened his gray woolen scarf.

But Manya ignored him. She was already shoving her boot tip into the stirrup.

Aztec snorted and began to high-step in circles on the slippery ground.

"He's so jittery this morning," Manya said, settling into the saddle.

"Calm down, boy," she cooed. "You'll need your wits about you when we get on that ice." She whistled softly and his ears pricked up. "Are you listening? We have to get to the other side."

She saw his slender legs reflected in a rain puddle. With a sudden, prancing step, he sent water splashing over the cobbles.

THIRTY-NINE

*C*lucking his tongue, Helling squeezed the wagon through a narrow side street in Frauenburg.

Manya rode close behind the wagon, her eyes never straying far from Joshi's face. He sat with his knees drawn to his chest, his thin fingers clutching the beaver-fur blanket she had given him hours before. Mostly he had slept since leaving Braunsberg, his head lolling sideways onto Leonid's shoulder. Whenever he awoke, she would try to hold his gaze, but no matter how hard she willed it, his eyes would flit straight past her into the distance.

Hoping to engage him, she trotted closer to the wagon. "Joshi, are you all right? Do you still feel feverish?"

"I'm fine," he mumbled.

But as the hours passed, he became more and more withdrawn, and she could not suppress the growing feeling that he had cut himself off from her.

By early afternoon, Helling had steered the wagon into one of the two refugee columns that faced the phosphorescent ice on the Frisches Haff. Many of the fleeing horse breeders, anxious to save their beloved Trakehners, had strung additional horses to one another and attached them to their carts, lengthening and slowing down the lines. Flurries of fresh snow had begun to fall, making it impossible to see the dunes along the narrow strip of land called the Nehrung.

"How far is it to the other side, Herr Helling?" asked Manya, riding up beside him.

"At its narrowest point, the inlet is seven miles wide," he said. "From what I gather, though, we'll be crossing it diagonally. That means we'll have to go about fifteen miles."

Near the shore, at the front of the column, a policeman was waving a baton and shouting orders. "People, for God's sake, rid your wagons of the extra weight. Throw everything out before you get on the ice. Everything except blankets, and food for yourselves and your horses."

A loud clamor arose from the crowds. "Our families have been murdered," a stern-faced woman railed back at him. "Our homes, plundered. And now you want us to throw away the last memories we own? What about our horses? You can't expect us to leave them behind. They're our only worldly wealth."

"Do it or you'll drown," the policeman barked. "If you don't have the heart, then stay back. But I warn you, you'll meet hell's fury when the Red Army arrives."

"God knows that's the truth," muttered a young woman in the wagon to Manya's left. She was clutching a silver picture frame, and as she turned toward Manya, her pale blue eyes filled with anguish. "So many women have suffered." She sighed. "But, there'll be no sympathy. People will say we got what we deserve." She lifted the frame for Manya to see. "This is my husband. If he comes back from the front, I'll never tell him how many times I was raped. It would kill him if he knew. Ach, I wish I'd died with my two sisters."

She tucked the frame into the front of her coat. "I'm sorry," she said, suddenly embarrassed to have said so much. Wiping grimy tears from her eyes, she lowered her face. "Here I am burdening a stranger with my sorrows."

"Don't say that," said Manya. She thought of the Russian who had attacked her in Nemmersdorf, remembering his fishy breath, his broad Mongolian features made ugly by the cruelty in his gray eyes, lurking beneath a heavy black brow. Unforgettable, that face.

Shivering, she gave the woman what she hoped was an encouraging smile and forced her mind to return to the present. In the crowd in front of them, she saw hundreds of refugees waiting for their turn to move onto the ice. She watched them discard their last possessions: silverware, photo albums, antique boxes, love letters. Even family Bibles, the cornerstones of every household, were cast out and trodden into the snow and horse manure. A Bible lay next to Aztec's front hoof, its leather binding splattered with mud. She leaned forward to scrape the dirt off the cover with her riding crop.

"Is there anything holy anymore?" she asked absently.

"Certainly not in that book."

She turned to see Joshi slouching over the edge of the wagon, peering down at the snow. He leaned around to face her and dropped one arm over the side. "It's all rubbish," he said, pointing at the Bible.

"Stop it," she said tersely.

Joshi shrugged and turned away from her.

She pushed her crop back into its holder. *I've been riding behind him for hours,* she thought, *and he won't give me a smile, a word, anything. It's not just the camp that has changed him. He's lost his parents, his clan. And even if the priest gave him hope, he must be afraid that Sofia is dead. Any man would break under the strain. Any heart would turn bitter.*

She pulled her arm close against her stomach to stop the ache and gazed across the Frisches Haff.

FORTY

The wagon rolled onto the bobbing ice field that covered the Frisches Haff lagoon. Manya held her breath, bracing against every creak and snap, fearing the ice wouldn't hold and the wagon would tumble down into the murky darkness. Hour by hour they moved slowly forward.

Trembling with cold, Leonid pinched the skin on his cheeks. "This is worse than Siberia."

"It's below freezing," Joshi said, his voice almost lost in the white mist. He brushed fat snowflakes from the blanket and pulled it up to his neck. Lillian had given him an extra piece of bread smeared with goose fat, and for that he was grateful. Still, his legs ached down to his bones. He tried to stretch his hamstrings, but his back felt locked and stiff.

From the trestle, Helling lifted his gloved hand and held it open. "It's warming up a bit," he said. "I can tell by the size of these snowflakes."

Manya followed Helling's gaze. "As long as the sky is cloudy, the Russian bombers can't see us," she said, trying to sound encouraging.

"Maybe they can't see us," said Lillian, her voice tense. "But I can't see the wagon in front of me, either. The police in Frauenburg warned us to stay fifty yards apart so that the ice would hold, but I don't know how far away I am. If it's true that the Russians have shot craters into the ice—" She shivered. "I don't want to fall into the water."

"No worrying," Helling said gently. "You're doing fine."

"I'm not doing anything," Lillian said. "I'm simply trusting Shambhala and Topsie to know where the ice is strong. Their instincts are better than mine."

"Do you want me to take the reins?" he offered.

"Absolutely not," she clucked. "Keep your hands in your pockets. You too, Zarah," she added sternly. "Stop rolling those crayons between your fingers. Children are far more susceptible to frostbite than adults. You don't want black fingers, do you?"

Zarah frowned and shoved her hands back inside her coat.

The snow squall had just begun to lessen when the wagon came to a stop in front of a man-made channel. Near the channel's jagged edge stood a group of soldiers, their faces lined with exhaustion. They spoke kindly to the refugees, assisting the horse-drawn wagons and limping pedestrians across a makeshift bridge.

One of them threw a fearful gaze back and forth across the Haff. "We're done for," he said, his accent betraying him as a Berliner.

Beside him, a boy in uniform feebly puffed on a cigarette that kept freezing to his lips. "Yeah," he muttered, "but if I die on this ice, I'll have saved a few lives first."

The Berliner nodded and kicked at a mound of ice. "Hitler had weeks to get these people out of here before the winter arrived," he spat. "Now it's too late. You and I will be shot or sent to Siberia." He grimaced. "But at least we're men. God have mercy on the women." He looked up at the sky. "What a hellhole! All of these people could have escaped. We had ships, but no orders. And now, we have orders and no ships."

The young soldier took another drag of his cigarette and stared at the column of refugees. "There won't be any epitaphs for them or for us," he muttered. He pointed to a dark spot some thirty yards away where the ears of a drowned horse were sticking up out of the ice. "Loyal to the end," he said, and stubbed out his cigarette beneath his boot.

A hissing crack rose in the frigid air. The soldiers spun around.

Joshi had been listening to the ice make strange noises, creaks and moans, and he too jumped back in fright. His eyes flew toward the trestle, where Helling sat motionless. He knew the old blacksmith was looking out over the ice, studying it carefully so that he might discern the exact point of danger. He followed Helling's gaze and shuddered. In the channel, black waves were crashing up between the few flat planks meant to support the wagons as they rolled across the water.

"This ice will hold," Helling said, his voice measured and even.

The soldiers, however, weren't taking any chances.

"Move!" they shouted, pointing at Lillian.

"Manya," she called, with a hard shake of the reins. "It's our turn."

As Joshi eyed the flimsy planks, he heard Manya cry out. Aztec refused to budge.

"Hold on, Fräulein Manya," Leonid shouted, leaping over the side of the wagon onto the ice.

Frightened by the commotion, Aztec began to pivot on his hind legs, nearly throwing Manya out of the saddle.

"*Los!*" the soldier commanded. "Move!"

"I can't," Manya yelled.

Joshi's limbs went numb. He watched Leonid grab Aztec's halter and lead him onto the swaying planks past the churning, black water.

"Easy, boy," Leonid coaxed, looking straight ahead. "Easy."

Joshi held his breath.

When they reached the other side, Manya closed her eyes. "Thank you, Leonid," she said. "Aztec has a mind of his own."

Leonid smiled, his weary eyes lighting up with pride.

As Topsie and Shambhala led the wagon behind Aztec, Joshi saw a look of affection pass between Leonid and Manya. A flash of jealousy ran down his spine.

By midafternoon, the overhanging clouds had blown eastward, leaving only a few silvery strands in the sky. Although the snow had stopped falling, the temperature plummeted.

"I'd rather be up to my ears in horse manure than in this cold," Joshi grumbled.

The frost had nearly glued his eyelashes shut. He wiped them with his fingers and saw Manya riding close behind the wagon.

Catching his gaze, she smiled.

I wish you would ride ahead, he thought, *so I wouldn't have to look at you*. Although he was exhausted, he resisted sleep because of the terrible images that arose in his mind. He saw his mother standing in fright just before the bullet struck her forehead. He saw his father lying dead on the ground, anguish on his face. Every smile Manya offered reminded him where he had been that night, and every nod of her head made him think of the warden and Gesa. Even worse, when he looked at her, he couldn't help thinking that she was here and Sofia was not.

A pain rose behind his eyes, cutting through his brow like a knife. He pressed his forehead to his knees and, despite the ache, fell into a sleep in which his limbs could rest. But the faces rose up again.

"Wake up, sleepyhead," Joshi heard Manya say some time later.

He groaned and turned his head sideways. She was crouched beside him, her hair falling in tangled strands from beneath her cap, her eyes a little too bright in the flickering dusk.

"We're stopping for the night," she said, her breath white on the frosty air. "Leonid and Helling are blanketing the horses. But you have to eat something before you turn into a snowman."

She touched his arm and pointed to a covered plate on the floor. "Lillian has prepared some potatoes. I brought you coffee." She smiled sweetly and handed him a flask. "There's no sugar left, but it's warm."

She looked out onto the Frisches Haff. The night was glass clear, and the ice was speckled with other wagons and human shapes. Beneath them, the water gurgled. "Listen to that. It's maddening," she whispered, her eyes wide and vulnerable.

"I don't want dinner," he heard himself say in a hardened voice. "No coffee either. Thanks, though." He pushed the flask back into her hand.

"But you *need* food."

He shrugged.

"Don't be a fool," she urged. "You've been so ill. Please."

"I can take care of myself."

"Joshi," she whispered. "Have I done something wrong?"

She was just inches away. He could see the pale freckles on the side of her nose, smell the salt and snow on her skin. Her closeness overwhelmed him, and all at once he drew back, pressing his head against the side of the wagon. He knew he had hurt her deeply when he had spoken. Her face was white, questioning him. It hurt him to see her like that. For a moment, he thought he might pull her close and weep into her hair.

"Let me sleep beside you tonight," she whispered. "Our nerves are so raw, and perhaps it will comfort us."

The pleading in her voice was unbearable. He slid away from her, and the gap between them filled with a rush of icy air. "Please, Manya," he said. "Stop."

His eyes blurred as he watched her step away, his heart contracting into a tiny black disc. He felt a terrible loneliness, but for the life of him, he couldn't call her back.

FORTY-ONE

Golitsin took a bite of raw potato, tiny bits of grit catching between his teeth.

"Tastes like shit," he mumbled.

"Ground recon missions are never a holiday," Afanasiv murmured, peering through the tangled shrubs in front of them.

Golitsin grunted. He was cold and hungry. They'd been walking all night through enemy terrain, making their way south from the girl's house in Guja toward Görlitz, where Hitler's headquarters were supposedly located. About nine miles north of their destination, they'd happened upon a potato field embedded with airplane tire tracks. The tracks were fresh, so they'd decided to wait in a dense patch of forest by the edge of the field to see if any military aircraft would return.

Afanasiv nudged him and pointed at the sky. "Look, an airplane's coming."

Golitsin spit out the mouthful of potato. Peering through the thickets, he saw the fabric-covered fuselage of a little plane. It appeared to hover over the treetops.

Afanasiv let out a low whistle. "A German Fieseler Storch." He grinned admiringly. "What a bird, all feathered up with slats. I've always wanted to fly one. That plane can land backwards on top of an outhouse."

They watched the aircraft touch down on the field and lurch to a halt. Moments later, the door swung open and the pilot jumped out, holding a large green net. Across the field to their right, a man was running out of the forest just yards away from them.

"Captain," the man called. "Did she check out all right?"

"Flies like a dream after the tune-up. But we better roll her into the bushes and cover her with the net. The Russians are everywhere. It's just as I expected. They've made it to the Führer's headquarters in Görlitz. And from what I've heard, Hitler's flown the coop to Berlin."

"That's good information," murmured Afanasiv, following most of their German.

Golitsin said nothing. He was disappointed. He'd dreamed of meeting Hitler face to face. He knew it was probably impossible, but he wished he could have been the one who dragged the son of a bitch in front of a Russian commander. His eyes focused on the plane. The pilot and the mechanic were already pushing it between two large spruce trees.

"Have some breakfast, Captain," said the mechanic. "I'll do the rest. When are you going up again?"

"This morning. Eleven o'clock," the pilot replied. "I'm flying one of our wounded ground troop commanders to the military hospital in Danzig and bringing back his replacement and supplies for our troops near Jankendorf."

The mechanic nodded.

"I filled her up this morning, so you're fine for petrol. You've got the extra canister as well."

"Thanks," said the pilot. "I just hope we get through alive." He saluted the mechanic and disappeared into the forest.

When they heard a vehicle drive off, Golitsin turned to look at Afanasiv. "What the hell are you smiling at?" he whispered.

"We're going storching today, Yuri," Afanasiv murmured with a wink. "We'll cover a lot of ground if we take that baby up. Commander Koslov will be very happy with the surveillance information we bring him. We'll be able to describe all the access roads and German troop locations and tell him what bridges and railroads are still intact. We'll fly up the Baltic coast as well, to check out the ports." His eyes were gleaming with excitement. "She's a recon pilot's dream. Flies so low and slow, you can read a newspaper on the ground. You in?"

For a moment, Golitsin hesitated. He hated planes. But this was the opportunity he had been waiting for. He reached into his pocket and felt for the piece of paper he studied every night, the girl's route to Danzig.

"All right," he whispered, pointing his chin toward the mechanic, who was unfolding the net. "I'll take care of him."

Slipping through the brush, Golitsin crept around the edge of the field. When the man's back was just feet away, he pulled out the knife he'd taken from girl's house and lunged forward, slitting the unsuspecting fellow's throat. His pulse raced with a new urgency.

Afanasiv was right. The information they gathered would be invaluable to Russia. And, along the way, he needed to even a little score. Even now, the girl's eyes seemed to follow him everywhere, as though she were laughing at him. But it was he who would have the last laugh. It was his duty, really. He dragged the mechanic's body into the brambles. After washing his hands in the snow, he waved Afanasiv on.

FORTY-TWO

$\mathcal{H}$elling rolled out from under the heavy duvet that covered him, Lillian, and Zarah. As he stretched his creaking joints, he studied the ice. The sky over the Frisches Haff was clear, but its sunny brilliance was deceptive. The ice atop the lagoon had refrozen. Already, hundreds of travelers were on the move, the wheels of their wagons snapping against the frigid surface.

Troubled, he turned his attention back to Manya, Joshi, and Leonid. Joshi was awake, propped up in a corner and wrapped in the beaver fur. Manya lay on the other side of the wagon, as far away from him as she could get.

"The sooner we get off the ice, the better," Helling croaked, blowing his nose and pulling his jacket tighter.

"How long will it take us to reach the Nehrung?" Joshi asked.

Manya sat up. Without a glance in Joshi's direction, she kicked off her covers and went to prepare the feed buckets for the horses.

"If we're lucky, we should be on the spit tomorrow," Helling replied, his eyes darting sideways at Manya. He was well aware of the tension in the wagon.

Joshi folded his blanket and shook Leonid's shoulder. "Wake up. It's time to go."

Leonid yawned and nodded. Soon he and Joshi were storing their pillows and duvets in the heavy canvas duffle bag that safeguarded them against the rain and snow. Helling gently roused Lillian and Zarah, careful not to let his worries show.

When they were up, he climbed into the trestle and pulled on his gloves. "Manya," he said. "Should we try the studs on the horses? I'm of two minds.

The ice is slippery, but in this dry cold, the pressure of the metal could split their hooves."

Manya was massaging Shambhala's legs with a towel. Joshi saw her raise her head to answer, but when she noticed him looking, she quickly turned away.

"Let's try without first," she said, wringing out the towel. "We can always stop later and put them in if we have to."

"Is there anything we can do to help you, Miss Manya?" Leonid offered.

"No, thanks," Manya said. With a shake of her head, she strode back toward Aztec.

"All right then, Joshi," Leonid continued. "Let's take a little walk. My bladder is about to burst."

They went behind an abandoned cart, pausing when they saw two boys rolling a dead woman up into a carpet. *Poor souls*, Joshi thought as they hoisted the woman onto their wagon. She was probably their mother. He winced at the thought of his mother's suffering and of Sofia, who surely had seen her slaughtered. If it weren't for Sofia and the speck of hope he held on to for finding her, he would gladly let himself fall through the ice. Death would be quick, and he would be at peace.

When they returned, Lillian was sitting in the trestle, cutting slices of the black bread Herr Thiele had given them and smearing the tops with goose fat. Helling stood near the mares, drying their harnesses. He called for Leonid to help him.

"Is there anything I can do, Lillian?" Joshi offered. "Everyone seems to have a job except me."

She lay the knife down on her small cutting board and leaned forward until her copper-colored eyes were level with his.

"That girl's heart is breaking," she murmured fiercely. "What's going on between you two?" Lillian shook a finger at him. "Have you any idea how hard she fought to save your life?"

Joshi nodded and looked down at his scuffed boots. "I know," he said.

The raw pain in his voice slid right through Lillian's skin. "I understand," she said softly. "My own husband died because I'm a Jew. All the same, silence is a lonely death." She handed him the sandwich. "Now eat this. And don't play games with me like you did with her. Your bones are poking through your skin. Chew every bite slowly so you don't throw it up. Our food is precious."

"Yes ma'am," Joshi said with a weak smile. Stepping onto the wagon, he hunkered down under his beaver throw and began to eat.

"Klaus Helling," he heard her call. "You look like death warmed over. Come get some food."

"I'll eat on the way," Helling said, smiling at her and hoisting himself into the driver's seat.

As Joshi chewed his food, he watched Manya swing her leg over Aztec's saddle and push her boot tips into the stirrups. She looked at him. Once again their eyes met, but this time she quickly pulled her woolen shawl over her cheekbones, hiding her face. Leaving her usual place behind the wagon, she passed him with indifference and settled in beside Lillian.

A sharp twinge of sadness struck him. He wished he could tell her that he was sorry. But things were different between them now. He wasn't the same man anymore.

"Topsie, Shambhala. On you go, my dears," Helling urged.

Afanasiv bounded across the field and climbed up the gear leg into the strange plane. Golitsin followed and closed the hatch behind him. Glancing at the cockpit, he saw that it was cluttered with cranks and wheels and levers.

"She's just like some women I know," Afanasiv laughed. "Ugly on the outside. Beautiful on the inside. Do you want to have a go when we're up? Didn't you once say you know how to fly?"

"I know how, but I don't want to," Golitsin muttered. "I'll stay back here and keep my eyes wide open."

He settled himself on the gunner seat and pulled out his binoculars. His throat was dry. He didn't want to tell Afanasiv that he was afraid of flying.

"Are you ready?" Afanasiv called, looking back and flashing Golitsin a grin.

Golitsin nodded in a rush of anxiety, the taste of leftover potato was like acid in his mouth. But he found comfort as he held the piece of paper the girl had left behind. Coordinates swam through his head in anticipation. Yes, he would be happy to navigate. After all, they had work to do. And he was still the best damn tracker in the Russian army.

The Storch rattled to the end of the field. Turning her into the wind, Afanasiv let out a whoop of exhilaration and throttled her forward, pulling back on the stick until she was airborne and skimming the treetops.

They had been traveling for three hours across the northern lagoon. Sunlight fell from the center of the sky, but its warmth came with a price. The top layer of ice had melted again, making the ice slick as grease. With each step, the horses' legs threatened to slide out from under them.

"It's time for the studs, Manya," Helling said when Topsie nearly tripped. "The horses can't carry on like this."

"We could put them on there," Manya replied, pointing to an empty stretch of ice just outside the column. "Do you think it's safe?"

Helling squinted against the glare. "It looks all right, but let Aztec take the lead. He won't go where there's danger."

Manya nudged Aztec toward the gleaming expanse.

"Give him more rein to sniff the ground," Helling suggested. "And watch for any change in the lift of his hooves."

"He seems fine," Manya murmured, relaxing a little in the saddle. "I trust him."

They stopped in a wide circle of glittering ice shards. Bombs and artillery flak still rumbled in the distance, but the spaciousness was soothing, and the world seemed pure and fresh. In the crowds, they had not been able to hear the wind. Here, it blew like a song from horizon to horizon.

Helling jumped down onto the ice. Joshi followed, inhaling the moist air and letting the heavenly sunlight warm his skin. He saw that Manya had dismounted from Aztec and taken off her cap. She had shoved it into her stirrup and had draped her red woolen scarf across Aztec's haunches. As she moved, the sun caught her hair, illuminating each strand.

He felt his pulse quicken. She was so striking. His eyes traveled to her right hand, pressed against her right hip, the one she favored. He knew that stance so well, the wide plant of her boots gripping the ice.

"Aztec is the most beautiful horse I've ever seen," Leonid murmured, interrupting Joshi's reverie. "Like a sculpture."

Joshi nodded. Aztec *was* a living work of art. Somehow the trek had matured him. Although he was thinner now, his spirit had grown, as if he had knowingly taken on the responsibility of the journey.

Shambhala nickered, and Aztec's nose touched hers. Mesmerized, Joshi watched their moist breath swirl into the air, then fade back into nothing.

"It's magic, isn't it?" Leonid murmured.

"Yes," Lillian said, climbing down to join them on the ice. "And we all need a bit of that. Look. Shambhala is kissing his cheek." She laughed and turned to Joshi.

"Lillian, we can't waste any time," Helling said gruffly, approaching the trestle. "Leonid, please bring my toolbox and help me hammer in the studs. Joshi, would you keep an eye on the reins?"

"Ach," Lillian said. "If the world wasted a little more time on love, we wouldn't have to be here."

Glad to have a task, Joshi climbed onto the wagon's bench. Zarah scooted sideways to make room for him, while Lillian rummaged through a low, built-in cupboard for a tin of biscuits.

From high up in the driver's seat, Joshi had an uninterrupted view of the sun glancing off the ice. In the breeze, Manya's scarf slid off Aztec's rump and fell onto the ice. He watched her pick it up and sighed. Beside him, Zarah was coloring as usual, her small, gloved hand drawing shapes on the frozen piece of paper she held in her lap. A woolen blanket lay on the bench between them.

"May I use that blanket?" he asked.

She paused and smiled at him before pushing the blanket his way.

"Thanks," he said, covering his knees with it. He looked out at the ice again.

Helling held Topsie's leg in the crook of his arm. He worked with swift confidence, cleaning each hole in her hoof with a stiff brush before tapping in the studs and tightening them with a wrench. Leonid was crouched beside Helling, one hand on Topsie's halter, the other on the toolbox.

Manya was leaning against Aztec's neck, and her tousled blond hair flying off her face like a bright, jagged halo.

The drone of an airplane slowly registered in Joshi's mind. Shielding his eyes against the sun's glare, he turned to look at the sky behind him. A small plane, its wings festooned with flaps and slats, was skimming above the refugee column. Then, strangely, it veered off. Flying remarkably slowly, it headed toward their wagon.

The horses began to fidget.

"Don't worry," Helling shouted above the loud hum. "It's a German plane. I see the swastika on the tail. They won't shoot." He rubbed his chin with his hand, adding thoughtfully, "It's a Fieseler Storch. Only they can fly that low. That's a search plane. You can almost see the color of my eyes from a Storch!"

The plane began to circle them, dropping lower with each turn.

"Why is he coming so close?" Manya asked indignantly, stepping in front of Aztec to grip both sides of his halter.

She craned her neck around to swear at the pilot, and the plane veered off. Like a raptor, it swooped around to hover above the ice to the left of the horses. Aztec's neigh grew belligerent, his hooves angry as they pawed the ice.

Joshi stared in disbelief. Zarah turned, looking up at him in terror. He was just about to grab hold of her when Lillian climbed into the trestle.

"What in God's name are they doing?" she yelled above the din, her arms circling the terrified girl.

"I don't know!" shouted Joshi. "Maybe they're trying to land."

The aircraft loomed closer. Now only feet away, it looked as if it were going to stall directly in front of Aztec. The side hatch hinged up and out on the wind.

A man holding a gun was kneeling on the floor at the opening. *What the hell is going on?* thought Joshi, his eyes focused on the padded khaki jacket in the hatch. *That's a Russian uniform!* "Duck!" he yelled, but his throat was too dry. Horrified, he realized the word never came out.

Raising his weapon, the man leaned forward. The sun struck his face, illuminating his high cheekbones and dark brow. A scream pierced the air. Joshi turned to see Zarah pointing at the man. The crayon in her hand dropped like a tiny arrow.

Lillian tried to pull her down, but Zarah twisted away, her eyes on the plane. Zarah knew that face. He'd looked into her window in Nemmersdorf, had locked eyes with her. She saw her Mama's kind eyes turn frantic with fear, saw the soft pink dimples in her cheeks harden into white marbles. Before the front door crashed open, Mama's hands, hard as tongs, had shoved her under the bed.

"Mama!" she'd cried.

"*Sei still!* Keep silent, Zarah!"

And she had kept silent, even when one of the men in khaki had dragged her out from under the bed, wrapped her up in Papa's old coat, and carried her out the back door.

"Shh," he whispered as he brought her to the oak tree beside the village, the one where she and the other children played hide and seek. "Shh," he said again, lifting her up into the dark hollow.

But the blood, the screams. Maritza. Mama. Their cries still rang in her ears, especially at night when the man with the dark brow stalked her dreams. Now, he was here to kill her.

Manya saw the Russian's face too. She blinked, trying to make sense of what was happening. Why was he in a German plane?

The glint of a pistol brought her to her senses. Unlike Nemmersdorf, though, there was no place to hide on this icy desert. Her eyes darted around in panic.

She felt a sharp tug on her arms as Aztec yanked the reins from her grasp. Unable to keep her balance, she fell onto the ice.

A shot blasted through the air.

Aztec reared. She saw his powerful body rise up against the sky, felt his shadow fall like a shield across her face.

To her left, Helling was shouting for Joshi to grab Aztec's reins. She saw Joshi leap from the wagon but knew it was too late.

Striking at the air with hard hooves, Aztec was prepared to fight or run, but he knew nothing about bullets. And the one that hit him flew too fast.

It ripped past muscle and bone, into his heart. He crashed onto the ice, a crimson rush of blood staining the hard-packed snow.

Manya twisted to her knees. "No!" she screamed, burying her face into his mane. "Not you. Please God, *please*, no!" Desperate, she pressed her hand against the blood pulsing from the bullet hole, but the force of Aztec's beating heart was too powerful. Releasing the wound, she scrambled forward and looked into his big, almond-shaped eyes.

The aircraft gathered speed and roared off into the sky.

"Aztec," she pleaded. "Don't leave me. You can't leave me."

Aztec's eyes widened, as though he'd heard her. But then he blinked and his eyes lost their light.

Panicking, Manya turned to Helling, her grip on Aztec still firm. "Do something!" she shouted.

She pressed her cheek against Aztec's girth, smelled the metallic tang of his blood. "Please," she begged. "You can do it. I know you can do it." And in that moment, her beloved stallion's slender legs jerked forward, and he was still.

Helling let out a long, low moan. Quietly, he walked over to Manya and placed a hand on her shoulder. He felt a tremor grip her body, and with a heart-ripping wail, she collapsed against Aztec's chest.

Joshi sprinted over to Helling, who nodded and quickly stepped aside. To see her hunched over, her bloodied hands cupping Aztec's face, was unbearable. "Where the fuck are you, God?" he shouted. "Where have you gone?"

"Joshi," she sobbed, as he rushed to hold her. "Bring him back to life."

He laid his palm on Aztec's barreled chest. "I wish I could," he said.

He kneeled on the ice and pulled her close, ashamed that he could not ease her sorrow and ashamed that he could not cry.

She began to rock, her bloodstained finger tracing the star beneath Aztec's forelock. "I love you," she whispered. "I love you."

Love is dead, Manya, Joshi thought bitterly.

Helling moved to comfort Manya again, his fingers clumsily pulling back her hair. Not a man for words, he leaned over and pressed his lips to the top of her head.

Manya lifted her eyes. A darkness fell over her face. "The bullet wasn't meant for him." Her voice shook with fury. "It was meant for me."

"What?" said Helling, his breath catching in his throat.

"That man in the plane was Russian. He was the one who tried to kill me in Nemmersdorf. He was there when Karin and Maritza died. I'd know him anywhere." She turned to Zarah, her eyes narrowing to points. "You recognized him too, didn't you?"

Zarah's thin body swayed like a reed in the wind. Gripping Lillian's hand, she nodded. Helling broke into sobs at the mention of Karin and Maritza. Although Zarah did not cry, her brow was etched in a deep, anxious groove. Keeping her eyes fixed on her father, she reached inside his pocket and handed him his handkerchief, waiting until she heard the familiar honk of his nose. Then, as if reassured by the sound, her face relaxed a little.

Leonid cleared his throat. "Miss Manya," he murmured. "I saw what happened. Aztec reared to protect you. Horses know more than we humans think they do. They feel things."

"I believe you," she sobbed. "But God, I wish I had killed that man when I had the chance!"

FORTY-THREE

"Shit! I missed her," Golitsin cried. After such painstaking attention to detail, he had actually missed his target! He tore at the binoculars around his neck.

At first the binoculars had been a godsend, magnifying everything within sight. He'd almost been stunned to see the fan of wild blonde hair looming larger than life in the powerful lenses. He'd imagined it differently a hundred times over. Something had told him that she was alive. And he was right!

He had zoomed in on face after face, carriage after carriage, almost directing Afanasiv to swoop down so many times. His stomach had turned cartwheels as they flew over Görlitz, headed toward the Baltic coast. And then, when they were flying over the Frisches Haff lagoon, skimming close to the columns of refugees, his attention to detail had paid off.

He had never imagined such a stroke of luck. But there she was, on an empty stretch of ice, unmistakable, her blond hair like a cloud of gossamer against the stallion's jet-black coat.

He'd crouched like a cat before the kill, calling to Afanasiv from the back of the plane.

"Over there, comrade! See that wagon off to the side?"

"Sure do," Afanasiv had shouted.

"Well, show me how low this Storch can go! Let's have some fun. I want to see the color of their eyes. Are you up for that?"

Afanasiv had protested, but he was intrigued by the horse, and so he had flown as low as the plane would allow at practically zero groundspeed.

Golitsin peered out the window. At closer range, the stallion was striking, his mane flashing like strands of opals in the sun. Beside him the girl had stood tall, full of confidence, like the damned aristocrat she was.

Kneeling on the floor, Golitsin kept his target until the plane was almost upon her. Swiftly and with as much strength as his bad shoulder could muster, he'd shoved the Storch's hatch open. He'd grasped his sidearm and aimed straight for the girl's head. Such an easy shot. At least that's what he'd thought. But he'd missed. Goddamn it! The stallion had reared, and the girl had fallen on the ice just as he pulled the trigger. Now, instead of her, the horse lay dying.

Desperate for another chance, he twisted around and crawled onto the gunner's seat, forcing his gun barrel out the rear canopy window. If he could just open fire one more time, surely he'd get her. But he couldn't do it. Everything was in his way, starting with his swinging binoculars. Further foiling him was the fact that the swivel mount for the machine gun was stupidly missing from the plane.

"Afanasiv, turn around!" he shouted frantically over the noise of the engine. "I'll get her this time."

FORTY-FOUR

*H*elling's hands shook as he took hold of the reins. He could barely look at the spot where Aztec lay butchered.

"Come on, Shambhala," he urged, his voice cracking. The mare's harness jangled defiantly. He slapped the reins against her rump, but she wouldn't budge. Neither would Topsie. Behind him, Manya was sobbing. "She'll lose her mind if we don't get her away from here," he whispered anxiously to Lillian.

He slapped the reins again. Harder.

Lillian grabbed his hand. "Don't do that," she said. "Max once told me that horses won't pass close to another horse that has died. I used to think it was an old wives' tale, but obviously it isn't. Let me see what I can do."

She slid off the wagon and crossed in front of Shambhala, grasping the crownpiece that ran over the mare's head. Resting her chin on Shambhala's forehead, she began to talk, her words tipping into the wind.

Helling felt a hollow in the pit of his stomach. How strange, Lillian's desire to keep going, he thought. All he wanted was to lie down on the ice beside Aztec and never wake up.

"It's time to say good-bye, Shambhala," he heard Lillian say. "*Meine arme Süsse*—my poor darling. Your Aztec was a hero, a one-of-a-kind stallion. But his legacy lives inside you, so you must keep going."

Shambhala nickered softly, and, dropping her muzzle to the ground, she sniffed at the crimson crystals of blood. "That's it, girl," Lillian coaxed softly. "You tell me when you're ready." It took a minute, but soon Lillian was nudging both mares backward. When their hooves stood free of the blood-drenched snow, she turned them around and led them back to the trail of refugees.

"What the hell are you thinking?" Afanasiv yelled back, pushing the plane throttle forward. "This is a recon mission, and you're shooting at civilians! Are you fucking crazy?" Afanasiv looked down through the angled glass to the ground. "You shot that horse! Damn it, man, what did you do that for? I have enough on my hands flying this bird. If a German fighter pilot saw what just happened, we're dead."

"Turn back!" Golitsin bellowed. Frustration clawed at his chest. "It's her! It's the German girl who maimed me. I need to finish her off. Please. Surely, you understand. I must do this."

Afanasiv twisted his head to stare at his comrade. It took him a moment to grasp what Golitsin was saying. Then it hit him. "Jesus, you *are* mad. I knew you'd put us in danger. To hell with you, man!"

He yanked at the tall stick, fighting to gain altitude, but the Storch's tail weighed a ton. His feet, strapped into the aluminum pedals, pumped up and down, working the rudder. To his astonishment, nothing happened. Thinking quickly, he wedged his shoulder against the throttle and gave the stick a hefty shove. He felt the nose lunge upward, and then, with a gasp of relief, he headed toward the Baltic Sea.

"Golitsin, come to your senses," he shouted when he had relaxed a bit. He checked his airspeed indicator. Everything looked good. He shook his head. "All this because I had to fly a Fieseler Storch."

He leveled off, concentrating on the cranks and levers labeled in German. He'd fly over the Danziger Bay and check out the ports and ships. At low altitudes, he would be able to see where the enemy troops were positioned. Then he'd fly back toward Angerburg. He had an extra canister of petrol right beside him. The Storch didn't use much, especially when flying this slow. He had a map, too. He could find Guja again, and the house on the hill where his battalion was stationed. No need for a runway. The Storch could land on a penny.

He licked at the beads of sweat that, despite the cold, had formed on his top lip. Golitsin, that disturbed son of a bitch, had really shaken him up. He pulled his jacket down.

"My ass will be rubbed raw by the time I'm through flying this thing," he muttered.

Golitsin seemed to have calmed down. Afanasiv relaxed. Flying a

Storch was not simple, but what a plane. Ugly, spindly, ungraceful, yet ever so honest. In spite of the debacle on the ice, he was pleased at how he'd managed so far.

And then he felt the solid barrel of a pistol pressing into the soft flesh of his neck.

"Turn back," said Golitsin, crouching behind him. "I don't want to fly this thing, but if you don't do what I say, I will."

Afanasiv's surprise turned to loathing. He glanced at the controls to make sure everything was in order.

Golitsin shoved the gun into Afanasiv's Adam's apple. Afanasiv coughed. "I'm not afraid to die up here," he declared calmly. "The Storch will make a nice coffin. But you, Golitsin—" He gave a sharp snort of laughter. "Watch this."

Pulling back on the throttle, he cranked the flaps sharply. The plane's nose dipped downward. Golitsin shrieked. "See?" Afanasiv cried, yanking the plane back up. "Shoot me if you want, but I'm not turning back. I have a duty to perform."

Afanasiv scowled. A shadow had fallen across the plane. Anxious, he looked up. Hovering just above the right wing was an IL-2 Russian fighter plane. Desperate, he tried to stall the Storch so that it would spiral down out of the Russian gunner's path, but the Storch was stubborn and refused to fall. Gunfire roared out of the IL-2, hitting the petrol canister beside him. Seconds later, the cockpit burst into flames.

Afanasiv's eyes burned like coals. With terror, he realized he couldn't see. And then, too late, the plane plummeted.

"Now you stall, you old bird?" Afanasiv cried.

Behind him, Golitsin was yelling. "Afanasiv, do something. Oh shit, I'm burning up. My clothes, my face!"

"I can't see," Afanasiv shouted, groping for the controls. "Take the plane!"

Another explosion rocked the plane and it fell toward the sea. In those final seconds, Afanasiv pictured the horse lying on the ice and all the people who had died under his command.

"God forgive me," he whispered.

The horses plodded on, the black water gurgling menacingly under the thin ice beneath their hooves.

By late afternoon the Nehrung rose in the west like a smoky mirage against the darkening sky. Behind, the horizon had turned a fierce, unnatural red. Frauenburg, Braunsberg, and Königsberg—all of the mainland cities—were in flames.

The gruesome sights seemed to grow worse. On the ice were human corpses, burned out wagons, and dead horses. Russian, French, and Polish prisoners of war limped alongside German soldiers, their foreign words mingling in the wind.

"What now?" Helling grumbled as the wagon came to a stop.

Joshi looked out over the side of the wagon and saw a thin, pock-faced boy in a baggy army coat sidle up to the trestle.

"You can't go on land here," the boy told Helling, brandishing a pistol. "No one can."

"Why not, for heaven's sake?" Helling asked, exasperated.

A flush of shame joined the pockmarks on the boy's cheeks. "This—this crossing is for Nazi officials only," he stammered. "You have to go toward Kahlberg."

He pointed left. "It's another six miles. I'm afraid you'll have to overnight on the ice, but trust me, it'll be safer to cross onto land in the morning. The edges thaw in the day and freeze at night." He tipped his green field cap. "Good luck."

"To hell with all of them," Helling muttered, pointing the horses in the direction the boy had indicated. The horses plodded on, the drone of airplanes hovering nearby.

Manya covered her ears. "I hate that sound," she whispered.

When the ice was finally swallowed up by darkness, Helling pulled the mares to a halt. The yellow moon hung low in the sky. On the shore, not far away, a few small fires blazed between the ragged tree trunks. They reminded Joshi of his people—his mother and the older women cooking by the stove, his father drinking honeyed wine by the fire. He thought about Sofia, how she loved to sit on a bench with the other children, weaving arm bangles out of wildflowers and grass. *Could she still be alive? Did Klawan really try to help her?* He pulled at the piece of red yarn Nuri had given him. *What if there is still a chance? I have no right to ask, but please.*

"It's time to eat," he heard Helling say. "Kahlberg is just over the dunes. We should be able to cross onto land at dawn."

"Helling?" Joshi asked, his voice quavering. "If we make it onto the Nehrung tomorrow, how long until we get to Stutthof?"

"It should be a day," Helling replied. "But don't count on anything."

✦

"There are no more biscuits," Lillian announced when they were all huddled in the back of the wagon. She turned the biscuit tin upside down, and the rose tissue lining fluttered away in the wind. "Not much else, either. It's taken longer than we thought to get this far."

"And more mouths than you expected," Joshi said. "Leonid and I are quite used to not eating, so please give what you have to the others."

"Don't be ridiculous," Helling snapped. "Whatever we have will be shared among all of us." He looked at Lillian. "What's left?"

"A few walnuts, some dried ham. Enough for a meal."

"Well, then, that's our dinner."

✦

Joshi sat beside Manya, cracking the small pile of walnuts that Lillian had rationed out. Two by two, he pressed them together in his palm. The cold had made his bones feel painfully brittle. Still, he dug at the meat, giving the fleshier pieces to Manya and keeping only the tiniest for himself. After an hour, Helling blew out the lamp. "Let's get some sleep," he said. "Tomorrow will be a long day."

Joshi rolled the beaver fur into a pillow and pulled an eiderdown over himself while Manya huddled between him and Zarah. He shifted his hips against the hard floor to try to find a comfortable position, but the oily walnuts churned in his empty stomach. He was so cold, and the pain in his ear never ceased. Still, he could hear the even whisper of Manya's breath. It was deep and steady, and he knew that in spite of her grief, she had fallen asleep.

Her hair lay like a tangled net of silver over the fur, a few strands grazing his cheekbone. He dared himself to inhale. She smelled of gunpowder, horse blood, sweat, and birch oil. For as long as he had known her, she had used birch oil on her skin.

"The camphor in the oil relieves my aches and pains whenever I ride too much," she used to tell him.

I wish it could take away the pain you're left with now, he thought sadly. *I wish it were that simple.* He swallowed, trying to wet his throat, but he felt so dried up, so empty. He was scared, too, because Manya could read him like a book. If he let her see the man he'd been in Schichau, she would turn away from him in disgust.

He stared at the moonlight creeping across the dunes. She'd lost everything—her home, her parents, Aztec. But it was different for her. She hadn't lost her soul. She was good. She could still find something to live for. Someone.

FORTY-FIVE

At dawn, Helling maneuvered the wagon off the ice. "We made it," he muttered when the wheels rolled onto the narrow isthmus that separated the Haff from the Baltic Sea.

He twisted around to look toward East Prussia and felt his body shake as he tried to swallow his tears. Manya followed his gaze. East Prussia lay behind them like a line of dark blue ink dissolving in the mist. She pulled her overcoat tighter, as if it could protect what was left of her spirit.

Helling's sobs broke the stillness. "I'll always see them," he said. "My darling Karin by the fireplace in our cottage. Maritza reading at the table. It's winter, and here I am remembering the handfuls of raspberries they picked for me in summer." He bowed his head and squeezed the bridge of his nose with his gloved fingers. Lillian put her hand on his arm and hugged Zarah closer.

"I didn't know how much this part would hurt," he said. As if to fortify himself, he shook the reins and moved the wagon forward once again.

Panic shot through Manya. "Wait!" she cried. "I'm not ready. We can't leave!"

"I'm sorry, child," Lillian said. "They're waving us into the column."

"Where are Mami and Father?" she asked, choking on her words. "I have to tell them about Aztec."

Lillian's eyes moved to Joshi, pleading for him to do something, but his face was white, his body motionless. "Oh Lord," she whispered, bringing her hand to her throat. "She's breaking my heart. Leonid, please—"

Shooting Joshi a confused look, Leonid moved to the back of the wagon. Gently, he took hold of Manya's hand. "What are you thinking?" he asked quietly, his voice kind and inviting.

Manya felt the pain lessen. Breathing in the cold, fresh air, she raised her head to stare at the horizon. "Just memories," she murmured after a while. "Of Guja."

"Share one with me—anything," Leonid said, squeezing her fingertips.

Slowly, she fixed her eyes on him. Warming to the kindness in his eyes, she murmured, "I see my mother playing the piano, my father's mandolin hanging on the wall. I see river spiders on the water." She looked at Joshi. "You and I watching them as children. Do you remember how quickly they moved across the surface? They never left a ripple."

Joshi nodded, but he said nothing.

She sighed, her gaze traveling back over the side of the wagon. "Guja was like a golden frame. I could look through it and see beauty and wildness everywhere."

When a flock of geese rose up from the Nehrung forest, cutting a dark "v" against the sky, Manya looked at Joshi once more. "What's it like for you?" she asked.

He stared into her eyes. "It hurts," he said, "to abandon the graves of my people. They were always with me, even though I was not always with them." He shrugged and twisted the red yarn on his wrist. "All I can do now is try to find out what happened to Sofia. If I don't, it won't matter how far I travel—I'll always want to come back and look for her. And so I welcome moving on."

FORTY-SIX

The forest that bordered the road running along the Nehrung spit was a gloomy one. It appeared to have risen out of an apocalyptic fairy tale. Every foot of pavement was covered with refugees moving westward, every inch between the trees taken up with litter.

Manya was surprised to find that people still had things to throw away, but she soon realized that the living had cast their last memories, the ones they'd preserved even across the ice, aside. Hairbrushes and dolls, books and candlesticks were among the debris that lay strewn on the ground. Above her, loose garments flapped in the pine branches like forgotten ghosts waiting for a familiar body to inhabit them. Sprays of feathers from torn eiderdowns flew up on the wind, only to settle back down like lost wings into empty shoes and open suitcases.

Manya's mind wandered to the things she had left behind and those few things she still had. She reached for the butterfly amber.

It was gone.

"What's wrong?" asked Joshi, seeing her dismay.

"The amber you once gave me. I must have lost it on the ice."

"No," he mumbled. "I have it."

She stared at him. "That's impossible."

"I know," he said in a baffled voice. "But I found it in my pocket this morning when I went to brush my teeth. I thought maybe you'd returned it when I was sleeping because—" Joshi cut himself short.

A prickle ran along the back of her neck. "No," she breathed. "I didn't."

He reached into his pocket and pulled out the shiny piece of orange resin. Bewildered, she stared at it. "I must have given it to you in my sleep," she murmured.

He gestured for her to take it, but she shook her head no.

"I have my ring," she said, looking down at her hand with a quiet smile. "Both our mothers are sitting right here on my finger, so I'm protected. You keep that piece for now."

Helling interrupted their conversation.

"We had better find shelter," he said. "I've been keeping an eye on those black clouds, but the air is starting to smell like metal. We're in for a blizzard. Unfortunately we're already at the western end of Kahlberg. There aren't many houses out here, and people are fighting to get into every one we pass."

Manya hadn't noticed it before, but there *was* a tension running through the refugees. People were pulling over, trying to find shelter from the oncoming storm.

"Surely there must be somewhere for us to stay?" she said.

"The Kahlberg Resort is our only hope," Helling answered, pointing to a large manor in the distance.

As the wagon drew closer to the resort, the awful smell of human waste overwhelmed them. Hundreds of people crowded the once elegant lawn. Most were sick or starving, and some were dead.

Lillian gagged and pulled her scarf over her nose. "Keep moving," she instructed. "We'll catch a disease if we stay."

Manya glanced at Zarah, whose frightened face said what words could not.

Leonid, attentive as always, caught Manya's eye and gave her a knowing nod. "Zarah," he called. "Why don't you come back here with me? Maybe you can show me how to draw a horse."

Zarah crawled over to him, red and black crayons clutched tightly in her fist. As soon as she was preoccupied, Manya spoke with Helling and Lillian.

"What are we going to do?" she asked.

"Keep going," Lillian said. "We'll find shelter somewhere."

Snow had started falling in big, soggy flakes, making progress on the overcrowded road even more difficult. When they finally rolled out of Kahlberg, Helling pulled the horses to a stop under a cluster of fir trees. Wrinkling his nose, he sniffed at the air like a hunter. Moments later, he hollered a quick giddyap and urged the mares over the brush-covered embankment and onto a rocky deer path.

"Why are we leaving the road?" Lillian asked, astonished.

Helling set his head against the gusting wind. "This road will become a wind tunnel. We have to find shelter elsewhere before the blizzard worsens."

Joshi was leaning over the side of the wagon. "Over there," he called, pointing to the right.

Helling scanned the wooded area and nodded. The snow was whipping down in clumps now, and Manya had to squint to see the large outcropping of rocks for which they were headed. Within minutes, Helling had pulled the wagon to a stop beside the rocky formation. He and Joshi leaped to the ground, and together they began tearing down pine boughs, which they leaned against the wagon frame and secured with mounds of snow.

"Leonid!" Helling shouted, reaching up to saw off another branch with his knife. "Go! Gather some stones and set them in a pile over there." He pointed to a bare spot beside the wagon. "Manya! Lillian! See if you can find firewood."

For twenty minutes they worked at an urgent pace. Soon a fire burned in a shallow pit Helling had dug and lined with Leonid's stones. The snow blew even harder, stinging their faces.

When they had done what they could to secure the wagon and the mares against the wind and snow, they climbed back inside. Helling lowered himself onto the wagon's bench and lit a lantern.

"Now, we just have to wait," he said, letting out his breath.

⚜

They sat huddled together in the wagon, the wind rocking them from side to side, the snow railing down from above. Still, they had a fire outside, and every hour they took turns gathering warm rocks, which they wrapped in fur to keep their hands and feet warm. Helling sat near the front, keeping his nerves in check by whittling a small doll for Zarah out of a smooth pine bough. As he carved, he looked to the back of the wagon, where Leonid was entertaining Zarah and Lillian with shadow puppets.

Joshi sat on the floor, his back propped up against a cushion, his eyes cast upward away from the group. He didn't want anything to do with their games. Every time he looked at Zarah he thought of Sofia, and dread would rip through his chest, so hard it hurt.

When Leonid started singing a silly Russian song about geese called "Gusi Gusi, Ga–Ga–Ga," Zarah erupted in laughter. Manya laughed, too. Sliding from her bench, she moved closer to Joshi. Tenderly she touched his arm, hoping to share the lightness of the moment. Joshi pulled back.

His forehead hurt where the old scar cut though his eyebrow. Annoyed, he rubbed it. "I can't do this," he snapped, shaking Manya's hand off his arm. Manya looked at the others, who were still laughing at Leonid's puppets. She hesitated, but then she gathered herself and leaned toward Joshi. Her eyes fell over his hard jaw, his tightly compressed mouth. "What's wrong?" she asked in a hoarse whisper. "Can't you feel some happiness for Zarah, some relief that she's laughing?"

He shook his head. "I can't pretend to be happy, nor do I feel one bit of relief. You expect me to laugh? All I see is Sofia in prison and my parents dead in the snow!"

Manya inhaled, feeling the hard, familiar knot in her stomach that Joshi's presence so often elicited now. Outside the wind howled. She was hungry and cold.

"You're not the only one who has suffered, Joshi," she hissed. "What about Helling? And Lillian? My parents? And Aztec?"

Her voice, suddenly so vehement and full of bitterness, took Joshi aback. Until now she had been patient with him, but this sharpness in her was like a slap in his face.

"What the hell do you know?" he snapped. "Those losses amount to nothing, *nothing* compared to what other people suffered in this war." He snorted at her. "But how would you know? You have no idea what happened in Stutthof or in Schichau. You weren't arrested and hauled away, were you? But I was. So were Sofia and Nuri. *I'm different from you.*"

His voice had grown loud, and Leonid stopped his shadow play, turning with the others to face him, but Joshi took no notice. He carried on, spitting his words at Manya. "They would *never* have taken *you*. *You're* not Romani. *You're* a German. Your can trace your history back to blond, blue-eyed princesses."

"Enough, Joshi!" Helling commanded, but Joshi ignored him, his eyes taking on an even harder glint as they narrowed in on Manya.

"And now, even *you* are acting like a Nazi to preserve a bloodline." He let out a nasty laugh. "A bloodline of horses, mind you. Tell me, do your Trakehners have more value than Gypsies or Jews?"

Helling slammed his fist against the bench. "Enough, I said!"

Tears stung Manya's eyes.

"Joshi," Helling growled fiercely. "I think you'd better go change out the rocks. This batch seems to have cooled off."

"It would be my pleasure," Joshi spat.

"Oh, sweetheart," Lillian said, moving toward Manya when Joshi had gone.

"I've tried to save my horses because I love them," she pleaded. "Not because I'm—"

"I know," Lillian murmured, smoothing back her hair.

"I hate him!" Manya sobbed.

"He's been through a terrible time."

But Manya's jaw was set in a hard line. *How dare he?*

When Joshi returned to the wagon, he announced in a surly voice that all was well with the horses. Manya shot him a hateful look. Sullen, he sat down in a corner.

Manya's thoughts fell in line with the sound of the blizzard hammering at the wagon. Eventually, however, she drifted off to sleep, only vaguely aware of Leonid and Helling taking turns throughout the night to check on the fire.

When morning came, a deep, insulating stillness had spread over the woods. Manya rose and peeked through the pine bough covering the rear of the wagon. The snow had fallen with ferocity for most of the night, swallowing much of the woods in its wake.

"We're going to have to dig ourselves out of this one," said Helling, coming up beside her. "Snow won't stop the Russians."

Manya nodded.

"Joshi, Leonid," Helling called. "Wake up. And bring the ax, please."

Joshi brushed by Manya wordlessly. She didn't care. She had nothing to say to him. When the crunch of his boots faded in the snow, she set about boiling tea with Lillian, relieved that he was gone.

Helling, Joshi, and Leonid spent much of the day digging out the wagon. When they finally succeeded in clearing a path back to the road, Helling climbed into the trestle. Manya, Lillian, and Zarah joined him up front to lighten the weight in the rear. Clicking his tongue, he coaxed the stiff-legged mares to a walk. With creaking wheels, the wagon rolled back over the embankment, onto the road.

But the column had frozen to a halt.

As Manya's eyes scanned the trail of wagons, she saw that many people had not survived the storm, and many more were sick and injured. She and Lillian exchanged a look, and after wrapping Zarah in another layer of blankets, they left the wagon and waded down the snowy road, administering help wherever they could. Pressing their heads against the wind, they comforted the dying and covered frostbitten limbs with whatever makeshift bandages and blankets they could find. Helling, Joshi, and Leonid joined the effort to clear the mounds of snow blocking the way.

Nightfall came and, almost imperceptibly, the column started to move forward again. Helling called Manya and Lillian back to the wagon. As much as she didn't want to see Joshi or hear his voice, she climbed back in.

FORTY-SEVEN

*T*he dunes of the Frische Nehrung stretched along the Baltic coast. To Joshi they looked like giant mammoths resting under an enormous blanket of sand and snow. He sniffed at the salty wind, a memory blowing across his mind—of a childhood summer years before when his clan had camped here. He had eaten smoked eel and rhubarb strudel with his mother and had searched with her for cobbles of amber along the beach.

A sharp bump jolted him out of his reverie.

"You all right, Helling?" he asked, glancing up. "These potholes could knock the breath out of any man."

"I'm managing," Helling answered. "If only these Nazi bigwigs in their fancy Mercedes Benzes would stop blowing their horns. The horses hate it." He shook his head. "Idiots. Kept us trapped for months, and now they can't get away fast enough."

A lorry slowed down beside them.

"Do you want us to take your women to Danzig?" hollered a soldier with a bandaged arm. "They won't make it otherwise. The Russians have broken through the front lines."

Zarah winced when she heard their loud voices, and Lillian quickly placed a protective arm around her shoulder. "Thanks for offering," she said, waving them on. "But we're staying together."

"I hope to God it's the right choice," Helling mumbled.

They carried on along the curving road, sand and ice grinding beneath the wheels until they finally arrived in the little fishing village of Bodenwinkel, the last on the Nehrung spit. The sun broke through the clouds, turning the sand dunes into golden canopies.

"Look," Manya murmured, momentarily forgetting her anger at Joshi and pointing to a bunch of wet pine needles. "It's almost as if a thaw is settling over the land."

"Isn't it something?" Helling asked. "No matter how harsh the winter, how devastating the war, the trees still hold their branches to the sun. Eventually the ice melts and winter turns to spring."

"And one day this war will be over," breathed Lillian.

The wagon rattled on. After two hours, Joshi noticed that the dunes had stopped converging and the straggly juniper bushes had become a forest of firs. The air smelled of resin more than sea.

"We're coming up on Stutthof, aren't we, Herr Helling?" he asked, a ripple of terror passing through him.

"Yes," Helling answered, handing the reins to Lillian. "But listen, your search for Sofia could be very dangerous for all of us." His voice caught in his throat. "You will have to move quickly to locate her. If the police get wind of this, we'll be in serious trouble."

Joshi nodded coldly, pushing down a wave of nausea. The mere proximity of Stutthof prison made him feel weak and small, like a panicked child in the shadow of a monster, but the thought of not finding Sofia was even scarier.

As Manya watched him, her gaze fell on his chest. She saw that he was breathing too fast. He turned to look at Leonid, who sat clutching a Russian Bible he had found on the Haff.

"We've come full circle to the forest of the dead," he whispered, his face ashen.

Manya's cheeks burned with guilt and remorse. She would never know what they had been through at that camp.

All at once, Leonid's scarred eyes fastened on a point beyond the wagon. "Look," he cried in a hoarse whisper. "Over there."

Joshi's gaze drifted sideways. Rising out of the ground between the leafless trees were the kommandant's quarters and the guardhouse. His breath stopped. The Death Gate stood open. Hundreds of refugees were filing through the gate, into the Stutthof Prison Camp and onto the Himmler Allee.

"What are they doing?" he asked, his mouth so dry he could barely speak.

"They're looking for shelter," Helling replied.

"Why would anyone stay there?" Joshi shook his head in disbelief. "Who can find rest among the tortured? The murdered?" His eyes stung from keeping them open so long, but he couldn't blink. How many had died in the camp, he wondered. Ten thousand? Fifty thousand? One hundred thousand?

His gaze met Manya's, catching her off guard. Quickly she looked away, her resolve hardening. Just yesterday, he had likened her to a Nazi. She couldn't forgive him for that.

Twenty minutes later, they rolled into the village of Stutthof. Joshi began to fidget, his eyes fixing on every window, every door. Helling pulled the wagon to a stop near the sidewalk and called to a young boy who was standing in a doorway, holding a yellow cat.

"Son, do you know where the seamstress lives?"

"Frau Kniep? Two houses back, on this side of the street," the boy answered. "Just knock. It might take her a while, but she'll answer."

Helling tipped his hat. "Be careful, Joshi," he murmured, turning around, but Joshi had already jumped off the wagon.

"I'm coming," Manya said before Joshi could protest. "It's better if a woman is with you."

He shot her a concerned look. "That might not be a good idea."

"Don't argue," she said. "Let's just go."

Joshi's eyes softened. "Are you sure?"

Manya refused to meet his gaze. "I'm not coming for you, Joshi, but for Sofia." And with that she headed off in the direction of Frau Kniep's house.

⁂

Joshi caught up with her and knocked at the seamstress's door, his heart pounding hard against his ribcage. When the door opened, he found himself peering into the soft brown eyes of a petite older woman with a seemingly gentle disposition. In her left hand, she held a tape measure case embroidered with a colorful display of flowers.

"Frau Kniep?" Manya asked in friendly voice. "Sorry to bother you, but we're looking for a young girl named Sofia."

Joshi saw the color drain from the woman's face. "There's no one here by that name," she said, recovering quickly.

"Please," Joshi said. "We haven't come to harm her."

"Who are you?"

"Joshi Karas. I'm her brother."

The seamstress sighed, her eyes searching the street. For a moment, he thought she was going to call for the police or slam the door shut. But, to his relief, she invited them in.

"Who told you?" she asked, locking the door behind her.

"A prisoner, a priest from Stutthof who knew Officer Klawan," Joshi said.

"Franz Klawan was my stepbrother," she said, her eyes misting over. "Like so many, he's dead now. Ach, he made a terrible choice when he joined the SS, but he wasn't all bad. He tried to save a few. He knew how much I love children, so he brought your sister to me."

Joshi tried to swallow. "Sofia? Is she—?"

Frau Kniep smiled tenderly and pointed to the ceiling. "She's here. I keep her hidden in the attic. Come," she motioned. She steered them past a sewing table and led them up two flights of stairs to a dimly lit hallway, where she opened a trap door in the ceiling. Joshi's knees shook as he followed her up the ladder. It couldn't be this easy. Something awful was going to happen. He pulled himself through the scuttle hole and looked past the sloping rafters.

She *was* there. His Sofia—huddled up as if she were trying to make herself as small as possible, reading on a cushion. Hearing a noise, she turned to look. A cry escaped her lips.

Crouching down, he gathered her in his arms. How light she had become, a small wren of a thing. He kissed her face again and again, as if to assure himself that she wasn't a ghost.

"I knew you'd find me!" she cried, bursting into tears. "Just like the last time."

Her thin shoulders shook, and she pressed her forehead to his chest. He held her close, talking to her in Romani and soothing her with his hands. After a while, she grew still, wiped her nose with her sleeve and let her gaze fall on Manya. "You're here too?" she asked. "How did you find me?"

Manya considered how to answer for a moment, and then she bent down to brush the tears from Sofia's cheeks. "It's a long story," she murmured, kissing Sofia's head. "But right now, we must go. The others are waiting."

From beside the scuttle hole, Frau Kniep began to cry. "I can't let her go without the coat I sewed for her," she wept, making her way down the ladder. "The scarf and the gloves. She's thin as a rail. The cold will kill her."

Joshi glanced at Manya. "You go first," he whispered. "Sofia and I will be right behind you."

When Manya's head had vanished down the hole, he gripped Sofia's hands and lowered her onto the ladder. Returning to the front room, Joshi anxiously watched Frau Kniep take a small brown coat off the coat rack by the door. What if she changes her mind, he thought? What if she screams? If only they were in the wagon already.

"Come, child," Frau Kniep murmured, slipping the sleeves over Sofia's arms and fastening the coat buttons one by one. Joshi heard a dog bark outside. *Why is she dallying*, he wondered in panic. But then he saw her face, and he understood. Frau Kniep loved Sofia.

He stepped forward to lay a hand on Frau Kniep's shoulder. "Thank you," he murmured sincerely. "For everything you've done, for risking your life."

"She's like my daughter," Frau Kniep whispered, bowing her head.

After a moment, however, Frau Kniep gathered herself. She picked up a piece of fabric from the floor and wiped her eyes. "Where is your transportation?"

"Just up the street," he said quietly.

"My neighbors have prying eyes," she warned. "So when you exit my door, pretend nothing's happened. Don't run."

"Auf Wiedersehen," Sofia whispered, hugging the woman. "I'll never forget you."

"God be with you, my darling," Frau Kniep said, stroking her cheek. And she unlocked the door.

***

Leonid saw the trio approach and waited to help Sofia and Manya into the wagon. Helling stood like a sentinel in the trestle, watching the street.

"Is everything all right?" Helling asked.

"Yes," Manya said, pulling out a blanket for Sofia from the canvas duffle. "We were very lucky."

"Are you being followed?"

"I don't think so," Joshi answered, "but let's go." He placed a cushion on the wagon floor and lifted Sofia onto it before sitting down beside her.

When she was settled, Sofia shyly acknowledged Zarah, who sat in the trestle with her face pressed into Lillian's coat.

Helling slid into the driver's seat and slapped the reins. The wheels turned, throwing up a spray of dirty snow. Overhead, the winter sun had left the sky, its orange rays tapering off into long dark fingers.

When they were nearly out of the village, Sofia pointed to a stone cottage set back off the street. "Klawan's house," she whispered, hardly moving a muscle. "That's where Nuri died."

Joshi pulled her close.

"Can you tell me what happened?" he asked softly.

She paused, as if to summon her courage. "On the night we were supposed to start on the march, he told me to hide in the trunk of his car, and he brought us to his house. Nuri was so sick. She had sores on her face and all over her body, and she was coughing up blood."

A nerve twitched under her eye, and Joshi tenderly tried to still it with his finger.

"Nuri told me she was beyond help and that Klawan had given her a poison capsule, something he kept in case he was captured by the Russians. She told me straight out that she was going to take it. She knew Frau Kniep wanted me, and she made him take me there that same night."

"You know for sure that Nuri is dead?" Joshi asked gently.

"Yes," she said, and began to cry. "Frau Kniep told me." Sofia pushed up her sleeve and began to pull on a red string looped around her wrist. "I still miss her. But Nuri gave me this. She said you had one, too."

"I do," Joshi smiled, showing her his wrist.

A dreamy look passed across Sofia's eyes. "She said as long as I wore it, you would find me."

"She was right," Joshi nodded. He looked up at the sky and sighed. "I kiss your wise hands, Nuri."

As the road curved out of Stutthof, Joshi kept his eyes fixed on Klawan's house. When it was just a matchbox against the aubergine-tinged sky, he imagined Klawan standing in front of him.

Did you care about Nuri, Joshi thought. *Maybe. About my sister? I doubt it. But then who can trust the kindness of killers? Nevertheless, however contemptible you are, you kept your promise to Nuri. Sofia is alive. For that, I thank you.*

⁂

Manya sat at the back of the wagon, watching Joshi and Sofia. They sat side by side, the blanket resting on their legs. Every so often Joshi would touch his sister's face, a look of awe filling the deep creases that ran down the sides of his mouth.

They spoke in low tones, their heads touching. As they spoke, sometimes Sofia cried, but for the most part, she was filled with adoration for her brother.

Zarah, who had been watching, climbed down from the trestle and crawled next to Sofia to stare at her with curious gray-green eyes.

"You remember Sofia, don't you, sweetheart?" Helling said, craning his neck to look at her. Zarah was silent.

"I remember you," Sofia smiled, leaning forward to peer at the younger girl in the dusky light. "You came to our caravan site with your Papa last year. You rode a bay mare. My Papa said your seat in the saddle was the best he'd ever seen in a girl."

Zarah began to chew on her gloved knuckles. Sensing that something was amiss, Sofia moved toward her, gently uncurling her fingers until her palms faced the sky. Tenderly, she placed her palms on top of Zarah's and looked her straight in the eye.

Does she hear what Zarah can't say? Manya wondered.

All at once, a grin splayed from ear to ear across Zarah's face. Her little hands began to move in unison with Sofia's, their silent communication unfolding. But suddenly, Zarah froze. Needing reassurance, she turned toward Lillian, who was watching from the trestle, her jade-colored scarf trailing behind her in the rolling wind.

"It's all right, precious heart," Lillian cooed. "You can stay there. Now you have another friend."

Zarah blushed. Lowering her head, she smiled into her collar.

They reached the Vistula River bank at sunrise. The refugees lined up on the shore made the busy little ferry look like a bobbing toy on the water. Luck was with them, though. After only an hour, they were able to board. The ferry left the shore, its wide bow plowing through the ice chunks that floated in the river, its stern churning up a foamy path in the brown water.

Manya sat between Joshi and Leonid, while Zarah and Sofia slept, curled up like sisters beneath a heavy duvet thickly crusted with mud.

Leonid leaned forward, his cheeks half buried in the collar of his coat.

"Does either of you know the date?"

Manya squinted at the sky and counted the days. "February 8, 1945," she said with a start. "My mother's birthday."

Her throat seized, and she found it impossible to swallow. Who would lay the table with flowers for her Mami today? Tears fell over the bridge of her nose and onto her lips. She licked at them, the salt bitter on her tongue.

Joshi, overcome by her sadness, reached out to touch her shoulder.

She turned to face him. "No, Joshi. We aren't the same people anymore, right?"

She wanted to press her cheek into his coat, but his hateful words still echoed in her mind. She was no better than a Nazi.

"I just wanted to—" Joshi started, then stopped.

"What?" Manya shot back.

"Vavara used to say that water guides the soul," he whispered.

A soft sob escaped her. "But where is it taking us?"

"I don't know," he answered in a hushed voice. "Wasn't it you who once told me that faith always holds out its hand?"

"Maybe I was wrong," Manya said wearily.

Joshi said nothing but passed her a pillow that was lying at his feet.

Nodding, she hugged it to her chest.

She slept, even when the wagon rolled onto a second barge that ferried them across the last arm of the Vistula River. It wasn't until much later, when the mares' hooves were clip-clopping along the firm road to Danzig, that she finally opened her eyes.

FORTY-EIGHT

Manya gazed at Danzig's St. Mary's Basilica, taking in the high, arched windows and graceful turrets decorating every corner of the building. Untouched by bombs, the beautiful church still stood in its full majesty. Outside its massive doors, parishioners were offering travelers hot coffee and buttered buns. At the sight of food, Helling pulled the wagon to a stop. An elegant elderly woman wearing a black cloche hat came up to hand him a steaming cup of coffee.

"Welcome, welcome," she said warmly.

In the trestle, Lillian and Helling exchanged a look. The serene atmosphere of the city felt surreal, almost uncomfortable.

Helling cleared his throat. "Madam," he asked courteously. "In every other town we've passed through, the people are fighting to get out. Why is everyone so calm here? Do you know something we don't?"

The woman placed a hand on the sideboard of the wagon to steady herself and laughed. "The Russians won't get this far. Our city has been declared a stronghold."

Helling sipped his coffee and looked at her with solemn eyes. For a moment, he was too shocked to speak. "I'm sorry to tell you this, but we encountered Russian soldiers not far back, and we were lucky to escape them."

The woman waved him away. "Look around you," she said. "If there were danger, wouldn't the citizens be panicking? Closing down their stores and running for their lives?" She shook her head. "We can't let the Russians change our way of life or they'll win. Besides," she smiled, "we must follow our own God-given guidance and the guidance of the Führer."

Hearing her, Lillian's eyes grew wide. How many people were still in this kind of denial, she wondered.

Helling, however, did his best not to let his feelings show. Coughing politely, he thanked the woman for the food and watched her hobble away.

Another woman passing by had heard their conversation. Her arms balanced a load of heavy bags, but she paused and turned to Helling.

"Sir," she said, fear running through her eyes. "I believe what you say about the Russians. A few trains are still running west through Pomerania to Stettin. The women and the two girls can probably find a passage. But I warn you. The *Wehrmacht* police are very strict regarding men. You won't be able to flee. And they're enforcing the same policy for ships leaving the harbor."

"Thank you for letting us know," Helling called to her, but she had already disappeared into the crowd.

Lillian mumbled something under her breath.

"What did you say?" Helling asked.

"I said, *mit gegangen, mit gefangen, mit gehangen.* If we go together and are caught, we die together."

The wagon jostled on and turned into the *Lange Strasse.*

"What shall we do, Manya?" Helling asked, worried. "I'm at a loss. If we go near the docks, we may find a soup kitchen and a refugee tent, but no shelter for the horses. And Shambhala needs rest. She's fast approaching her time. Her udder is beginning to swell."

Manya stared out at the blur of shops and people crowding the busy thoroughfare that ran toward the water. "If only we knew someone here," she said, struggling to maintain her composure.

Her mind raced. If Shambhala gave birth now, the foal would not make it to the West. If they risked taking the coastal road, the foal would be too vulnerable to withstand the journey. Most likely it would mean death for them, too. Red Army battalions were stationed in pockets all over the countryside now, in Prussia, Poland, and Pomerania. At least that's what a fisherman in Bodenwinkel had told them. In this city, people still held out hope, but the Russians were working their way systematically across the Oder River into Berlin.

Panic struck her. Why hadn't she thought this through? "I guess I was a fool to believe we could get out," she said, moving from the touch of Joshi's hand against the small of her back. She saw him flinch, but she needed to admit the truth. "We've come this far, but the Russians are all around us. It's hopeless. The road west spells death. The trains won't take you or the horses. Neither will the ships. We won't make it."

"Come on," he murmured. "It's not like you to give up."

She shook her head numbly and stared at the stately homes running alongside the curved street.

"It's no use. And we don't know anyone here."

"I just thought of someone," Helling mumbled, rubbing his chin thoughtfully and looking at Manya. "Dr. Eckert, our family doctor from Nordenburg. He was called to Danzig because the army needed him. I went to see him back home about a year ago, when your father's horse kicked me in the knee. You remember?"

"I do. But how would you know where he is?"

"He told me. His aunt who passed away had a house here." He scratched his head. "If I could just remember. I believe he said it was on the outskirts of the city, in Steffens Park, near the water."

"Where?" asked Manya. "What street?"

"It's—ach, it's on the tip of my tongue. He mentioned it as I was going out the door. Said I was welcome any time. Wait, I know. It's *Schiller Strasse*."

Lillian clapped her hands together. "Your brain still works! And if we can find him, he's in for a surprise."

By late afternoon, they had located the quiet residential avenue lined with elm trees.

"I'll go knock on the doors," Manya offered, hopping off the wagon.

"Not alone, you won't," said Joshi, following her.

"I'm coming too, then," Leonid declared.

The three of them set off, leaving Helling, Lillian, and the girls at the bottom of the road.

⁂

Helling tapped the stiff fingers of his right hand against his armrest.

"It's been fifteen minutes," he said impatiently.

"For goodness' sake, Klaus," said Lillian. "It's probably a long street."

They heard the loud beep of a horn. Frowning, Helling watched as a military vehicle resembling a steel tub with wheels braked to a halt beside them.

"Damn soldiers in their *Kübelwagens*," he muttered. "What do they want now?"

"You there," called a young man in uniform who was already exiting the vehicle. "You've got one too many horses!"

Helling stared, forcing himself to behave with a sense of calm he did not feel.

The soldier strutted up to Shambhala and Topsie, his boots clicking against the icy pavement. After giving both mares a scrutinizing look, he began to unhitch Topsie.

"What are you doing?" Helling cried.

"I'm requisitioning your mare," the soldier declared matter-of-factly. "For the German army."

"But she's not yours to take," Helling protested.

"The army has the right to take whatever it needs. We'd take her, too," the soldier said, pointing to Shambhala. "Except she's mighty pregnant."

Helling's breath caught in his chest. Suddenly he felt old, helpless. "Please, don't take our mare," he begged. He could feel his mouth quivering. "She belongs to our—" But he couldn't say the word "family." It would have cracked him open, and the soldier might have laughed. Thinking he could plead for Topsie one last time, he stood up in the trestle. However, his knees shook so badly that the soldier grew alarmed and reached for his revolver. Helling heard a click. He even knew the pistol: a Walther P38.

A hand yanked at his belt, and he plopped down hard on the trestle.

"For God's sake, Klaus, sit down," Lillian hissed.

"Look at him," Helling mumbled under his breath. "The war has left him without a soul." Numbly, he watched the soldier tie Topsie to the back of the Kübelwagen and heard the vehicle shift into gear. It sounded so far away, as if it were coming from the edge of the world.

"Sorry, man," the soldier hollered. "I wish I could pay you for your Trakehner. But consider it a trade-off for not drafting you as well. The army needs men, too, even old ones." He snorted. "Put in a claim when the war is over."

The Kübelwagen drove away with Topsie, good-natured as always, trotting behind, her graceful neck stretched long in a valiant effort to keep up.

When the clip-clop of her hooves had faded, Helling pressed his palms to his eyes and wept. "I tell you one thing. If we ever get out of here, we will owe our lives to Topsie and Shambhala and Aztec. All those wagons back there on the trek, all those thousands of people on the run—the horses are the ones saving them from death and rape and prison camps in Siberia. Ach," he lamented. "Topsie gave her all, and I did nothing to save her."

"You couldn't, Klaus," Lillian whispered.

Hearing footsteps, he pulled himself together and glanced up. Manya was running down the sloping street toward the wagon.

"Good news!" she cried. "We've found Dr. Eckert's house."

Helling slid out of the trestle. Limping up to Shambhala, he began to rearrange the harness traces so she could pull the wagon alone.

"You're on your own now, girl," he murmured, running his fingers along Shambhala's chin groove. "But Manya mustn't see us upset."

A siren was whining into the night. He fastened the second breech strap and waited for Manya.

"Where's Topsie?" she asked when she reached the wagon.

Helling watched her excitement dwindle, saw the shock of the new loss in her eyes when he told her what had happened. "There's nothing we can do," he said quietly. He bent over to pick up Topsie's bellyband and wiped the buckle that lay heavy against his palm. "Don't cry, child. Shambhala's here." He forced himself to smile. "So am I. They nearly drafted me too."

Manya looked beyond him, her eyes searching the darkness for a glimpse of Topsie.

Turning wordlessly on her heels, she began to walk up the street.

Helling gripped Shambhala's noseband. "I could use a walk, old girl," he said. "And you could use a teammate. At least for this stretch."

⁂

Half an hour later, after Shambhala was safely ensconced in Dr. Eckert's garden shed, they found themselves sitting at a round, copper-topped table near a potbellied stove that stood in the center of his large kitchen.

The doctor was a kind-faced elderly man who looked as if he had been broad-shouldered once. He ambled around the chairs in a pair of thick woolen socks.

"I'm so glad you found me," he smiled. "It's rare to see anyone from Guja now." He took a frying pan out of a cupboard and began to fry three eggs and a few chunks of liver. "Wish I had more food, but ration cards don't buy much these days."

The tantalizing smell of sizzling meat wafted off the stove, and Manya's mouth began to water. She wasn't fond of liver, but she nearly swooned when the good doctor set a plate in front of her. She ate slowly, savoring every bite and every sip of the sugary tea he had offered her. After the plates had been washed and dried, Dr. Eckert poured himself a drop of wine and sat down at the table.

"Danzig will fall," he said, cracking his knuckles. His gaze came to rest on Manya. "I have connections. I can get you out on a train, possibly even the men."

"What about my mare, Shambhala?" Manya asked.

"Leave her behind."

Manya looked down at her hands. Her fingers felt stiff and wooden. She twisted her ring, and the amber caught the light of the stove.

A sharp stab of guilt went through her. She could no longer risk the others' lives for the sake of a horse. Not if Dr. Eckert could get them to safety. But she could stay with Shambhala. She owed it to Aztec.

She blinked at the candle wax dripping onto the table.

Across from her, Dr. Eckert was opening the lid of a small bonbon tin. He passed it around to his guests.

"A little dessert to sweeten your dreams," he said, smiling at Zarah and Sofia. "And then we must all go to bed."

Manya rose from the table. "I want to look in on Shambhala," she said. "She's so pregnant, and after what happened to Topsie, I need reassurance or I won't sleep."

"The shed is locked, but I understand," Helling smiled, reaching into his pocket. "Here's the key."

"I'll come with you," Joshi said.

He rose to fetch their coats.

"Use my lamp," Helling offered. "It's in the wagon. I just refilled it with oil."

※

Joshi and Manya walked along the ice-crusted path that led through the garden, a slim crook of the moon giving off just enough light for them to see the shed and the wagon. When a gust of wind jarred the snow from the leafless branches and whipped it into Manya's eyes, she nearly fell.

"Be careful," Joshi warned, reaching out to catch her hand.

"I'm fine," Manya snapped.

Inside the shed, Shambhala greeted them with a welcoming neigh.

"Ah, my beauty," Manya murmured, offering her the bonbon from her pocket. "I'll do everything within my power to make sure you and your foal are all right." Smoothing out the mare's knotted mane with her fingers, she watched Joshi place the lamp on a dusty rack lined with jars and rusted tools.

In the corner to her right stood a broken handloom covered in cobwebs. A threadbare oriental carpet lay beside it on the floor. Joshi bent over to pick up a fallen broom with worn bristles and began to sweep the dried leaves from the carpet's surface.

"What do you want, Joshi?" asked Manya.

He stared at her. "Can we sit here for a bit? It's cold. I'll get an eiderdown from the wagon."

She looked away, but when he returned a moment later, she sat down next to him and spread the eiderdown over their knees.

Outside, the wind howled, while inside, the sound of Shambhala's steady munching soothed the awkward silence.

Finally, Joshi spoke. "Will you let me apologize?"

"What's there to apologize for?" Manya gazed at Shambhala, who looked so peaceful. "Besides, I wouldn't understand."

"All right, I deserve that," Joshi murmured. He was silent for a long moment. "But then you can let me thank you, can't you? For saving my life and for helping me find Sofia. It could have gone terribly wrong."

Manya shrugged. "Sofia is family."

He turned to look at her, the glow of the lamp softening the creases in his face, but she wouldn't meet his eyes.

"Manya, look at me," he pleaded.

"I can't, Joshi." She began to shake. "What, so that you can push me away again? What is it that you want from me?"

Joshi looked away.

"You were my, my—best friend," Manya continued, "and I thought—I really thought—I didn't deserve that from you!" Tears rolled down her cheeks. "Still, I—I'd like to know—"

"What would you like to know, Manya?" Joshi felt his stomach tie in knots.

"What changed you so?" She finally turned to face him.

He stirred uncomfortably and reached out to stroke Shambhala's muzzle.

"It's not what you think, Manya," he said, shaking his head sadly. "I didn't mean to hurt you!"

"Don't pity me. I couldn't bear it," Manya spat out.

"No," Joshi countered. "You don't understand. Believe me, you wouldn't want me now. The things I went through—they're ugly, not something you want to hear."

"How would you know? You didn't try to tell me anything. Except that I was a Nazi! You looked at me like you didn't even know me."

"I'm sorry," Joshi said quietly, reaching out to touch her arm.

"Please don't," Manya cried.

"I was so afraid that you would turn away from me. I guess I did it for you."

"What?"

"I—I did some things," he said finally, his cheeks flushing red, his voice shaky. "In Schichau, at the shipyard where I worked. They were terrible. I lied to myself. I said I was doing them to save Sofia, but really, I would have done anything for a crust of bread."

He let out a bitter laugh. "On my very first day in Stutthof, a guard hit me and I lost half my hearing. At first I was so upset. Me? Deaf in one ear? What about my music? But later, it almost made me happy, because I felt I was paying for my sins—at least a little." He paused and looked at her uncertainly, shame frozen in his eyes.

But Manya said nothing.

"Manya, my feelings for you haven't changed," he continued. "But I'll never be the same man. I just can't see things the same way."

He took another breath and hesitated.

"I wouldn't have left you," Manya whispered. "No matter what you told me. I loved you!"

"What about now?" he asked quietly.

"Tell me," she murmured.

"If I tell you this, you may never want to be near me again. And honestly, I'll understand." His eyes focused on her. "So, my question to you is, do you really want to know?"

"Yes," she whispered.

The events of the past months spilled out in broken sentences. As Manya listened, the awful fragments fell into place. When he described what the warden made him do, she shuddered. At times Manya thought that if she heard another word, she would run away. But then it struck her. How many others *had* run away from wanting to know?

His voice grew stronger as he shared what had happened to Andras and

Vavara, how he had found them, and how he had dressed and buried them. "I should have been there," he said, his voice shaking with anger.

"Oh God, stop!" she broke in, grabbing the chafed knuckles of his hand and pulling him close. "I'm sorry, Joshi. I'm so sorry." She reached for his face and cupped it in her hands, kissing him softly on the lips. His lips met hers more urgently, and he wrapped his arms around her waist, pulling her so close to him that she felt the bones of his ribs press against her own.

Suddenly he pulled away and gripped her shoulders. "I love you, Manya," he said, seeking her eyes. "That never changed. But I also can't change the past."

He began to cry, and she held him until his sobs subsided.

"I was so sure you would leave when you found out, but you're still here, you're still holding me," Joshi whispered. "Can you still love me?"

His voice had grown so quiet that she barely heard him.

"Of course," she said, kissing the rough stubble of hair at the crown of his head.

"If life is still possible," he said haltingly, "where do we start?"

"Right here," she whispered, pressing her palm against his chest and feeling his heart beat.

"But there are so many ghosts inside me," he murmured gravely. "I've been so afraid that if I get too close to you, something—"

"Something terrible will happen?"

He nodded.

"Come," she murmured, drawing him down beside her on the carpet. "Just lie with me a while, so you know it isn't so."

FORTY-NINE

"Dr. Eckert, you should have a wife," Lillian said, flashing the elderly man a warm smile from the far end of the table where she, Zarah, and Sofia were wiping cutlery.

Helling grinned and bent down to light the candle in the copper tea warmer. "Leave the poor man alone."

"No, no," Manya laughed, setting a stack of plates on the table. "Lillian is right. Dr. Eckert is too good a man to be single. First he heats water so we can all have baths. Then he lays out fresh towels and lemon-scented soap as if we're in a fancy hotel."

"What about using the last of his ration cards on eggs and flour?" Lillian added. "And cooking for us. All this on his day off."

Dr. Eckert blushed and turned back to the *Kaiserschmarrn* pancakes he was frying.

He slid the crispy pancakes onto a platter, dusted them with sugar, and brought them to the table.

"Listen," he sighed, the pleased expression on his face turning earnest. "I don't want to put a damper on things, but you must go. You won't be safe anywhere this side of Berlin."

He sat down at the table and glanced anxiously toward the window. "Get out of Danzig. You too, Leonid," he urged. "Go someplace where your landsmen won't find you, at least until the war is over. I've seen too much. They won't treat you kindly when they hear you've survived a POW camp."

Manya sat quietly under the weight of his words. A glint of sunlight on the windowpane beside her caught her eye. Looking closer, she saw fingerprints smeared in the low corners of the glass. She wiped them away with her napkin and noticed that her hand was shaking.

"What time is it?" she heard Joshi ask.

"Three o'clock," Helling replied.

"Let's go down to the docks, Leonid, and see what we can find," said Joshi.

His voice sounded urgent, and Manya instantly sensed that he was contemplating a way out of Danzig.

"I'm ready," Leonid said, rising from his chair. "If you remember, I was sent to Danzig shipyard from Stutthof, so I know my way around."

"I'm going too," said Helling.

Dr. Eckert sighed and cracked his knuckles nervously. "Do what you must. I tell you, though—it's mayhem down there. A train would make more sense."

The Vistula River canal that flowed into the Danziger Bay was indeed a scene of mayhem. Every foot of water, every inch of dock space was taken up with trawlers, navy vessels, merchant ships, even life rafts.

"These boats aren't here to win the war," Leonid told Joshi. "They're trying to save civilians."

Thousands of people were on the piers. Joshi looked to his left, where several cranes hovered over the crowd. Honking vehicles reversed in and out of the human masses, creating even more chaos. On the other side of the quay, a merchant ship floated in the water, its engines still idling. Women and children leapt from the stern onto a dock.

"What are they doing?" Joshi asked a weather-beaten sailor who was walking beside him.

The sailor looked out over the water. "They've come from ports further north, like Pillau and Königsberg," he replied. "Those ships don't stop. They're the angels of the sea. They turn around and sail right back for more desperate souls."

Near a roped-off area, Joshi noticed four armed port officers dressed in trench coats and black boots. An old man with an amputated leg had fallen on his one knee in front of them and was begging for a ticket to board. Several feet away, at the edge of the wharf, a distraught woman was throwing her baby to a stranger on board a moving ship. Joshi walked over to the elderly woman standing behind her.

"How long have you been waiting here?" he asked.

"Days," she replied wearily.

She pointed to a well-dressed woman in a mink coat climbing up the crowded gangway. "The rich are luckier. Most of us don't have the means."

We'll never get out like this, Joshi thought. *And a horse hasn't a hope in hell.*

A fight broke out beside them.

"This way," Leonid said, grabbing Joshi's arm and pulling him forward.

They made their way along the canal, dodging in and out of the throngs of people.

Leonid pointed to a large, columned building in the distance. "That's the Danziger shipyard. I know it well. Maybe we'll have more luck in that area."

They hurried past the hulking masses of ships moored at the quay. Nipping between skids stacked high with broken crates, they pressed on, vigilant for armed guards or SS storm troopers who might be on patrol.

The smell of ropes and tar hung heavy in the air. Overhead, hungry herring gulls shrieked and swooped. Somehow, the sight of them flying free filled Joshi with hope.

After ten minutes, Leonid slowed the pace. The bank was noticeably quieter here. Dusk was falling, but the sky still held a faint yellow glow, enough to light up the wide concrete piers that ran perpendicular to the main waterway.

"My old stomping grounds," Leonid grinned, pointing to his right. "I sweated buckets in those brick warehouses beside the railway tracks. What you see ahead are the repair docks."

Joshi looked up. Tugboats, freighters, and barges were everywhere, but there were hardly any people.

Leonid read his mind. "The refugees don't come to this area because these vessels all need work. They've been towed here so as not to interfere with those ships that are loaded and ready for departure."

"Goddamn it!" roared an angry voice from the dock beside them. "We'll never get out of this hellhole. After all I've risked hauling supplies and flea-bitten refugees in and out of this harbor. Now I have a mechanical problem, but has one official offered to help? No."

Joshi, Helling, and Leonid looked at each other. A glimmer of hope flashed between them. At the top of the dock, they saw four men standing beside a rusty barge bearing the name *Euphoria*. The tallest of the men was beardless with long, sun-bleached sideburns poking out from beneath his captain's hat. Exasperated, he rubbed his red face with a wind-chapped hand and turned to his crew.

"We need a friggin' fairy to patch our steam line," he muttered angrily, shaking his arm at the docked barge. He began to pace the dock, choking on his curses. "Damn bomb shrapnel. Killed my steamfitter," he cursed. "The Ivans will be here any day. We might as well kiss our asses good-bye. We'll never see Lübeck again."

Helling looked at Joshi and Leonid, his face lighting up. "All right," he whispered. "Let's see what we can do."

They walked toward the end of the pier, where the men were still talking. "Excuse us," Helling called.

"Who the hell are you?" shouted the captain, folding his arms in front of his chest.

"I'm a blacksmith," Helling replied, squaring his shoulders.

"A blacksmith? You look like a peddler to me."

"I heard you say you have a broken steam line," Helling said, ignoring the insult. "Do you want me to take a look? Maybe I can help."

The captain unfolded his arms and craned his neck forward. "Listen, man," he growled, his eyes studying Helling suspiciously. "You better not mess with me, or I'll tear all three of you into pieces and feed you to the sharks." The captain pulled out his pistol.

"We're not messing with you," Joshi assured him. "My friend here is a skilled blacksmith, honest."

"And I was a mechanic on the docks," said Leonid.

The captain kept his pistol out and pondered the group before him for a moment. Then he motioned toward the gangplank that led onto his vessel. "All right, then. Get up there."

He brought them on board and down a hatch, into the stuffy engine room, where he lit a torch and showed them the damage. "Bomb shrapnel," he muttered. "It exploded right through the deck. Killed my good man Hans, too."

"Sorry to hear it," Helling said, bending over to take a look. "It's ruptured the main pipe to the boiler. Pretty bad break. Are your steamfitter's tools on board?"

"Of course, man. On my ship, everything's in order. But I need someone who knows what the hell they're doing."

"You certainly do," Helling said matter-of-factly. "And you need two flat pieces of steel."

"I know," said the captain. "But where the hell do I find them? I'm not a goddamn magician. I can't pull them out of my seaman's cap."

"I know where to find them," Leonid said quietly.

"What?" Joshi asked in a hoarse whisper.

"Excuse us a minute, Captain," Leonid murmured, pulling Joshi aside. When they were out of earshot, Leonid continued: "You strike the bargain to get Shambhala out. I can't do the talking. He won't trust my accent."

"Where the hell are you going to find steel?"

"Leave that to me," Leonid said with a curt nod. "You make the deal."

Joshi cleared his throat. "Captain—what did you say your name was?"

"I didn't say, but it's Bock. Jürgen Bock."

"Well, Captain Bock, this is what I propose. If we find the steel, and Blacksmith Helling here patches your steam line, then you will transport us to Lübeck—but with two women, two girls, and a horse."

The captain gave Helling a crooked smile, his eyes narrowing to glittering slits. "Hmm. Women and children I understand. But a horse?" he said. "That makes seven of you *and* the horse. I'm desperate, so I'm going to say yes. But if you're lying, or if you mess up this job, I promise that I'll kill you."

They followed the captain back up through the hatch. Before stepping onto the gangway, Joshi cast a quick look around. It was almost dark, but the captain's torch revealed a large, boxlike structure midway along the flat deck.

"Is that where you transport livestock?" Joshi asked.

The captain nodded.

"So our mare would go in there?"

"And so will you."

Joshi took another look. It was plenty big for Shambhala, and it appeared solid. Except for the shrapnel hole, the deck looked sturdy too. Evidently, Captain Bock was a stickler for neatness, because everything was in place. Any extra rope was coiled in tidy circles. The hatches to the holds were properly closed, and the winch that held the heavy anchor above water looked fine. "We'll be back, Captain Bock," he said.

As they stepped off the barge, he prodded Leonid with his elbow. "Where are you going to find steel without getting killed?"

"It's risky," Leonid said, his voice falling to a nervous whisper. "But it's our only chance. I'm sneaking back into the shipyard. I know a way. There's a machine workshop to the right of the administration building. I worked with the smithy there. He was a good man. Had a conscience for Stutthof prisoners. Used to hide a key in a cracked eave. Told me I could always go in if I needed a rest. He keeps scraps of metal hidden under his cot. Said he hated wasting them on U-boats that were bound to lose the war." He looked at Helling. "What size do you need?"

"Good Lord!" Helling groaned. "What if you get caught?"

"Don't go soft on me now, Blacksmith. Tell me what you need."

"Two pieces, sixteen by twenty-four inches. Or something close to that. I'll have to heat them and make half cylinders." He scratched his head. "Some rivets would be good. I'll pound them into the flanges so the seal stays watertight."

Leonid grinned. "I'll leave those details to you. Are you both ready?"

"God almighty," Joshi murmured, pulling his cap down over his brow.

"It's not far," Leonid said. "Just along the railroad tracks, past the barracks. The buildings are dark; that's good."

They walked on briskly. Joshi held his breath and waited for the familiar shout of a guard, the harsh "*Achtung*" and click of a trigger, but none came. The only sound was the melancholy whistle of the wind. They stopped under a footbridge, and Leonid told them to wait.

"If I'm not back in twenty minutes, get out of here," he said.

"Take my matches so you can see," Helling whispered.

Joshi pressed his back against the cold arch of the bridge. Helling was beside him, and he could hear Helling's teeth chattering in the wind.

In the distance, a ship's siren whined. Joshi blew into his cupped hands, trying to keep them from freezing. Rain began to fall. It dripped down the side of the bridge, forming a puddle near his shoes. He thought of Leonid, memories falling into the skein of oil that floated on the puddle's surface. Somewhere in the night, he heard a muffled gunshot and the tinny sound of a motorbike.

Get back here, he prayed. *Please.*

Half an hour went by. Then another ten minutes.

"Do you think we should leave?" Helling's whisper was flat, as if he were trying to hold on to his terror.

"No."

They heard a soft scuffling sound. Joshi balled his fists, ready to strike. A shadow jumped past and Leonid appeared.

"Thank heavens," Helling gasped with relief.

Joshi's hands trembled as they cupped Leonid's shoulders. "Did you get what you needed?" he asked.

"Yes," Leonid nodded, pulling a square piece of metal from the front of his jacket. "I have two. You take this one. Stick it under your coat. Careful of the rough edges. The sizes aren't perfect, but beggars can't be choosers. Neither can thieves. I snatched a few rivets, too, on the way out."

"Did someone try to shoot you?"

The circles under Leonid's eyes seemed to grow darker.

"Yes. Let's move."

The rain had stopped when they slipped out from beneath the bridge, the moon breaking through the clouds in a misty halo. They hastened back to the dock, passing a few sailors and refugees along the way, but no one seemed to notice them.

The captain was waiting on the *Euphoria's* upward-sloping bow, his bushy sideburns floating off his cheeks in the breeze.

"If it isn't the three musketeers," he said, peering over the edge when they arrived on the dock. "Have you got the goods?"

"We do," Joshi called up to him, giving him a glimpse of the metal in the moonlight.

"Then what the hell are you waiting for? I want to sail before daybreak."

Joshi passed the steel sheet to Helling, the moon's milky tendrils lighting it with an eerie glow. "You're on, my friend," he murmured. "Good luck. Leonid will assist you. I'm going to get the others and Shambhala. Whatever you do, don't finish the job until you hear my whistle and you know we're on this dock." He glanced up at Bock's bulky shadow. "I wouldn't put it past that scoundrel to sail away without us."

FIFTY

At five a.m., Helling heard Joshi's shrill whistle.

"Thank heavens," he muttered. "It's about time. Leonid, go help them."

He pulled his sweaty shirt collar away from his neck before pounding in the last rivet. It had taken muscle and concentration to forge the steel plates into two exact half cylinders. However, hard as that was, the real task had been drawing the job out for hours. To top it off, he'd had to listen to Bock's obnoxious ranting. The captain was no fool. He had noticed right away that Helling was stalling, and his impatience had verged on abuse.

Helling picked up a metal file from the toolbox and smoothed off the last burrs on the pipe before applying the tin solder. Despite the distractions, it was a solid fit. When the steam pressure expanded the pipe, the seal would hold. The barge would move again.

"Damn it, man, are you done?" Captain Bock bellowed. "I want to sail out of the Danziger Bay before daylight."

Helling slammed the toolbox lid shut. "Yes, I'm done." Scowling, he followed Captain Bock up the ladder, wishing on every rung that he could reach up and yank the man's stupid-looking sideburns.

Yet, when he crawled through the hatch to the deck, his irritation faded. He glimpsed the arch of a new dawn, thin, tangerine-colored threads feathering the wide horizon. *We're so close*, he thought.

He glanced toward the dock where Manya and Joshi stood holding Shambhala. Lillian, Leonid, and the two girls were already at the bottom of the boarding plank, waiting to step onto the barge.

Captain Bock stopped short when he saw them. He called out to a crewman. "Horst, fire up the boiler and lube up the old girl so she gets cooking." Then he turned to the group. "I'm going to have to charge you two hundred marks," he said. "For the additional weight."

Helling was ready to punch Bock in the face when he heard Manya call out.

"This is all I've got," she said, holding up the amber ring her mother had given her. "It's worth far more than the fare you're demanding." She walked up the gangplank and pressed the heavy gold ring into his palm. "It's yours. Now, may we board?"

Captain Bock felt himself blush. The young woman had caught him off guard. Her bearing was so imperious, he found himself tongue-tied. His lips burned, and a fresh sweat broke out on his brow. He glanced down at the ring resting in his calloused palm. Two diamonds, at least a half carat each, were set on either side of the amber and sparkled like stars. A tingle zigzagged into his wrist. *Yes*, he thought, *this will make a lovely gift for my wife.*

"Captain?"

He looked up. By damn, she was pretty. Breath-stopping, actually. And he had a penchant for blondes. He shoved the ring deep into his pocket.

"All right. I'll take it."

He signaled his deckhand, Dieter. "Set up the wide loading plank with slats so the mare doesn't slip. Lay down some straw in the livestock hold and secure the tarps. Let's go."

The hold was big and warm. Lillian, Zarah, and Sofia quickly settled themselves on one of the benches that served as a side support for the makeshift shelter. Fashioned out of chicken crates and planks nailed neatly together, the structure was covered with tightly laced canvas. Manya helped Zarah and Sofia spread out their blankets while Helling found a place for his lamp.

As Joshi surveyed the area, the engine coughed and kicked over. He glanced toward the entrance of the hold and saw Leonid eyeing him with uneasy seriousness.

"What's wrong?" Joshi asked, his nerves ready to break.

"Dear friend," Leonid said, approaching him. "I won't be coming with you. And please don't try to stop me. I've made up my mind. I'm Russian. I don't belong in Germany."

"Where will you go?" Joshi asked, his voice filling with worry. "They'll shoot you when they find out you survived a German prison camp. They'll call you a traitor."

Leonid's scarred eyelids twitched, and Joshi's heart turned over.

"Maybe," said Leonid. "But I want to go home to Minsk, see another spring there. So—I'm going to wait for my comrades."

The engine gave off another noisy clang. "Untie the ropes!" called Captain Bock.

Leonid crossed the deck and leaped from the barge, landing on the dock just as the *Euphoria* surged forward, her engine hissing steam.

"Until we meet again, Gypsy," he shouted. "You're a damned fine doctor. And if there's a God, I know he's on your side."

From the wheelhouse, Captain Bock watched the scraggly Russian waving on the dock. He was surprised to hear the gnome call the tall fellow Gypsy and doctor. Who the hell knew? Still, there *was* an educated aura about the man. Bock had never met a Gypsy who went to university, nor had he ever seen one cry while waving good-bye.

He felt the barge slide forward and turned his attention to the helm. Maneuvering the *Euphoria* past vessels moored in the harbor, he counted the heads on the dock, wincing at the numbers. Lots of money there. Refugees dug deep into their pockets for a passage out. He felt the weight of the ring in his pocket. Even if they had no money, desperate people always found something to pay with when it came to the crunch. But he couldn't stop now. The chaos at the docks had grown to dangerous levels. And he wanted out of Danzig.

His eyes scanned the water for a minesweeping trawler that might be escorting another vessel through the danger zones. Luckily, in Neufahrwasser, just before the Vistula Canal entered the Danziger Bay, he spotted one and steered into its wake, mumbling the first two lines of the Seaman's Prayer out of habit: "The Lord is my Pilot. I shall not drift."

He didn't believe in God. But the prayer couldn't hurt. Once they rounded the crescent-shaped tail of the Hel peninsula, they'd be in the Baltic Sea and on the home stretch to Lübeck. As long as they didn't meet up with a Russian U-boat or a bomber, they'd be in good shape.

He grinned and looked down. The two women were on deck now. They shouldn't be out there, he thought, but hell, it's none of my business.

"Stick your finger down your throat," Manya suggested.

Lillian gripped the side of the barge with one hand and stuck the other in her mouth. Seconds later she was vomiting into the sepia water churning beneath her. "That's better," she groaned when the heaving had stopped.

Leaning against Manya, she stared at the spits of land passing on either side of them. The Neufahrwasser lighthouse stood to their left. Slender and distinguished, it marked the entrance to the Bay of Danzig. A warship with a tattered German flag was moored to the pier below it. In the distance, two slim church spires shimmered in the early-morning sun, while along the riverbanks the houses remained shrouded in the rising mist.

Dieter, the deckhand, stood near the bow and pointed to a dark cluster of poplars on their right. "We're passing the Westerplatte," he said somberly. "That's where the war started, where the first shots fell."

Lillian gave him a solemn nod. "September 1, 1939," she said. "Think how many shots have fallen since." She made a sweeping gesture over the water. "'Noble be man, merciful and good.'"

Dieter shot her a questioning look. "Who said that?" he asked, scratching his head.

"Goethe," she answered softly.

Dieter stared at the poplars again. "You'd better go inside now," he sighed when the waves in the bay grew choppy and the barge began to rock. "I'll fetch you a slop pail to puke in."

⚜

Captain Bock gripped the spokes of his wheel and let out a satisfied grunt. They had survived the first twenty-four hours. Thanks to the blacksmith, the *Euphoria* was chugging through the sea at a speed of three knots. Slower than normal, but steady nonetheless. He craned his neck forward to peer at the night sky. Tomorrow the temperatures would drop and the seas would take on a roll. He was sure of it. He looked down to the inky black water, pierced dimly by bursts of phosphorescence riding the sea crests. Those bursts could mean a surfacing U-boat. But so far, so good.

He raised his eyes again. A shooting star streaked across the western sky, brief and bright and almost gone before he could see it.

"Get me to Lübeck," he muttered, making a wish. Smiling to himself, he added, "And if Vibekke gives me a piece of ass, I promise to be a better man."

God, she made him weak. He'd met her in a pub in Copenhagen just before the war. A fisherman's daughter, she was also a true Dane—blond and bold and kindhearted, but tough to the core. They'd made love on the second night they'd met. He'd taken her on board for a glass of fine Riesling wine. In turn, she'd taken him right in the cloth hammock in his cabin, her legs weaving themselves around his bare buttocks. Crazy for her, he'd plunged between her thighs, climaxing in a way he'd never imagined possible.

He'd never had sex like that before. It was tender, too. And all because she cared for him. She cared for other people as well, albeit in a different way. Something in her passion and kindness whitewashed his soul. When she grabbed hold of his sideburns and pulled his lips close to hers, it was like going to confession. And he needed that, for deep down, he knew he was an unscrupulous and mercenary man who needed saving.

They'd married quickly, and she'd come to Schleswig-Holstein, where they'd set up house in a red brick cottage on the Elbe-Lübeck Canal. They couldn't keep their hands off each other whenever he was home. When he sailed, she never asked whether he was transporting weapons or flour. And he never told her. It was only when the Nazis in Lübeck started killing Jews that she began to meddle in his affairs.

One day in the kitchen, while she was scaling a codfish and he was reading the newspaper, he heard her say, "I don't like what's happening in this town. The Nazis are murdering innocent people and shipping them off to work camps. Slave camps, I think." She'd raised her knife high and brought it down hard, chopping off the fish head. "You need to do something, Jürgen."

He had looked at her in surprise.

"Really, you do," she repeated. "Use your barge to get them out of here."

"It's too goddamn risky," he snapped.

"That's an excuse," she said. He had argued until his mouth was dry, explaining that he'd be strung up by his balls if the authorities found Jews on his vessel. And where the hell could he take them, anyway?

"Denmark," she countered. "The Danes won't turn them away. My brother Steen works with the Danish resistance. He'll get them to safety from there."

"No! No! No!" he bellowed. "A thousand times no."

Without challenging him further, she fried the fish to a brown crisp, just the way he liked it. She even made him a hot toddy, smiling while she measured out an ounce of the dark Cuban rum he'd brought back from his voyage south a few years before.

But that night in bed, when his hand reached for the warm plummy flesh between her legs, she turned to ice, brusquely pushing him away.

From that moment on, she refused to have sex. During the day, she cooked, scoured the floors, and washed his salt-crusted underwear. She even tallied his ledgers. When he was home, her conversations were amiable, full of fresh anecdotes, but at night, in bed, she gave him nothing.

For months she refused him. It was only in the last weeks that she'd shown signs of softening. It happened right after the German authorities pressed the *Euphoria* into service, evacuating refugees from the east. He'd sailed back and forth to Danzig numerous times carrying arms, coal, grain—anything for a fee—but last month, when he sailed into Lübeck with a load of grimy passengers, Vibekke had been on the dock, chatting with the fishmongers. From his perch, he'd seen the surprise on her face.

As soon as the ropes were secured, she'd walked up the plank without caution for wind or weather, swinging her delectably curved hips and moving through the crowd, consoling mothers and children. Finally, she was in the wheelhouse. Looking into his eyes, she demanded to know whether he'd charged the refugees for the trip. Naturally, he lied. Under no circumstances would he have mentioned the money and jewelry hidden in the metal box under the helm. She would have left him if he'd told her.

Later, as they lay together under clean sheets, Vibekke laughed her throaty bedroom laugh. Pulling him close, she kissed him with a sweetness that made him feel he was being baptized anew. Groaning, he pulled her on top of him, but she slipped high up onto his ribs, her iridescent eyes so intense he nearly cried.

"Not all the way tonight," she laughed, rubbing her pubic bone against his chest. "But I promise, the more refugees you save, the more pleasure you'll have."

He pushed his hand into his pocket. The amber ring rolled onto the end of his pinky. Holding it up to the brass lantern on the wall behind him, he examined it. It would suit Vibekke well. He'd tell her he bought it in Danzig, the amber capital of the world. He'd ask her to wear it with the tight yellow blouse. Suddenly, though, he felt a pang of guilt. Had he taken advantage of those passengers?

"Nah," he muttered crossly, shoving the ring back into his pocket. "Every man deserves to make a little profit." Cocking his head sideways, he listened to the sea. The wind was picking up. Soon there would be rolling swells on the Baltic. He checked the compass and pushed the throttle up a notch. The sooner he got home, the better.

FIFTY-ONE

*M*anya awoke to hear Shambhala whinnying and groaning. "Shambhala's in labor," she cried, throwing off her blanket.

Helling hastened to light his lamp, raising it high above his head so the light fell on Shambhala. The mare was on the floor, nipping at her flanks.

"Her water's broken," Joshi said when a gush of clear yellow fluid poured out. "Won't be long now."

Shambhala rolled to her side, snorting with each powerful contraction. Soon, the sac appeared, thin and translucent white.

"How long?" Manya asked, glancing at Helling and Joshi. "What if the foal doesn't make it? Oh, I wish the hooves would come."

"Give it some time," Joshi answered calmly. "If Shambhala has trouble, we'll help her."

They waited. Every so often a large wave would break over the bow of the barge, dousing the floor with icy water. Shambhala's groans grew louder.

"I think the foal's shoulders are stuck," cried Manya.

"Lillian," Joshi called. "Give us a dry cloth. We need to pull out the foal." Lillian handed him a pillowcase.

"I want to do it," Manya whispered, taking it from Joshi. "Will you help me?"

Joshi nodded, but his eyes were serious. "The feet will be slick. Hold them with the cloth. Where's your knife? You'll need it to break the sac."

Silently, she pulled it out from under her belt.

Helling opened a bottle of iodine from his tool kit and poured a few drops over the blade.

Sliding forward on her knees, Manya moved up to Shambhala's rear. She knew what to do. She'd seen the maneuver many times over, but she'd never done it herself. It had always been Schwitkowski or a veterinarian from

Trakehnen. Carefully, using just the tip of her knife, she pierced the birth
sac. "I have them," she whispered, grasping the foal's tiny hooves.

"Pull down, not out," Joshi instructed, his hands supporting the small of
her back. "Take it slow. We don't want to rupture the umbilical cord."

With the next mighty heave of Shambhala's flanks, the foal slipped out
and into Manya's arms.

"You have to activate its breathing," Helling urged.

Joshi began to squeeze the foal's ribs.

"That's not doing the trick," Helling cried anxiously. "Manya, blow into
its nose."

Manya nodded. Taking a deep breath, she placed her mouth on the
foal's wet nostril. Seconds later, the foal quivered and took its first breath.

"A colt." Helling's eyes shone. "Look at him. Onyx-black like his father,
but with amber-colored fetlocks."

Manya pressed her hands against the foal's beating heart, and it dawned
on her that she had seen him in her dreams more than once.

Shambhala arched her graceful neck to greet her baby and lick the
blood and fluids from his coat. Soon, however, instinct drove her to stand.
Helling and Joshi hastened to steady her.

"Twist the cord, Manya," Joshi urged. "Right near the foal's navel."

Manya's knuckles whitened as she snapped the cord in two.

"Well done," he murmured.

She looked at him and beamed when she saw his admiration.

Zarah knelt beside Manya and held on to her jacket, her heart pounding
with excitement. "You can do it," she whispered to the foal, her lips moving
with solemn determination. "Up you go."

She felt a rush of heat in her throat. The foal was up! He was so tiny, so
precious. She saw him wobble, saw the uncertainty in his spindly legs. "Stay
up," she commanded. But the boat pitched and he crashed to his knees.
"Don't worry, little one," she crooned. "I'll help you."

He blinked his long black lashes and her heart somersaulted inside her.

"Come, Zarah," said Manya. "You *can* help him."

Slowly, so as not to frighten him, Zarah moved forward to cradle his muzzle in her hands. It was all wet. She giggled, the warmth of his breath dissolving the knots in her stomach.

Someone sniffled and she glanced up. Why was her Papa laughing and crying at the same time? He must be happy about the baby foal too. And Lillian? She looked around. Lillian's eyes were squeezed shut, as if she were praying.

"What shall we call him, Manya?" asked Zarah.

Manya's eyes were full of tears too. "How about Amber Dancer?"

"That's a good name," Zarah said, twisting her fingers into the foal's wispy mane.

Shambhala whinnied.

Zarah felt an arm encircle her waist and draw her away from the foal.

"Let's see if Amber Dancer lives up to his name," Manya whispered. "Now it's time for him to bond with his Mama."

Zarah nodded.

As if on cue, the foal stood up. Although he wasn't steady, Zarah was content to see that he was managing on his awkward legs. He took a few wobbly steps and shoved his nose under Shambhala's sweat-soaked belly.

Her Papa let out a long sigh.

"He's found gold, Zarah," she heard him say as he stooped to take her hand in his.

And although her voice felt scratchy, she tried the weight of the word upon her tongue: "Gold."

"Ach," Bock moaned.

Why the hell couldn't he sleep? Something hard was pressing into his thigh. He rolled over on his back and felt his pocket. The damned ring. Annoyed, he dropped it into the empty cupholder that was bolted to his nightstand.

"Barbados rum," he muttered, reaching under his bunk and taking out a bottle. "Maybe that'll help."

He unscrewed the cap and took a swig, fluffed up his pillow, and plopped his head back down. The rum soon warmed his belly, and, cradled in his cot, he let his mind wander to the passengers on deck.

He had decided to check on them a few hours earlier. After handing the helm over to Dieter, he'd gone to see how they were holding up in the rolling seas. Lifting the canvas, he'd peered through a crack in the crates. What a scene! The mare was in labor. The blond beauty had scooted herself right up to the horse to pull the foal out, with no regard whatsoever for the mess spilling over her clothes. She was listening intently to the Gypsy's instructions.

"He really is a doctor," Bock had muttered.

Gutsy thing, that young woman, he thought now, swallowing. Someone Vibekke would like. He sighed with longing.

He pushed himself up on his elbow and picked the amber ring up out of the cupholder, watching the gorgeous stone glimmer. *When should I give it to her?* he wondered. *Before we make love? After?* He felt his stomach knot.

"Ach, I'm just dog-tired," he mumbled, dropping the ring back into the cup.

He stretched out and closed his eyes. Something was nagging at him. Had he been unfair in taking the ring? Maybe a little. After all, the *Euphoria* would still be in Danzig if it weren't for the Gypsy and the blacksmith.

"Ach, don't be stupid," he muttered, shaking off his uneasiness. "All is fair in war."

He yawned and shoved the rum bottle back under his bunk. Turning on his side, he fell fast asleep. A dreamy mist carried him away. He was in a garden full of red-tongued hibiscus, overlooking a gin-colored lagoon. The blond woman and the Gypsy were walking on the beach. He heard voices and turned to see two other women standing next to him on the sand.

"Give it back," one said, wagging a finger in his face.

"Help them," whispered the other.

He woke with a start. Inside the brass cupholder, the amber ring rolled back and forth to the rhythm of the sea's swell, clinking softly against the sides.

I need some fresh air, he thought, getting out of bed and pulling on his jacket and boots. Snatching the ring out of the cup, he shoved it into his sock and left the stuffy cabin.

On the way up, he stopped by the engine room.

"Take those passengers a bucket of hot water," he told Horst, gruffly. "And some soap."

On deck, a blast of icy spray hit him squarely in the face, refreshing his senses. "Ach," he muttered, wiping the saltwater out of his eyes. "What am I worried about? It was just a friggin' dream."

FIFTY-TWO

For thirty-six hours, Bock stayed in the wheelhouse. He was hell-bent on reaching Lübeck harbor.

No bombs fell on the *Euphoria*. The Russian pilots seemed more interested in targeting the Luftwaffe than destroying an inconspicuous barge. Still, he held his breath.

On the fourth day, he sighted the beaches of Travemünde, just north of Lübeck, that marked the mouth of the Trave River. A quiet "hallelujah" escaped his lips. Soon Vibekke would draw him a hot bath. Soon she'd massage the tension from his neck. Feeling happier, he steered the *Euphoria* into the river entrance, where hundreds of tugs and barges were either docked or motoring back and forth.

He knew every inch of the Elbe-Lübeck Canal. It linked his city and Schleswig-Holstein to the rest of Europe's interior. As the *Euphoria* sailed through the waterway, he drank in the common sights he had come to love. The war had left its destructive mark on Lübeck's gothic architecture. Still, much of the medieval city had been left standing. He sniffed at the air, taking in the familiar smell of tar and oil, seawater and fish. Off to the port side, a flock of squawking gulls was hovering above a floating fish head.

His eyes traveled beyond them, seeking out landmarks: the church spires and old salt warehouses that had served as markers for as long as he'd sailed, the park where he and Vibekke picnicked every spring.

Leaning forward, he wiped the wheelhouse window with a clean towel. There it was. The dock that spelled home. Better news yet, his slip was free.

"Not long now," he murmured. "Once these passengers are offloaded, I'll be with my wife."

He took a gulp of the strong black coffee Dieter had brought him earlier and was relieved to feel the fog clear in his head.

Another vessel was motoring out, so he pulled the throttle into neutral and shouted for the deckhands to prepare the docking lines and secure the fenders. As he waited for the other boat to pass, he noticed a Danish tramp steamer moored behind his slip. *Vibekke's brother*, he thought. *I bet he's brought a load of grains or turnips from Denmark, but knowing him, he won't be going back empty-handed. If his underground contacts in Lübeck have any Jews to smuggle out, they'll be on that tramp steamer.*

He shook his head. Sometimes he wished he could do what Steen did, but he just wasn't hard-wired for that kind of thing. Steen lived on the edge of danger. No matter what port he was in, he always managed to charm the German harbor officials and slip from under their noses with Jews in his hold.

"Crazy son of a bitch," Bock murmured, reversing a little to make room for the other vessel. "I don't know how the hell he does it, but he gets them to Denmark and on to Sweden. Ah well, let the heroes be heroes."

The vessel he'd been waiting for passed his starboard side. He waved at the other captain and inched the throttle forward, bringing the *Euphoria* parallel to the dock while his eyes scoured the pier for any uniforms. He sure as hell didn't want to get caught unloading not one, but two horses. And God only knew what they'd do to him if they found a Gypsy on board, especially one who looked like he'd escaped from a concentration camp. But the coast was clear. Shutting down the engine, he strode out of the wheelhouse and onto the deck and called for the deckhands to prepare the gangway.

The young woman was standing in the door of the livestock shelter awaiting instructions, her big hands nervously tugging at her scarf, the gaunt Gypsy behind her.

"Good day," Bock said gruffly.

"Hello, Captain," she said, lifting her hand. "Thank you for sending up the hot water. It was a godsend."

Her smile, so dazzling and open, made him stop short. Something about her and the Gypsy softened him.

"I must be really tired," he muttered to himself, straightening up.

"Captain?" Dieter was calling to him from the dock. "Everything's ready. I've explained the disembarkation procedures to the passengers. They should be coming off now."

Bock turned his gaze back to the shelter, where the blacksmith and the mare were just emerging. The older woman and the two girls followed close behind with the colt, their hands gripping his makeshift halter.

"Captain?" he heard the Gypsy say. "Do you know where we might find shelter in the city?"

Bock's stomach knotted up, just like it had during the night. Vibekke's sweet face flashed through his mind. Without thinking, he bent over and pulled the ring out of his sock. Dazed, he stood up to find the blonde woman staring at him.

Give it back, he thought, and turned the ring over in his palm. He didn't believe in supernatural things, but—

The woman laid a hand on his wrist. "Captain? Are you all right? You look faint."

"Here, Miss," he mumbled, handing her the ring. "I can't take this. It's yours."

"But I have nothing else to give you," she said.

"It's all right, honestly. I was wrong to take it in the first place." He blushed. "Besides, my wife would kill me if she knew."

The woman smiled softly.

"Listen," he heard himself say warmly. "Where will you settle now?"

The woman's eyes widened with worry. "We're really not sure."

"I've been thinking," he said. "For many years, I've sailed the Caribbean. There's a group of islands at the edge of the Caribbean called the Bahamas. They're beautiful. You would be safe there and could start a new life. I don't mean to pry, but as I said, it's just a thought. And, uh, I have the means to help you."

"Thank you, sir." She didn't know what else to say.

The Gypsy was nodding eagerly, imploring him to continue.

"You see, I have a connection. And I get the feeling you might need a little bit of help?"

His gaze flew to Steen's vessel. "You'd have to go to Denmark first, then into Sweden, but if you can get papers, you could cross the Atlantic. The shipping routes will open as soon as this war is over. Trust me, it won't be long. You'll soon be able to sail."

He glanced up. The woman stood rooted to the deck, listening, her gold hair flying up into the Gypsy's face.

"Miss, I watched you the other night," he said. "I saw you catch that foal and snap the cord." He gazed at the man. "And I know you're a Gypsy, but are you really a doctor like your friend in Danzig said?"

"Yes."

"And were you in a concentration camp?"

"I was."

"Then there's really nothing here for you, is there?" He pointed to the dock, where the others were waiting in the drizzling rain. "Who's that girl over there? She looks like your sister."

"She is, sir."

"Well, take her too. It will be a long time before Germans like Gypsies, even educated ones. To be honest with you, I'm not fond of your people either." He paused, wondering whether he'd lost his mind completely.

"Go to the Bahamas," he continued. "Why not?"

"The Bahamas?" Joshi said.

"Yes. Trust me. The beauty would override the hardship. The waters are turquoise, clear as the sky and full of fish." He smiled. "The beaches are so pink, you'll think you're in heaven."

"But, just what would we do?"

Bock leaned toward Joshi like a conspirator. "Listen," he murmured, "I've been there. The forests are rich with yellow pines. I've seen lumber camps on some of the islands, but no doctors. Injuries and diseases, but only bush medicine." He glanced at the young woman. "They have wild horses there too. Descendants of Spanish Barbs."

He took a deep breath and exhaled. He was beginning to feel like himself again, thank goodness. "Enough talk," he grunted. "Do you want to get out of Lübeck or not? Make up your minds, because there isn't much time, and I'm not fond of risking my neck." He bent over to pick up the loose end of a rope. "Think about it while I check the hatches."

———※———

"I want to go," Joshi whispered.

Manya looked at him. Above her a flock of seagulls circled in the sky. "We need to think about this," she said.

"I want to go," he repeated, his voice firm this time. "With you and Sofia. Listen, it struck me while the captain was talking. Ragnar is in Sweden. He has connections in high places, and to embassies. He even has his own shipping line. He's helped me before, and I know he'll do it again. There's no purpose for me here, Manya, no life. They'll never let me work." He paused, searching her face. "What do you think?"

Manya turned her head toward Helling. He was waiting, his calloused hands patiently holding Shambhala's halter. *He's aged so much*, she thought.

He's tired of moving on. She wanted to reach out and push his lopsided hat into place. Shambhala was nuzzling Amber Dancer, and Zarah and Sofia were tickling his nose, fussing over him like little nannies.

A flapping noise on a pole at the end of the dock caught her attention. From where she stood, she could see a German flag.

A thought hit her with such force, it made her want to weep. *I don't want to live in Germany anymore, not in a place where Joshi is despised and people like Lillian are hated.*

She took hold of Joshi's hand, their fingers intertwining. He was still waiting for her answer, his eyes greener and more full of light than she'd ever remembered.

"Will you come?" he asked.

"My head is spinning," she said.

"But we don't have time." He gripped her fingers.

"Then, yes," she said, "I'll come." She felt herself sway with the weight of her words.

"You won't regret it," he smiled, pulling her close.

And for the first time in what seemed like ages, Manya saw something of his old boyish certainty glimmer mischievously in his eyes.

"What about Helling?" she whispered. "And Lillian and Zarah? Helling's always been there, and I've known Zarah since she was a baby."

"We can't wait," Joshi answered, his eyes sad but determined. "We have to tell them now." Taking her hand, he walked with her toward the captain, who was checking the anchor.

"Captain Bock," he said. "We want to take you up on your offer. However, we need to talk to our friends."

"Go ahead. But let me warn you: This is serious business. No horses on this trip."

Joshi shot him a grin. "I understand."

"All right." The captain's eyes scanned the dock. "The harbor officials must be having a coffee break. Be quick with your good-byes because I want you back on deck before they return. You'll stay in my quarters until someone named Steen comes for you. He's my brother-in-law." The captain tugged at his sideburns thoughtfully. "Most likely, he'll come before dawn. Don't answer any knocks until you hear the words 'black tea.' You hear me? Steen will take you to that boat." He pointed across the dock. "The *Migrant Bird.* After that, you're on your own."

"May I ask you something?" said Joshi, shaking Bock's hand. "Why are you doing this for us?"

Bock let out an irritated sigh. "Hell, I wish I knew. Something just came over me. Maybe I was thinking about my wife." His eyes fell on Manya's ring and he quickly looked away.

Manya stared at him, and, stepping forward, she kissed him on the cheek. "You're a good man, Captain," she said.

"Not always, but—but this time," Bock stammered. "I just hope my wife feels the same, because I haven't got a damn thing to give her when I get home."

FIFTY-THREE

*I*t took Manya ten steps to walk down the loading plank, each weighing more heavily than the one before.

How do I tell Helling in minutes what he has meant to me all my life, she wondered. She couldn't bear to look at Shambhala and Amber Dancer.

Her heart pounded as she fixed her eyes on Helling. Sixty-two winters had passed across his brow. He wouldn't leave Germany. His soul was fettered to the cool European forests. Lovingly she looked at his buckling shoulders, his crooked knees, and she realized how much Nemmersdorf and the trek had taken their toll. When her last step brought them face-to-face, she reached out and grasped his hand.

"Blacksmith Helling," she said, her voice a brittle whisper. "The captain has offered to help Joshi and me get out of Germany. Sofia too."

Shock and disbelief flitted across Helling's face, so she carried on quickly, hoping to explain.

"We don't know any details, except that Sweden will be our first stop. From there we plan to sail south to a place called the Bahamas." She swallowed. "At least that's where the captain suggests we go."

Helling struggled to take in what she was saying.

"But—"

Manya cut him off.

"I know this is all very sudden. But it's our only chance to make a new start." She glanced at Joshi, who cleared his throat.

"You know that Manya can't imagine life without you. She loves you so much," he said, picking up where she left off. "The choice is easier for me. Germans will always hate me. They'll always have the Führer in their eyes when they look at me."

Helling's kind blue eyes searched their faces. "You believe you can make a good life together in this new world, this place that I've never even heard of?"

They both nodded silently.

"Then you must go," Helling said, smiling sadly. "With my blessing."

"I would ask you to come along," Manya said, embracing him through her tears. "But—"

"No, child, I'm done running." He ran his hand over her hair. "But must you go now? Tonight? Have we no time to prepare for this kind of good-bye?"

"We only have a few minutes." She bit her trembling lip.

"But Shambhala? And Amber Dancer? You can't take them with you?"

"No."

Helling's shoulders slumped. In shock, he turned toward Lillian. She was standing on the other side of Shambhala, her rucksack slung over her shoulder, her fingers holding the mare's muzzle.

"What about you, Lillian?" he asked in a cracked whisper. "You're Jewish. Shouldn't you go too?"

"No, Klaus," Lillian said quietly, her dark hair flying across her face like birds' wings. "I'm staying with you and Zarah." She smiled uncertainly, but her eyes were bold as she waited for him to assure her that this was what he wanted too.

He looked at her in bewilderment. "Are you saying that we should stay together?" he stammered.

Lillian nodded, and suddenly his ashen cheeks turned deep red.

"But here, we have no home, nowhere to settle, nothing but dirt in our pockets." He rubbed his forehead, trying to catch up to the events unspooling before him. "I guess that doesn't matter now," he said, clearing his throat.

She smiled, reaching over Shambhala's mane to touch his face. "But what about you? I'm a Jew. I may be more of a liability than you bargained for."

"I don't care about that," Helling declared stoutly. "We'll find our way."

Lillian glanced at the barge and back at him. "We will have a lifetime to talk, dear," she said tenderly. She turned to Manya, her eyes turning grave. "What shall we do with Shambhala and Amber Dancer?"

Manya looked at the horses and thought of her beloved Aztec.

"Take care of them," she said softly. "If anyone can keep Aztec's lineage going, it's you."

"But I'm not really a horse breeder," Lillian said doubtfully. "Max was the one."

"Please. You and Blacksmith Helling know what to do. Even if I stayed in Schleswig-Holstein, I wouldn't want to breed horses anymore." She felt Shambhala nuzzle her cheek. Her heart breaking, she pressed her hands against Shambhala's neck. "My brave and beloved girl," she whispered. "I hope Lillian finds a Trakehner for you, one who made it across the Haff, too."

Reluctantly, she released Shambhala and opened her knapsack. From it, she pulled out Aztec's papers.

"You'll need these to prove Amber Dancer's bloodlines," she said, handing them to Lillian. "They've come full circle, back to your hands."

"Isn't it something," Lillian said softly. "A Jewish woman, deemed unfit to live among Germans, holds in her hands the papers to the proudest pedigree in the country."

"Zarah," Manya said, stepping close to the girl, whose arms were wrapped around Amber Dancer's neck. "I have something to ask you."

She bent down to kiss the top of Zarah's head. The colt tilted his head to look, and with a quiet sob, Manya buried her face in his fuzzy mane.

"So small," Manya murmured, "yet so much like Aztec." She paused. "Zarah, sweetheart? Joshi, Sofia, and I are going away, and I was wondering— would you look after Amber Dancer for me? There's a lot of work involved in raising a foal, but if you want to take that on, he's yours."

Zarah's cheeks blossomed. "Mine?" she asked, her eyes wide as saucers.

"Yes," Manya smiled.

"Oh!" Zarah exclaimed in a scratchy little voice. "Thank you." She leaned into Manya's arms. "I promise to groom him and oil his hooves. I'll teach him to lie down, too, when I'm in the saddle, just like you taught Aztec." She stopped to catch her breath. "But will you promise to come back and visit us? Like you used to in Nemmersdorf?"

"I promise."

"I love you," Zarah said. She looked at Sofia. "You too." Tears spilled down her cheeks.

"Don't cry, Zarah," Sofia murmured. "Look, here's my string." She took Zarah's wrist and tied the yarn, and as their little heads bobbed together in the salty wind, Sofia's newly sprouting strands of coppery hair mingled with Zarah's tawny locks. "We'll never lose each other now," Sofia said.

The captain's voice thundered over them.

"Are you almost ready? I want to go home to my wife."

※

Captain Bock was rocking with impatience. Dusk was falling, and all he could think of was Vibekke and hot glühwein spiced with cinnamon. *If only these people would hurry up.* He needed a rest. He needed to be on his sofa with his feet up, telling Vibekke about the trip and the close call he'd had with death in Danzig. And he had yet to inform Steen about the Gypsy and the woman and the girl.

"This way," he said when the three passengers finally climbed up on deck.

He opened the hatch that led down to the galley and his quarters. The woman went first, but she stopped short on the top rung of the ladder.

"Where will our friends stay?" she asked in a troubled whisper.

Her closeness made his breath stall.

"I'll point them in the right direction," he mumbled.

"Thank you," she whispered gratefully.

He rolled his eyes. *Christ*, he thought, *haven't I done enough good for one day?* He showed them into his cabin, where he pulled out blankets and pillows. The Gypsy girl sat bravely on a chair, pinching the folds of her coat, her stomach rumbling in the semidarkness.

"You hungry?" he asked.

"Yes," she whispered.

"All right, I'll see what I can scrounge up in the galley."

"Now I'm even feeding them," he grumbled as he went out to rummage through the galley cupboards.

Still, no one would be eating the leftover loaf of bread or the half-eaten jar of Vibekke's homemade jam. So he took them, along with a quarter bottle of Doppelkorn he found.

"The alcohol isn't for you, little lady," he grinned at the girl. "But, Gypsy, if you need to ease your nerves, have a sip."

The Gypsy rose to thank him, but, too tired for niceties, Bock told him to sit back down. "From now on, you'd better be as quiet as church mice. One suspicious sound and the authorities will have your necks."

He closed the door, leaving them in silence.

The drizzle had turned to icy needles when he stepped back on deck.

Home, he thought. *Finally*. He pulled his collar up around his ears and strode to the side of the barge.

"Damn it," he muttered. The blacksmith and his family were still on the dock. They stood with their backs to him, staring in the direction of the city, their shapeless bodies huddled together like lost sheep. "Don't you think you ought to be on your way?" he called as he sauntered down the plank. "It's going to be a cold one tonight, and you shouldn't be here when the police come snooping."

"Believe me, Captain," the blacksmith sighed, glancing over his shoulder. "If I knew where to go, I wouldn't be here. Have you any suggestions?"

Shit, Bock thought. *I wish I'd minded my own business. Why did I tell that woman I'd help out?* He felt responsible even though she'd likely never know.

"There are shelters on the outskirts of the city," he growled.

"How far?" asked the blacksmith.

"An hour or two, if you know the way. But they may not be open for horses. Where are you headed?"

"We have friends in Rabenkirchen."

"You won't get there tonight, not in this weather. Oh, for goodness sake. I told you, I'm not the Salvation Army. You people. Ach, to hell with it. Come with me before I change my mind."

He strode past them, his whiskers flying out like sails over his ears. As he brushed past the little girl, she squinted up at him with weary eyes. A tingling went through his chest.

"Well, Vibekke," he muttered ruefully as he walked down the pier. "Guess what I'm bringing you instead of a ring."

FIFTY-FOUR

Joshi was the first to hear the knock. He sat up with a start. *What time is it*, he wondered, his eyes adjusting to the dark. How many hours had they slept?

"Black tea," a hushed voice whispered.

"He's here, Manya," Joshi breathed, shaking her arm.

His heart raced as he unlatched the door, but when he saw the gentle, ashen-haired figure in the doorway, he relaxed. The man stepped into the cabin.

"I'm Steen," he said, introducing himself with a brief nod. "The captain's brother-in-law."

Manya and Sofia rose to greet him, but he held up his hand. "I'm afraid we don't have time to get to know one another," he told them with an apologetic smile. "We have to move fast." He motioned furtively. "Please, come with me."

They followed Steen off the *Euphoria* and onto the dock, the raw salt wind whipping at their faces. Manya pulled her jacket tighter to her chest and peered into the darkness.

When they reached the *Migrant Bird*, Steen paused and turned to them. "Wait here," he murmured, disappearing onto the boat.

They stood in silence, looking out at the rough, black water. A gust of cold wind blew over their heads parting the night clouds and exposing a row of stars. The horizon seemed to open like a dark chasm before them. Sofia's tiny voice pierced the air.

"I'm scared," she whimpered.

Joshi took her hand and slid it deep inside the folds of his coat. For a moment, she stood there, silent. Then, taking a step back, she pulled something out of his pocket.

"What's this?" she asked, holding up the chunk of butterfly amber.

He looked at the amber thoughtfully. "Mama used to say that amber holds the stories of the earth, the heartbeats of our ancestors," he answered softly. "She always carried a cobble in the folds of her skirt to protect us when we were on the road. So now we have one too."

Shivering, Sofia raised it up to the night sky, the stars shining through the orange resin in crisp slivers. She tried to run her finger along the milky edge, but her hands were too cold. Suddenly the amber slipped from her grasp, hitting the dock with a twang and bouncing into the angry water below.

"No!" she gasped. Falling to her knees, she leaned out over the dock, her small hand reaching for the water, but the amber had vanished.

"Sofia, don't!" Joshi cried, pulling her back from the edge and wrapping his arms around her. "Let it go."

"But it was all we had to take with us. And now it's gone." She looked down at the water. "I've lost it," she sobbed. "I've lost everything."

Manya kneeled beside her. "You haven't lost everything," she said, stroking Sofia's hair. "You're alive. We still have each other."

⁂

Steen led them into the hold. Once they were inside, he lit his torch, guiding them along a corridor toward a sooty room in which huge wooden bins, piled high with coal, lined the walls. To their astonishment, he leaned over and effortlessly pulled one aside.

"This one has rollers on the bottom," he explained in a whisper. "There's a built-in cubbyhole behind it that we use for smuggling people like you." He gave the bin another shove, and they found themselves standing in front of a secret entrance.

Stooping, he showed them into a small space, where he lit a brass lamp that was fixed to the wall. Pillows and colorful blankets were laid out on the narrow bunk beds.

Hastening to unpack a wicker basket he'd brought with him, Steen opened a fold-down table, setting out a loaf of bread and a generous wedge of soft cheese along with three hard-boiled eggs, a sausage, some gherkins, a small bottle of egg liquor, and a box of heart-shaped marzipan. "Compliments of my sister Vibekke," he said with a toothy grin. "Oh, and she wants me to tell you that your friends have eaten and are comfortably bedded down in her house for the night, the mare and the foal safe in the shed."

"Thank you so much for letting us know," Manya said, squeezing his hand. "I can rest easy now."

"Don't mention it." He gave an amused chuckle. "I could hardly stop her from coming with me to the dock. She was dying to meet you because she thinks her husband has come back a changed man."

"What do you mean?" Manya asked.

"Well, it seems my brother-in-law has discovered his humanitarian side. And Vibekke's over the moon."

He looked at his watch. "I must go, but before I do, let me explain a few things. Our first stop is Copenhagen. Don't be alarmed when you hear the engines shut down. That will mean we are in port. The authorities will come on board there to inspect the boat." He raised one eyebrow, glancing at Sofia. "You'll have to be completely silent during this stop."

He paused to make sure they understood the gravity of his words. When Joshi nodded, he continued. "Once we clear the authorities in Copenhagen, we'll be sailing the ferry route to Oslo. I can't take you to shore because I'm not allowed to deviate from my path." He glanced at his watch a second time. "However, you'll be met by a small fishing boat. The fisherman knows my pennant means I have a special delivery. He'll take you the rest of the way. That leg will be short. However, there's always a chance you'll be caught. If that happens, please don't spoil it for others or for my crew and me by spilling the beans. And, one last thing: Do you have any contacts in Sweden?"

"Yes," Joshi replied. "I have a close friend, a man named Ragnar Malmberg. He lives in Göteborg."

"You mean Ragnar from the shipping line?" Steen exclaimed.

Joshi nodded proudly.

"He's one of us," Steen continued. "He works together with Count Bernadotte of the Swedish Red Cross. Ragnar can worm his way into any embassy. If anybody can get you papers, he can."

"Is anyone else coming?" Joshi asked.

Steen's deep-set eyes clouded over.

"No. Unfortunately the police intercepted my other passengers. But don't be afraid. My crew is trustworthy. They're all family. They've been working for the Danish resistance since the beginning of the war."

"But—but how do we pay you?" Joshi asked.

Steen smiled. "Don't worry. It's all taken care of."

Joshi moved to thank him, but Steen just shook his head. "It's the least we can do. Now, get some rest. You'll be here for a while."

The *Migrant Bird* sailed from Lübeck just after dawn. After hours of riding in the cramped space with the noise from the engines humming in his ears, Joshi began to feel claustrophobic. There were no portholes, so he couldn't see outside, but he calculated that they had been pushing through the sea for more than a day. He knew that soon the ship would stop and the inspectors would board, and if the three of them were found, they would most likely be shot.

Anxious, he ran his hand through his hair and looked up at Manya from his spot on the bottom bunk. She was sitting at the small fold-out table with Sofia, studying a map she'd found in the cupboard. Sofia caught her brother's eye and shot him a fearful look.

I'd better pull it together, he thought. *She's not handling this very well.*

Rising, he put on his best smile and went over to her. "Sofia," he said, placing a hand on her thin back. "I need something to help me pass the time. Would you sing me a song?

"I can't," she said in a squeaky voice. "When I lost the amber, I lost all we had of Mama." Her eyes began to water again.

Manya glanced up at Joshi. His eyes were a reflection of his sister's grief.

"Sweetheart," she said, putting her arm around the girl. "I understand. But may I tell you something about amber?"

Sofia gave her a little nod, and Manya leaned closer so that their foreheads were touching.

"There's a myth," she began quietly, "that says amber was created when a young god named Phaeton was killed by lightning. He was riding through the sky in a chariot, trying to get to the ends of the earth, when a huge bolt struck him."

Sofia looked up, the accumulated shadows beneath her wet eyelashes dissolving briefly.

"And?" she asked.

"He fell straight into the Baltic Sea. Our sea. His sisters, who loved him very much, cried at the shore for a thousand years, until one day their tears turned to amber. And the sea, finally satisfied with their gift, gave back their brother." She paused. "You too have given the sea a gift. The amber you dropped is paying for *our* passage." She smiled and pressed her fingertips to Sofia's heart.

Sofia sat up a little straighter and folded her hands in her lap. Her voice faltered when she spoke, but her grief seemed to give way to a new strength. "I still hear the songs my Mama used to sing."

"Yes, see?" Manya said with a nod. "It's better we leave the amber behind than forget the songs. Besides, I still have my ring." She slid it off her hand, the stone glowing in the light like a yellow carnelian circle.

"Was that Mama's?" Sofia asked.

"Yes. Your mother gave it to my mother. My mother gave it to me."

Sofia's lips turned up into a little smile. Gazing at her brother, she began to sing in Romani.

"*Gelem, Gelem,*" Joshi murmured, humming along with her. He bent down, and, touching his lips to Manya's ear, he translated. "'*I have traveled long roads and stopped with happy Rom . . . so come with me now.*'"

Manya smiled and laid her head against the wall.

A half hour later, they heard the engines shut down and felt the freighter lurch forward. Joshi stumbled. Steadying himself against the splintery table, his gaze darted to the door and back to Manya. "Copenhagen," he whispered.

He drew in his breath. Without a word, he reached up and turned the brass knob on the lantern, dimming the light. Looking at Sofia, he put his finger to his lips. She nodded and gathered up a blue quilt from the floor beside her. Wrapping it tightly around her shoulders, she hunched over the table, her pale fingers picking at the fringe.

They heard the sharp thump of boots on deck. Snatches of German and Danish filtered through the walls.

⁂

They waited, tense and quiet, for nearly three hours. Finally the engines turned over with a loud belch, and the sulfur stench of burning coal filled their nostrils. The steamer lurched forward, her hull trembling under the strain.

Joshi breathed a sigh of relief as Manya let herself sink onto the bench beside Sofia. "Oh, thank God," she exclaimed, lowering her head to the table.

Sofia tugged at her sleeve. "How much longer now?" she asked.

"Sofia, my love, we still have a long way to go," Joshi said. "Maybe you should get some sleep. I'll wake you when it's time."

For a moment, Sofia looked as if she might protest, but then a wave of fatigue washed over her face. Conceding with a nod, she rose and climbed up to the top bunk.

"Sweet dreams," Joshi murmured, stepping over to the bed to stroke the side of her cheek. "All will be well."

⚜

When Sofia's breathing had evened into sleep, Manya folded up the map and moved onto the lower bunk. Holding out her hand, she motioned for Joshi to join her. For a long while, they lay together in silence, their bodies rocking to the gentle movements of ship's hull. Manya laid her head on Joshi's chest, the heat from his skin warm against her face. "Is this really happening?" she whispered.

Joshi squeezed her hand. "Hard to believe, isn't it?" he said.

"Yes," she breathed. "So strange. My body has no weight to it." She rolled over on her back and raised her arms, turning her fingers in the air as if she were seeing them for the first time. Suddenly she laughed and pointed to a scar near her right elbow. "No, I'm awake. That's a reminder of my first fall off Aztec, when he threw me into Mami's rosebushes."

"I feel strange too," Joshi said, running his finger down the curve of her neck. "For months I've been on the run, and now, unexpectedly, it's quiet. It feels too normal to be real."

"Would you have stayed with me in Germany if I hadn't wanted to come?" Manya asked.

"Yes," he said quietly, "but I wouldn't have been happy there."

"What a chance we've been given," she smiled, feeling the knots inside her loosen. "To leave it all behind. Start a new life." She sighed. "But do you *really* think we made the right choice?"

"I do," he assured her, leaning up on his elbow and looking into her eyes. "We would never have been able to make a life together if we'd stayed. I want something better. I want to be a doctor, even if that means settling down in one place with the gadje."

His face paled in the shadowy darkness, and he gave her a nervous smile. "I only hope that my mother and father, wherever they may be, are at peace." He leaned back on the pillow. "But I have to ask you something too, Manya, something that I feel is important—"

"You want to know about *my* parents, right? How I feel about leaving them?"

"Yes. You haven't spoken about it, and—"

"I know," she stammered. "I've been trying to put what happened out of my mind. But really, I can't." She closed her eyes. "My parents' names won't be posted on any refugee lists, nor will they be engraved on the headstones in Guja, but I just know—I know they're dead."

She swallowed. "I had a dream while we were still on the Haff. It was spring in Guja. The dandelions had sprung up on the meadow. Mami and Papa were wandering through hundreds of yellow flowers, up the slope leading to our house. I was crying in the dream, and Mami came to me and put her face next to mine. She said I shouldn't worry, and she looked so peaceful."

Joshi nodded and traced his finger along the high bone of her cheek. The lamp flickered and went out, but the bunk was warm now. Manya stared into the darkness until Joshi's breathing became light and regular.

"Bahamas," she whispered, trying out the word.

It felt new to her tongue, soft on the "h," like a slow exhalation of breath. What would those islands be like, she wondered. Would there be otters? No, too warm.

She closed her eyes and imagined Aztec galloping across the meadow in Guja. Her breath caught in her throat. The captain had said there were wild horses on one of the islands. Was it possible? Could she tame one? Cantering along a beach would be very different from cantering through the forests at home.

Home.

She heard the sea surging past, felt it move inside her chest. Her thoughts traveled to her mother, who had not been able to leave home, and to Vavara, who was content to wander. Two women so different, yet so attached to their own ways of life.

Joshi stirred beside her. She felt his breath tremble through his body as he pulled her close in his sleep.

"Bahamas," she whispered again.

Her eyes grew heavy. She drifted off into a soft sleep and dreamed of deep blue currents curving ever westward.

ACKNOWLEDGMENTS

I am grateful to so many people who have been part of writing this book and supporting my journey. To my editor Joy Stocke, who helped me radically refine and change the structure of this entire novel; led the way with optimism, skill, and integrity; and told me to keep breathing. To Kim Nagy, whose wise and caring spirit helped shape the book from the very first draft to the last, and Libby Bako, for her bright ideas and never-ending patience with the final edits. These creative women were handmaidens to *The Last Daughter*.

The story of Manya and Joshi was inspired by my East Prussian grandparents, Walter and Edith von Sanden-Guja. Even though they are long gone, their guidance has been with me throughout. I am especially grateful to my grandfather, Walter von Sanden, whose diaries and legacy of rare East Prussian photographs supplied me with unforgettable impressions of a forgotten land and whose books—particularly *Das Gute Land*, *Schicksal Ostpreussen*, and *Die Zugvögel*—gave me insight into what life was like in East Prussia and what happened on the trek.

There are other authors whose writings I found helpful, including Professor Ian Hancock, whose heartfelt books about the Romani people opened my eyes to another world; Patricia Clough, whose book about the trek never left my writing desk; and Fritz Schilke, Stasys Yla, Viktor Frankl, and Janina Grabowska-Chalka. Living as I do—on an island—the Internet was invaluable. It gave me enormous insight into the war, the Eastern Front, the Russian and German armies, the Romani people, and so much more.

I thank Erhard Schulte for sharing his invaluable knowledge about Trakehners and for allowing me to pick his brain. I am indebted to the famous Trakehner stallion Fetysz Ox, and my mother's loyal Trakehner, Dandy. When I learned of their heartbreaking stories, I knew they had to be remembered, as do all Trakehners that fought so valiantly to save so many.

My heart is full of gratitude to the following friends who put aside their own work to read and critique the manuscript and who unwaveringly embraced the vision of this book: Anne Hampson, my ever-present literary mentor and friend; Paula Boyd Farrington, my generous advisor and brilliantly gifted muse; Ruth Ann Harnisch, my sage counselor; Elly DeVries, my scholarly guardian angel; Christine Matthäi, my German sister of the heart and gifted friend who lent the image of the soulful woman to the cover; Dave Mackey, my talented media man; and Linda Marlin, Joyce Belmonte, and Shawnie Dickie, my cheerleaders.

I have deep appreciation for those conscientious teachers who helped me walk with faith through the years it took to write this book: Dr. Judith Schmidt, Karin and Ron Aarons, Alexis Johnson, Donna Evans Strauss, and Barbara Brennan. The close friends that I made in these transformative circles have been my spiritual backbone. You know who you are. I am thankful to my companions in the Grand Bahama Writers' Circle, who supported me from start to finish.

My sincere thanks to Capt. Robbie Nixon, whose aviation knowledge made the aircraft scene possible, and Donald Bertke, who patiently answered my many questions about barges and escape routes to Sweden. Thanks to Klaus Plikat for introducing me to East Prussian researcher Norbert Skowron—a living archive of information—and to Irek Golojuch, the angel who took care of me while I was in Poland researching the Danzig harbor and the Stutthof concentration camp. I thank my cousin Dr. Eckhard von Bock for his advice and knowledge of family history. Thanks to Shantae Bain, our skilled secretary, for copying the manuscript many times and assisting whenever needed.

It has been a pleasure and a privilege to work with my publisher, Wild River Books, nurturing and encouraging companions on the journey.

Thanks to designer Tim Ogline for creating such a beautiful composition and for being so patient and professional in bringing together the perfect elements for the cover.

I bow to my parents, Dr. Ejnar and Dr. Owanta Gottlieb, for the courage they had to step into the unknown and emigrate from Germany to the Bahamas. Threads of their brave lives are sewn into the fabric of this book. I thank my brother Frederik Gottlieb for his strength of character and support.

Last, but never least, I embrace my husband, James Sarles, for his constant emotional and financial support, for the space he gave me to write, and for urging me to travel back to Guja to find my roots. Hugs to my son, Nikolai, for taking that journey back in time with me, for tiptoeing around when I was writing, and for listening when I read out loud.

ABOUT THE AUTHOR

Raised in the Bahamas as the daughter of German immigrant parents, Marina Gottlieb Sarles worked as a physical therapist and energy healer for many years before drawing on her storytelling skills as the author of *Sand In My Shoes: A Collection of Island Stories*. She has been published in Macmillan's Caribbean anthology, *Under the Perfume Tree*, and ESPN produced a special feature based on one of her short stories. Her essay *Auschwitz, Stutthof and Remembrance* was featured in the online magazine *Wild River Review*. Marina and her husband and son live on Grand Bahama Island and spend a lot of time boating in the Abaco cays as well.

For further information about *The Last Daughter of Prussia*, please visit her blog:

http://www.marinagottlieb-sarles.com/